Nancy Drew DIARIES®

"No matter where you go, dark is still dark..."
–Nancy Drew

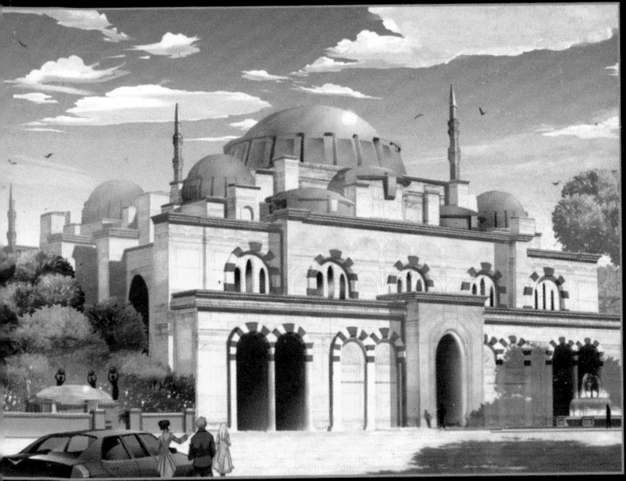

PAPERCUTZ

NANCY DREW DIARIES GRAPHIC NOVELS AVAILABLE FROM PAPERCUT

NANCY DREW DIARIES graphic novels are also available digitally wherever e-books are sold.

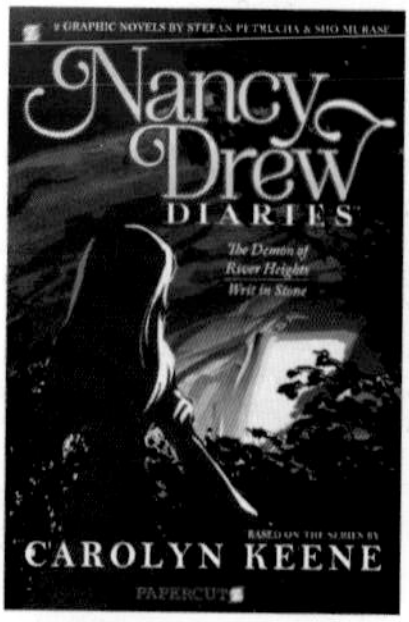

2 GRAPHIC NOVELS BY STEFAN PETRUCHA & SHO MURASE
Nancy Drew
DIARIES
The Demon of River Heights
Writ in Stone
CAROLYN KEENE
PAPERCUTZ

"The Demon of River Heights" and "Writ in Stone"

#1

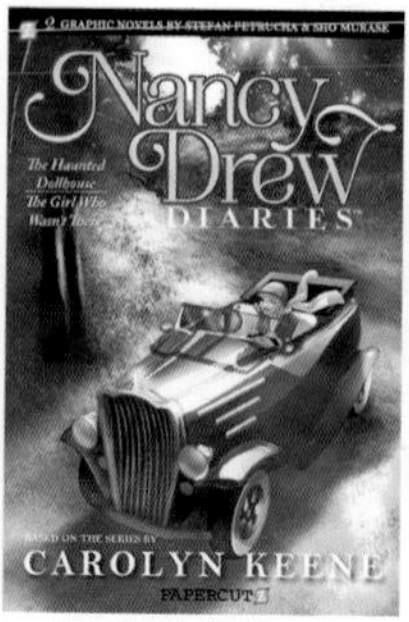

Nancy Drew
DIARIES
CAROLYN KEENE
PAPERCUTZ

"The Haunted Dollhouse" and "The Girl Who Wasn't There"

#2

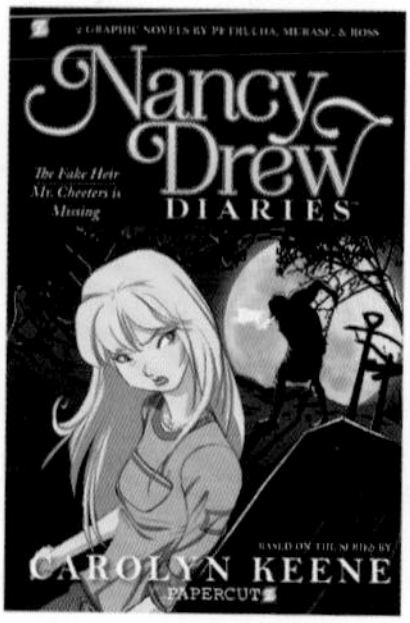

Nancy Drew
DIARIES
The Fake Heir
Mr. Cheeters is Missing
CAROLYN KEENE
PAPERCUTZ

"The Fake Heir" and "Mr Cheeters is Missing"

#3

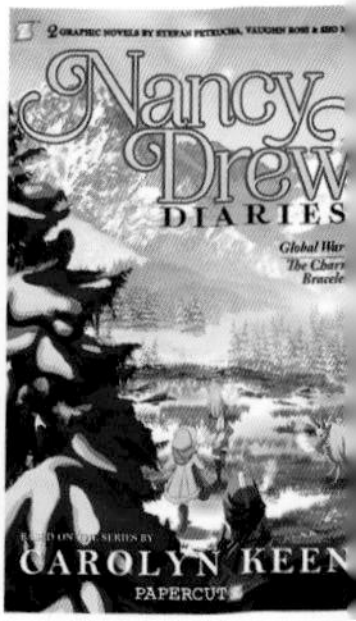

Nancy Drew
DIARIES
CAROLYN KEEN
PAPERCUTZ

"The Charmed Bracelet" and "Global Warning"

#4

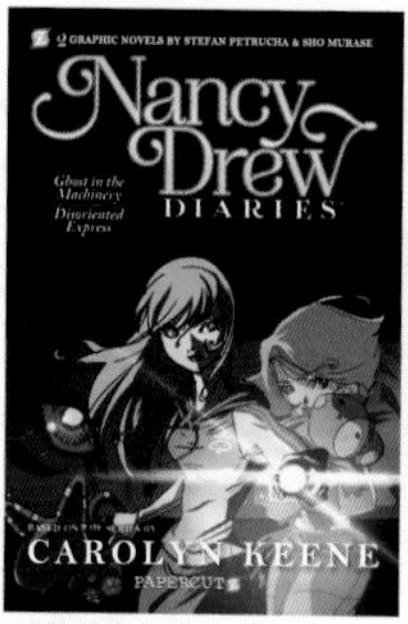

2 GRAPHIC NOVELS BY STEFAN PETRUCHA & SHO MURASE
Nancy Drew
DIARIES
CAROLYN KEENE
PAPERCUTZ

"Ghost in the Machinery" and "The Disoriented Express"

#5

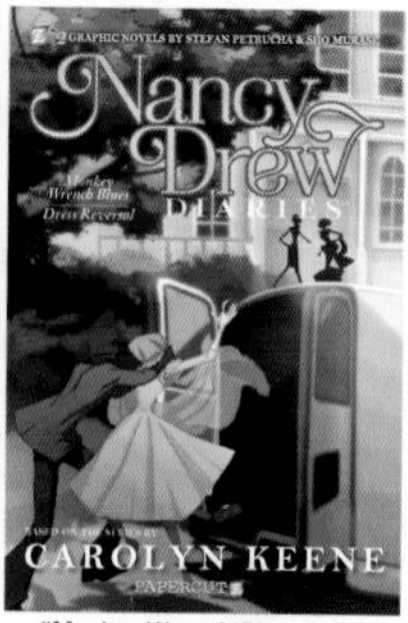

Nancy Drew
DIARIES
CAROLYN KEENE
PAPERCUTZ

"Monkey Wrench Blues" and "Dress Reversal"

#6

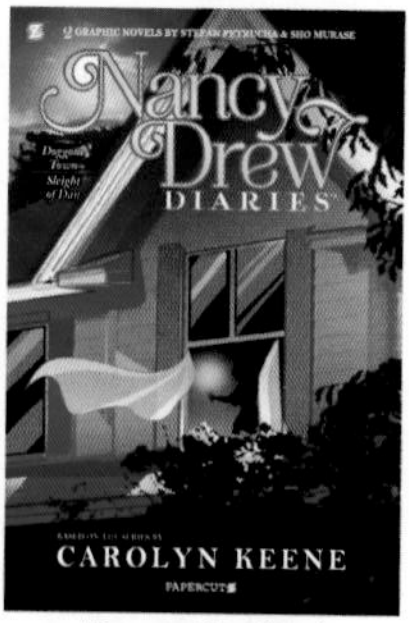

Nancy Drew
DIARIES
CAROLYN KEENE
PAPERCUTZ

"Doggone Town" and "Sleight of Dan"

#7

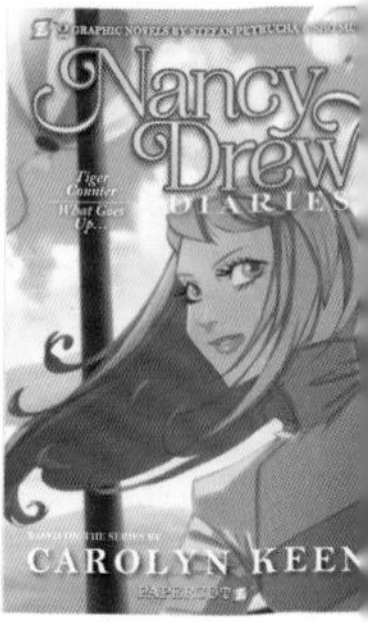

Nancy Drew
DIARIES
CAROLYN KEEN
PAPERCUTZ

"Tiger Counter" and "What Goes Up..."

#8

COMING SOON:

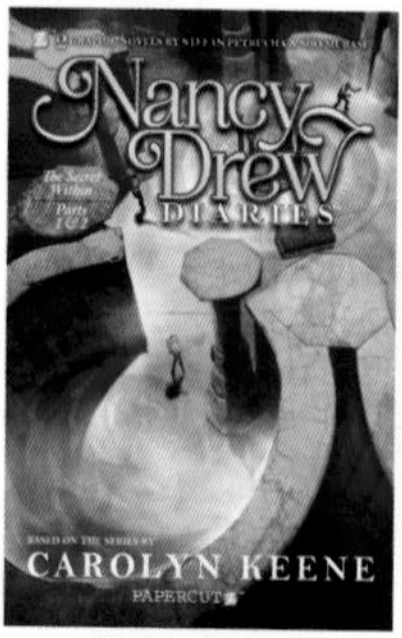

Nancy Drew
DIARIES
CAROLYN KEENE
PAPERCUTZ

"The Secret Within" Parts 1 & 2

#9

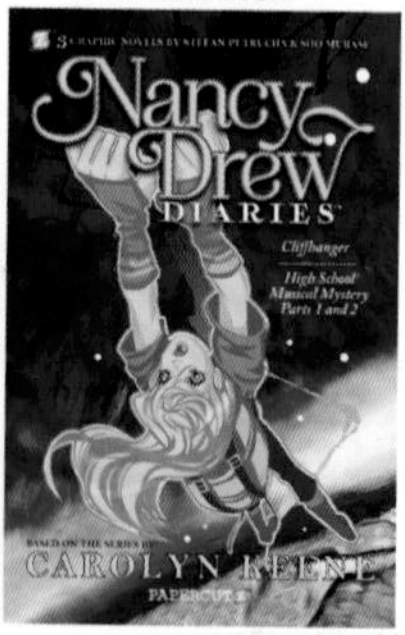

Nancy Drew
DIARIES
Cliffhanger
High School Musical Mystery Parts 1 and 2
CAROLYN KEENE
PAPERCUTZ

"High School Musical Mystery."

#10

See pages 80 and 175 for more NANCY DREW graphic novels!

NANCY DREW graphic novels are available at booksellers everywhere

NANCY DREW DIARIES graphic novels are $9.99 each and availa only in paperback. You may also order online at www.papercu com. Or call 1-800-886-1223, Monday through Friday, 9 – 5 E MC, Visa, and AmEx accepted. To order by mail, please add $4. for postage and handling for first book ordered, $1.00 for eac additional book and make check payable to NBM Publishing. Send to: Papercutz, 160 Broadway, Suite 700, East Wing, New Y NY 10038.

papercutz.com

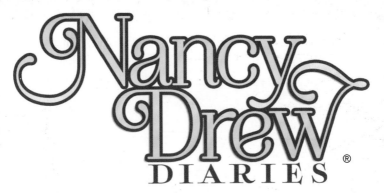

Nancy Drew DIARIES ®

#9 "The Secret Within"
Parts 1 & 2

Based on the series by
CAROLYN KEENE
STEFAN PETRUCHA & SARAH KINNEY • Writers
SHO MURASE • Artist
with 3D CG elements and color by CARLOS JOSE GUZMAN

PAPERCUTZ
New York

Nancy Drew Diaries
#9

"The Secret Within" Parts 1 & 2
Part 1: "Night of the Living Chatchke"
Part 2: "City Under the Basement"
STEFAN PETRUCHA & SARAH KINNEY – Writers
SHO MURASE – Artist
with 3D CG elements and color by CARLOS JOSE GUZMAN
BRYAN SENKA – Letterer
DAWN GUZZO – Production Coordinator
JEFF WHITMAN – Assistant Managing Editor
ROBERT V. CONTE –Editor
JIM SALICRUP
Editor-in-Chief

ISBN: 978-1-62991-742-9

Published by arrangement with Aladdin Paperbacks,
an imprint of Simon & Schuster Children's Publishing Division.

Printed in China

Distributed by Macmillian
First Printing

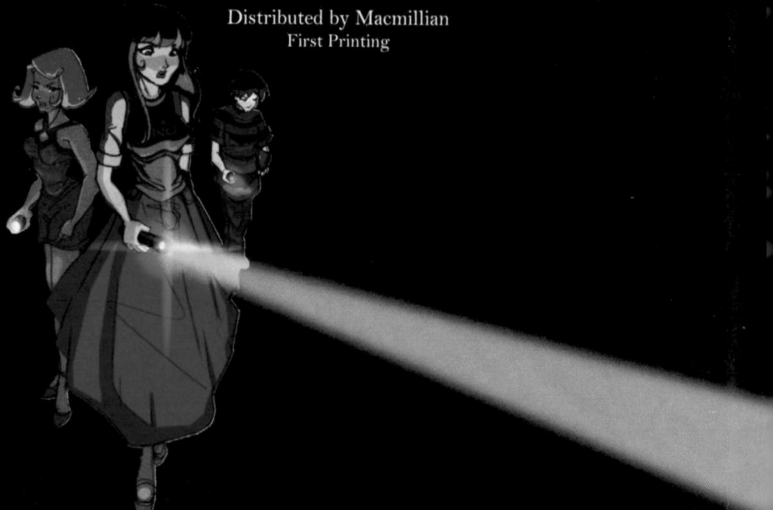

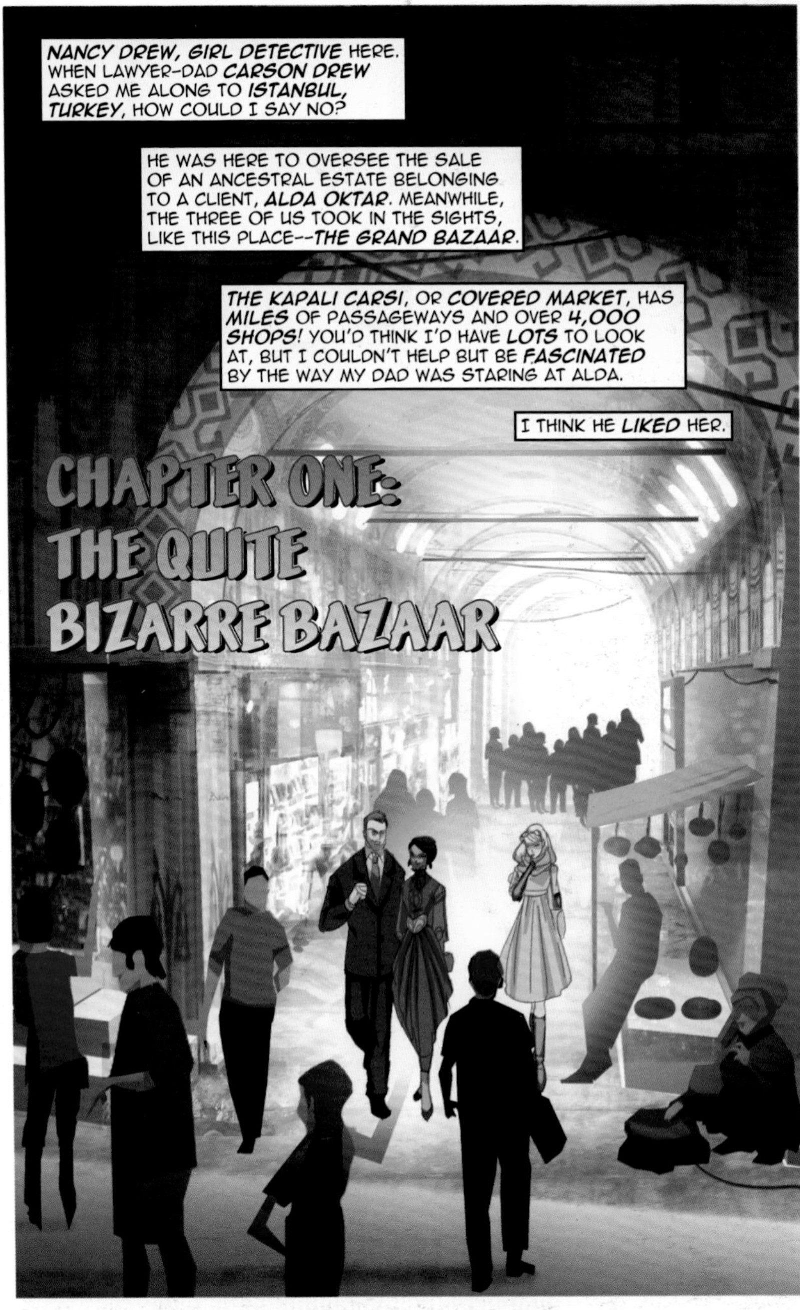
NANCY DREW, GIRL DETECTIVE HERE. WHEN LAWYER-DAD CARSON DREW ASKED ME ALONG TO ISTANBUL, TURKEY, HOW COULD I SAY NO?
HE WAS HERE TO OVERSEE THE SALE OF AN ANCESTRAL ESTATE BELONGING TO A CLIENT, ALDA OKTAR. MEANWHILE, THE THREE OF US TOOK IN THE SIGHTS, LIKE THIS PLACE--THE GRAND BAZAAR.
THE KAPALI CARSI, OR COVERED MARKET, HAS MILES OF PASSAGEWAYS AND OVER 4,000 SHOPS! YOU'D THINK I'D HAVE LOTS TO LOOK AT, BUT I COULDN'T HELP BUT BE FASCINATED BY THE WAY MY DAD WAS STARING AT ALDA.
I THINK HE LIKED HER.
CHAPTER ONE: THE QUITE BIZARRE BAZAAR

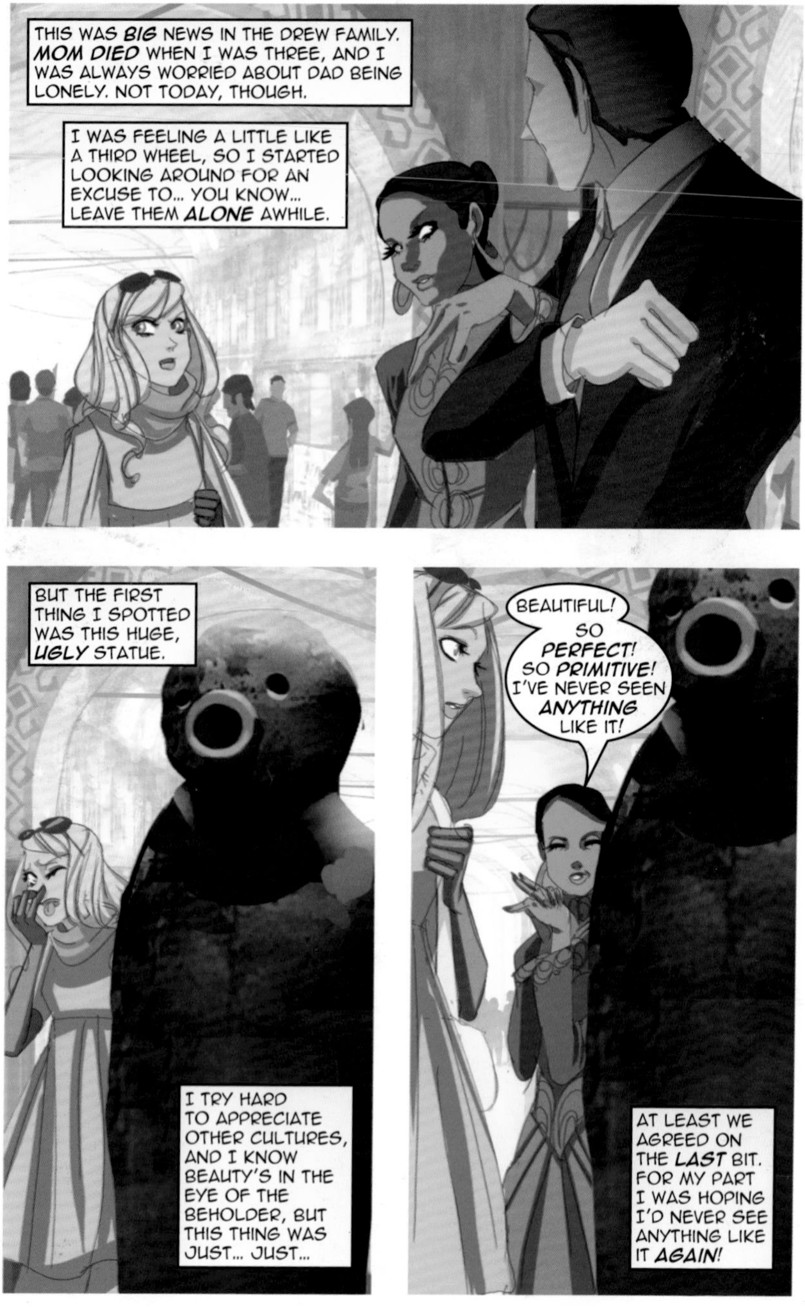
THIS WAS BIG NEWS IN THE DREW FAMILY. MOM DIED WHEN I WAS THREE, AND I WAS ALWAYS WORRIED ABOUT DAD BEING LONELY. NOT TODAY, THOUGH.
I WAS FEELING A LITTLE LIKE A THIRD WHEEL, SO I STARTED LOOKING AROUND FOR AN EXCUSE TO... YOU KNOW... LEAVE THEM ALONE AWHILE.
BUT THE FIRST THING I SPOTTED WAS THIS HUGE, UGLY STATUE.
I TRY HARD TO APPRECIATE OTHER CULTURES, AND I KNOW BEAUTY'S IN THE EYE OF THE BEHOLDER, BUT THIS THING WAS JUST... JUST...
BEAUTIFUL! SO PERFECT! SO PRIMITIVE! I'VE NEVER SEEN ANYTHING LIKE IT!
AT LEAST WE AGREED ON THE LAST BIT. FOR MY PART I WAS HOPING I'D NEVER SEE ANYTHING LIKE IT AGAIN!

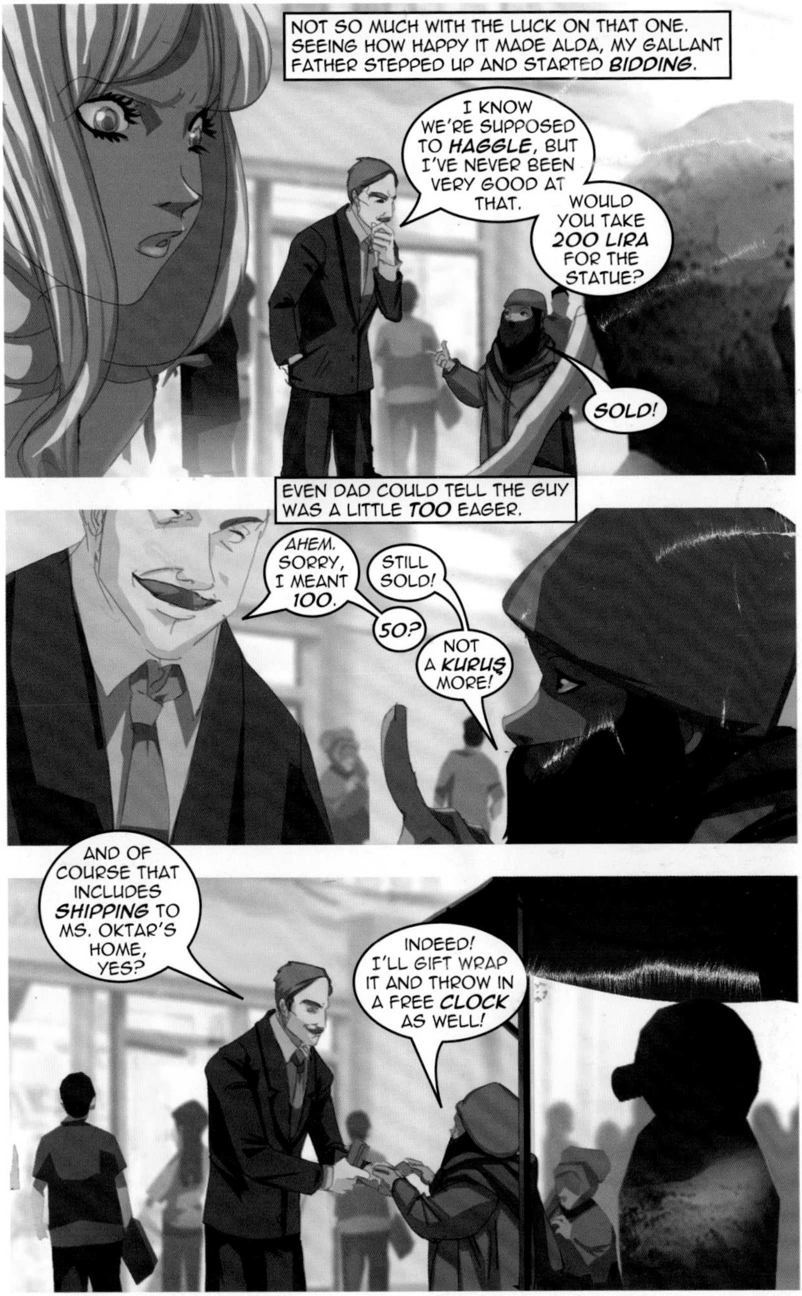
NOT SO MUCH WITH THE LUCK ON THAT ONE. SEEING HOW HAPPY IT MADE ALDA, MY GALLANT FATHER STEPPED UP AND STARTED BIDDING.
I KNOW WE'RE SUPPOSED TO HAGGLE, BUT I'VE NEVER BEEN VERY GOOD AT THAT.
WOULD YOU TAKE 200 LIRA FOR THE STATUE?
SOLD!
EVEN DAD COULD TELL THE GUY WAS A LITTLE TOO EAGER.
AHEM. SORRY, I MEANT 100.
STILL SOLD!
50?
NOT A KURUŞ MORE!
AND OF COURSE THAT INCLUDES SHIPPING TO MS. OKTAR'S HOME, YES?
INDEED! I'LL GIFT WRAP IT AND THROW IN A FREE CLOCK AS WELL!

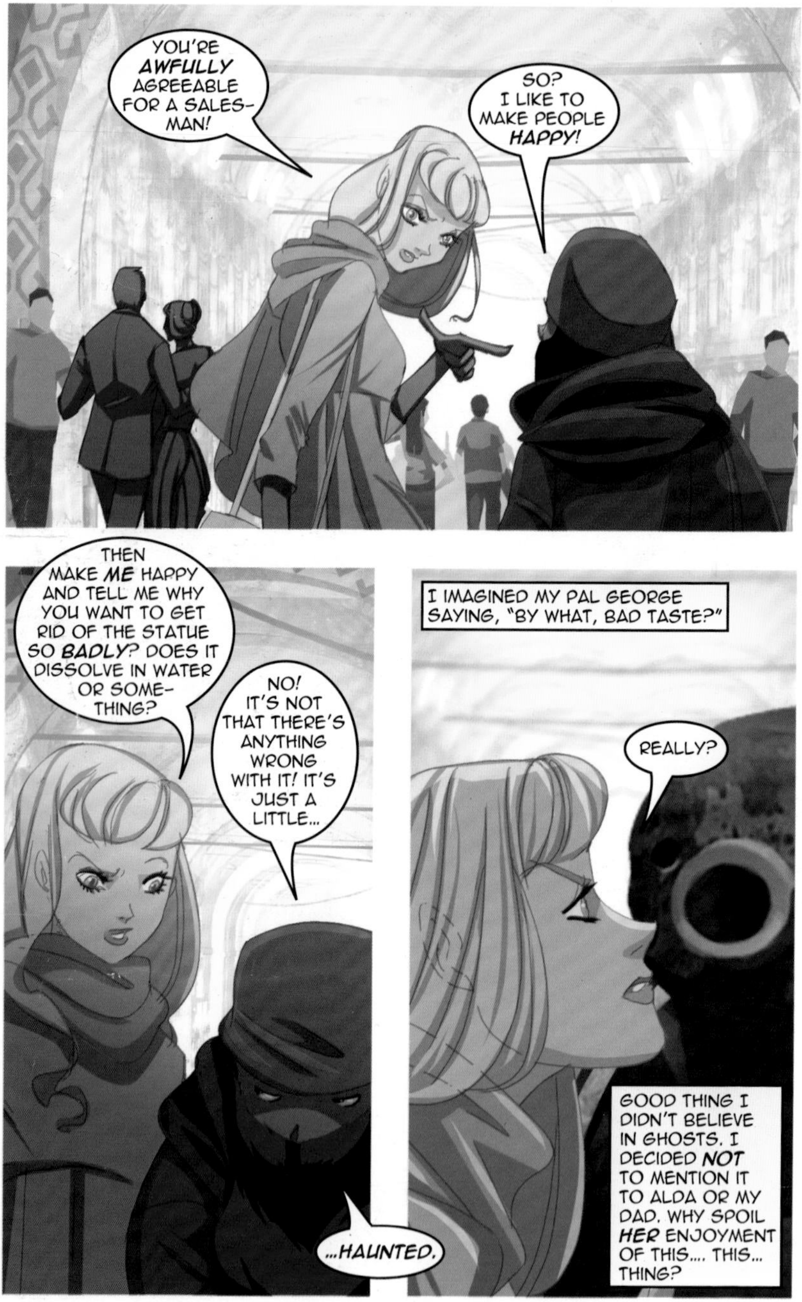
YOU'RE AWFULLY AGREEABLE FOR A SALES-MAN!
SO? I LIKE TO MAKE PEOPLE HAPPY!
THEN MAKE ME HAPPY AND TELL ME WHY YOU WANT TO GET RID OF THE STATUE SO BADLY? DOES IT DISSOLVE IN WATER OR SOME-THING?
NO! IT'S NOT THAT THERE'S ANYTHING WRONG WITH IT! IT'S JUST A LITTLE...
...HAUNTED.
I IMAGINED MY PAL GEORGE SAYING, "BY WHAT, BAD TASTE?"
REALLY?
GOOD THING I DIDN'T BELIEVE IN GHOSTS. I DECIDED NOT TO MENTION IT TO ALDA OR MY DAD. WHY SPOIL HER ENJOYMENT OF THIS.... THIS... THING?

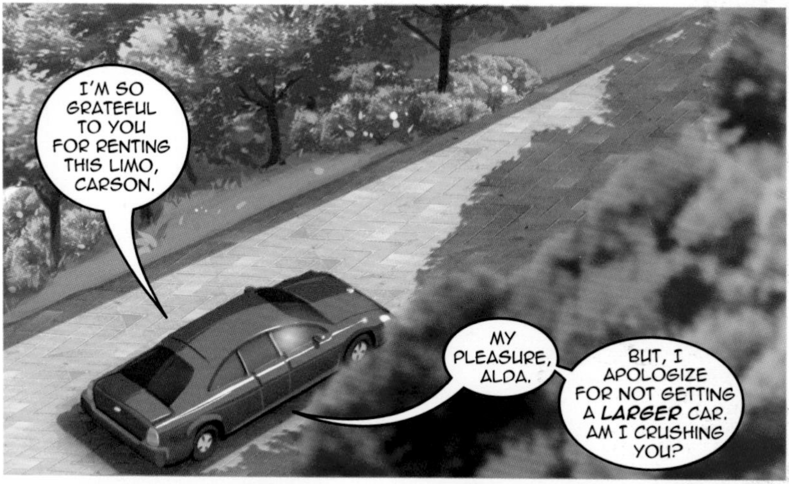
I'M SO GRATEFUL TO YOU FOR RENTING THIS LIMO, CARSON.
MY PLEASURE, ALDA.
BUT, I APOLOGIZE FOR NOT GETTING A *LARGER* CAR. AM I CRUSHING YOU?

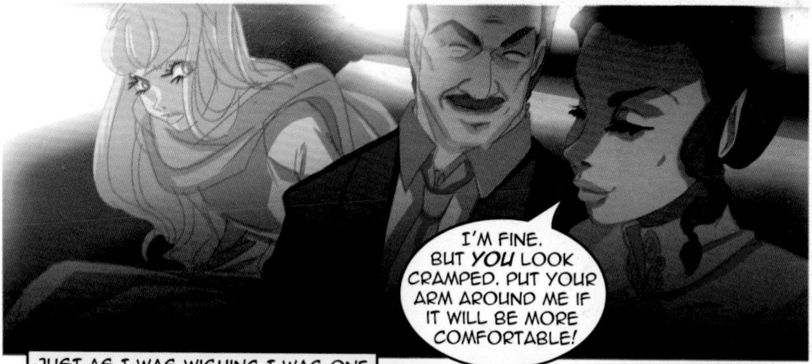
I'M FINE. BUT *YOU* LOOK CRAMPED. PUT YOUR ARM AROUND ME IF IT WILL BE MORE COMFORTABLE!

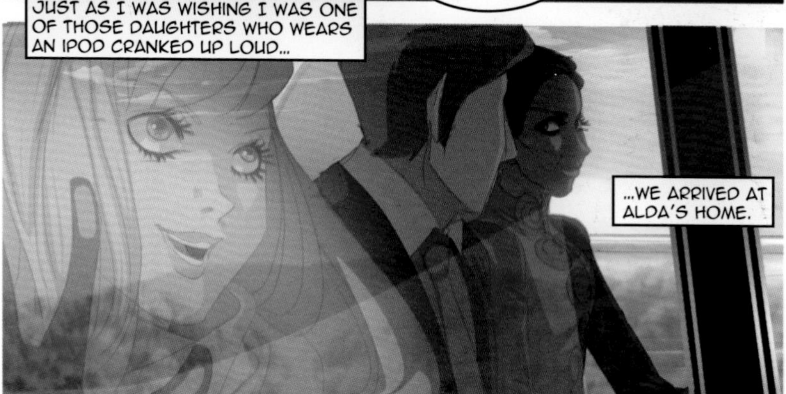
JUST AS I WAS WISHING I WAS ONE OF THOSE DAUGHTERS WHO WEARS AN IPOD CRANKED UP LOUD...
...WE ARRIVED AT ALDA'S HOME.

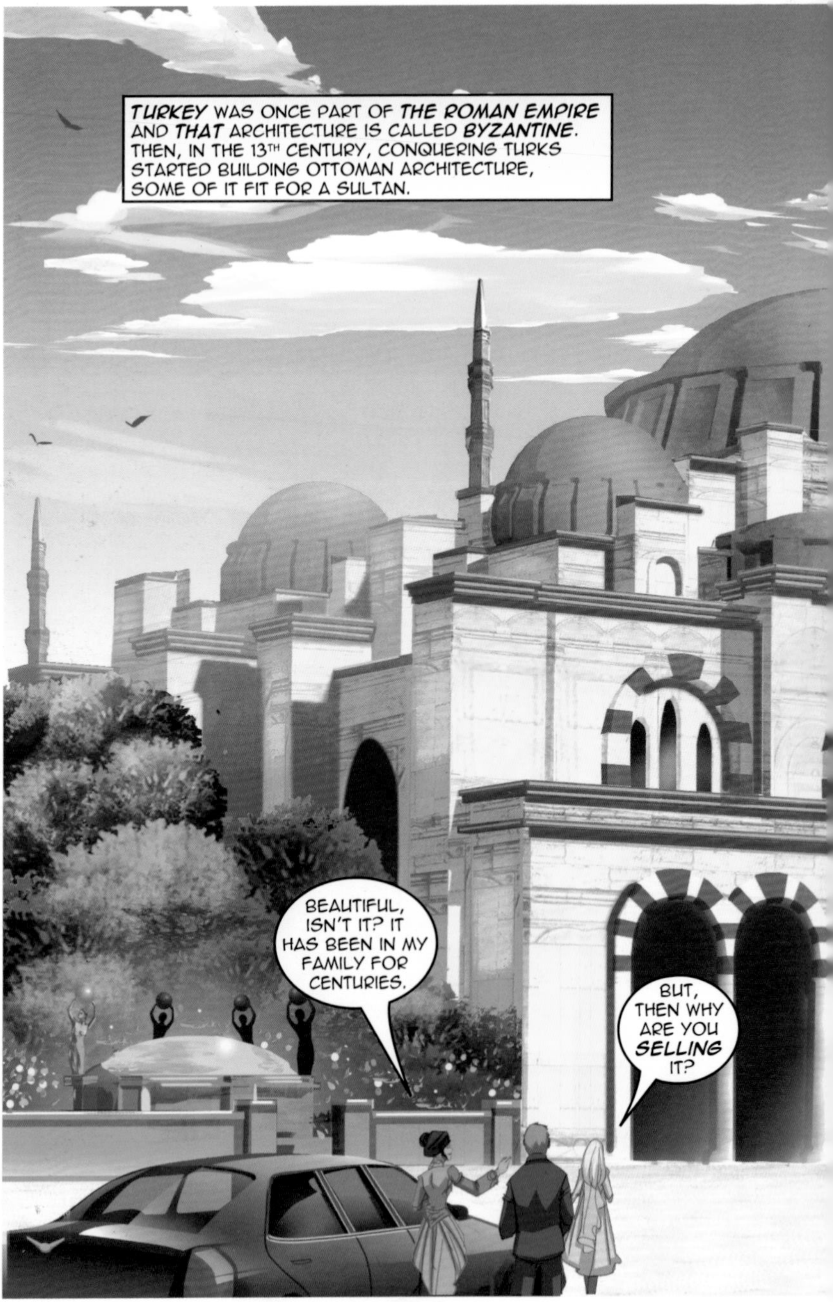
TURKEY WAS ONCE PART OF THE ROMAN EMPIRE AND THAT ARCHITECTURE IS CALLED BYZANTINE. THEN, IN THE 13TH CENTURY, CONQUERING TURKS STARTED BUILDING OTTOMAN ARCHITECTURE, SOME OF IT FIT FOR A SULTAN.
BEAUTIFUL, ISN'T IT? IT HAS BEEN IN MY FAMILY FOR CENTURIES.
BUT, THEN WHY ARE YOU SELLING IT?

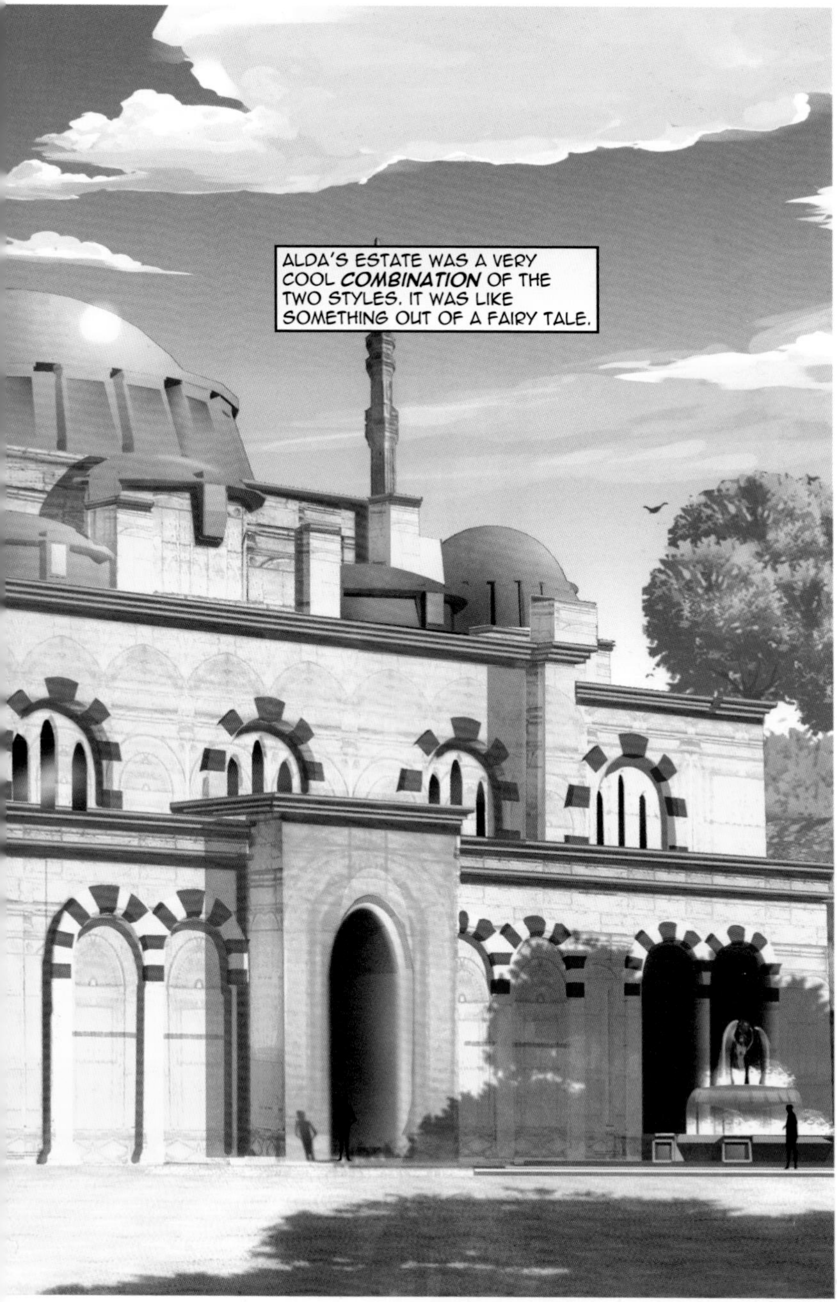
ALDA'S ESTATE WAS A VERY COOL **COMBINATION** OF THE TWO STYLES. IT WAS LIKE SOMETHING OUT OF A FAIRY TALE.

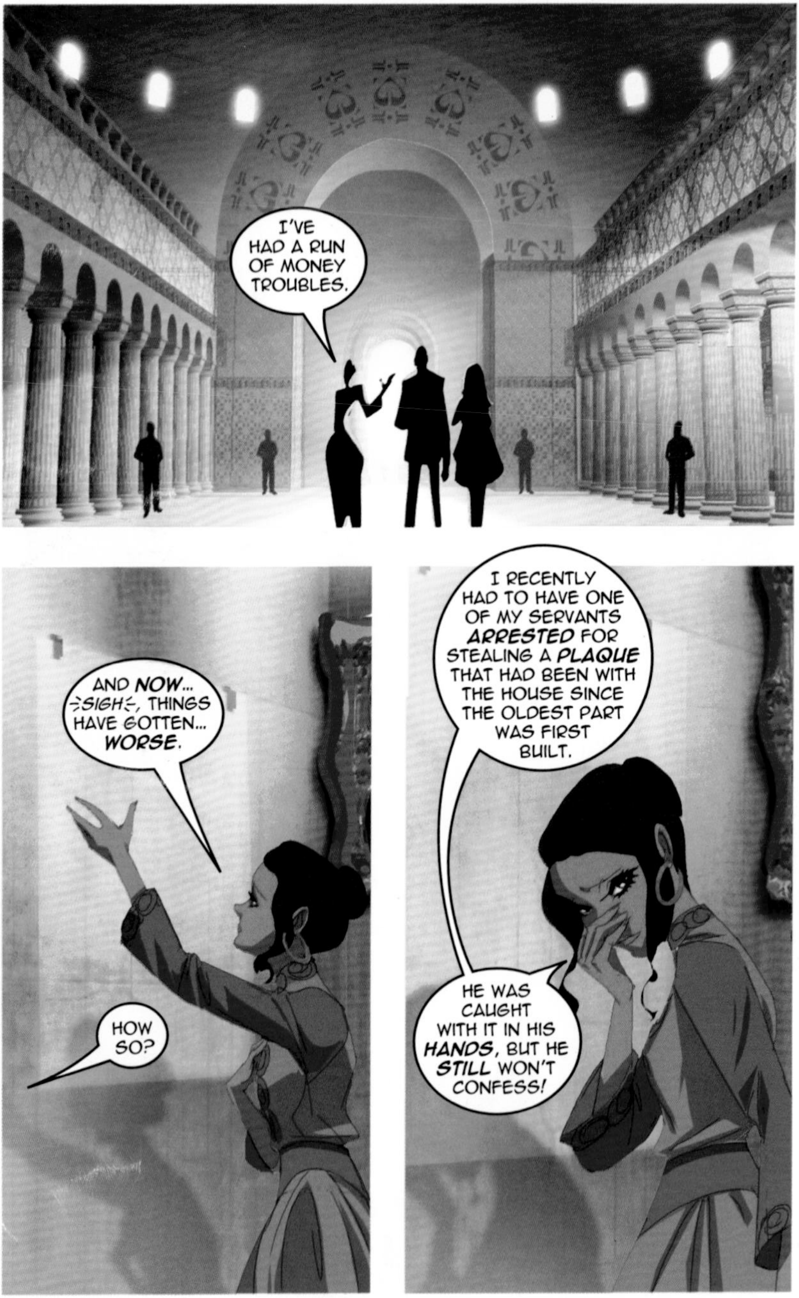
I'VE HAD A RUN OF MONEY TROUBLES.
AND NOW... ⇒SIGH⇐, THINGS HAVE GOTTEN... WORSE.
HOW SO?
I RECENTLY HAD TO HAVE ONE OF MY SERVANTS ARRESTED FOR STEALING A PLAQUE THAT HAD BEEN WITH THE HOUSE SINCE THE OLDEST PART WAS FIRST BUILT.
HE WAS CAUGHT WITH IT IN HIS HANDS, BUT HE STILL WON'T CONFESS!

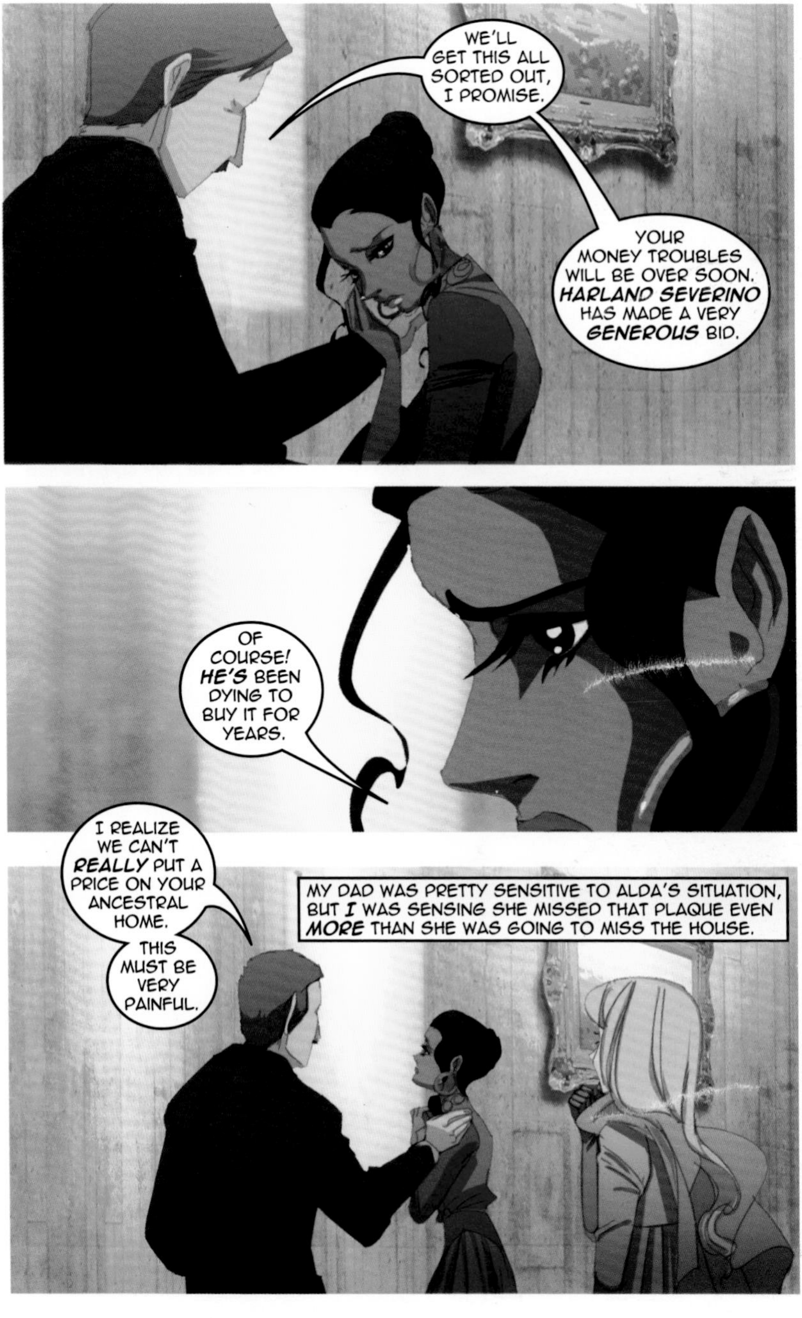
WE'LL GET THIS ALL SORTED OUT, I PROMISE.
YOUR MONEY TROUBLES WILL BE OVER SOON. HARLAND SEVERINO HAS MADE A VERY GENEROUS BID.
OF COURSE! HE'S BEEN DYING TO BUY IT FOR YEARS.
I REALIZE WE CAN'T REALLY PUT A PRICE ON YOUR ANCESTRAL HOME.
THIS MUST BE VERY PAINFUL.
MY DAD WAS PRETTY SENSITIVE TO ALDA'S SITUATION, BUT I WAS SENSING SHE MISSED THAT PLAQUE EVEN MORE THAN SHE WAS GOING TO MISS THE HOUSE.

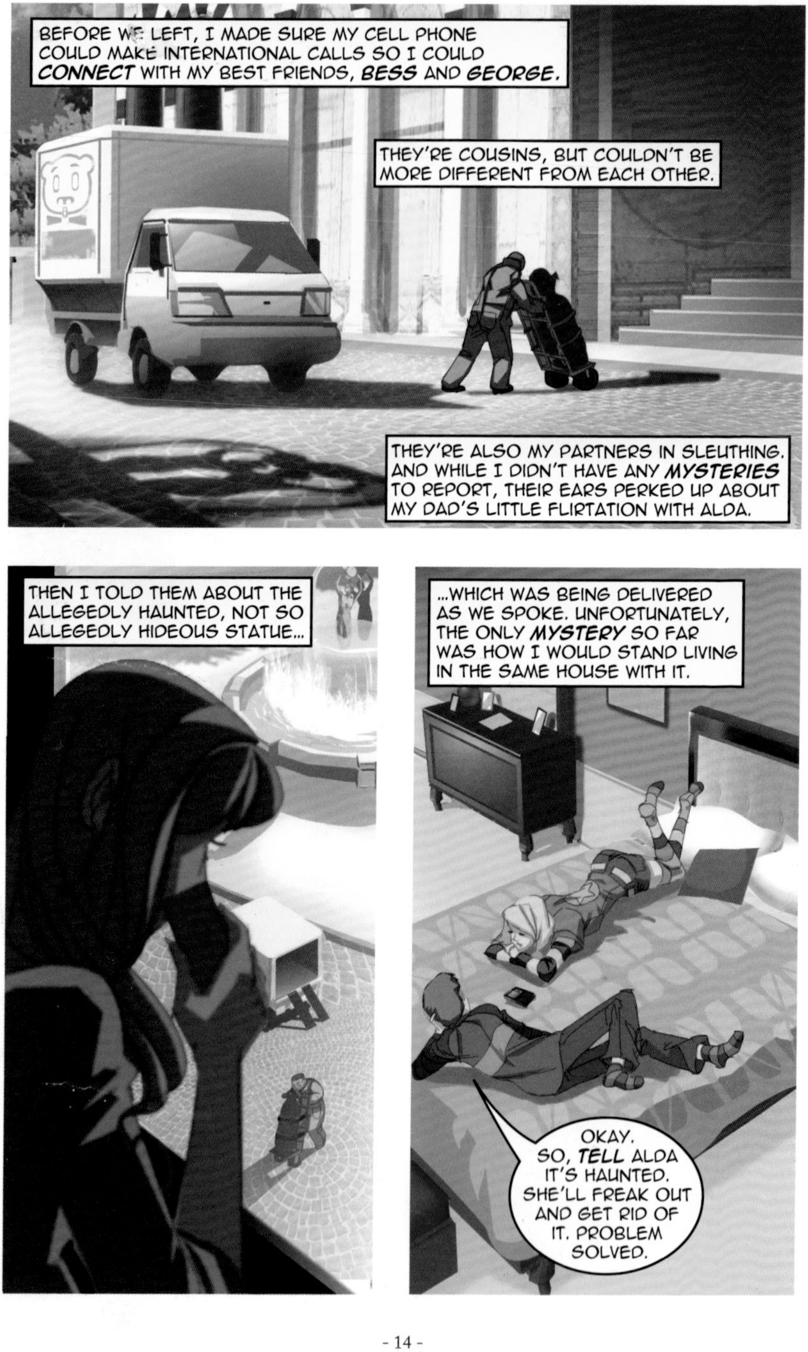
BEFORE WE LEFT, I MADE SURE MY CELL PHONE COULD MAKE INTERNATIONAL CALLS SO I COULD CONNECT WITH MY BEST FRIENDS, BESS AND GEORGE.
THEY'RE COUSINS, BUT COULDN'T BE MORE DIFFERENT FROM EACH OTHER.
THEY'RE ALSO MY PARTNERS IN SLEUTHING. AND WHILE I DIDN'T HAVE ANY MYSTERIES TO REPORT, THEIR EARS PERKED UP ABOUT MY DAD'S LITTLE FLIRTATION WITH ALDA.
THEN I TOLD THEM ABOUT THE ALLEGEDLY HAUNTED, NOT SO ALLEGEDLY HIDEOUS STATUE...
...WHICH WAS BEING DELIVERED AS WE SPOKE. UNFORTUNATELY, THE ONLY MYSTERY SO FAR WAS HOW I WOULD STAND LIVING IN THE SAME HOUSE WITH IT.
OKAY. SO, TELL ALDA IT'S HAUNTED. SHE'LL FREAK OUT AND GET RID OF IT. PROBLEM SOLVED.

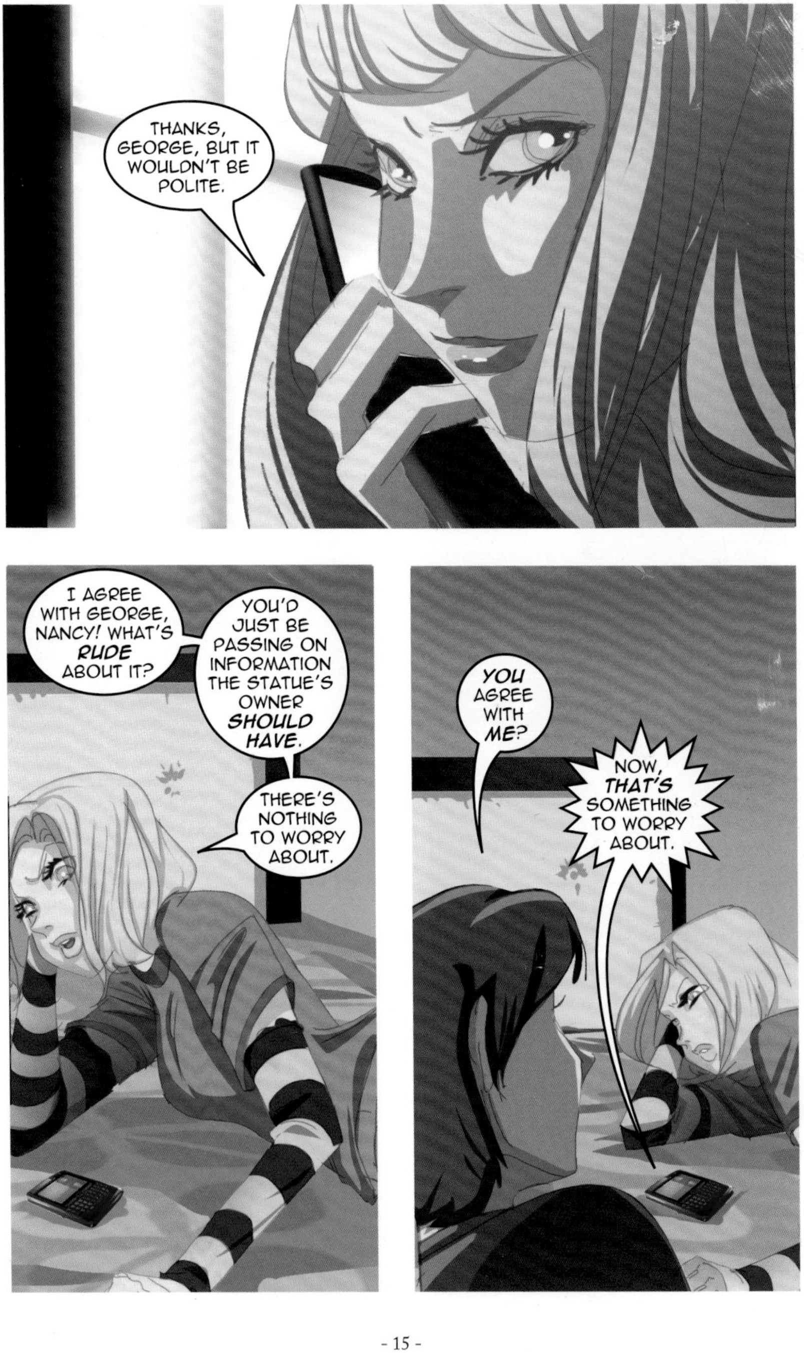
THANKS, GEORGE, BUT IT WOULDN'T BE POLITE.
I AGREE WITH GEORGE, NANCY! WHAT'S RUDE ABOUT IT?
YOU'D JUST BE PASSING ON INFORMATION THE STATUE'S OWNER SHOULD HAVE.
THERE'S NOTHING TO WORRY ABOUT.
YOU AGREE WITH ME?
NOW, THAT'S SOMETHING TO WORRY ABOUT.

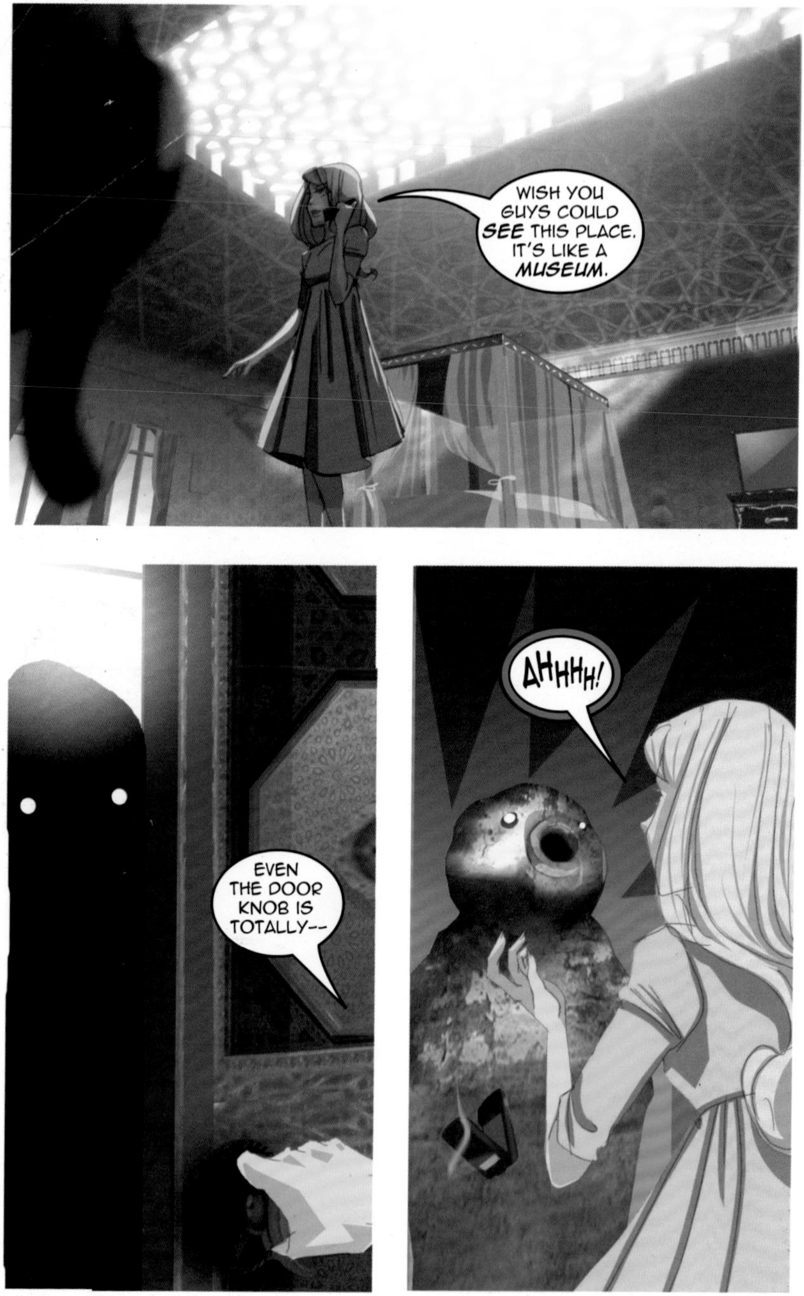
WISH YOU GUYS COULD SEE THIS PLACE. IT'S LIKE A MUSEUM.
EVEN THE DOOR KNOB IS TOTALLY--
AHHHH!

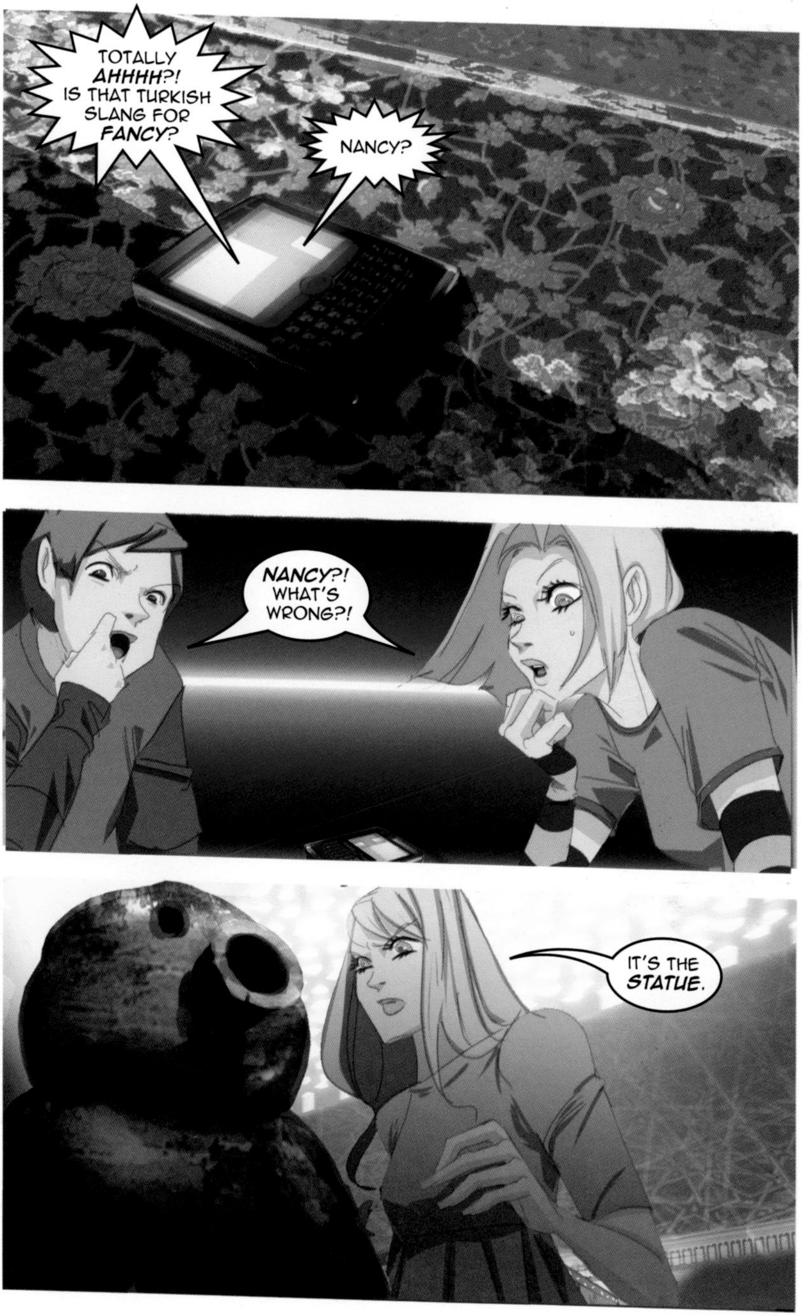
TOTALLY AHHHH?! IS THAT TURKISH SLANG FOR FANCY?
NANCY?
NANCY?! WHAT'S WRONG?!
IT'S THE STATUE.

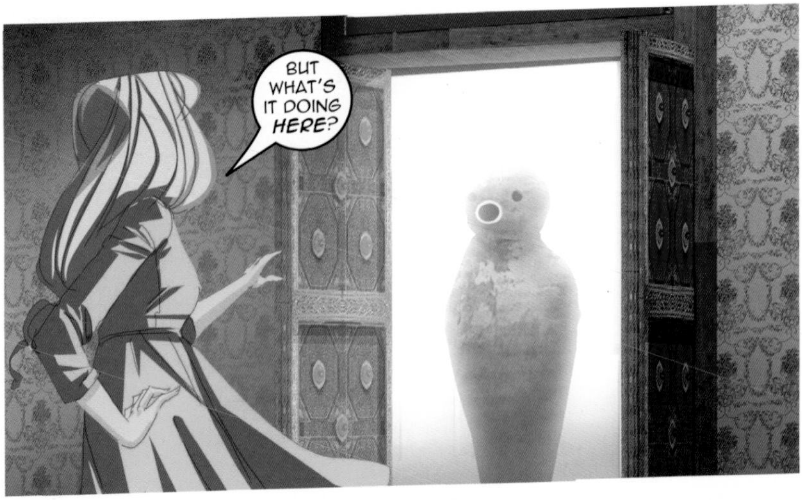
BUT WHAT'S IT DOING HERE?

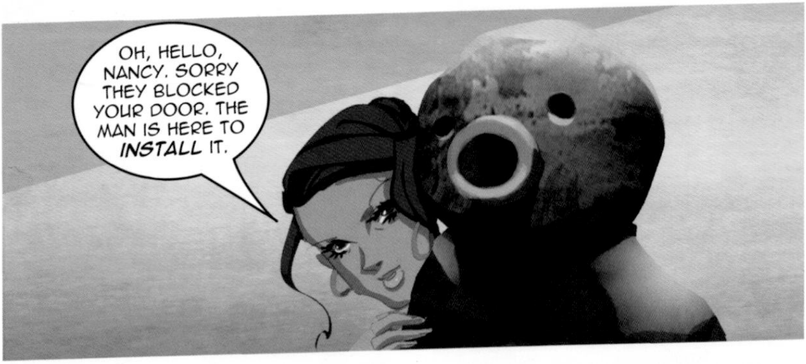
OH, HELLO, NANCY. SORRY THEY BLOCKED YOUR DOOR. THE MAN IS HERE TO INSTALL IT.

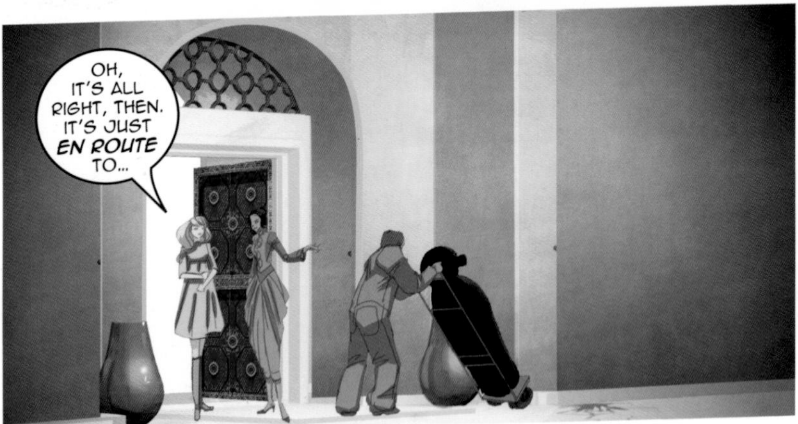
OH, IT'S ALL RIGHT, THEN. IT'S JUST EN ROUTE TO...

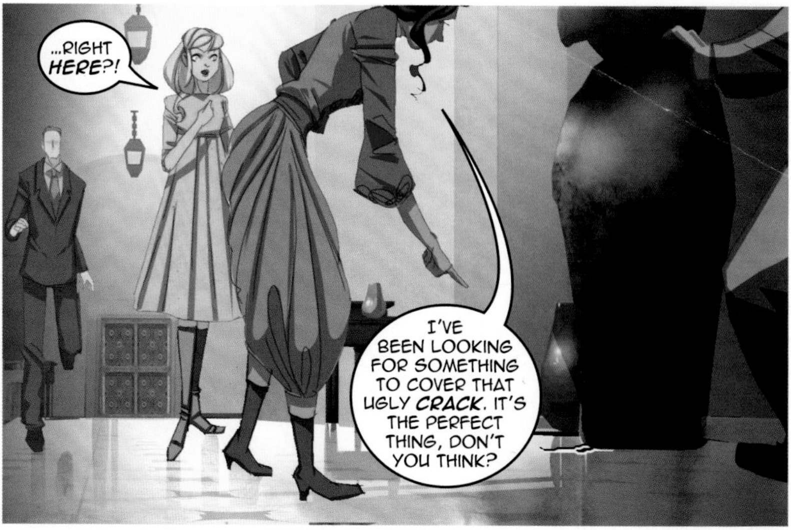
...RIGHT HERE?!
I'VE BEEN LOOKING FOR SOMETHING TO COVER THAT UGLY CRACK. IT'S THE PERFECT THING, DON'T YOU THINK?

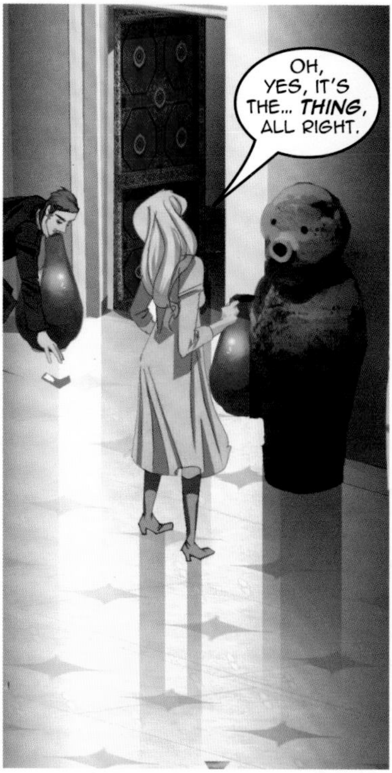
OH, YES, IT'S THE... THING, ALL RIGHT.

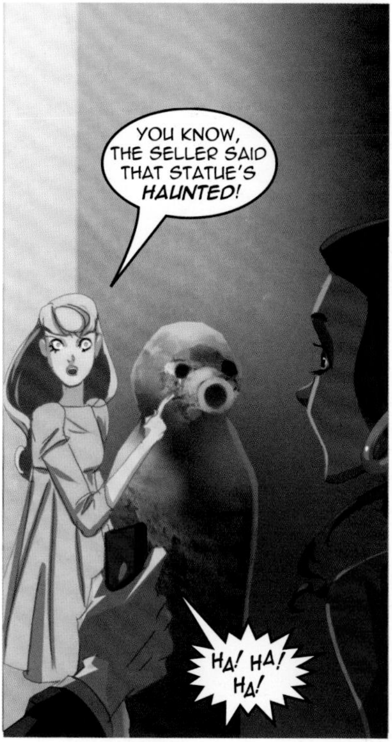
YOU KNOW, THE SELLER SAID THAT STATUE'S HAUNTED!
HA! HA! HA!

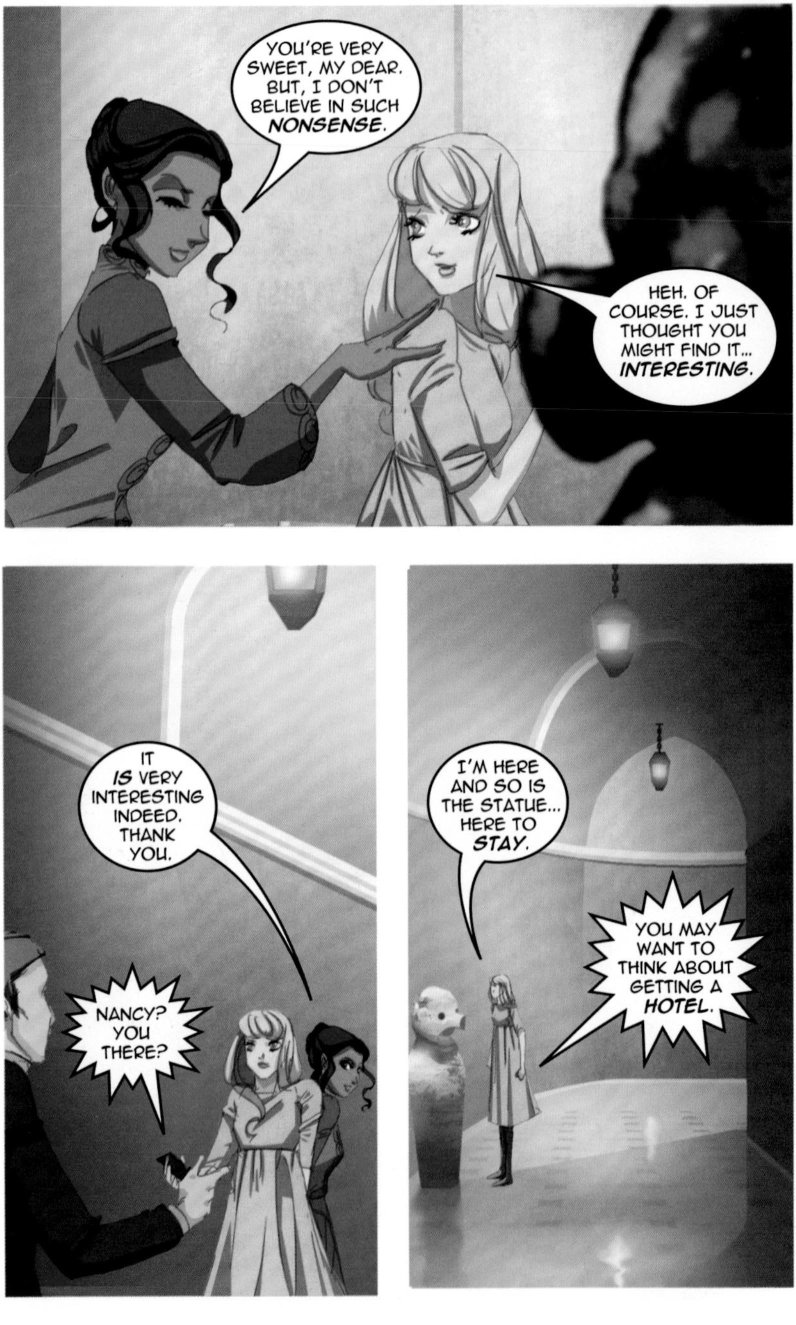
YOU'RE VERY SWEET, MY DEAR. BUT, I DON'T BELIEVE IN SUCH *NONSENSE*.
HEH. OF COURSE. I JUST THOUGHT YOU MIGHT FIND IT... *INTERESTING*.
IT *IS* VERY INTERESTING INDEED. THANK YOU.
NANCY? YOU THERE?
I'M HERE AND SO IS THE STATUE... HERE TO *STAY*.
YOU MAY WANT TO THINK ABOUT GETTING A *HOTEL*.

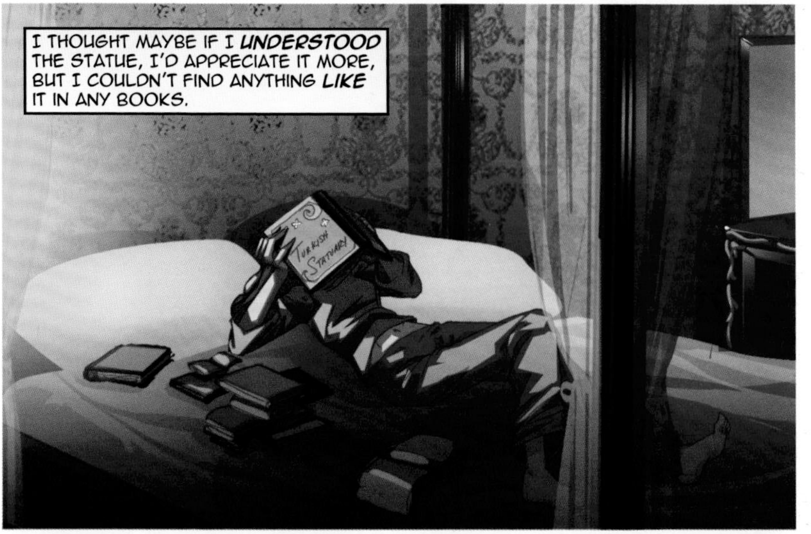
I THOUGHT MAYBE IF I ***UNDERSTOOD*** THE STATUE, I'D APPRECIATE IT MORE, BUT I COULDN'T FIND ANYTHING ***LIKE*** IT IN ANY BOOKS.
TURKISH STATUARY

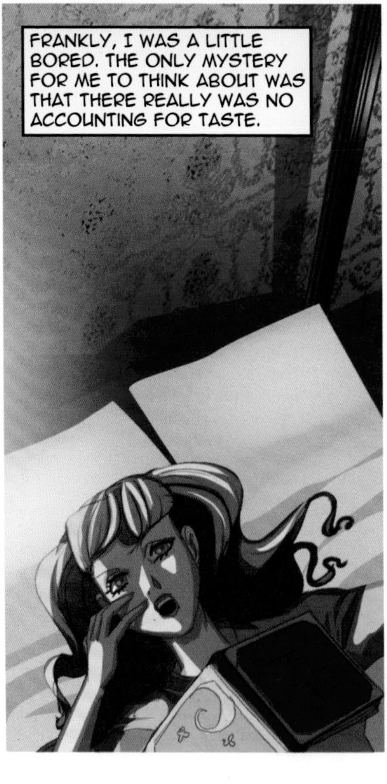
FRANKLY, I WAS A LITTLE BORED. THE ONLY MYSTERY FOR ME TO THINK ABOUT WAS THAT THERE REALLY WAS NO ACCOUNTING FOR TASTE.

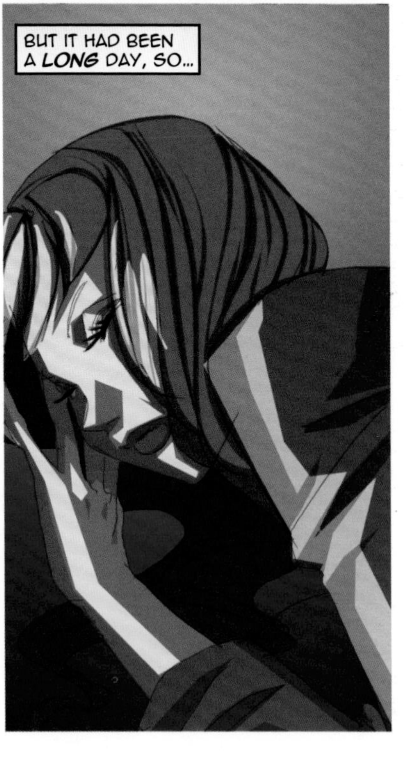
BUT IT HAD BEEN A ***LONG*** DAY, SO...

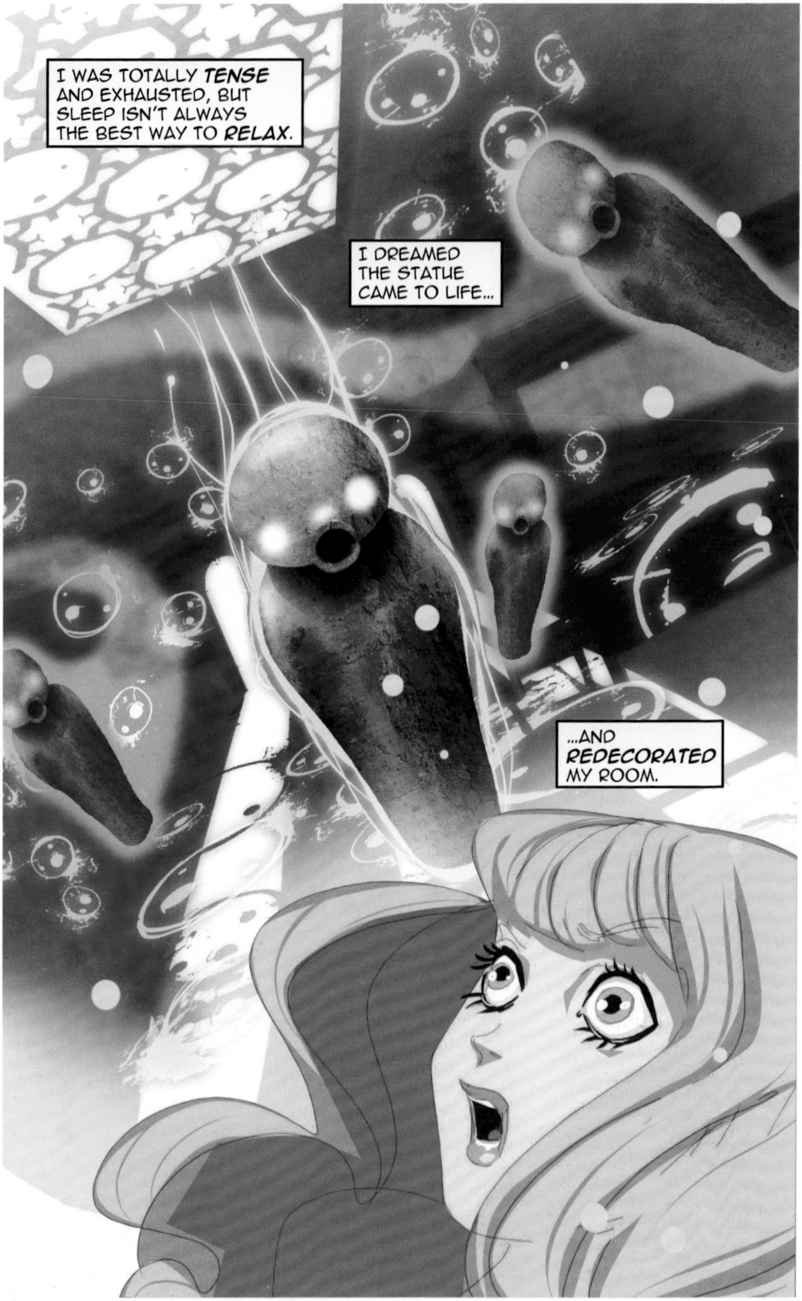
I WAS TOTALLY TENSE AND EXHAUSTED, BUT SLEEP ISN'T ALWAYS THE BEST WAY TO RELAX.
I DREAMED THE STATUE CAME TO LIFE...
...AND REDECORATED MY ROOM.

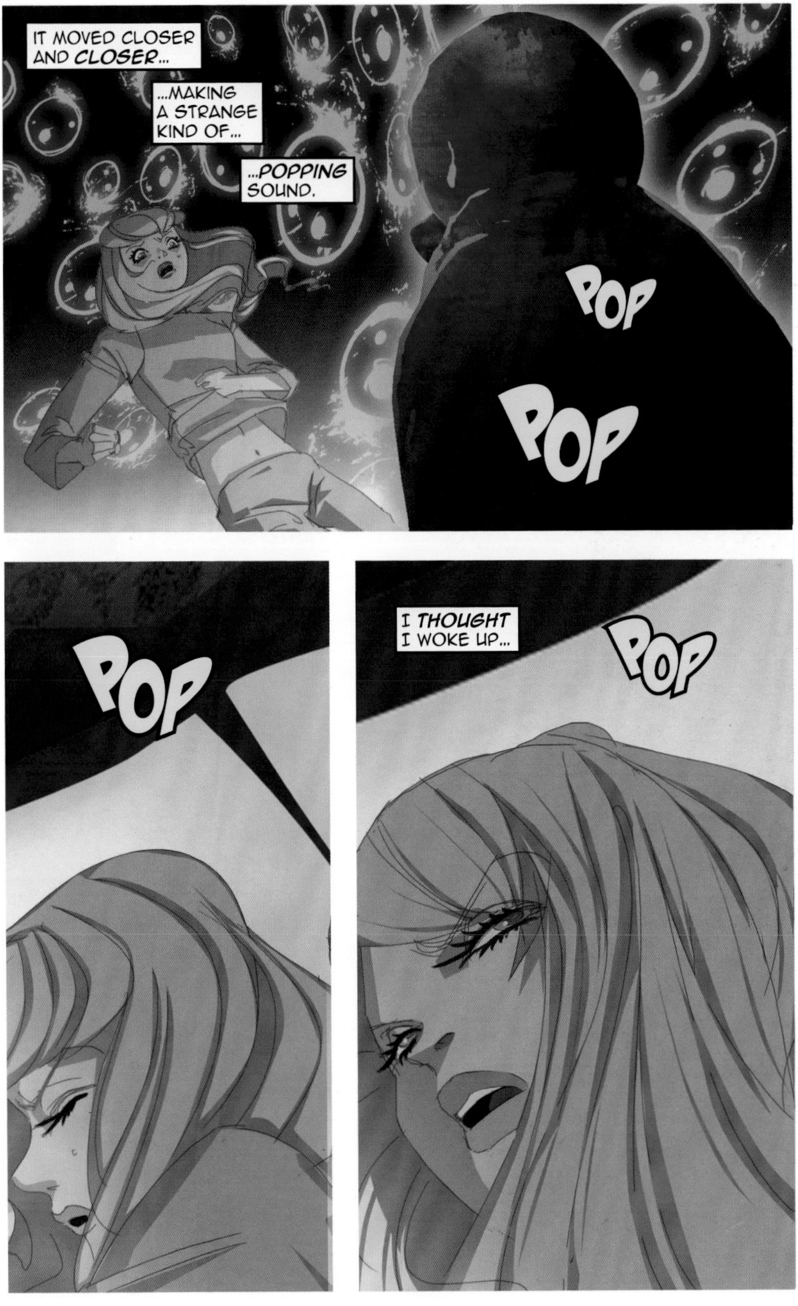
IT MOVED CLOSER AND *CLOSER*...
...MAKING A STRANGE KIND OF...
...*POPPING* SOUND.
POP
POP
POP
I *THOUGHT* I WOKE UP...
POP

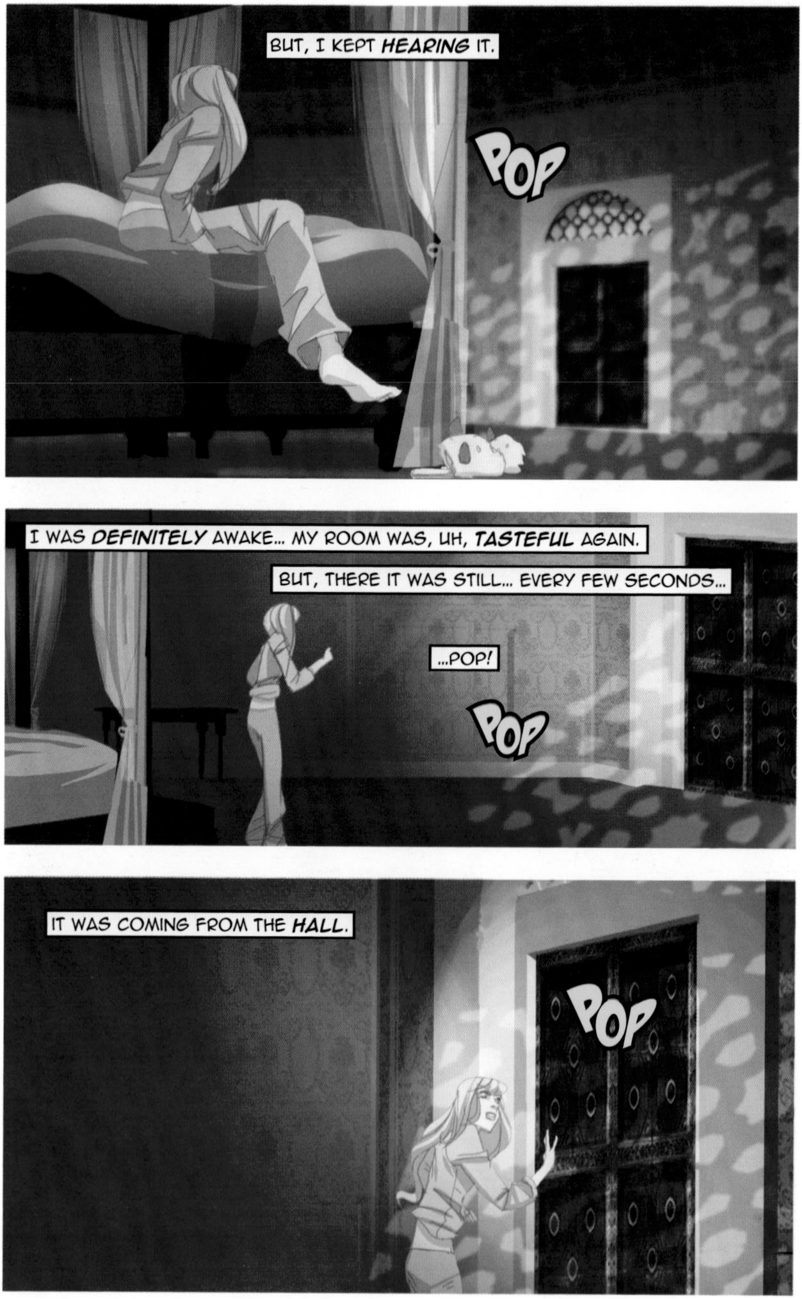
BUT, I KEPT HEARING IT.
POP
I WAS DEFINITELY AWAKE... MY ROOM WAS, UH, TASTEFUL AGAIN.
BUT, THERE IT WAS STILL... EVERY FEW SECONDS...
...POP!
POP
IT WAS COMING FROM THE HALL.
POP

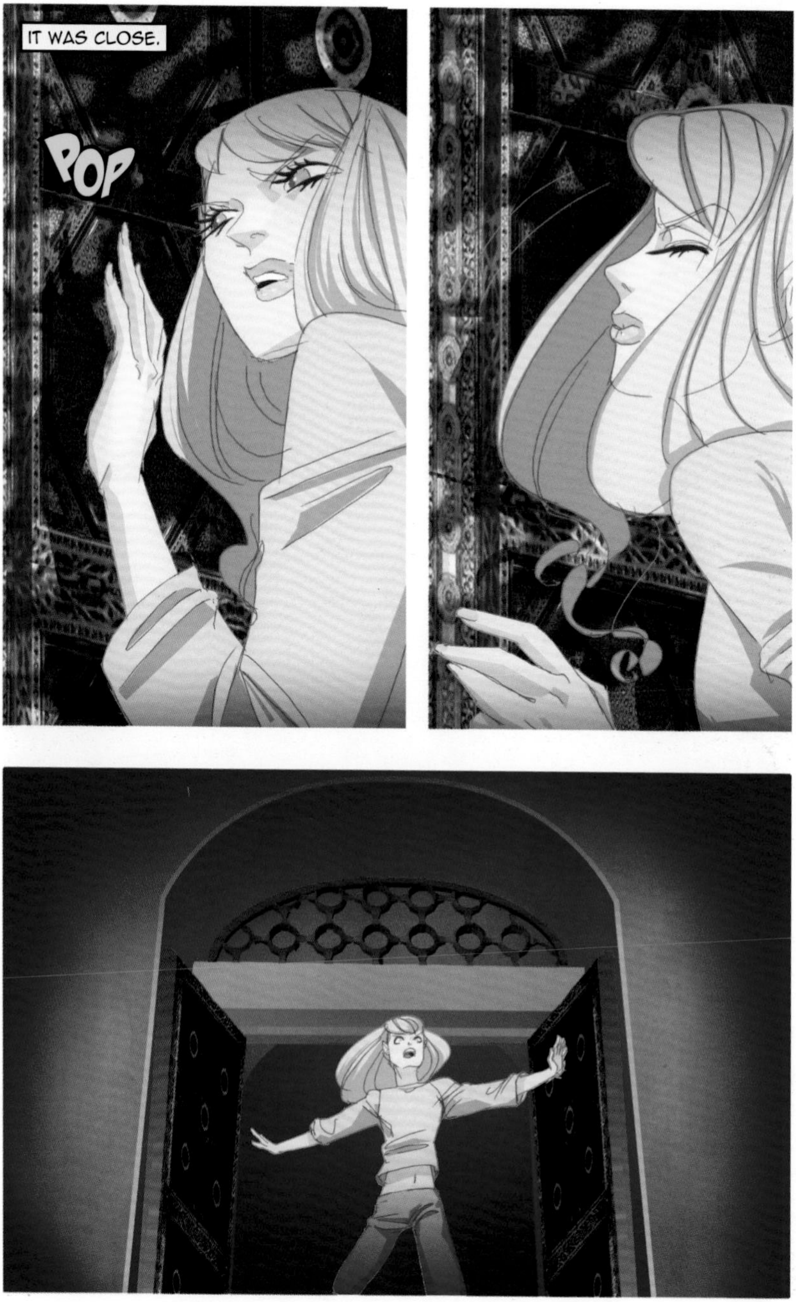
IT WAS CLOSE.
POP

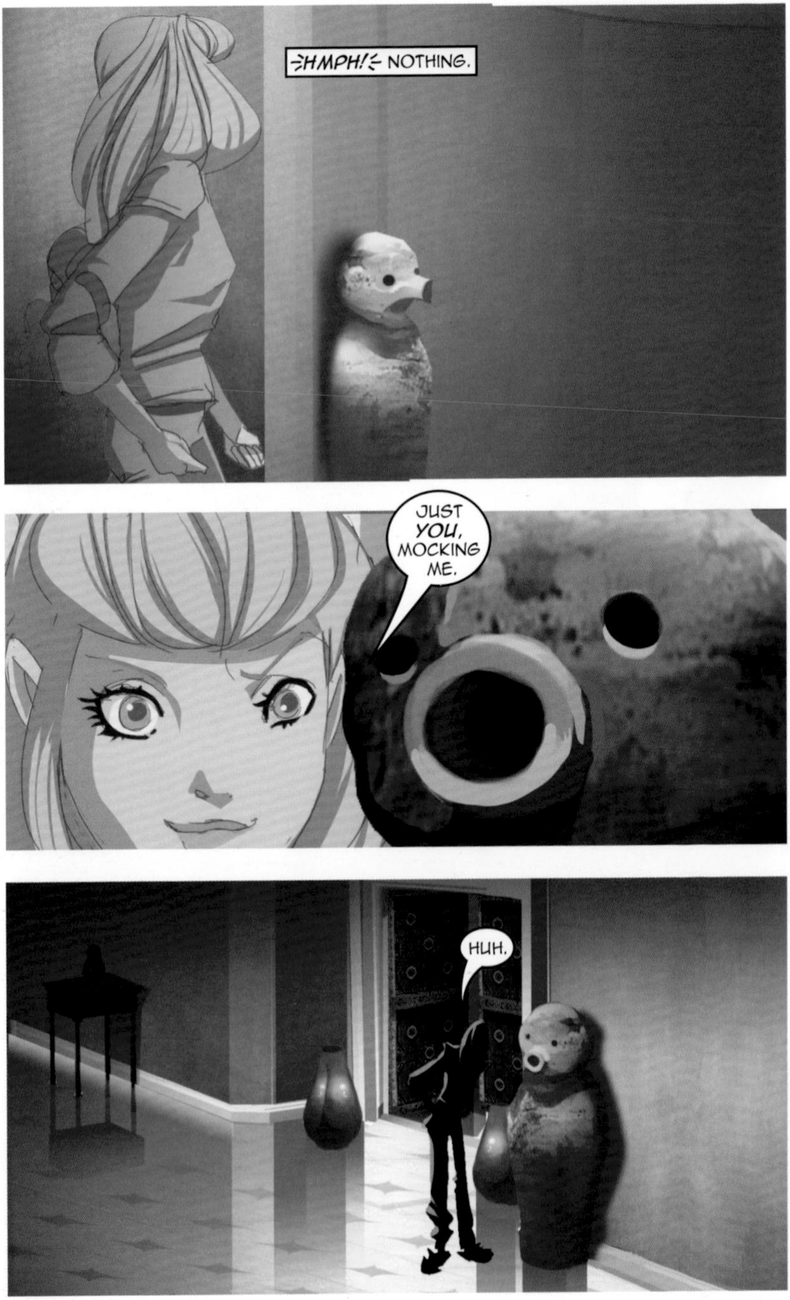
≡HMPH!≡ NOTHING.
JUST YOU, MOCKING ME.
HUH.

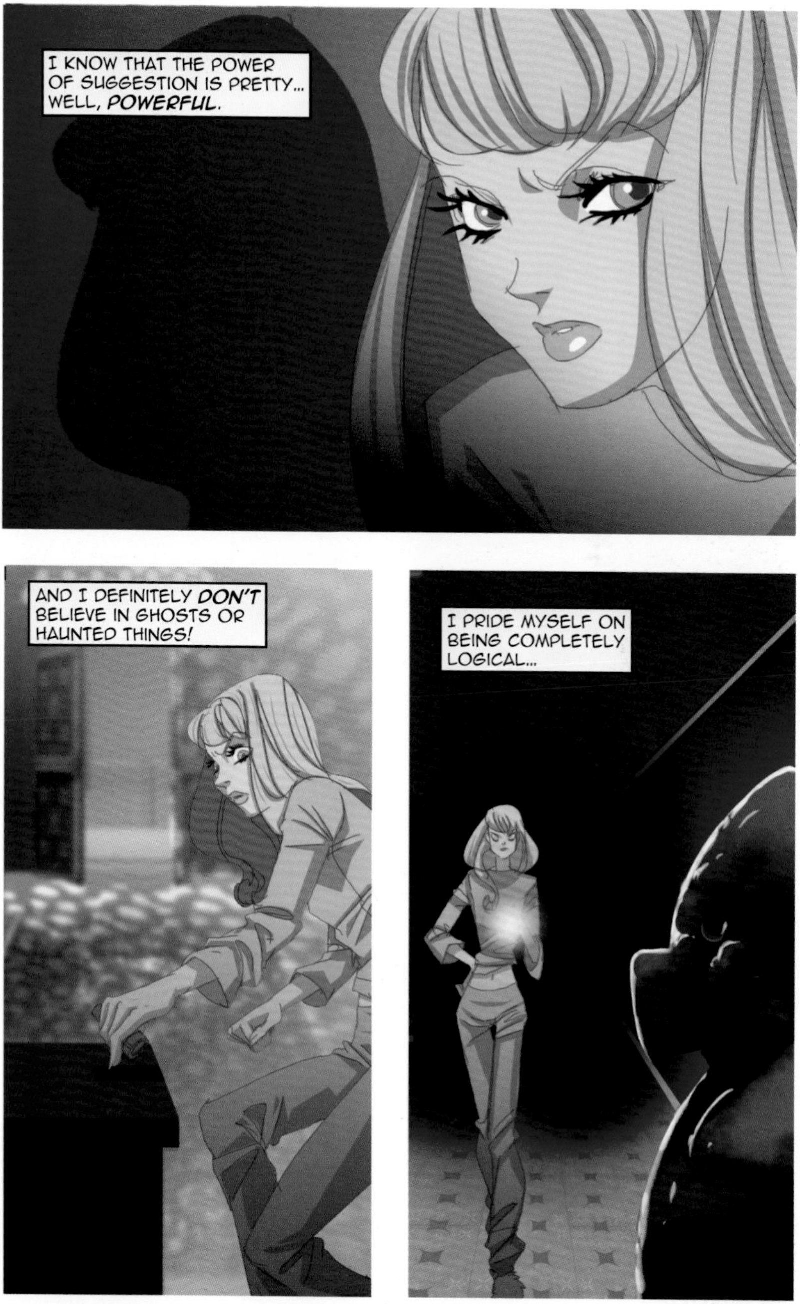
I KNOW THAT THE POWER OF SUGGESTION IS PRETTY... WELL, *POWERFUL*.
AND I DEFINITELY *DON'T* BELIEVE IN GHOSTS OR HAUNTED THINGS!
I PRIDE MYSELF ON BEING COMPLETELY LOGICAL...

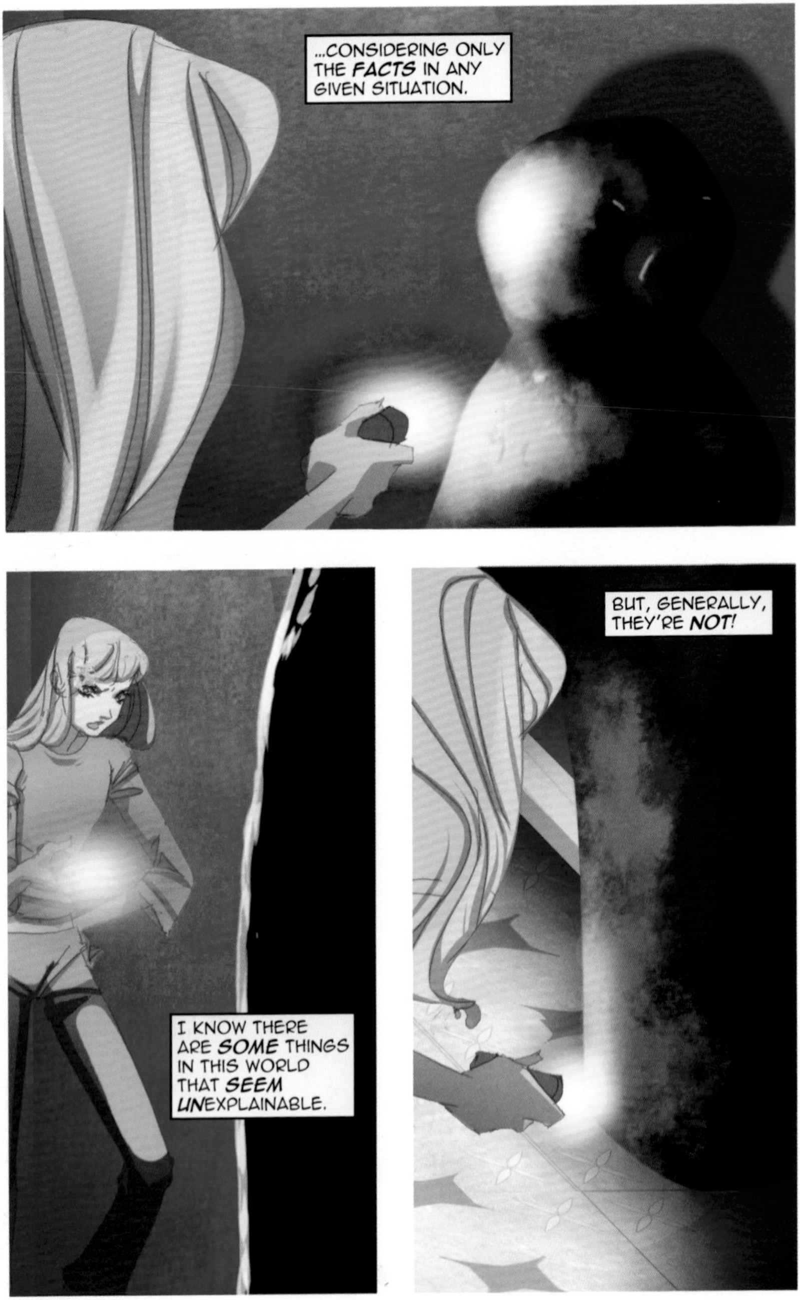
...CONSIDERING ONLY THE **FACTS** IN ANY GIVEN SITUATION.
I KNOW THERE ARE **SOME** THINGS IN THIS WORLD THAT **SEEM** **UN**EXPLAINABLE.
BUT, GENERALLY, THEY'RE **NOT**!

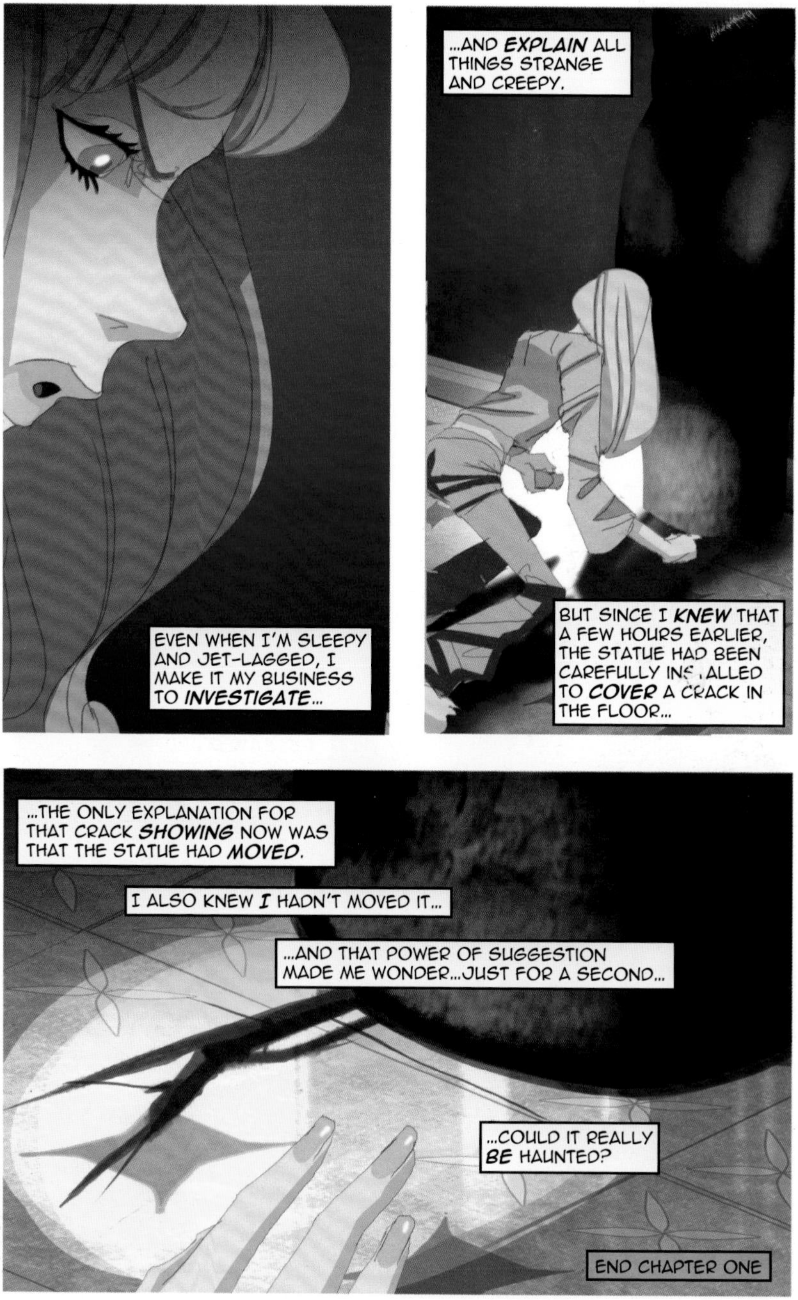
EVEN WHEN I'M SLEEPY AND JET-LAGGED, I MAKE IT MY BUSINESS TO INVESTIGATE...
...AND EXPLAIN ALL THINGS STRANGE AND CREEPY.
BUT SINCE I KNEW THAT A FEW HOURS EARLIER, THE STATUE HAD BEEN CAREFULLY INS ,ALLED TO COVER A CRACK IN THE FLOOR...
...THE ONLY EXPLANATION FOR THAT CRACK SHOWING NOW WAS THAT THE STATUE HAD MOVED.
I ALSO KNEW I HADN'T MOVED IT...
...AND THAT POWER OF SUGGESTION MADE ME WONDER...JUST FOR A SECOND...
...COULD IT REALLY BE HAUNTED?
END CHAPTER ONE

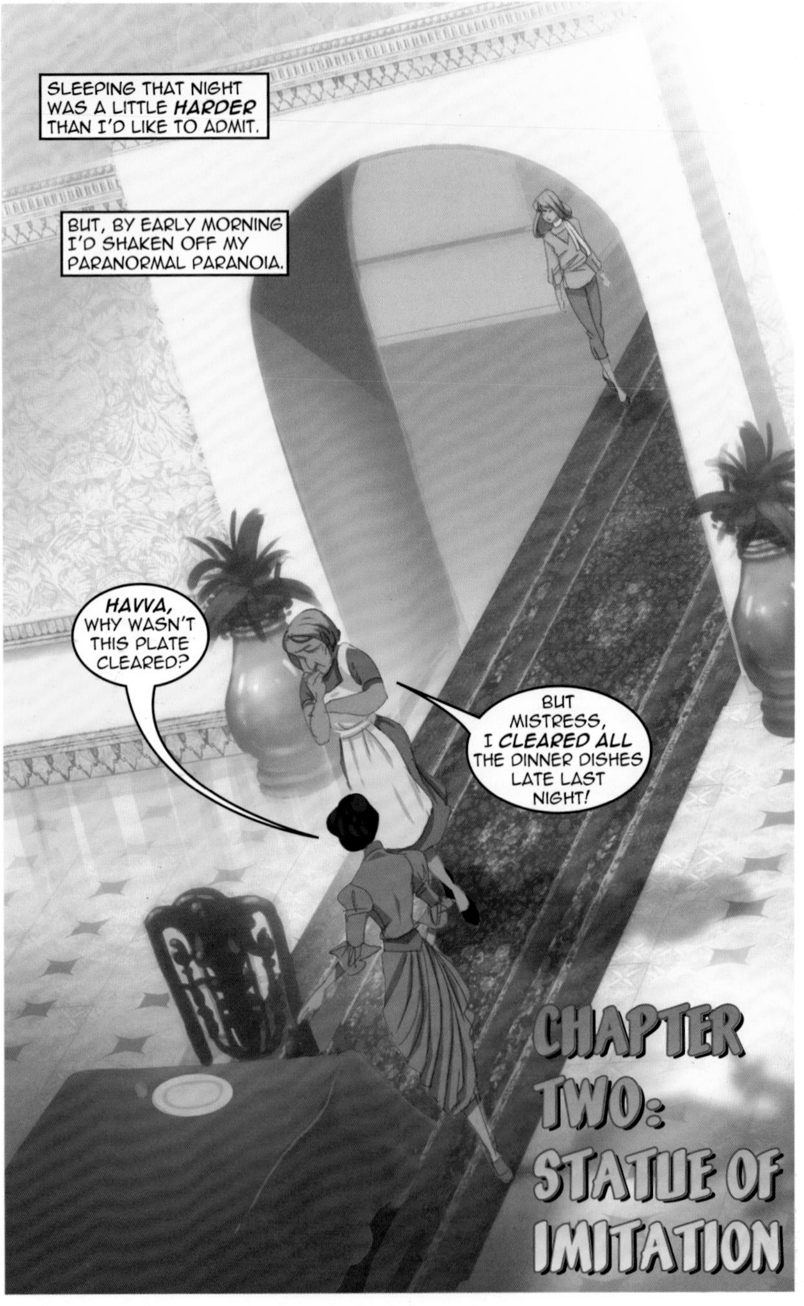

SLEEPING THAT NIGHT WAS A LITTLE *HARDER* THAN I'D LIKE TO ADMIT.
BUT, BY EARLY MORNING I'D SHAKEN OFF MY PARANORMAL PARANOIA.
HAVVA, WHY WASN'T THIS PLATE CLEARED?
BUT MISTRESS, I *CLEARED ALL* THE DINNER DISHES LATE LAST NIGHT!
CHAPTER TWO: STATUE OF IMITATION

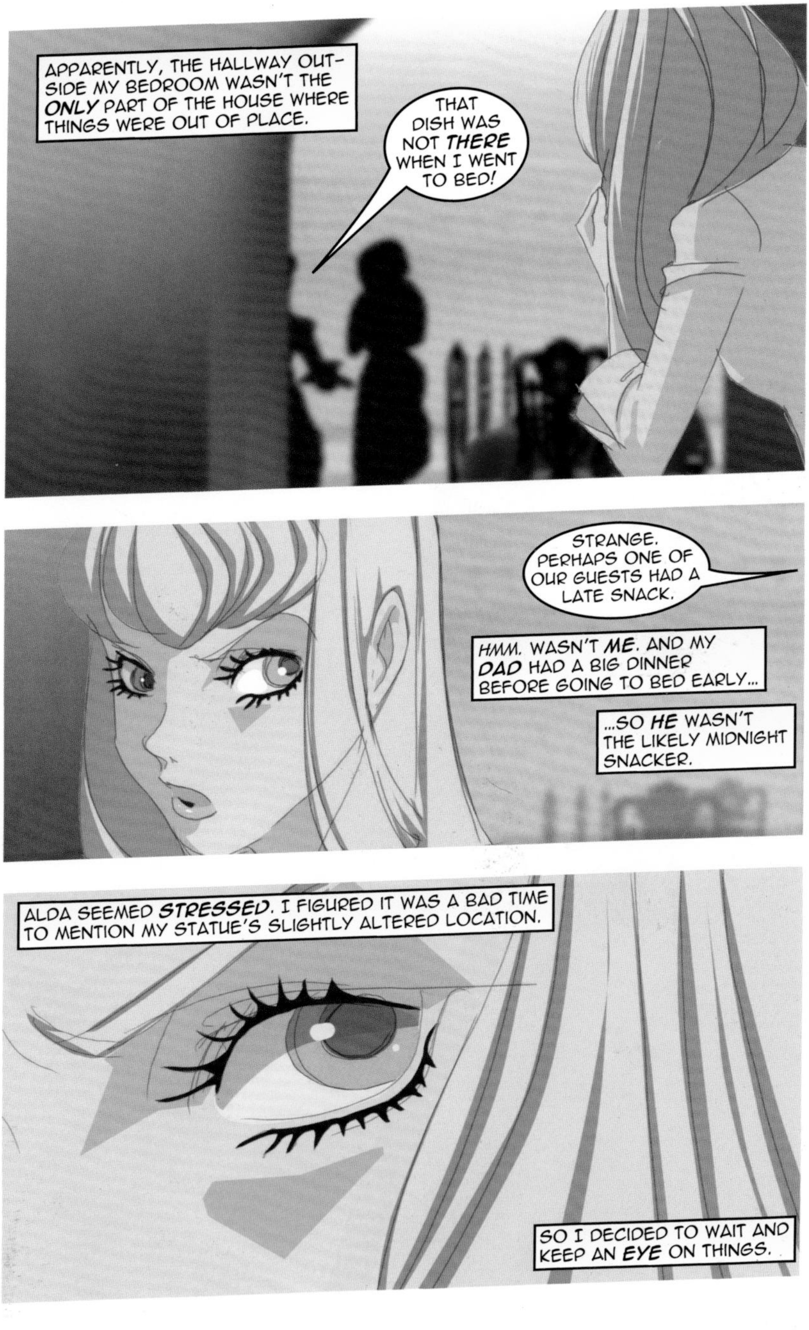
APPARENTLY, THE HALLWAY OUT-SIDE MY BEDROOM WASN'T THE ONLY PART OF THE HOUSE WHERE THINGS WERE OUT OF PLACE.
THAT DISH WAS NOT THERE WHEN I WENT TO BED!
STRANGE. PERHAPS ONE OF OUR GUESTS HAD A LATE SNACK.
HMM. WASN'T ME. AND MY DAD HAD A BIG DINNER BEFORE GOING TO BED EARLY...
...SO HE WASN'T THE LIKELY MIDNIGHT SNACKER.
ALDA SEEMED STRESSED. I FIGURED IT WAS A BAD TIME TO MENTION MY STATUE'S SLIGHTLY ALTERED LOCATION.
SO I DECIDED TO WAIT AND KEEP AN EYE ON THINGS.

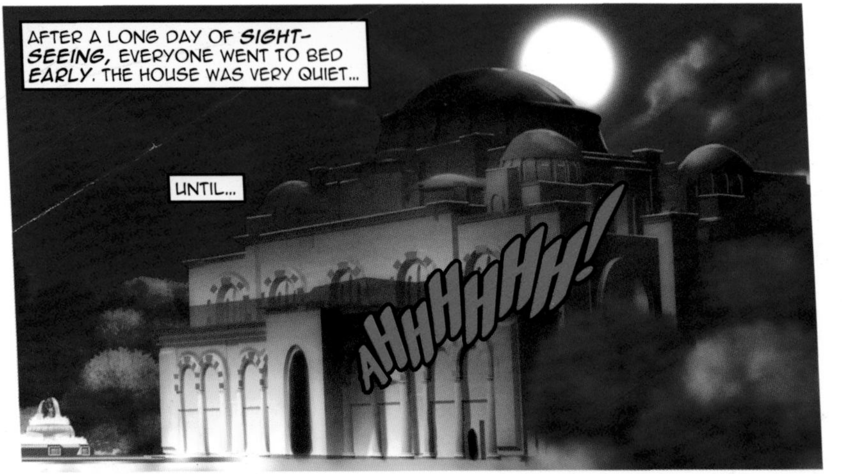
AFTER A LONG DAY OF **SIGHT-SEEING,** EVERYONE WENT TO BED **EARLY**. THE HOUSE WAS VERY QUIET...
UNTIL...
AHHHHHHH!

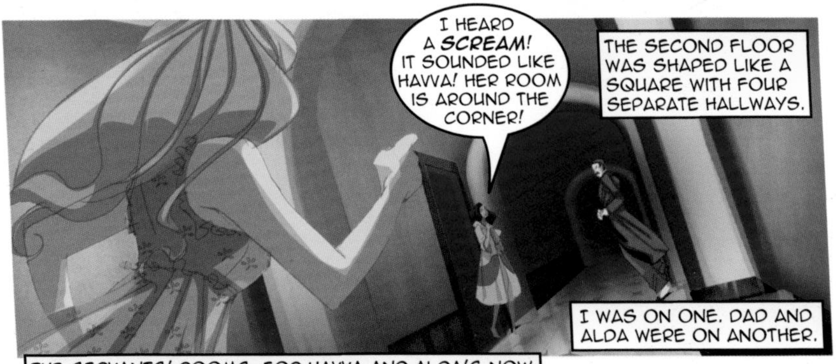
I HEARD A **SCREAM**! IT SOUNDED LIKE HAVVA! HER ROOM IS AROUND THE CORNER!
THE SECOND FLOOR WAS SHAPED LIKE A SQUARE WITH FOUR SEPARATE HALLWAYS.
I WAS ON ONE. DAD AND ALDA WERE ON ANOTHER.

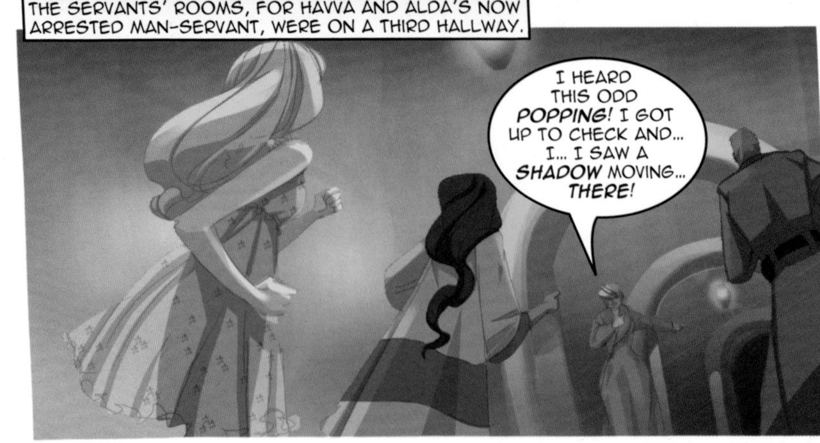
THE SERVANTS' ROOMS, FOR HAVVA AND ALDA'S NOW ARRESTED MAN-SERVANT, WERE ON A THIRD HALLWAY.
I HEARD THIS ODD **POPPING**! I GOT UP TO CHECK AND... I... I SAW A **SHADOW** MOVING... **THERE**!

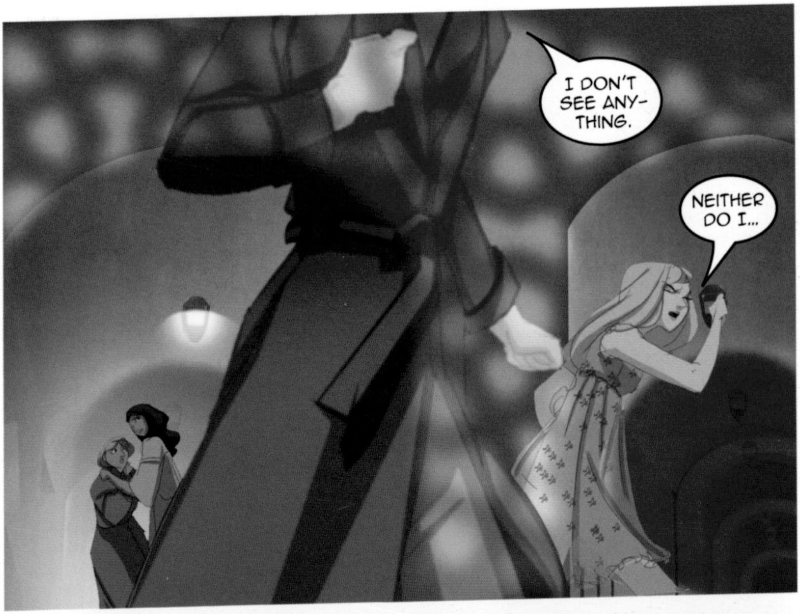
I DON'T SEE ANY-THING.
NEITHER DO I...

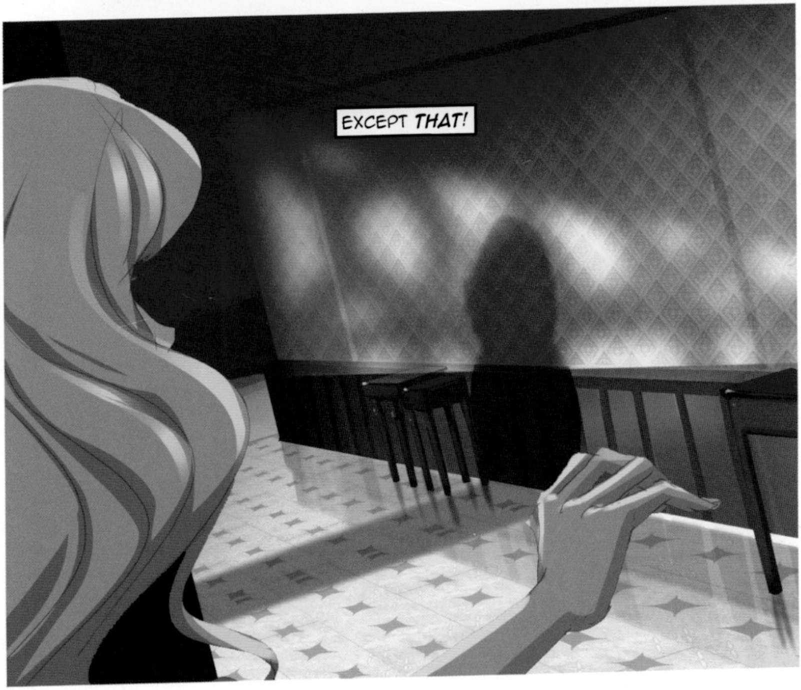
EXCEPT THAT!

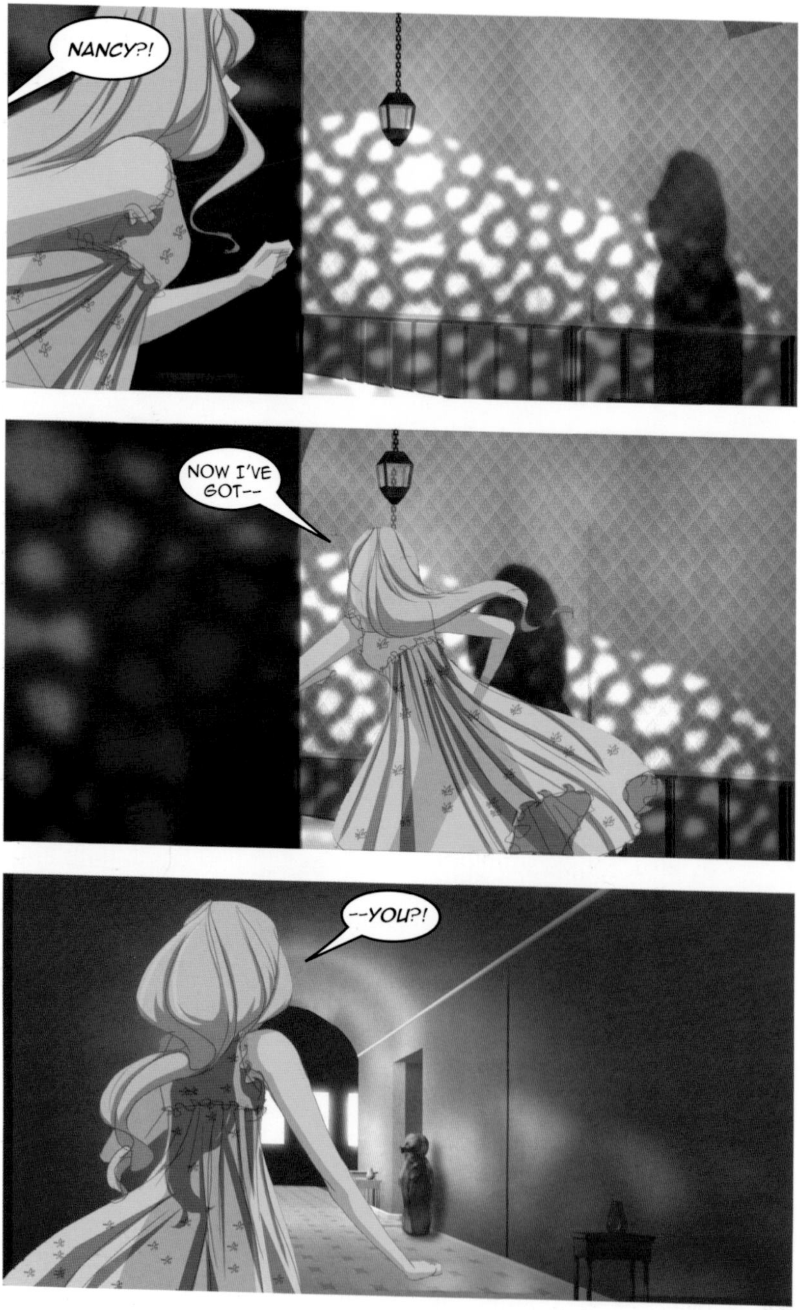
NANCY?!
NOW I'VE GOT--
--YOU?!

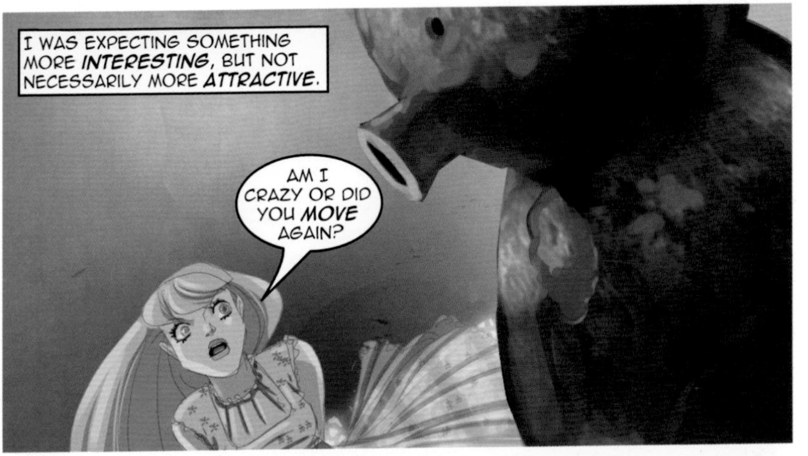
I WAS EXPECTING SOMETHING MORE INTERESTING, BUT NOT NECESSARILY MORE ATTRACTIVE.
AM I CRAZY OR DID YOU MOVE AGAIN?

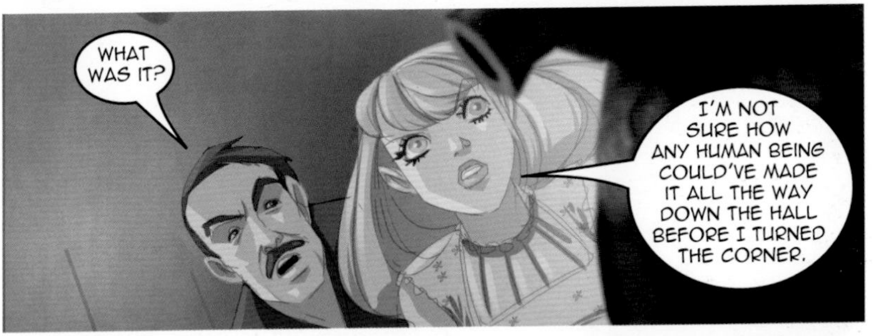
WHAT WAS IT?
I'M NOT SURE HOW ANY HUMAN BEING COULD'VE MADE IT ALL THE WAY DOWN THE HALL BEFORE I TURNED THE CORNER.

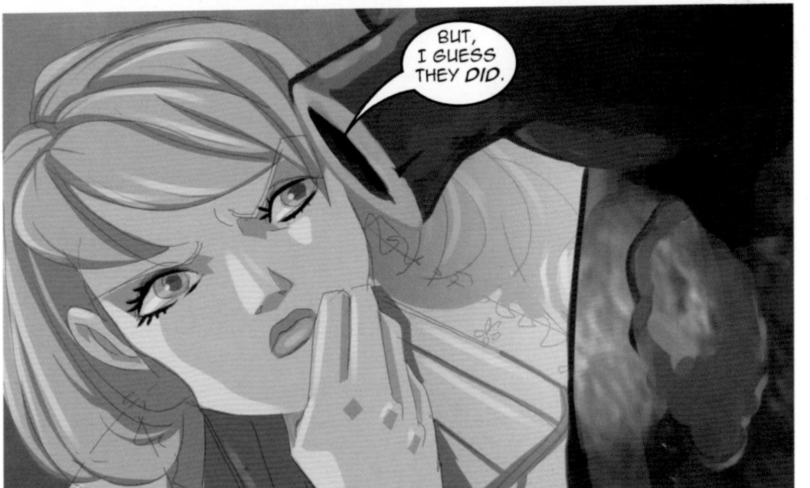
BUT, I GUESS THEY DID.

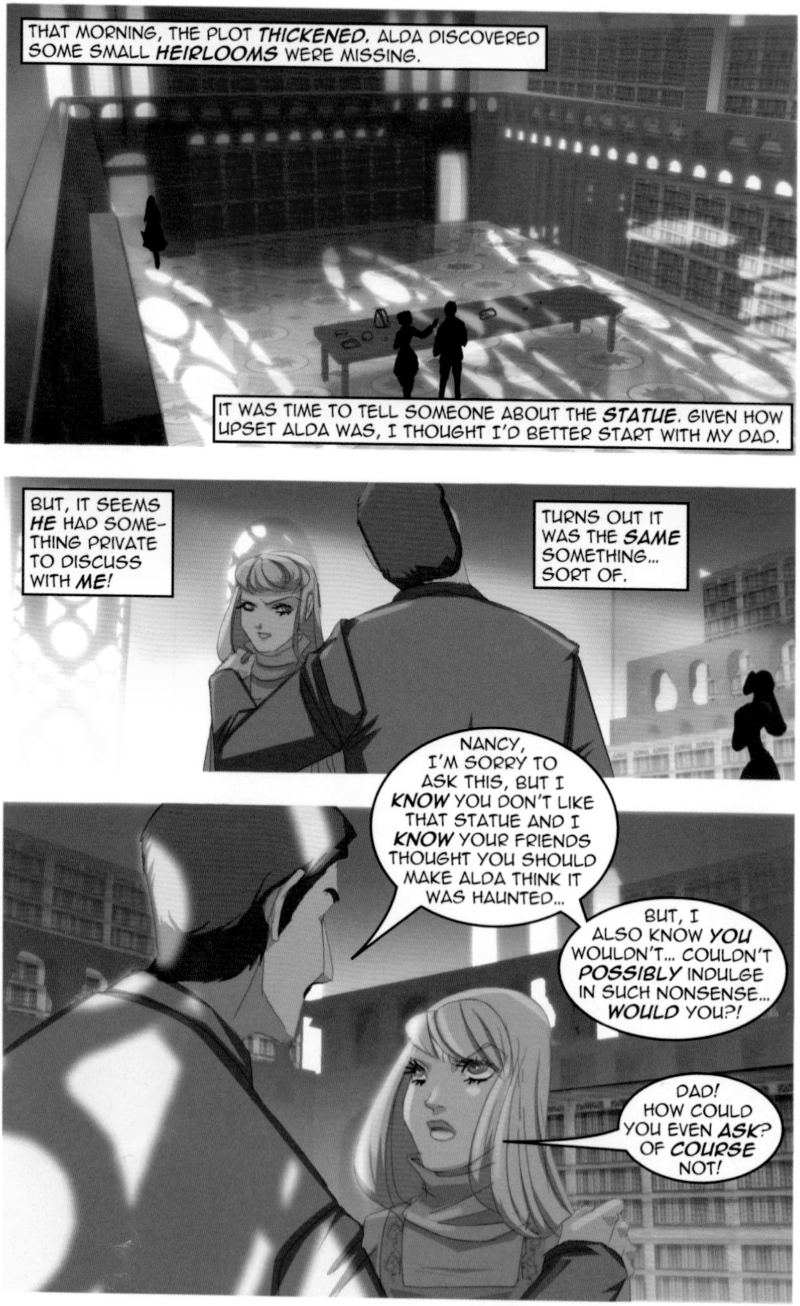
THAT MORNING, THE PLOT THICKENED. ALDA DISCOVERED SOME SMALL HEIRLOOMS WERE MISSING.
IT WAS TIME TO TELL SOMEONE ABOUT THE STATUE. GIVEN HOW UPSET ALDA WAS, I THOUGHT I'D BETTER START WITH MY DAD.
BUT, IT SEEMS HE HAD SOMETHING PRIVATE TO DISCUSS WITH ME!
TURNS OUT IT WAS THE SAME SOMETHING... SORT OF.
NANCY, I'M SORRY TO ASK THIS, BUT I KNOW YOU DON'T LIKE THAT STATUE AND I KNOW YOUR FRIENDS THOUGHT YOU SHOULD MAKE ALDA THINK IT WAS HAUNTED...
BUT, I ALSO KNOW YOU WOULDN'T... COULDN'T POSSIBLY INDULGE IN SUCH NONSENSE... WOULD YOU?!
DAD! HOW COULD YOU EVEN ASK? OF COURSE NOT!

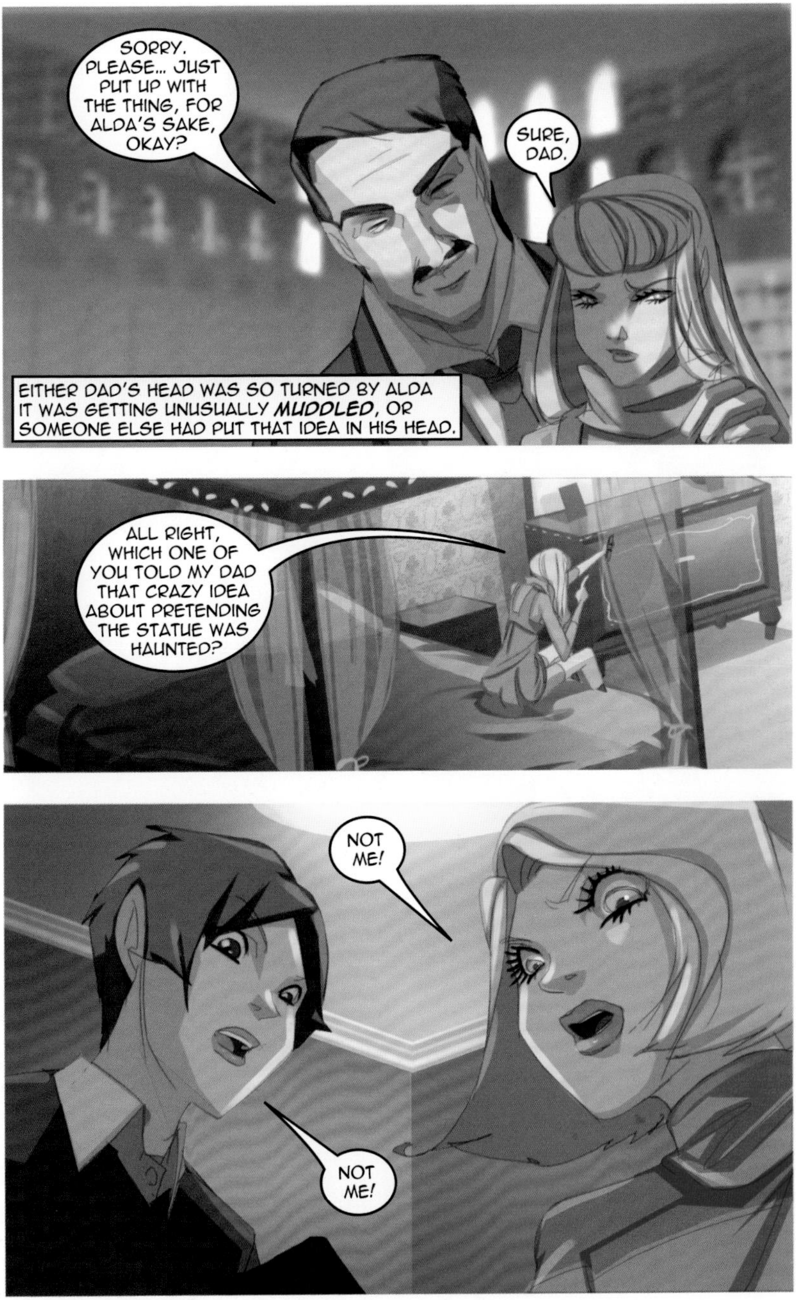
SORRY. PLEASE... JUST PUT UP WITH THE THING, FOR ALDA'S SAKE, OKAY?
SURE, DAD.
EITHER DAD'S HEAD WAS SO TURNED BY ALDA IT WAS GETTING UNUSUALLY ***MUDDLED***, OR SOMEONE ELSE HAD PUT THAT IDEA IN HIS HEAD.
ALL RIGHT, WHICH ONE OF YOU TOLD MY DAD THAT CRAZY IDEA ABOUT PRETENDING THE STATUE WAS HAUNTED?
NOT ME!
NOT ME!

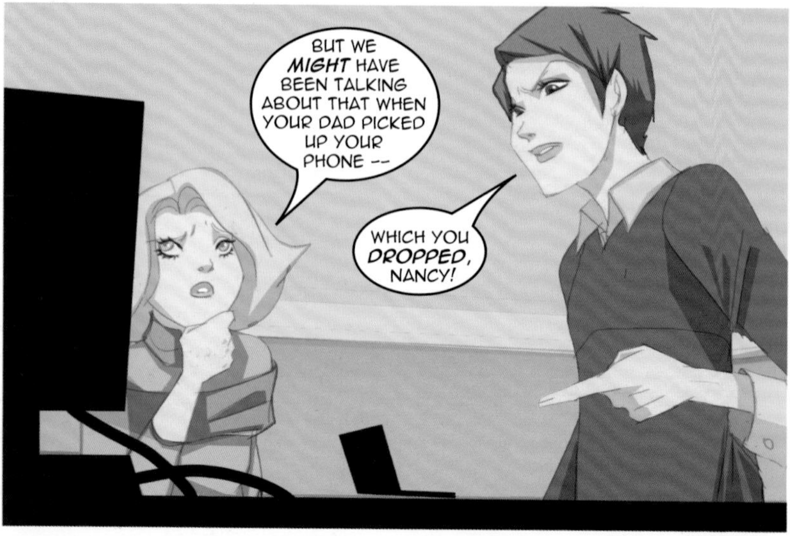
BUT WE MIGHT HAVE BEEN TALKING ABOUT THAT WHEN YOUR DAD PICKED UP YOUR PHONE --
WHICH YOU DROPPED, NANCY!

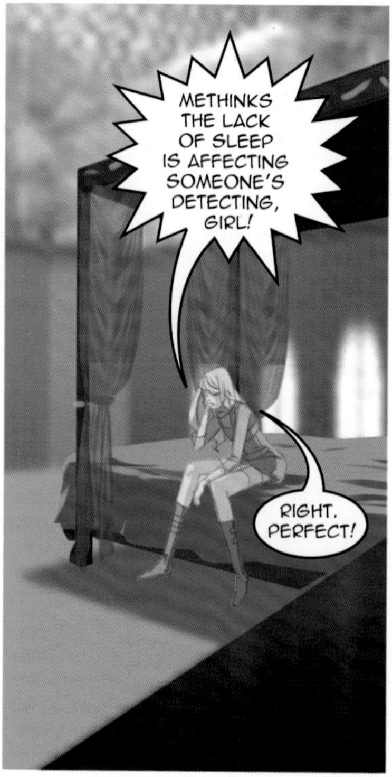
METHINKS THE LACK OF SLEEP IS AFFECTING SOMEONE'S DETECTING, GIRL!
RIGHT. PERFECT!

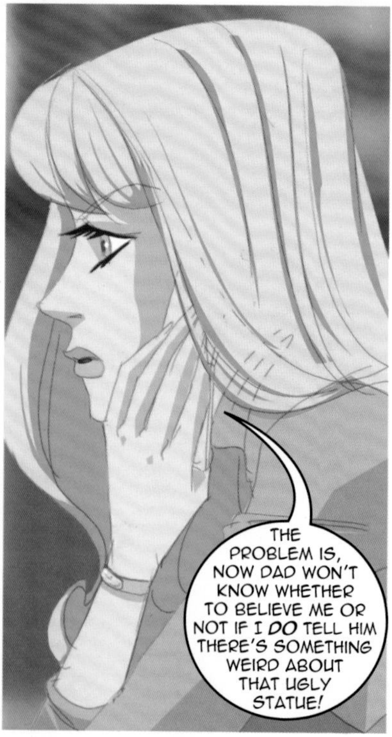
THE PROBLEM IS, NOW DAD WON'T KNOW WHETHER TO BELIEVE ME OR NOT IF I DO TELL HIM THERE'S SOMETHING WEIRD ABOUT THAT UGLY STATUE!

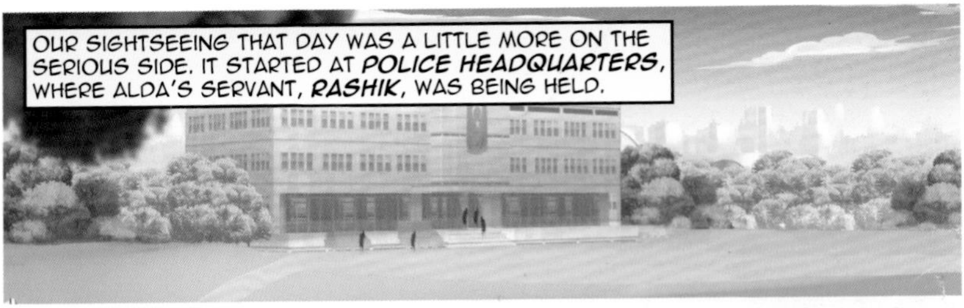
OUR SIGHTSEEING THAT DAY WAS A LITTLE MORE ON THE SERIOUS SIDE. IT STARTED AT POLICE HEADQUARTERS, WHERE ALDA'S SERVANT, RASHIK, WAS BEING HELD.

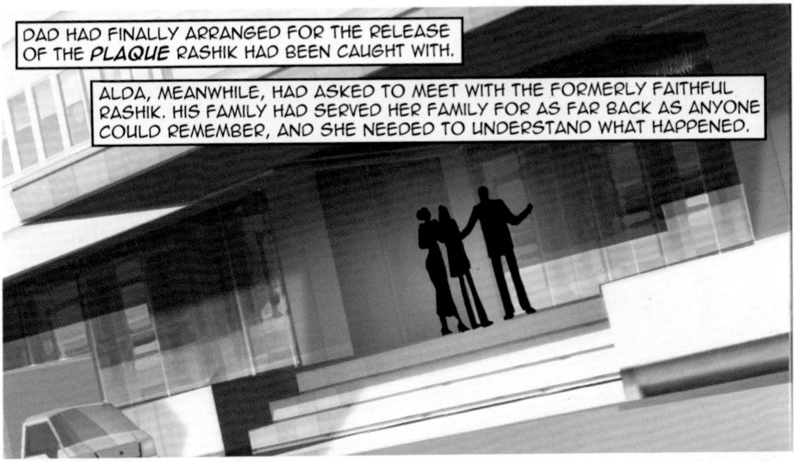
DAD HAD FINALLY ARRANGED FOR THE RELEASE OF THE PLAQUE RASHIK HAD BEEN CAUGHT WITH.
ALDA, MEANWHILE, HAD ASKED TO MEET WITH THE FORMERLY FAITHFUL RASHIK. HIS FAMILY HAD SERVED HER FAMILY FOR AS FAR BACK AS ANYONE COULD REMEMBER, AND SHE NEEDED TO UNDERSTAND WHAT HAPPENED.

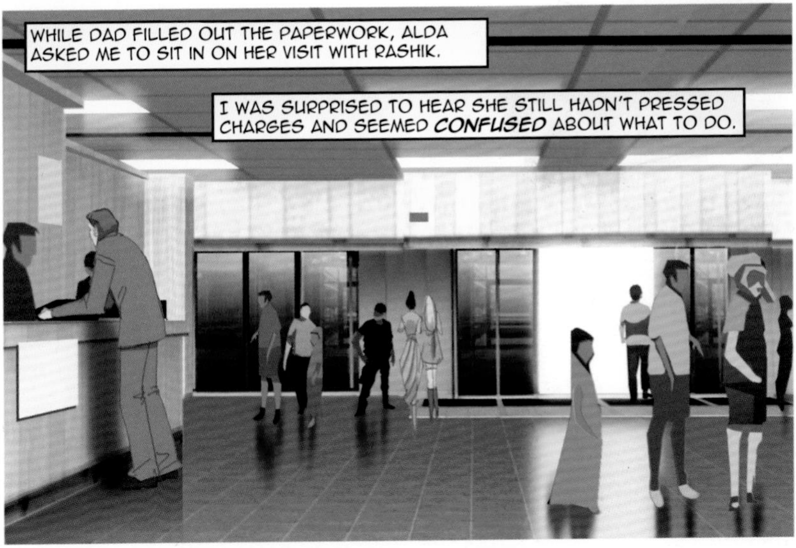
WHILE DAD FILLED OUT THE PAPERWORK, ALDA ASKED ME TO SIT IN ON HER VISIT WITH RASHIK.
I WAS SURPRISED TO HEAR SHE STILL HADN'T PRESSED CHARGES AND SEEMED CONFUSED ABOUT WHAT TO DO.

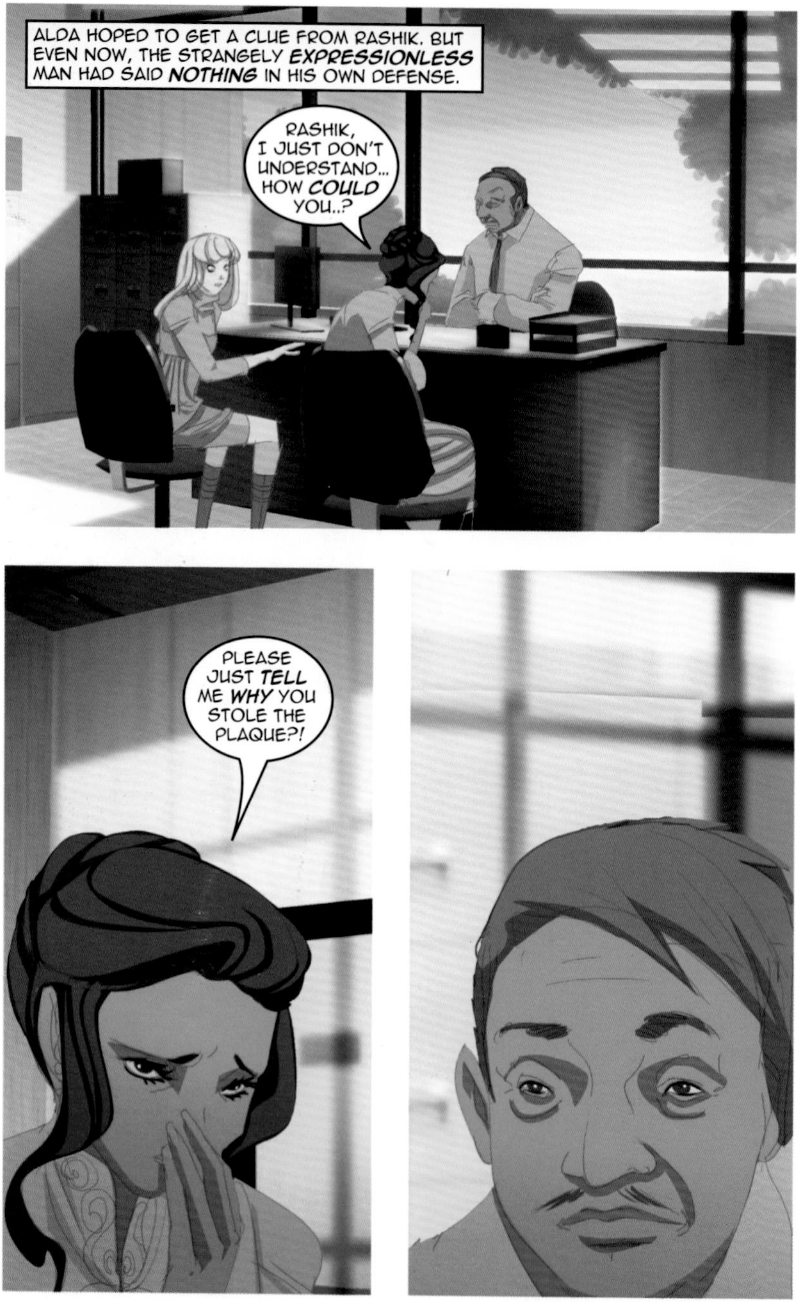
ALDA HOPED TO GET A CLUE FROM RASHIK. BUT EVEN NOW, THE STRANGELY *EXPRESSIONLESS* MAN HAD SAID *NOTHING* IN HIS OWN DEFENSE.
RASHIK, I JUST DON'T UNDERSTAND... HOW *COULD* YOU..?
PLEASE JUST *TELL* ME *WHY* YOU STOLE THE PLAQUE?!

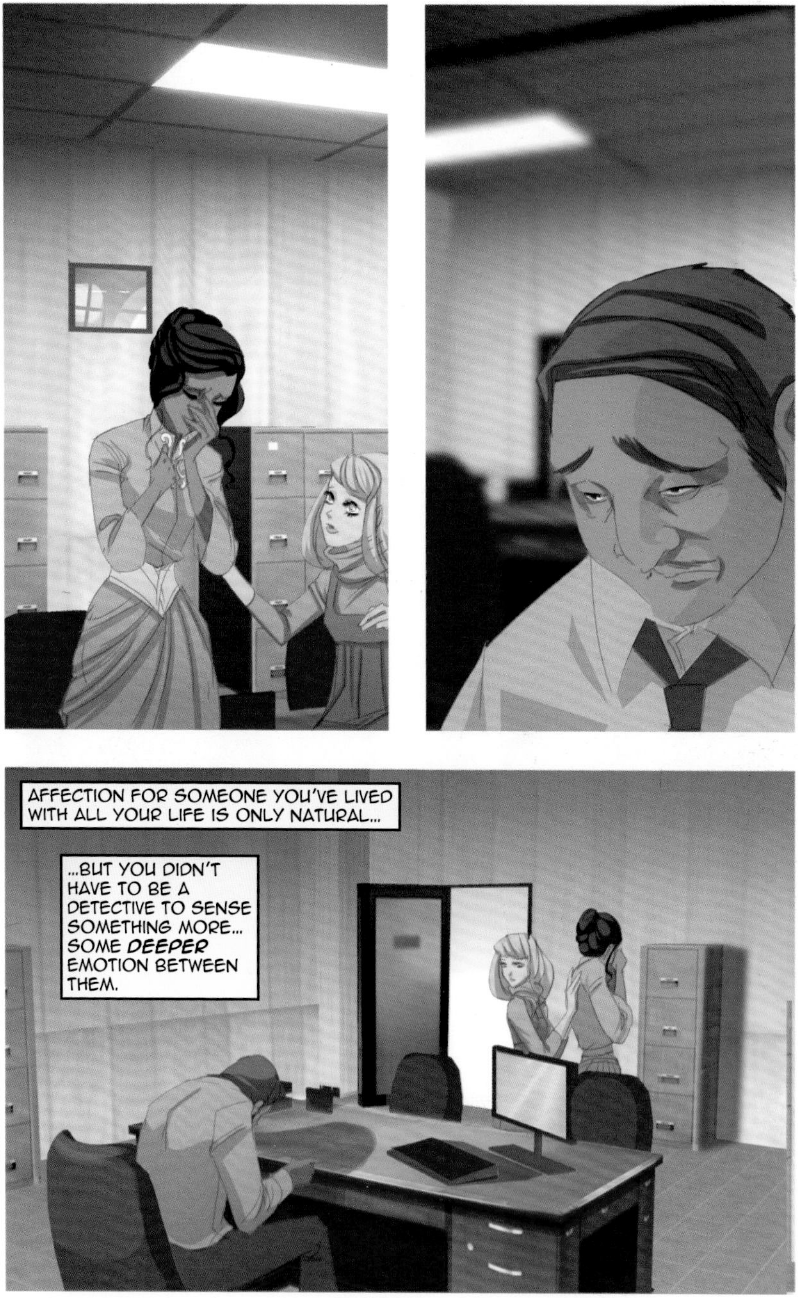
AFFECTION FOR SOMEONE YOU'VE LIVED WITH ALL YOUR LIFE IS ONLY NATURAL...
...BUT YOU DIDN'T HAVE TO BE A DETECTIVE TO SENSE SOMETHING MORE... SOME *DEEPER* EMOTION BETWEEN THEM.

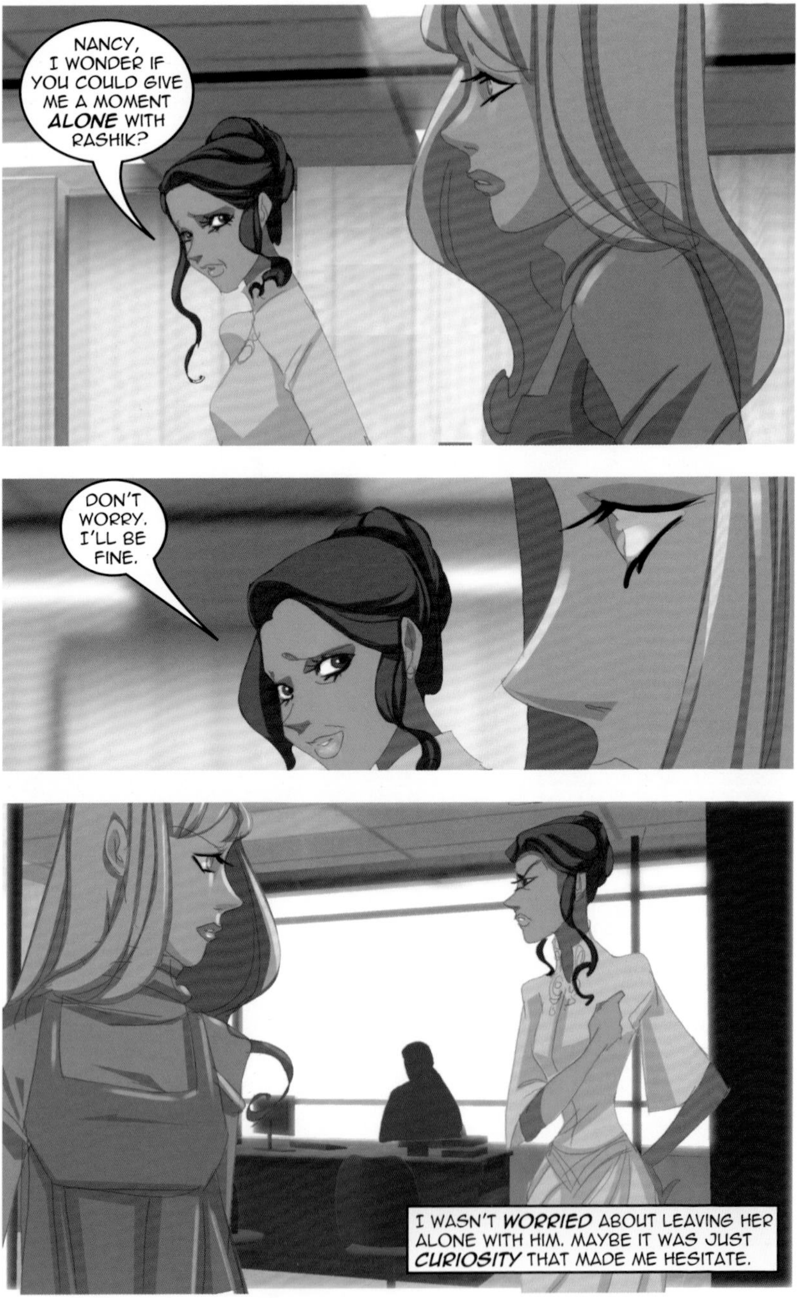
NANCY, I WONDER IF YOU COULD GIVE ME A MOMENT ALONE WITH RASHIK?
DON'T WORRY. I'LL BE FINE.
I WASN'T WORRIED ABOUT LEAVING HER ALONE WITH HIM. MAYBE IT WAS JUST CURIOSITY THAT MADE ME HESITATE.

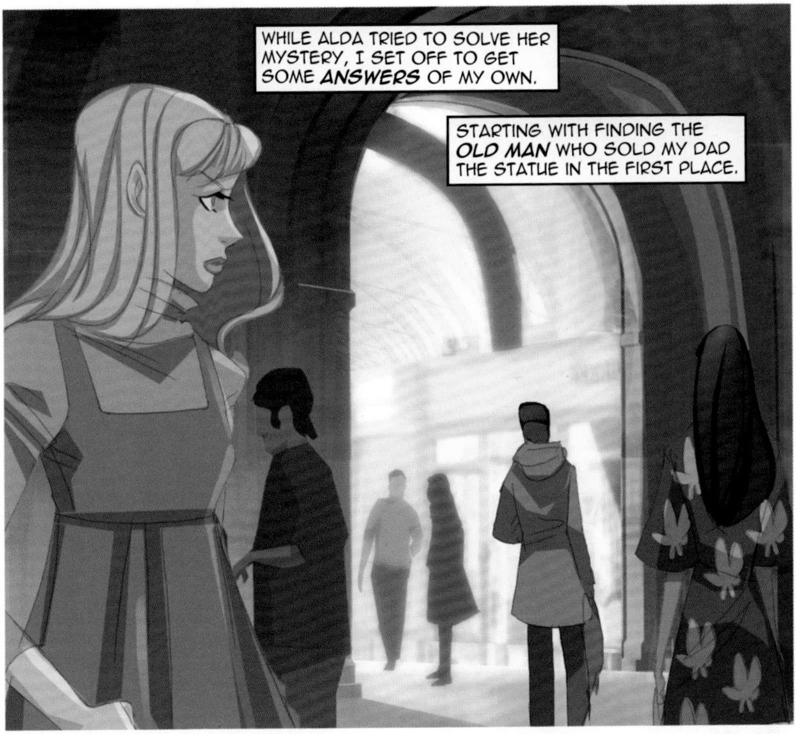
WHILE ALDA TRIED TO SOLVE HER MYSTERY, I SET OFF TO GET SOME ANSWERS OF MY OWN.
STARTING WITH FINDING THE OLD MAN WHO SOLD MY DAD THE STATUE IN THE FIRST PLACE.

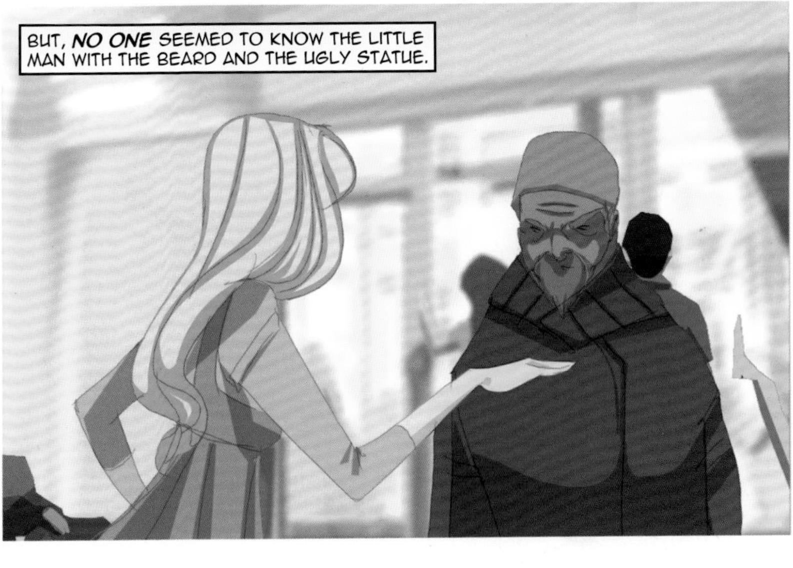
BUT, NO ONE SEEMED TO KNOW THE LITTLE MAN WITH THE BEARD AND THE UGLY STATUE.

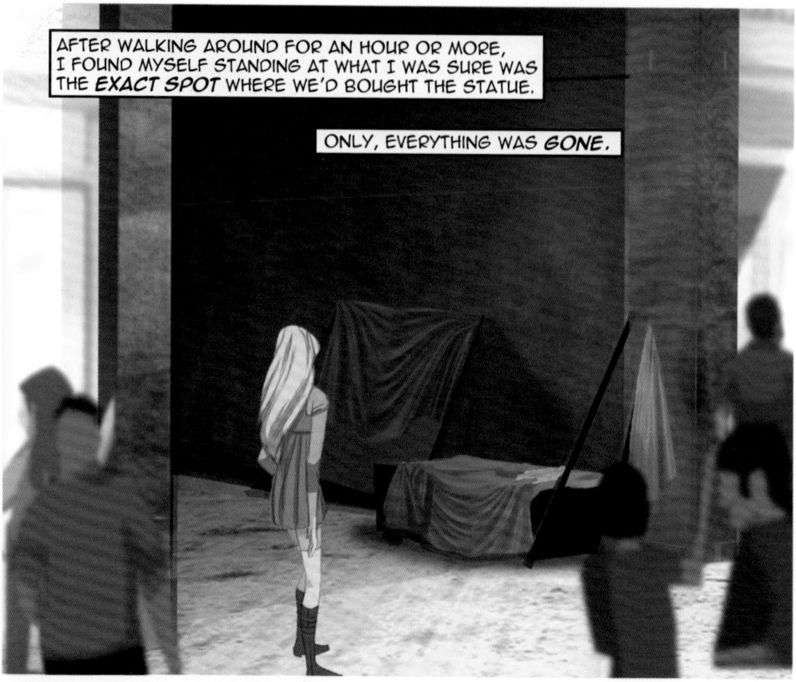
AFTER WALKING AROUND FOR AN HOUR OR MORE, I FOUND MYSELF STANDING AT WHAT I WAS SURE WAS THE EXACT SPOT WHERE WE'D BOUGHT THE STATUE.
ONLY, EVERYTHING WAS GONE.

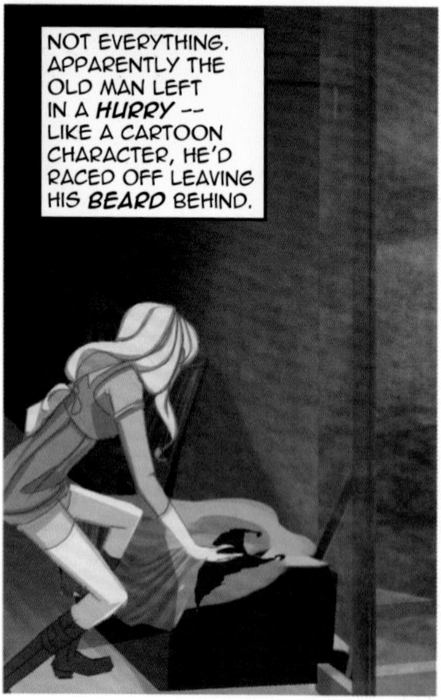
NOT EVERYTHING. APPARENTLY THE OLD MAN LEFT IN A HURRY -- LIKE A CARTOON CHARACTER, HE'D RACED OFF LEAVING HIS BEARD BEHIND.

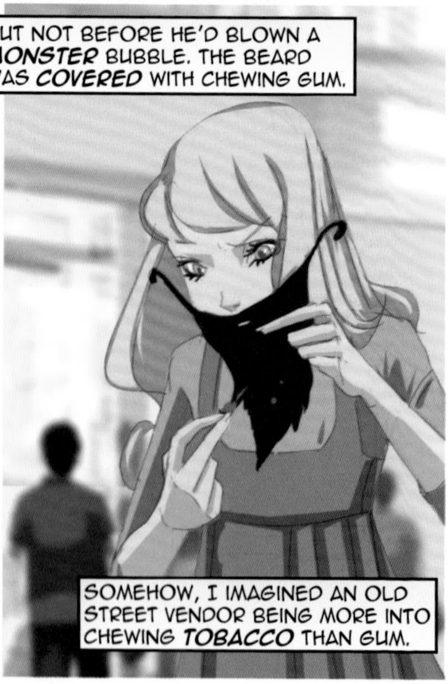
BUT NOT BEFORE HE'D BLOWN A MONSTER BUBBLE. THE BEARD WAS COVERED WITH CHEWING GUM.
SOMEHOW, I IMAGINED AN OLD STREET VENDOR BEING MORE INTO CHEWING TOBACCO THAN GUM.

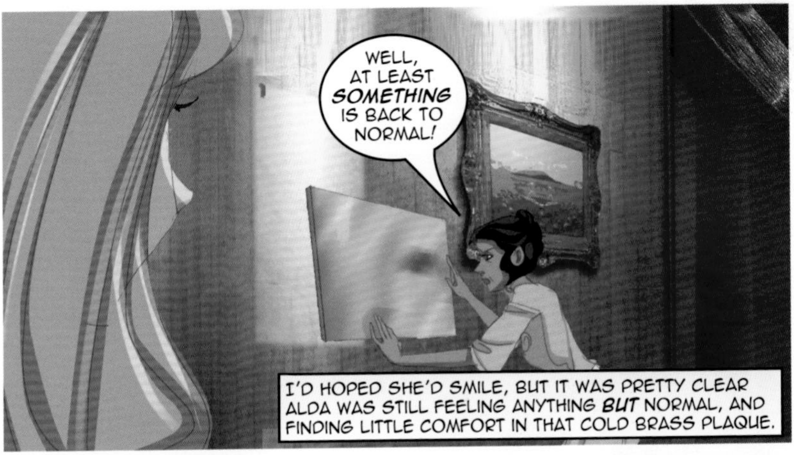
WELL, AT LEAST **SOMETHING** IS BACK TO NORMAL!
I'D HOPED SHE'D SMILE, BUT IT WAS PRETTY CLEAR ALDA WAS STILL FEELING ANYTHING **BUT** NORMAL, AND FINDING LITTLE COMFORT IN THAT COLD BRASS PLAQUE.

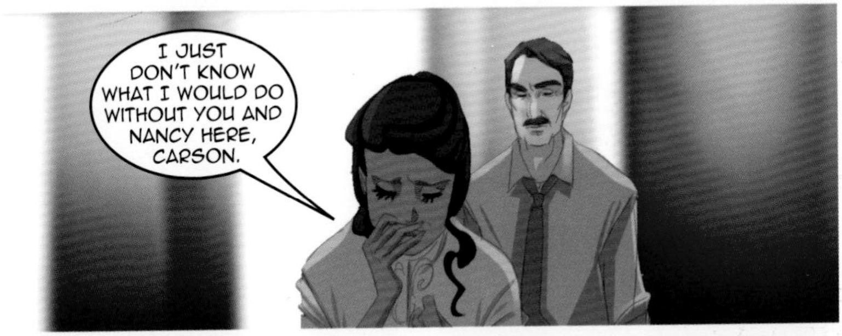
I JUST DON'T KNOW WHAT I WOULD DO WITHOUT YOU AND NANCY HERE, CARSON.

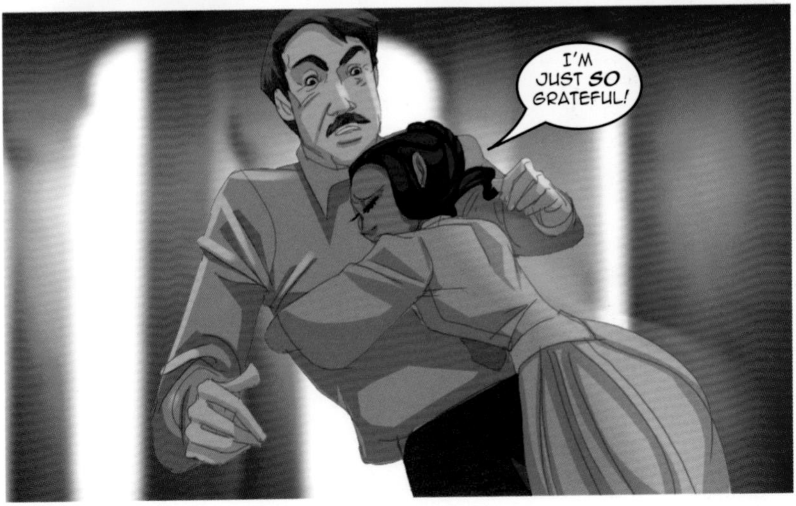
I'M JUST **SO** GRATEFUL!

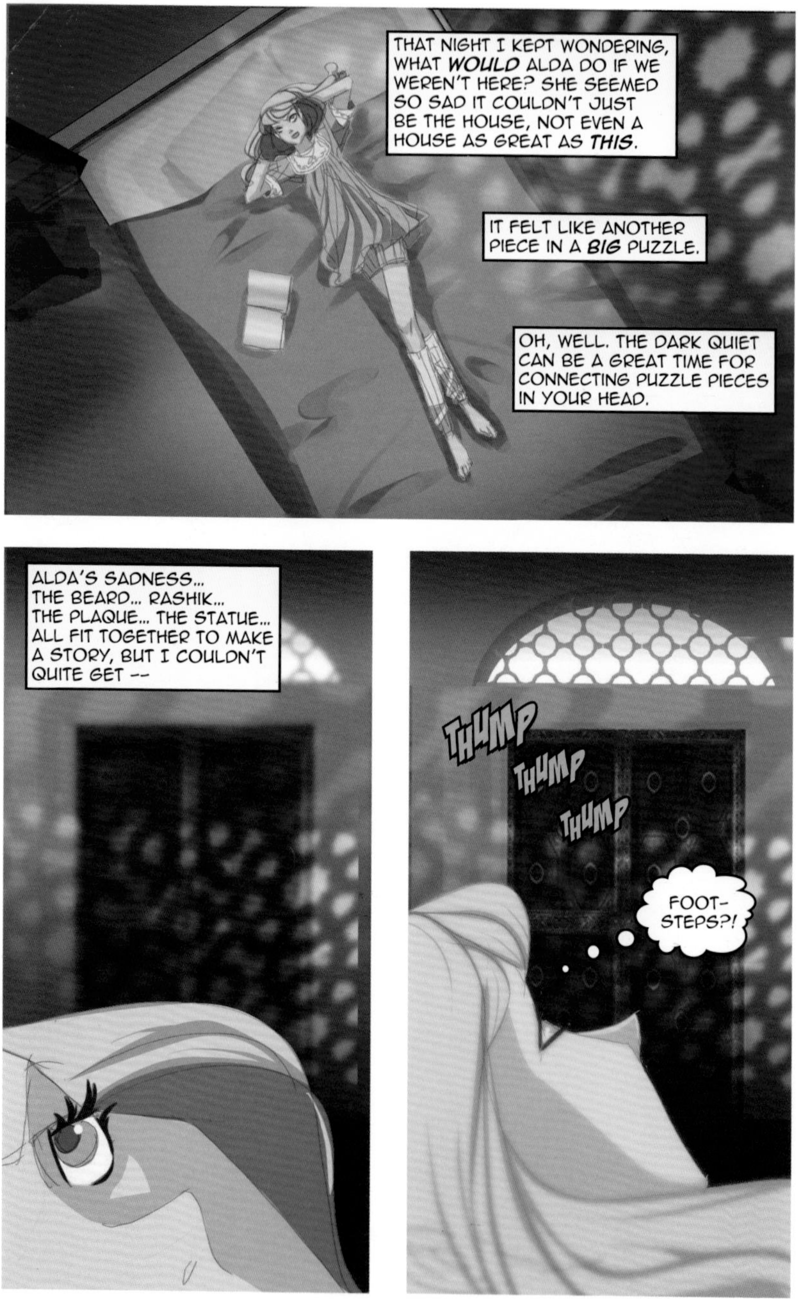
THAT NIGHT I KEPT WONDERING, WHAT WOULD ALDA DO IF WE WEREN'T HERE? SHE SEEMED SO SAD IT COULDN'T JUST BE THE HOUSE, NOT EVEN A HOUSE AS GREAT AS THIS.
IT FELT LIKE ANOTHER PIECE IN A BIG PUZZLE.
OH, WELL. THE DARK QUIET CAN BE A GREAT TIME FOR CONNECTING PUZZLE PIECES IN YOUR HEAD.
ALDA'S SADNESS... THE BEARD... RASHIK... THE PLAQUE... THE STATUE... ALL FIT TOGETHER TO MAKE A STORY, BUT I COULDN'T QUITE GET --
THUMP
THUMP
THUMP
FOOT-STEPS?!

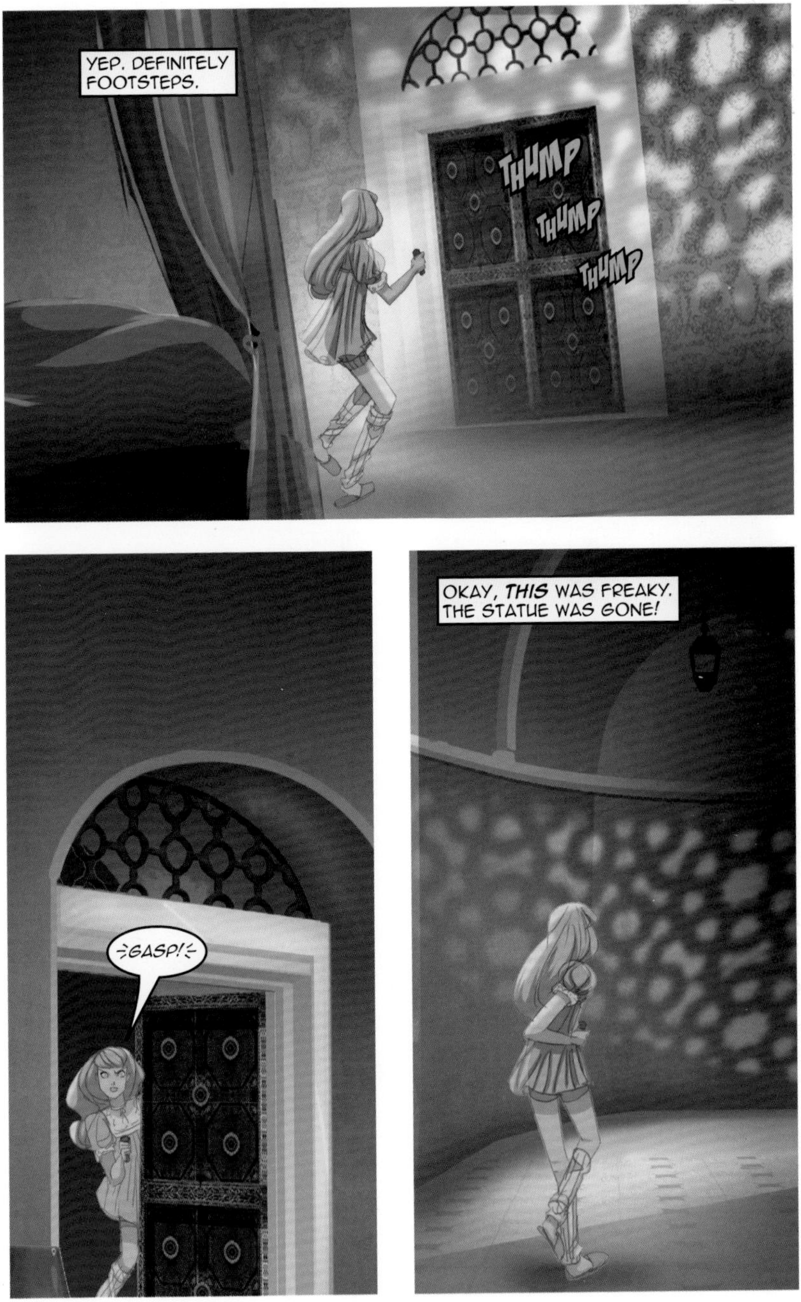
YEP. DEFINITELY FOOTSTEPS.
THUMP
THUMP
THUMP
GASP!
OKAY, *THIS* WAS FREAKY. THE STATUE WAS GONE!

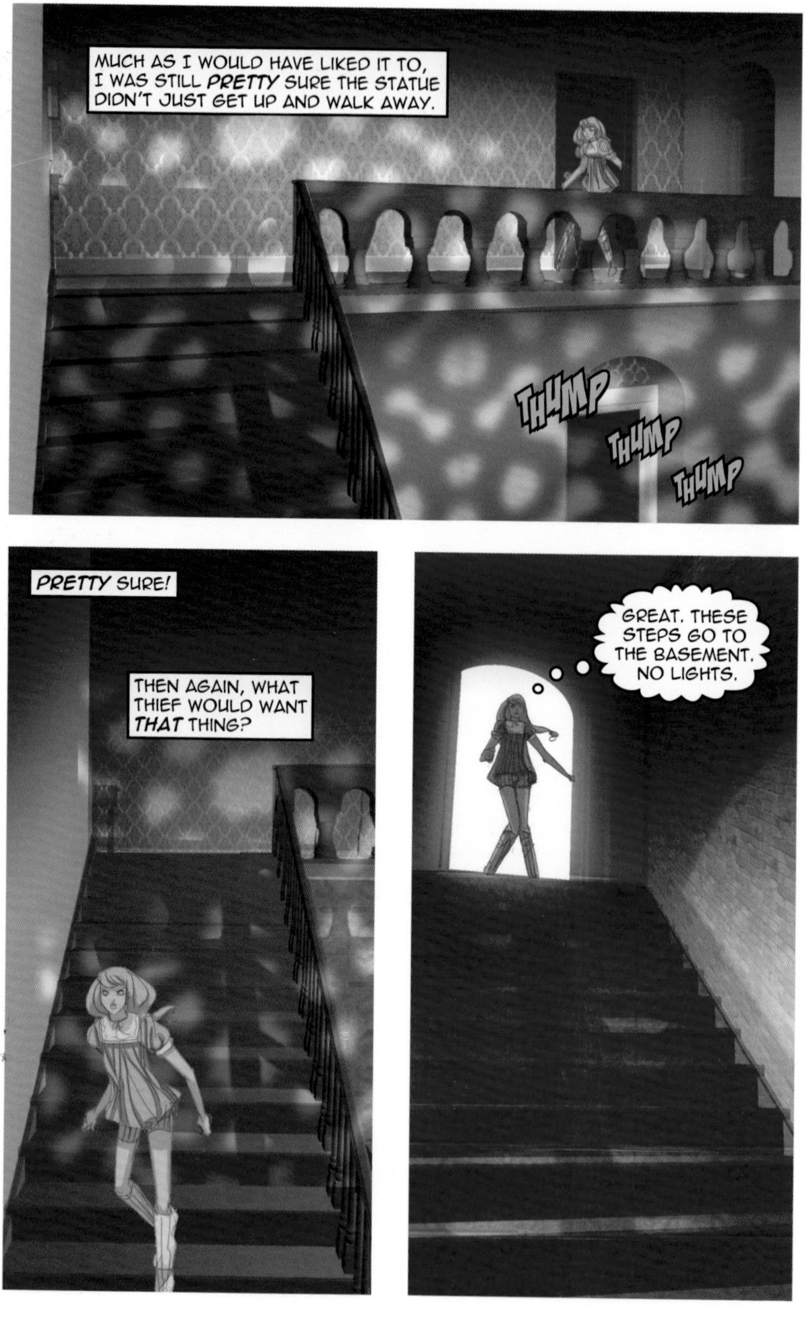
MUCH AS I WOULD HAVE LIKED IT TO, I WAS STILL PRETTY SURE THE STATUE DIDN'T JUST GET UP AND WALK AWAY.
THUMP
THUMP
THUMP
PRETTY SURE!
THEN AGAIN, WHAT THIEF WOULD WANT THAT THING?
GREAT. THESE STEPS GO TO THE BASEMENT. NO LIGHTS.

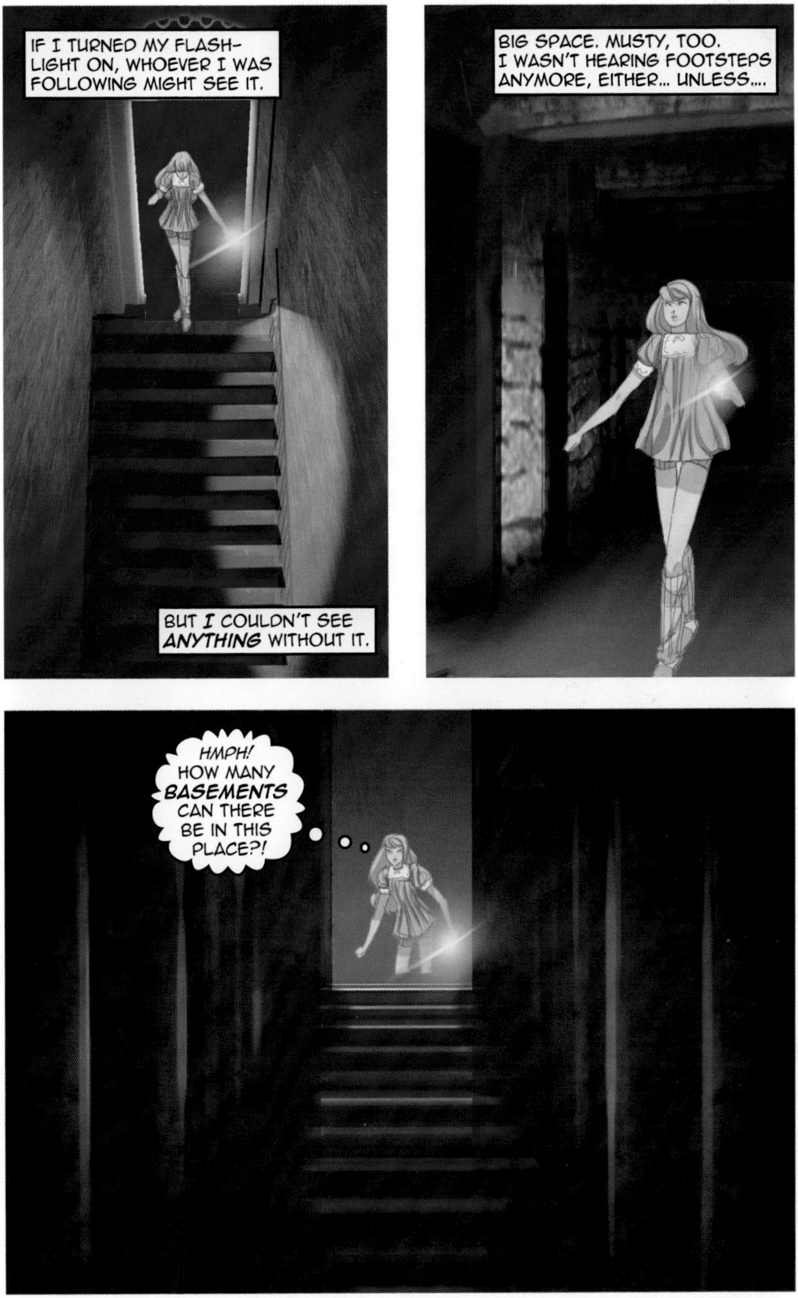
IF I TURNED MY FLASH-LIGHT ON, WHOEVER I WAS FOLLOWING MIGHT SEE IT.
BUT I COULDN'T SEE ANYTHING WITHOUT IT.
BIG SPACE. MUSTY, TOO. I WASN'T HEARING FOOTSTEPS ANYMORE, EITHER... UNLESS....
HMPH! HOW MANY BASEMENTS CAN THERE BE IN THIS PLACE?!

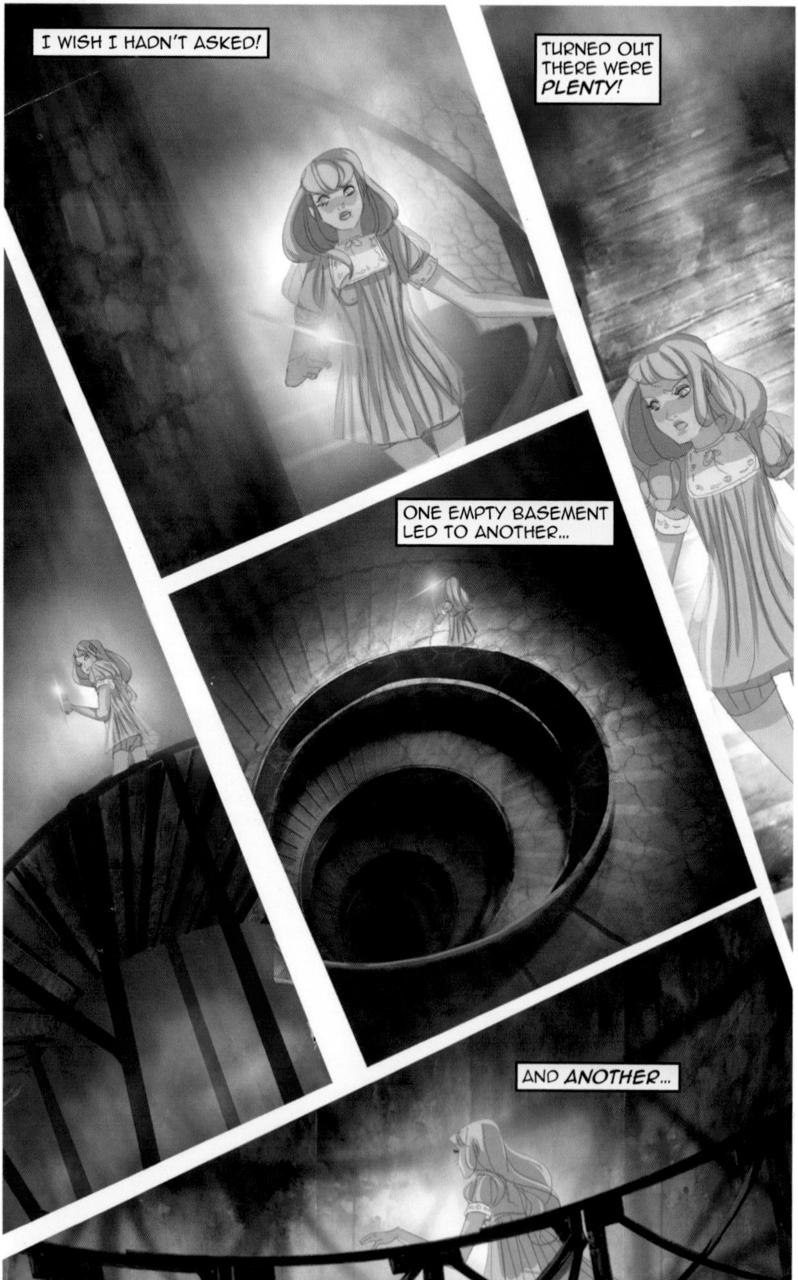
I WISH I HADN'T ASKED!
TURNED OUT THERE WERE *PLENTY!*
ONE EMPTY BASEMENT LED TO ANOTHER...
AND *ANOTHER...*

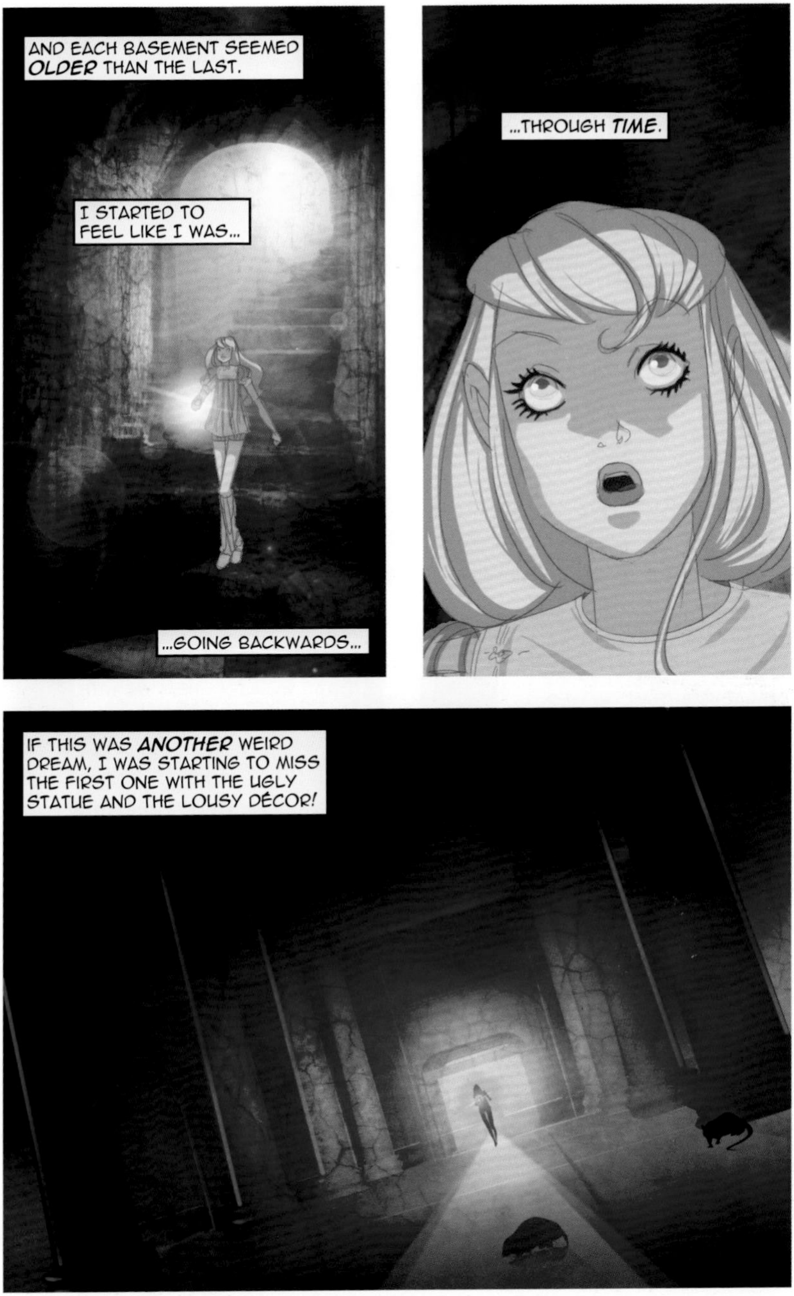
AND EACH BASEMENT SEEMED OLDER THAN THE LAST.
I STARTED TO FEEL LIKE I WAS...
...GOING BACKWARDS...
...THROUGH TIME.
IF THIS WAS ANOTHER WEIRD DREAM, I WAS STARTING TO MISS THE FIRST ONE WITH THE UGLY STATUE AND THE LOUSY DÉCOR!

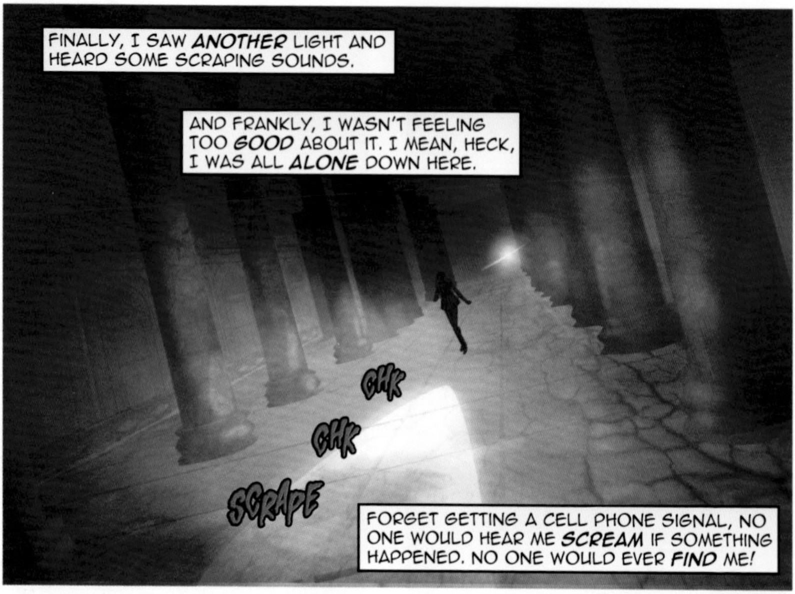
FINALLY, I SAW ANOTHER LIGHT AND HEARD SOME SCRAPING SOUNDS.
AND FRANKLY, I WASN'T FEELING TOO GOOD ABOUT IT. I MEAN, HECK, I WAS ALL ALONE DOWN HERE.
CHK
CHK
SCRAPE
FORGET GETTING A CELL PHONE SIGNAL, NO ONE WOULD HEAR ME SCREAM IF SOMETHING HAPPENED. NO ONE WOULD EVER FIND ME!

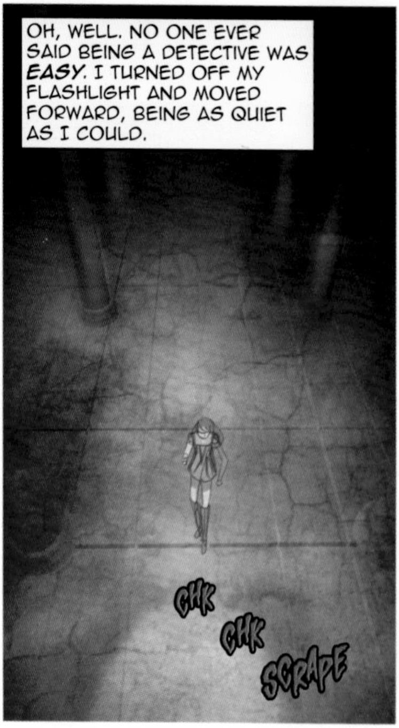
OH, WELL. NO ONE EVER SAID BEING A DETECTIVE WAS EASY. I TURNED OFF MY FLASHLIGHT AND MOVED FORWARD, BEING AS QUIET AS I COULD.
CHK
CHK
SCRAPE

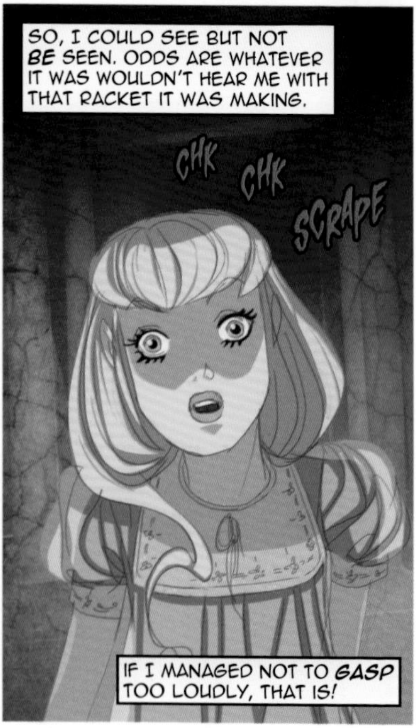
SO, I COULD SEE BUT NOT BE SEEN. ODDS ARE WHATEVER IT WAS WOULDN'T HEAR ME WITH THAT RACKET IT WAS MAKING.
CHK
CHK
SCRAPE
IF I MANAGED NOT TO GASP TOO LOUDLY, THAT IS!

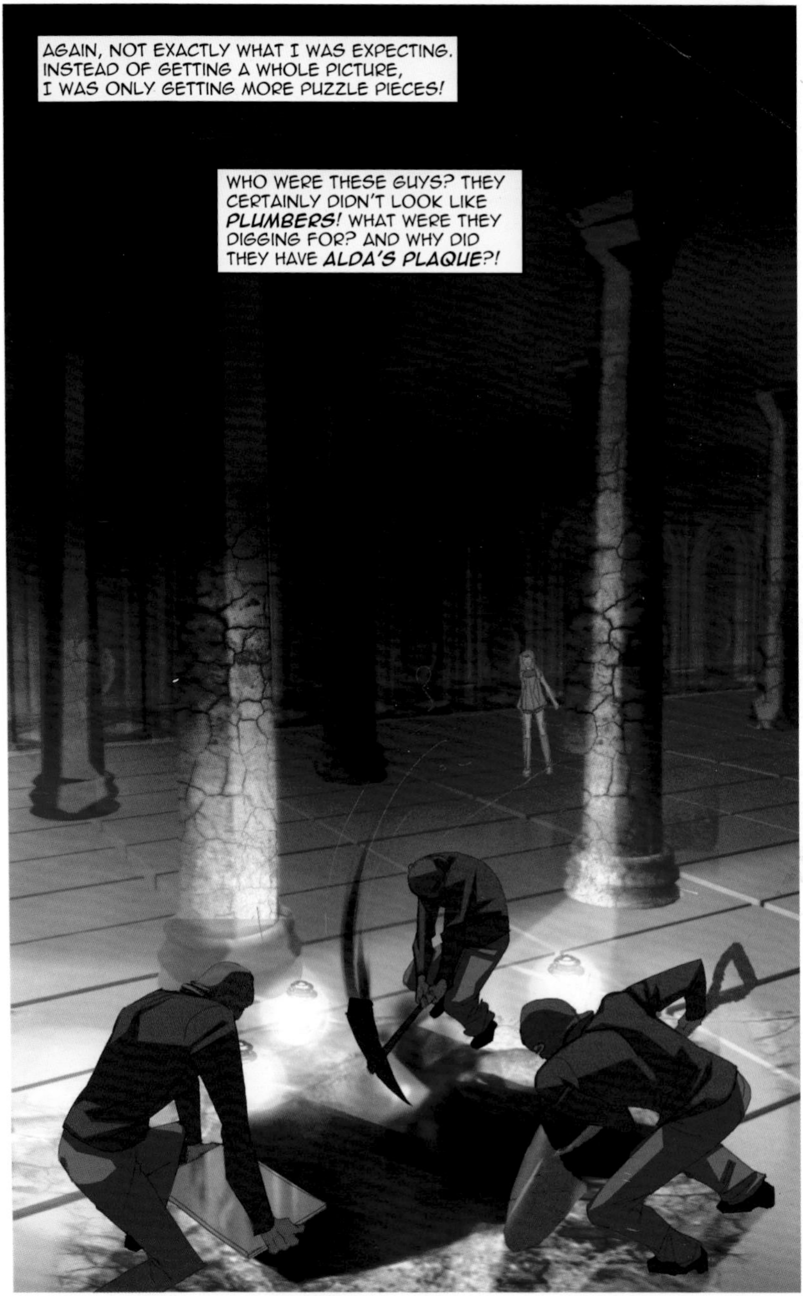
AGAIN, NOT EXACTLY WHAT I WAS EXPECTING. INSTEAD OF GETTING A WHOLE PICTURE, I WAS ONLY GETTING MORE PUZZLE PIECES!
WHO WERE THESE GUYS? THEY CERTAINLY DIDN'T LOOK LIKE *PLUMBERS!* WHAT WERE THEY DIGGING FOR? AND WHY DID THEY HAVE *ALDA'S PLAQUE*?!

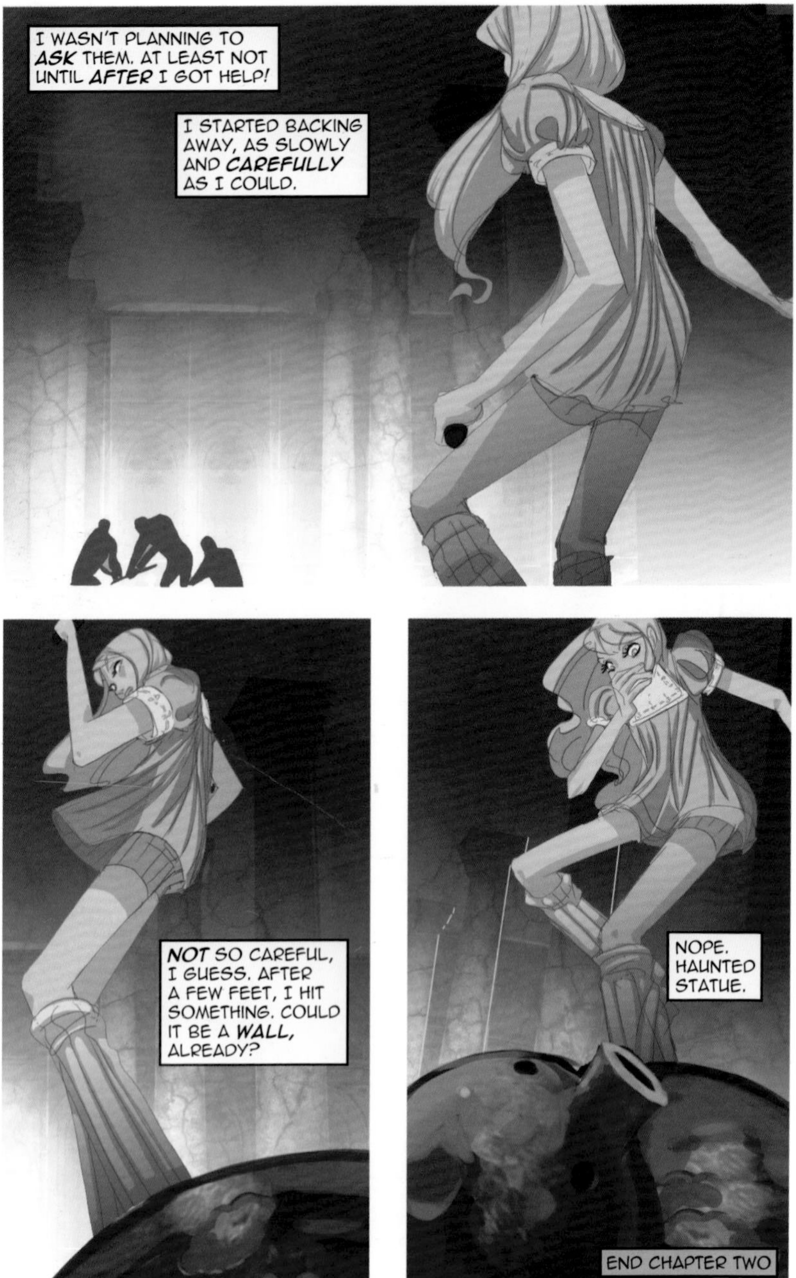
I WASN'T PLANNING TO ASK THEM. AT LEAST NOT UNTIL AFTER I GOT HELP!
I STARTED BACKING AWAY, AS SLOWLY AND CAREFULLY AS I COULD.
NOT SO CAREFUL, I GUESS. AFTER A FEW FEET, I HIT SOMETHING. COULD IT BE A WALL, ALREADY?
NOPE. HAUNTED STATUE.
END CHAPTER TWO

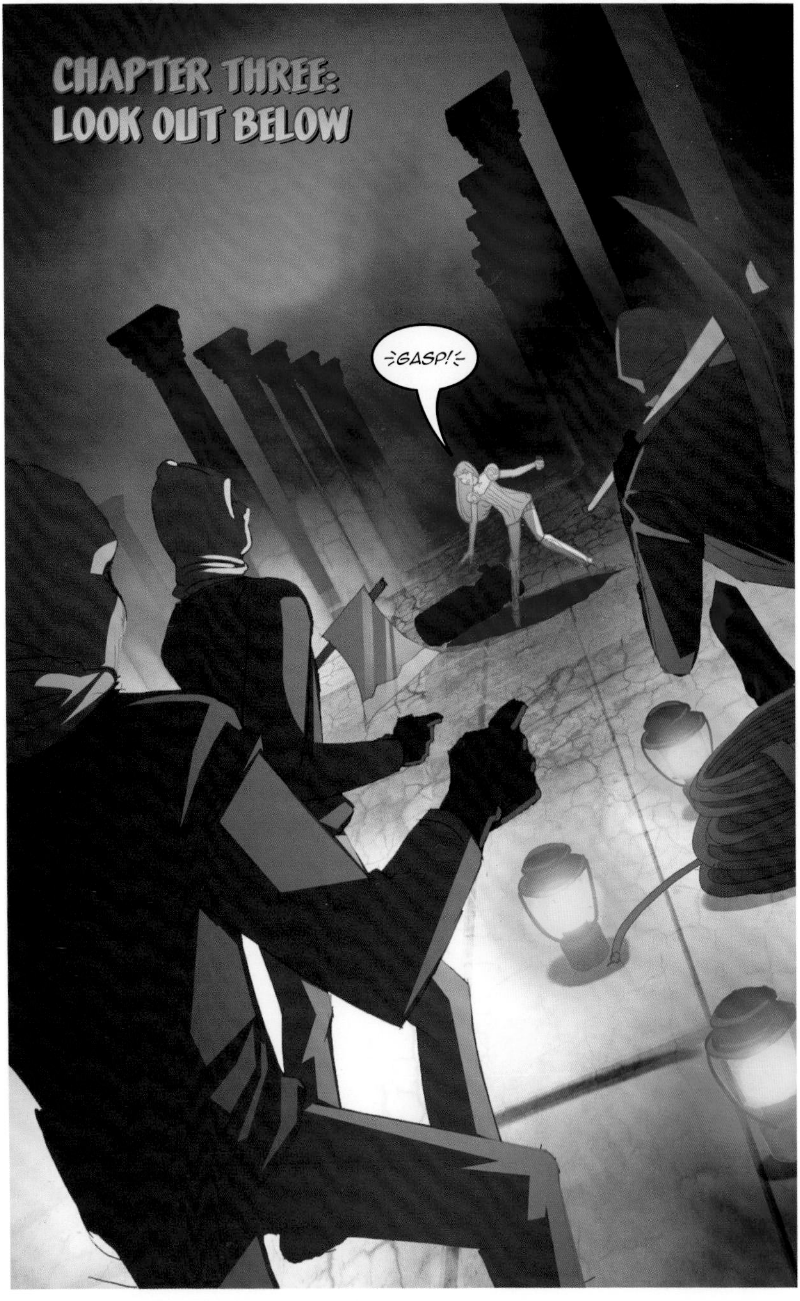
CHAPTER THREE:
LOOK OUT BELOW
GASP!

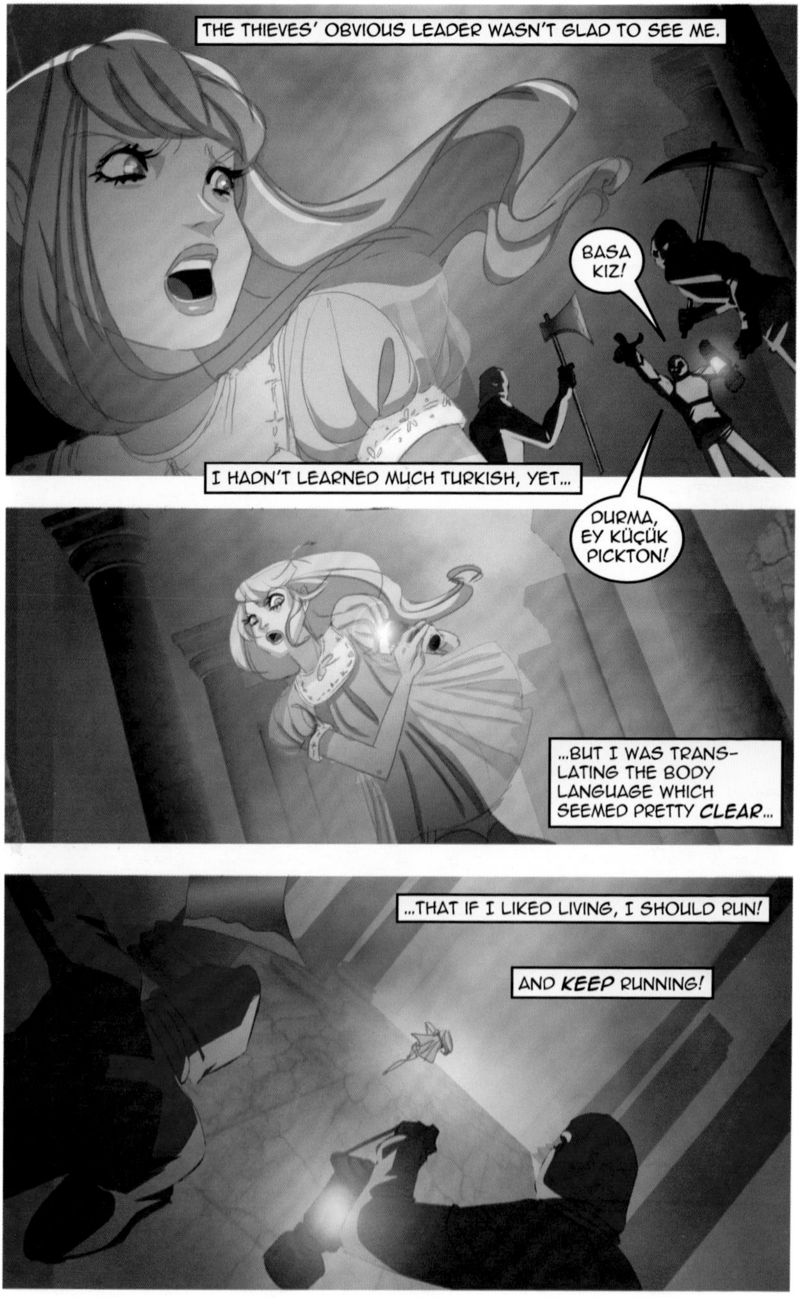
THE THIEVES' OBVIOUS LEADER WASN'T GLAD TO SEE ME.
BASA KIZ!
I HADN'T LEARNED MUCH TURKISH, YET...
DURMA, EY KÜÇÜK PICKTON!
...BUT I WAS TRANSLATING THE BODY LANGUAGE WHICH SEEMED PRETTY CLEAR...
...THAT IF I LIKED LIVING, I SHOULD RUN!
AND KEEP RUNNING!

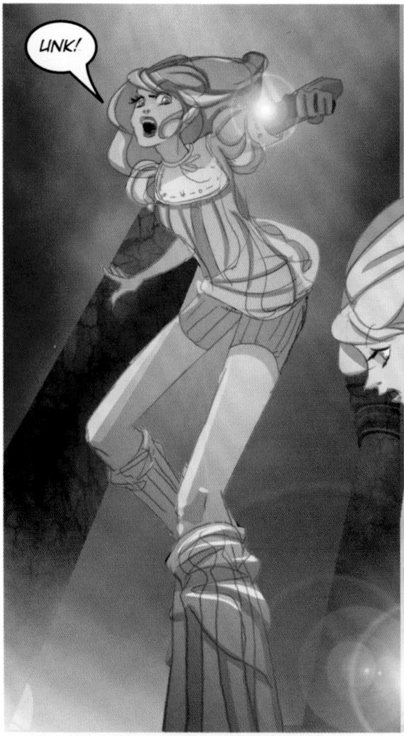
UNK!

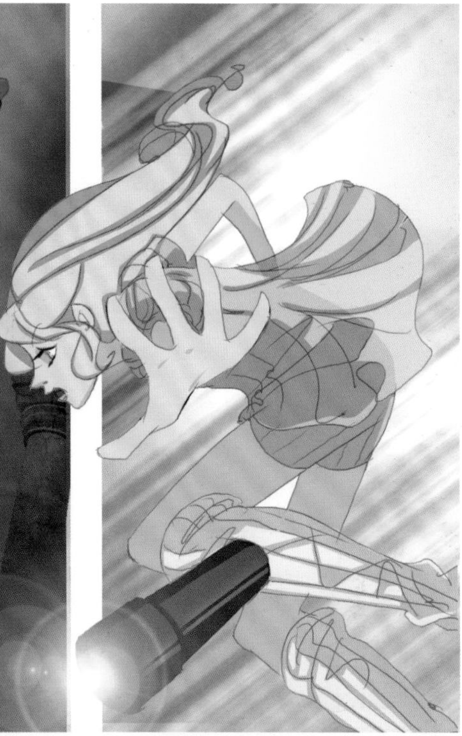

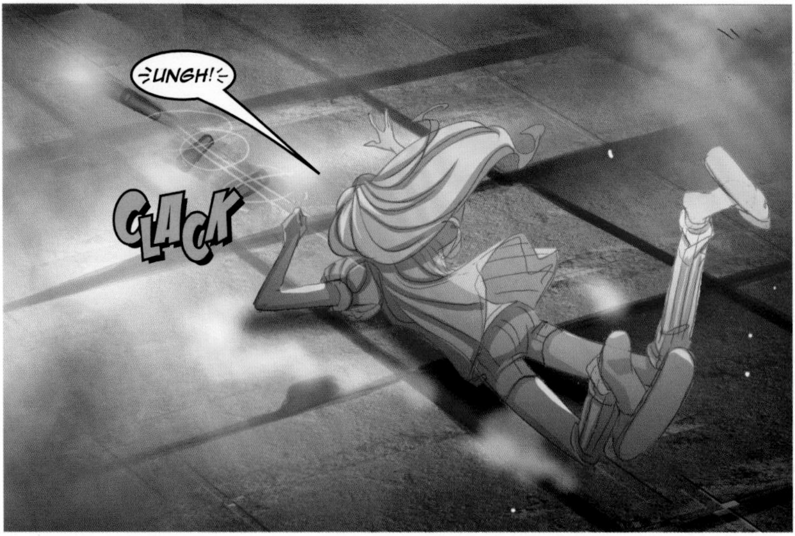
UNGH!
CLACK

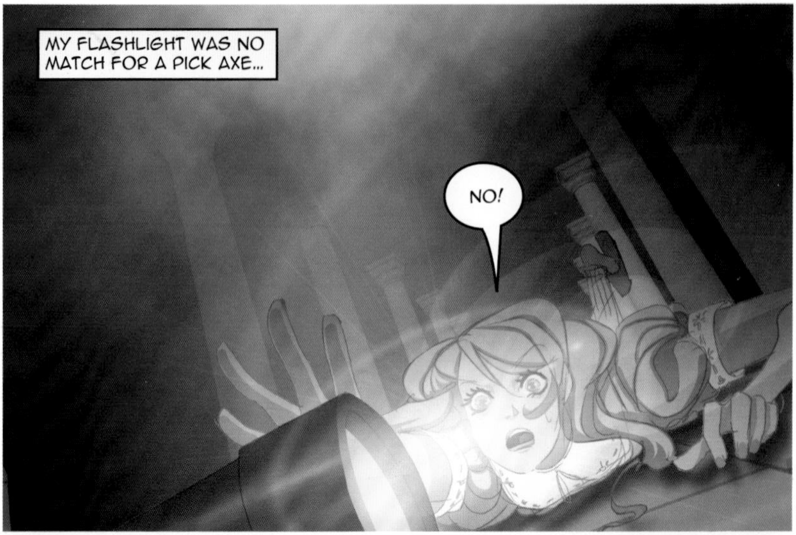
MY FLASHLIGHT WAS NO MATCH FOR A PICK AXE...
NO!

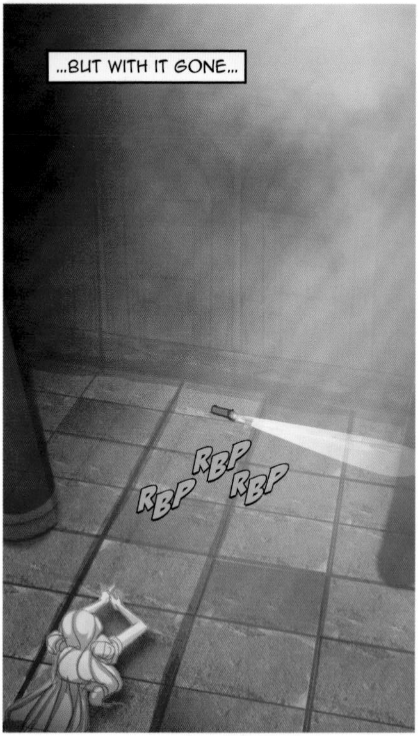
...BUT WITH IT GONE...
RBP RBP RBP

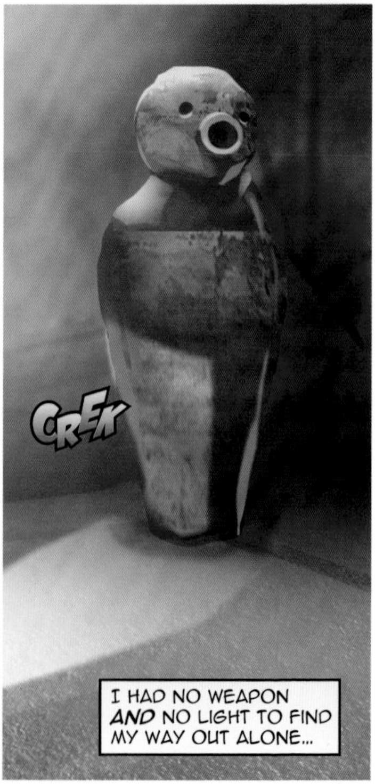
CREK
I HAD NO WEAPON **AND** NO LIGHT TO FIND MY WAY OUT ALONE...

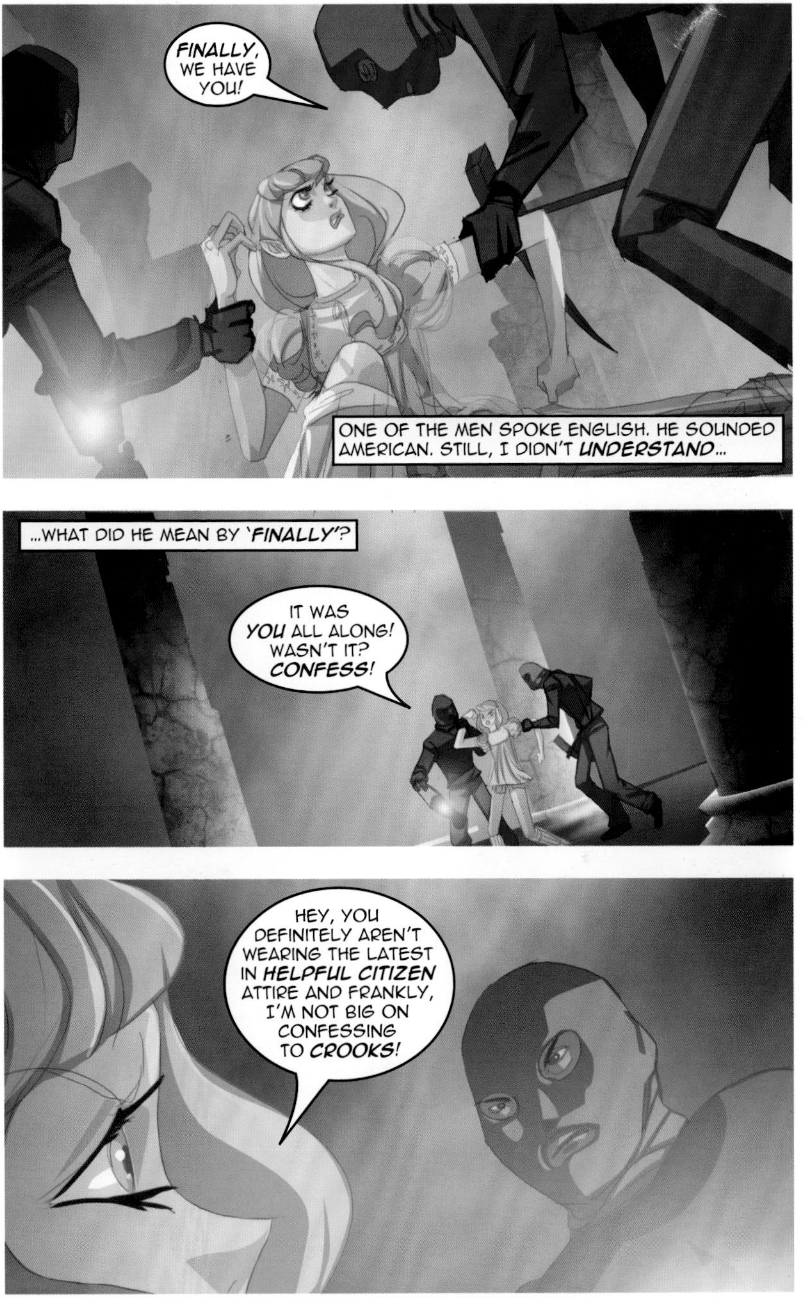
FINALLY, WE HAVE YOU!
ONE OF THE MEN SPOKE ENGLISH. HE SOUNDED AMERICAN. STILL, I DIDN'T UNDERSTAND...
...WHAT DID HE MEAN BY 'FINALLY'?
IT WAS YOU ALL ALONG! WASN'T IT? CONFESS!
HEY, YOU DEFINITELY AREN'T WEARING THE LATEST IN HELPFUL CITIZEN ATTIRE AND FRANKLY, I'M NOT BIG ON CONFESSING TO CROOKS!

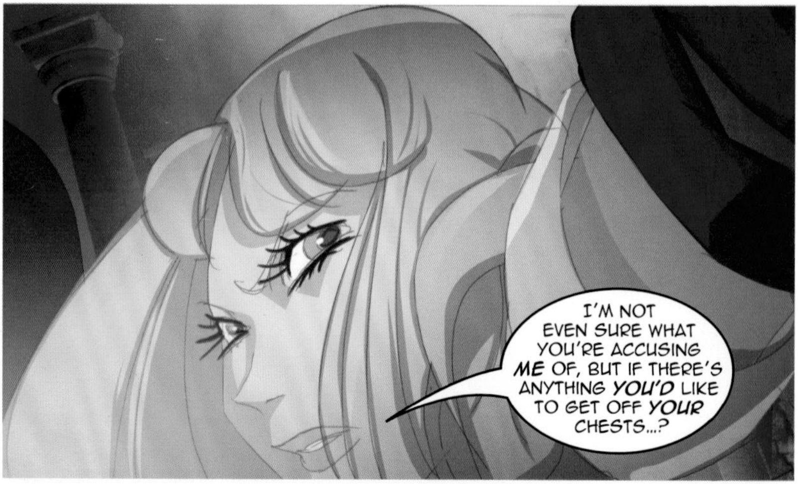
I'M NOT EVEN SURE WHAT YOU'RE ACCUSING *ME* OF, BUT IF THERE'S ANYTHING *YOU'D* LIKE TO GET OFF *YOUR* CHESTS...?

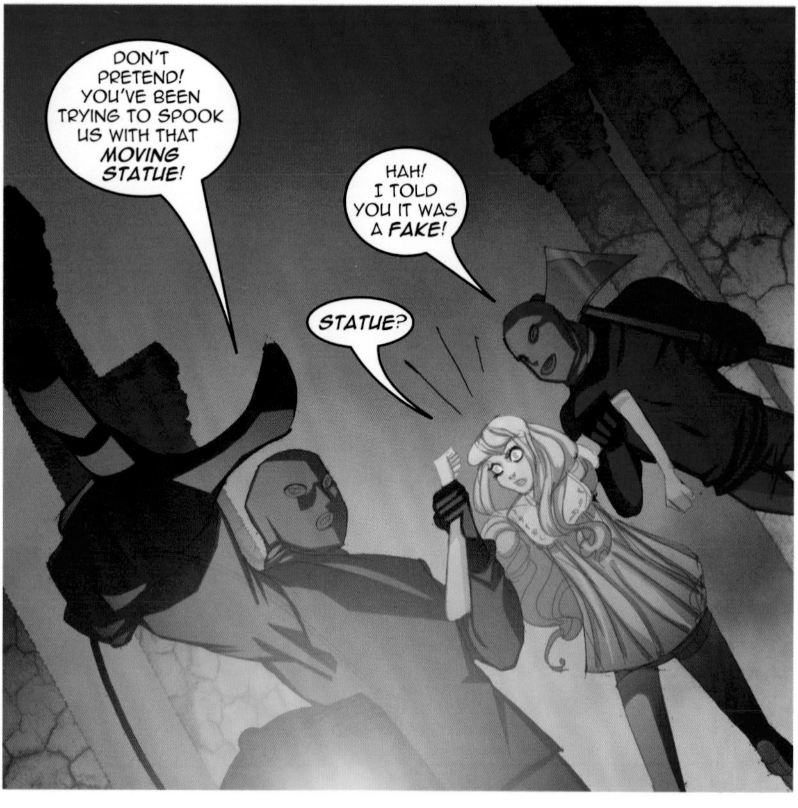
DON'T PRETEND! YOU'VE BEEN TRYING TO SPOOK US WITH THAT *MOVING STATUE*!
HAH! I TOLD YOU IT WAS A *FAKE*!
STATUE?

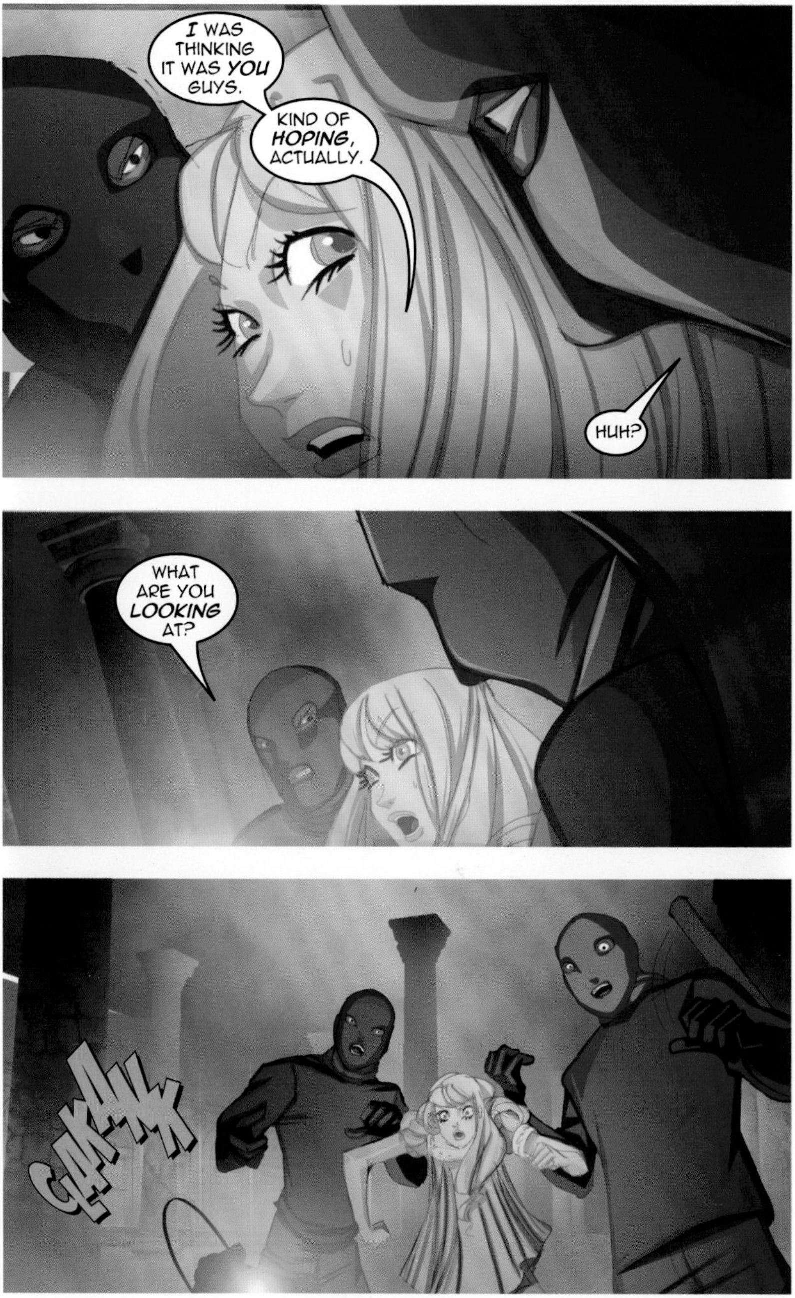
I WAS THINKING IT WAS YOU GUYS.
KIND OF HOPING, ACTUALLY.
HUH?
WHAT ARE YOU LOOKING AT?

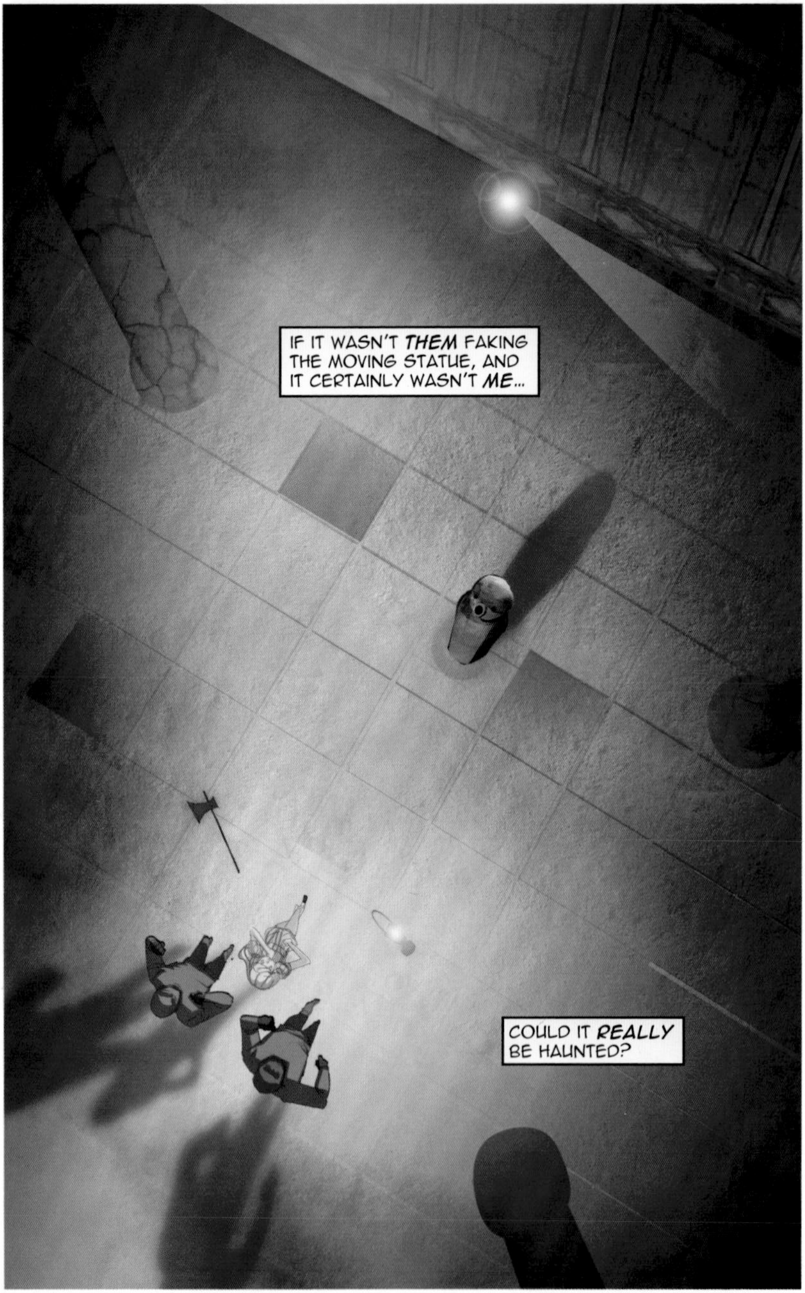
IF IT WASN'T THEM FAKING THE MOVING STATUE, AND IT CERTAINLY WASN'T ME...
COULD IT REALLY BE HAUNTED?

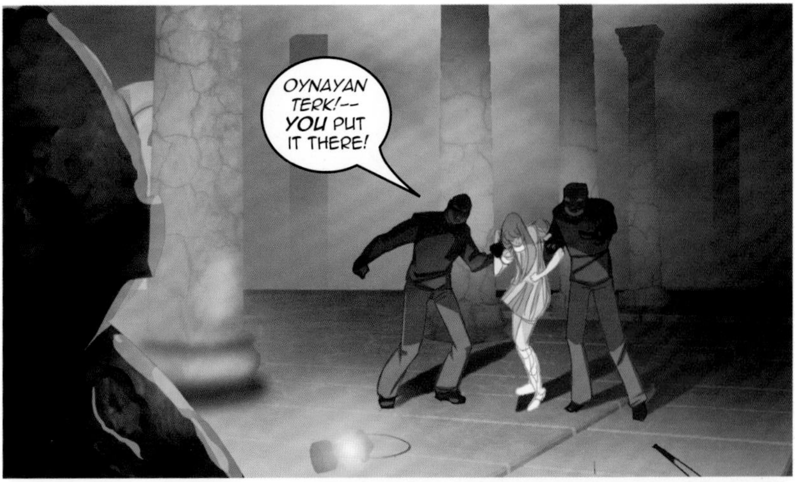
OYNAYAN TERK!-- YOU PUT IT THERE!

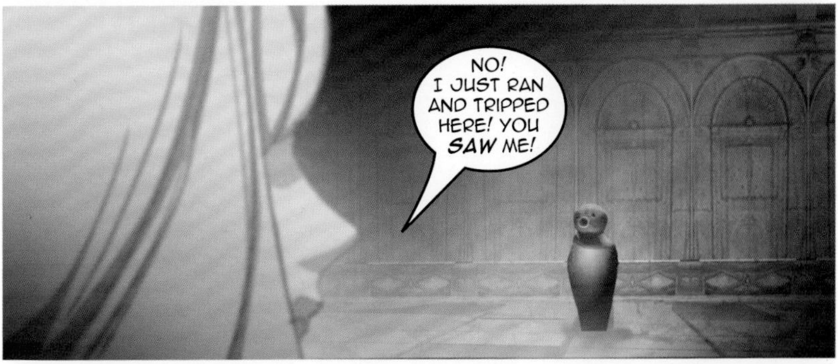
NO! I JUST RAN AND TRIPPED HERE! YOU SAW ME!

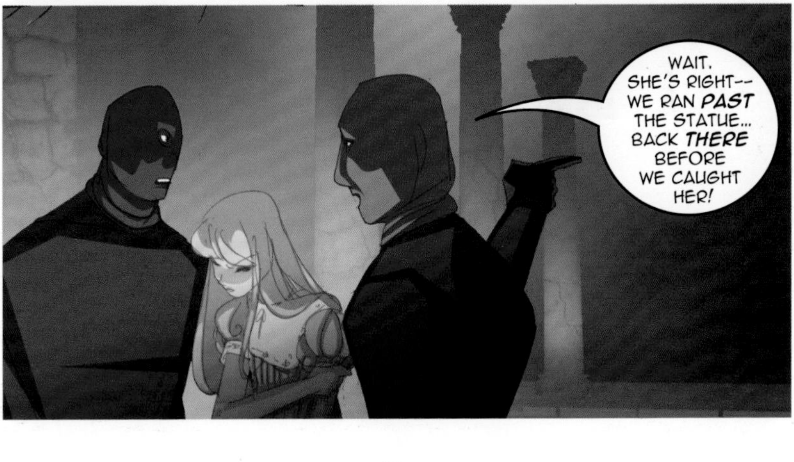
WAIT. SHE'S RIGHT-- WE RAN PAST THE STATUE... BACK THERE BEFORE WE CAUGHT HER!

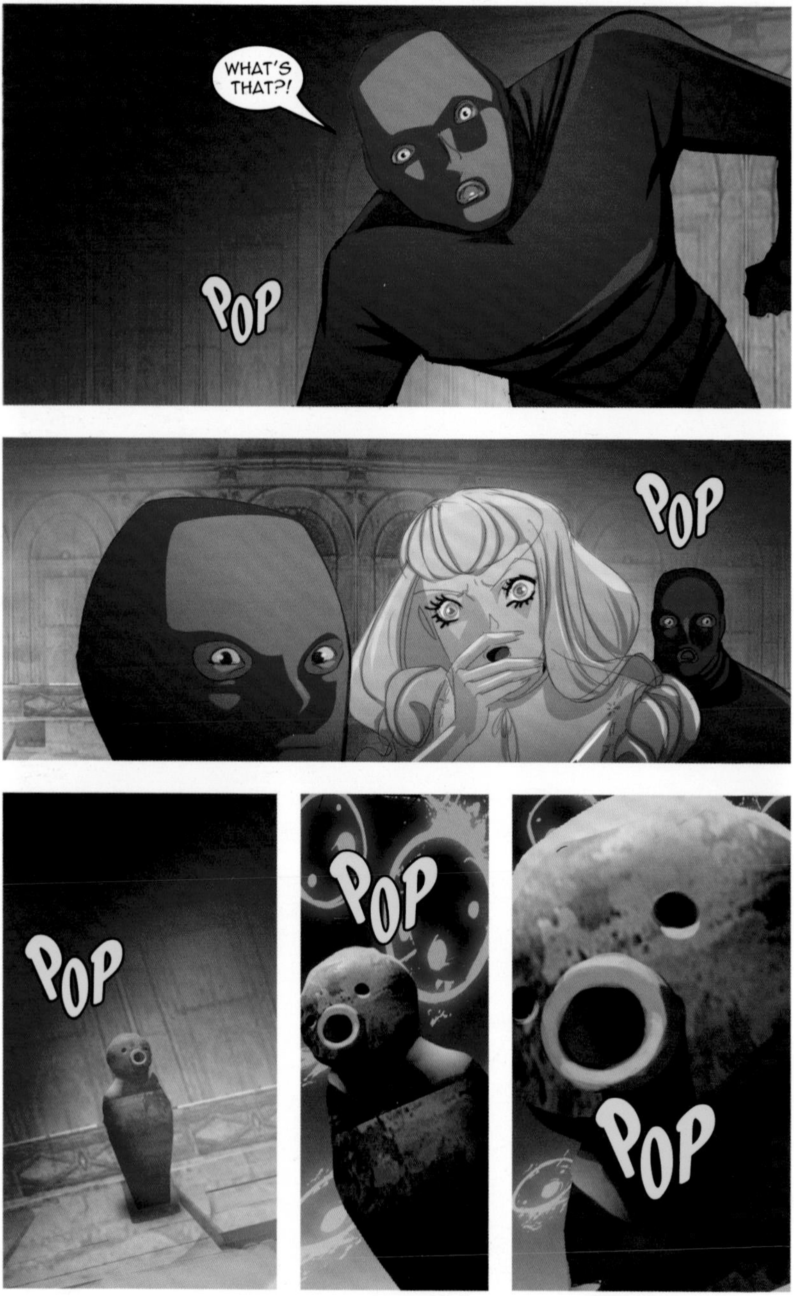
WHAT'S THAT?!
POP
POP
POP
POP
POP

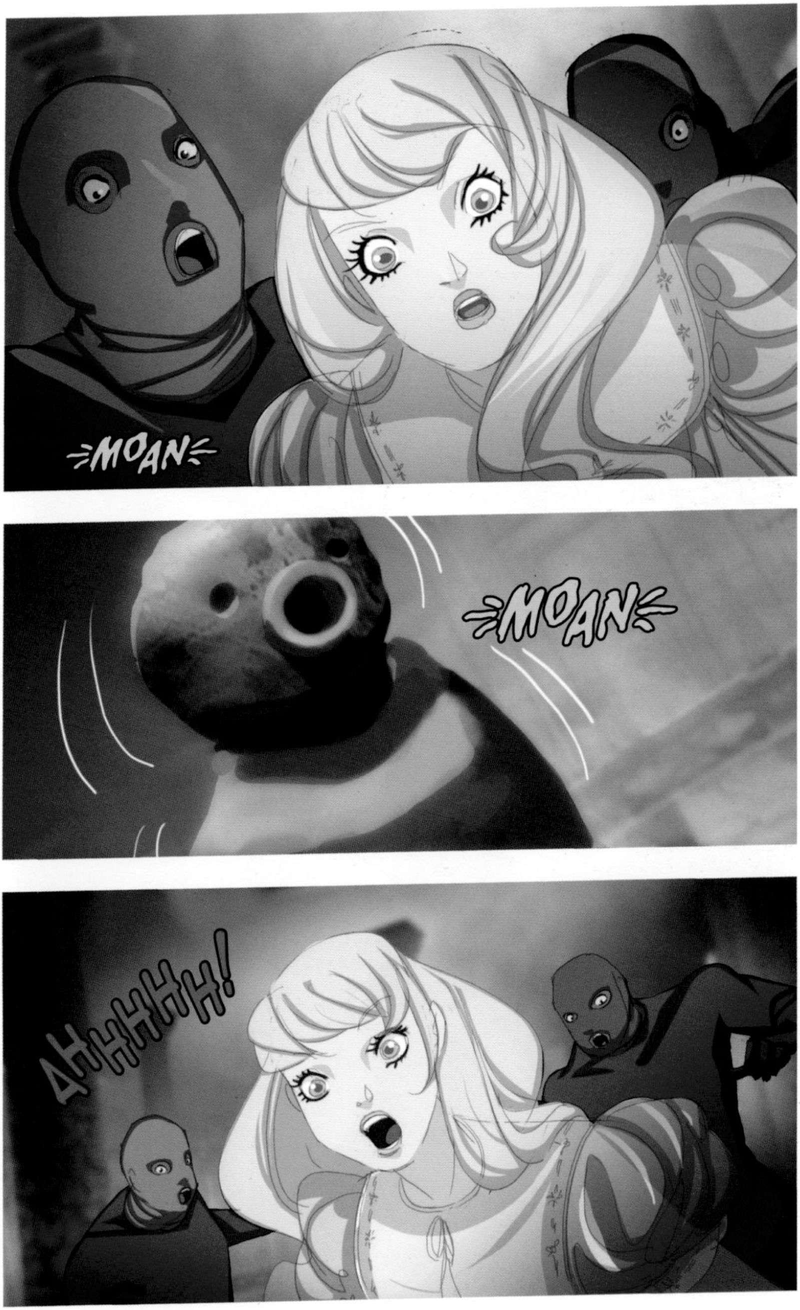
MOAN
MOAN
AHHHHH!

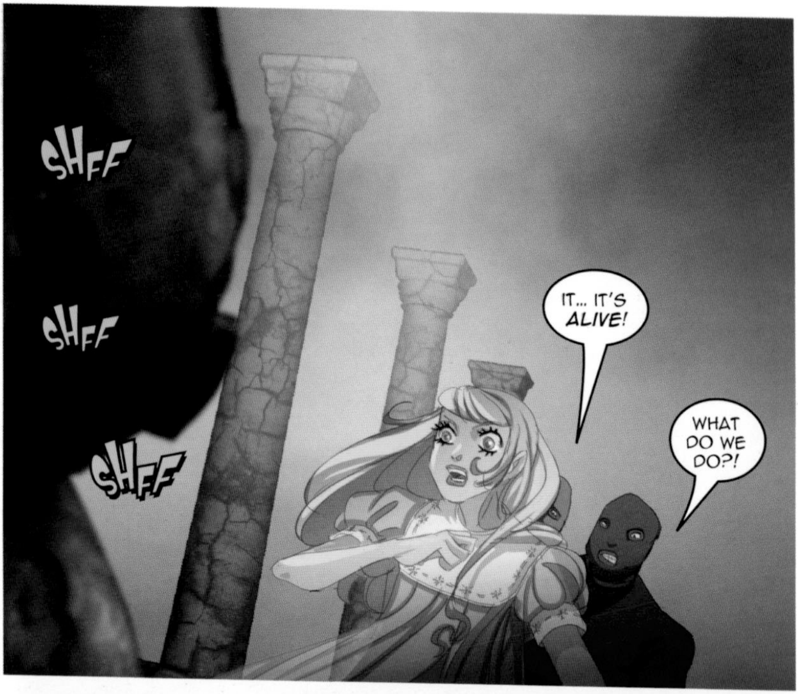
SHFF
SHFF
SHFF
IT... IT'S ALIVE!
WHAT DO WE DO?!

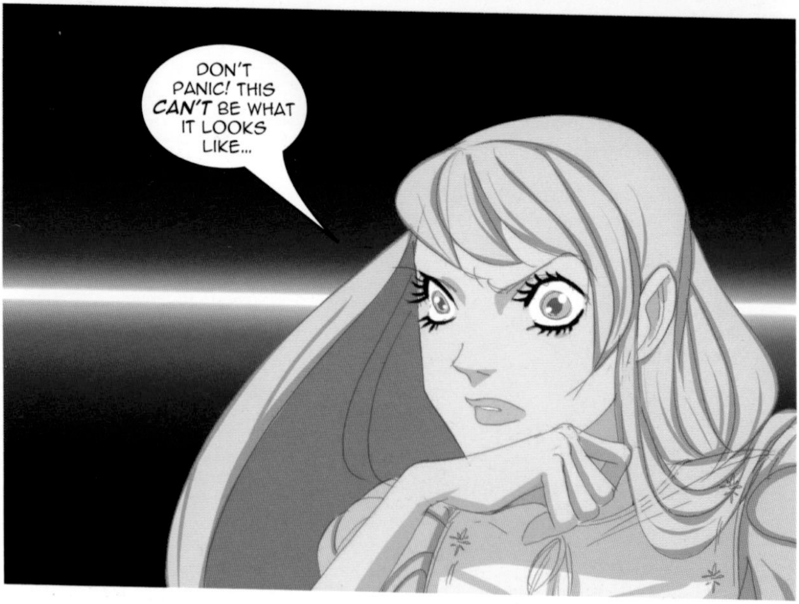
DON'T PANIC! THIS CAN'T BE WHAT IT LOOKS LIKE...

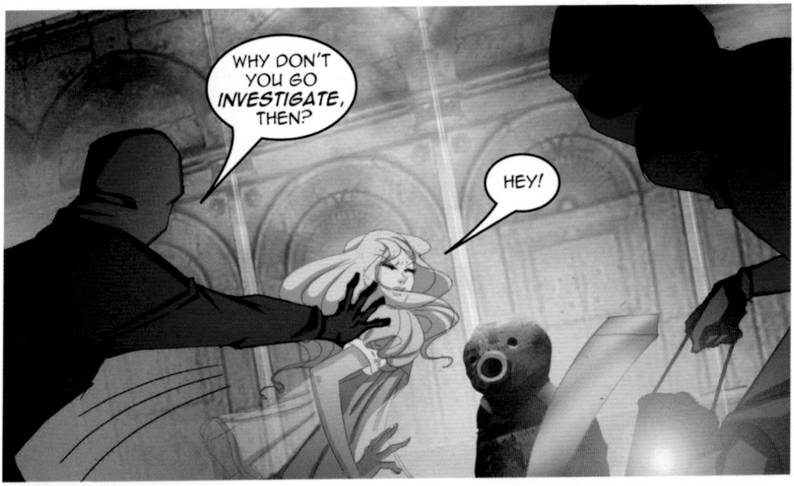
WHY DON'T YOU GO INVESTIGATE, THEN?
HEY!

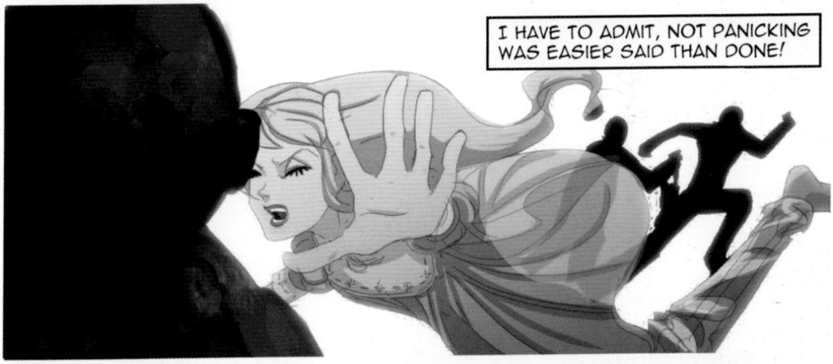
I HAVE TO ADMIT, NOT PANICKING WAS EASIER SAID THAN DONE!

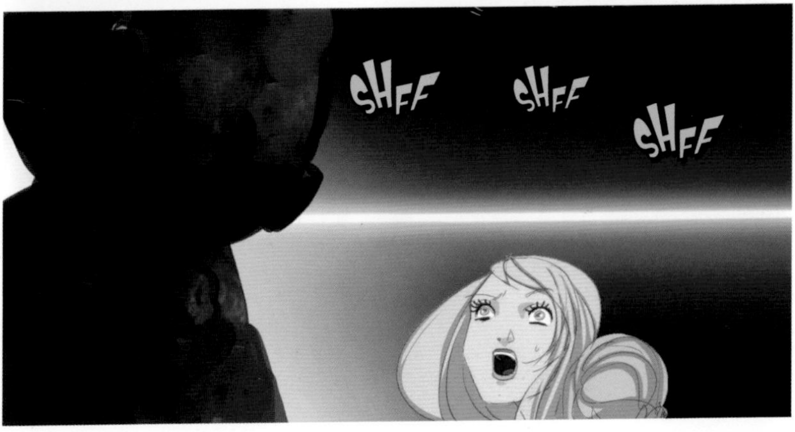
SHFF
SHFF
SHFF

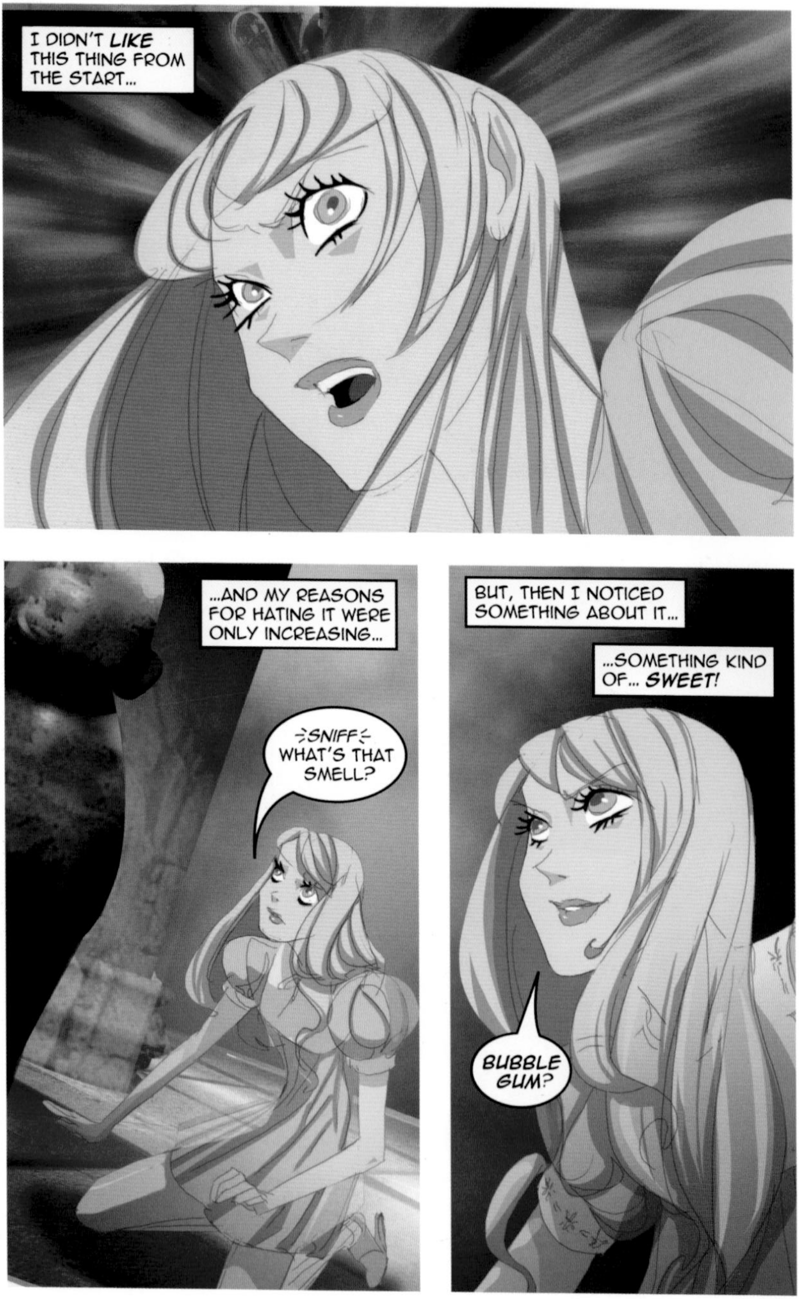
I DIDN'T LIKE THIS THING FROM THE START...
...AND MY REASONS FOR HATING IT WERE ONLY INCREASING...
SNIFF WHAT'S THAT SMELL?
BUT, THEN I NOTICED SOMETHING ABOUT IT...
...SOMETHING KIND OF... SWEET!
BUBBLE GUM?

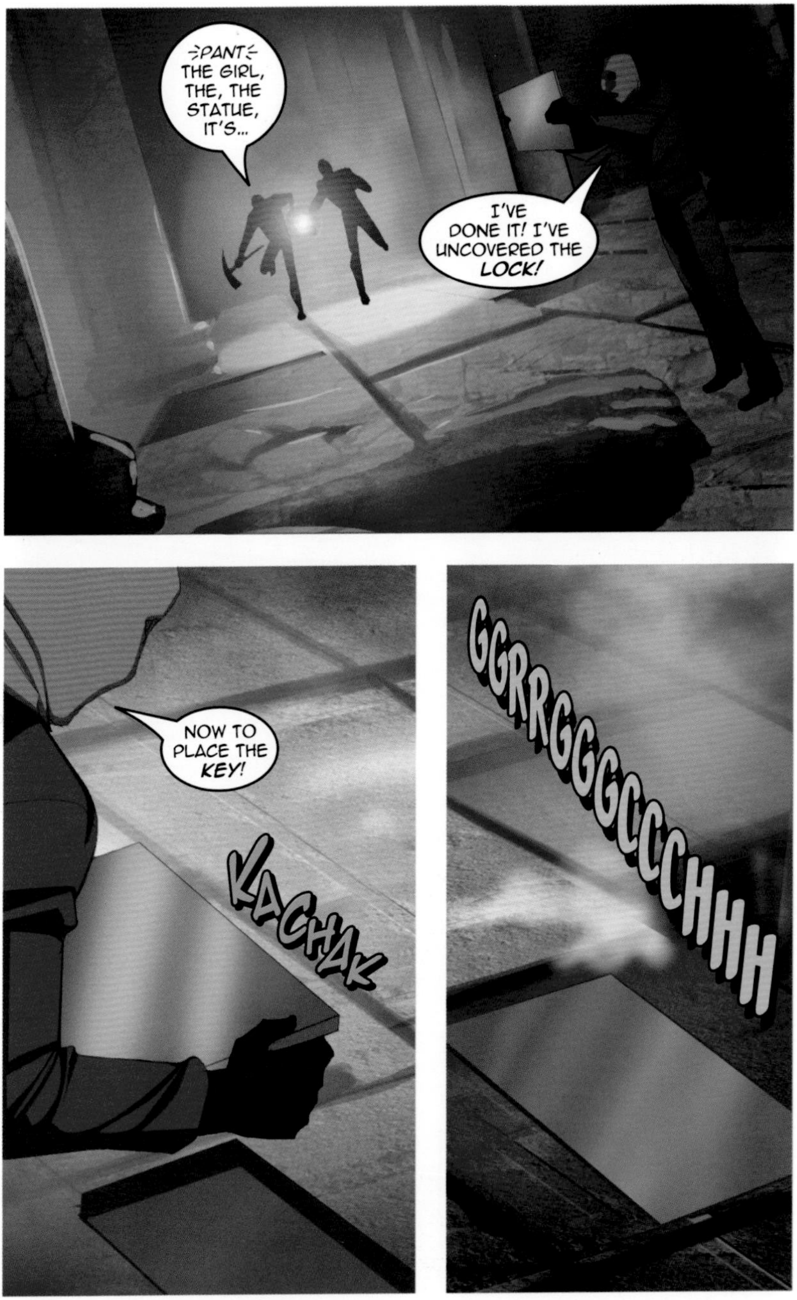

=PANT= THE GIRL, THE, THE STATUE, IT'S...
I'VE DONE IT! I'VE UNCOVERED THE LOCK!
NOW TO PLACE THE KEY!
KACHAK
GGRRGGGCCCHHHH

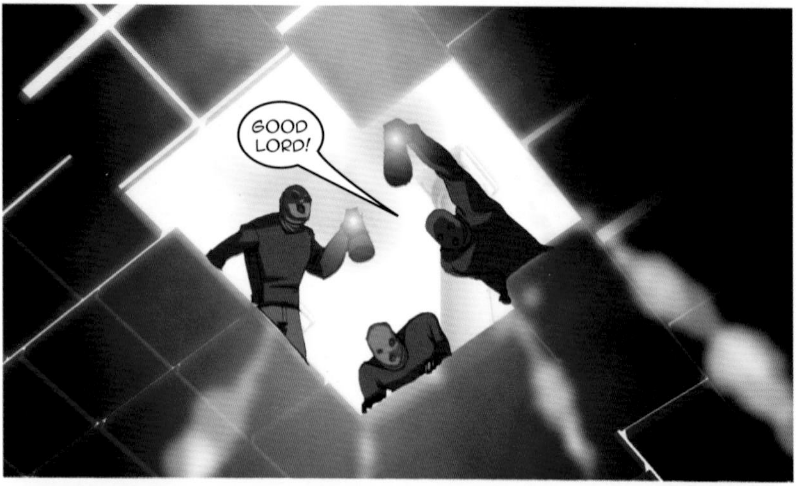
GOOD LORD!

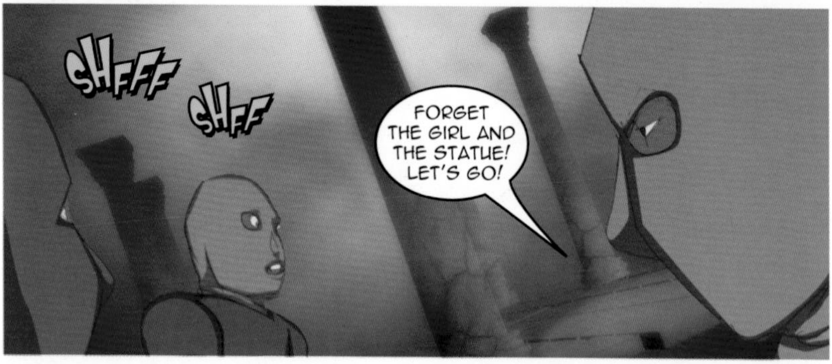
SHFFF
SHFF
FORGET THE GIRL AND THE STATUE! LET'S GO!

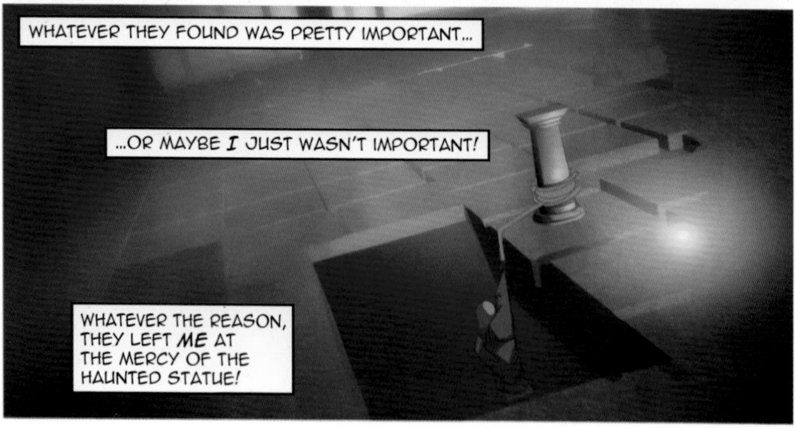
WHATEVER THEY FOUND WAS PRETTY IMPORTANT...
...OR MAYBE *I* JUST WASN'T IMPORTANT!
WHATEVER THE REASON, THEY LEFT ***ME*** AT THE MERCY OF THE HAUNTED STATUE!

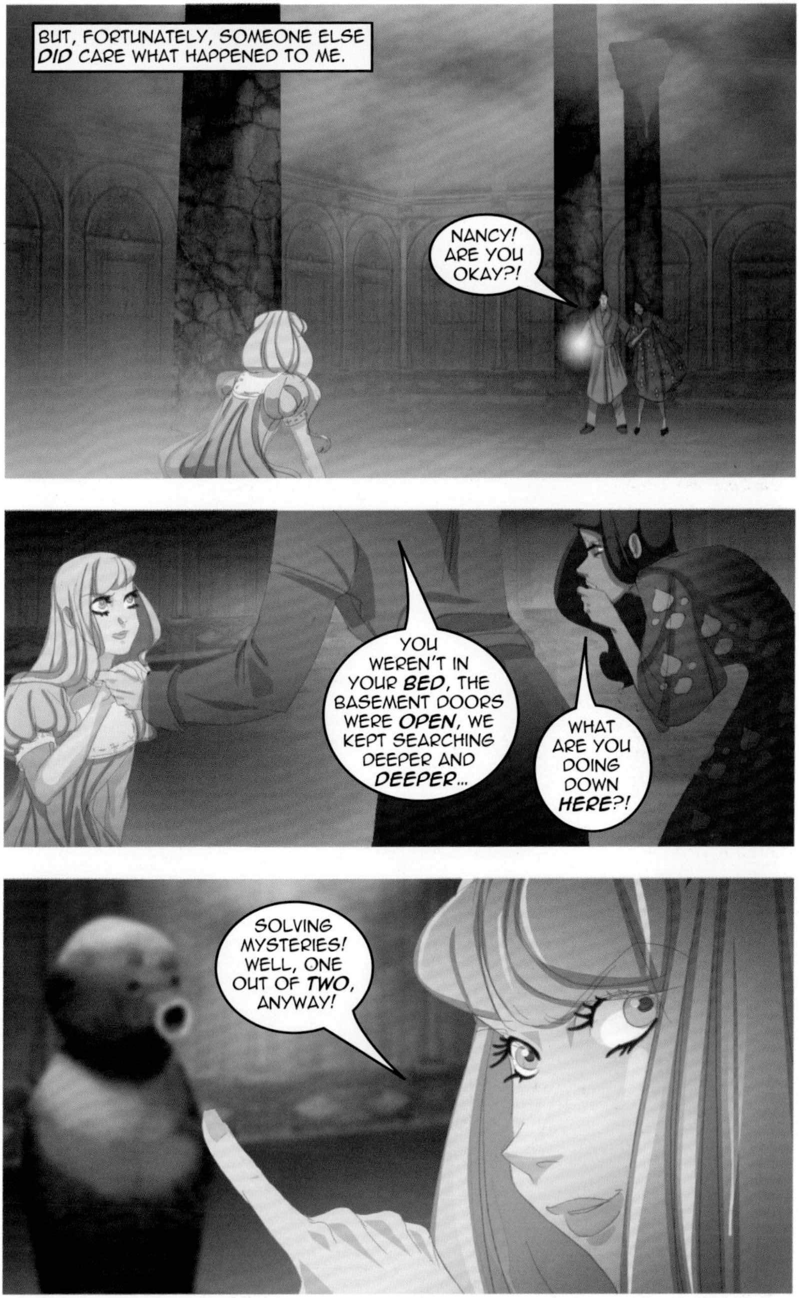
BUT, FORTUNATELY, SOMEONE ELSE DID CARE WHAT HAPPENED TO ME.
NANCY! ARE YOU OKAY?!
YOU WEREN'T IN YOUR BED, THE BASEMENT DOORS WERE OPEN, WE KEPT SEARCHING DEEPER AND DEEPER...
WHAT ARE YOU DOING DOWN HERE?!
SOLVING MYSTERIES! WELL, ONE OUT OF TWO, ANYWAY!

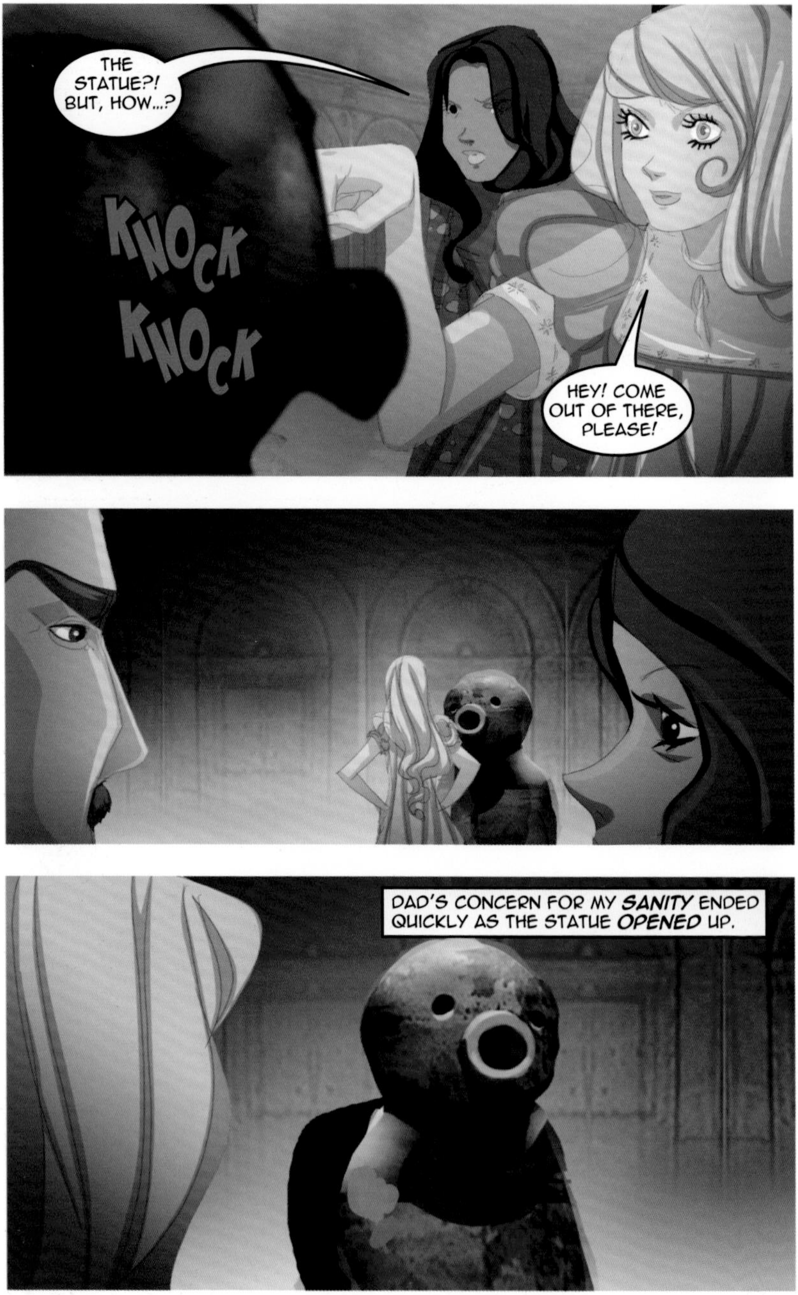
THE STATUE?! BUT, HOW...?
KNOCK KNOCK
HEY! COME OUT OF THERE, PLEASE!
DAD'S CONCERN FOR MY *SANITY* ENDED QUICKLY AS THE STATUE *OPENED* UP.

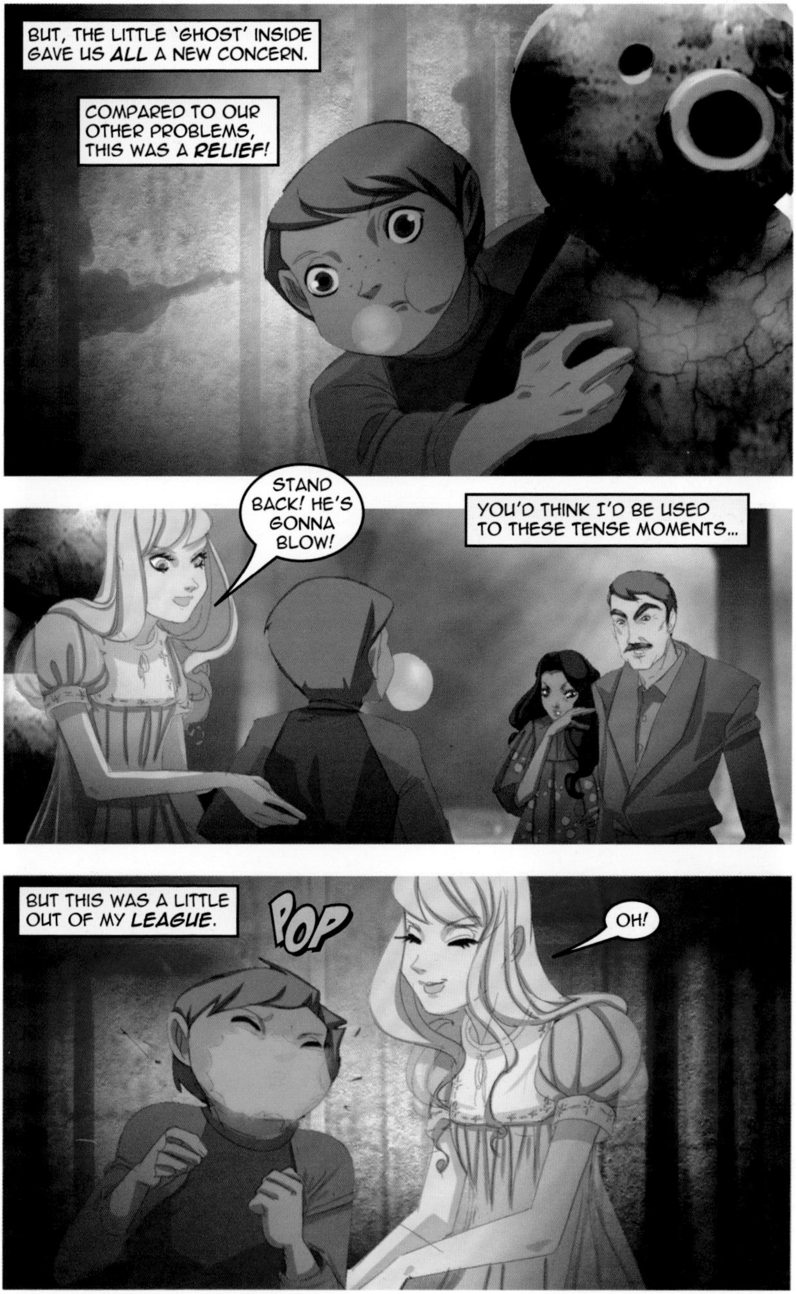
BUT, THE LITTLE 'GHOST' INSIDE GAVE US ALL A NEW CONCERN.
COMPARED TO OUR OTHER PROBLEMS, THIS WAS A RELIEF!
STAND BACK! HE'S GONNA BLOW!
YOU'D THINK I'D BE USED TO THESE TENSE MOMENTS...
BUT THIS WAS A LITTLE OUT OF MY LEAGUE.
POP
OH!

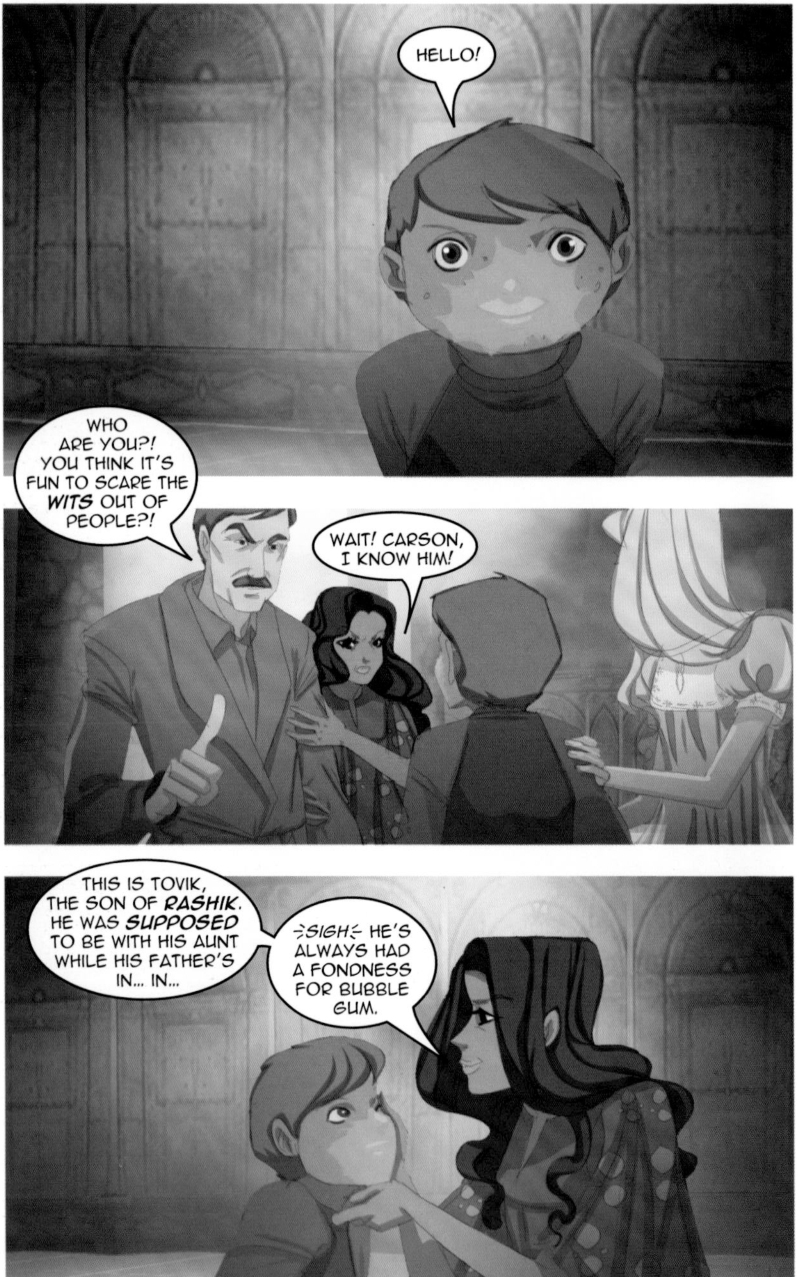
HELLO!
WHO ARE YOU?! YOU THINK IT'S FUN TO SCARE THE WITS OUT OF PEOPLE?!
WAIT! CARSON, I KNOW HIM!
THIS IS TOVIK, THE SON OF RASHIK. HE WAS SUPPOSED TO BE WITH HIS AUNT WHILE HIS FATHER'S IN... IN...
-SIGH- HE'S ALWAYS HAD A FONDNESS FOR BUBBLE GUM.

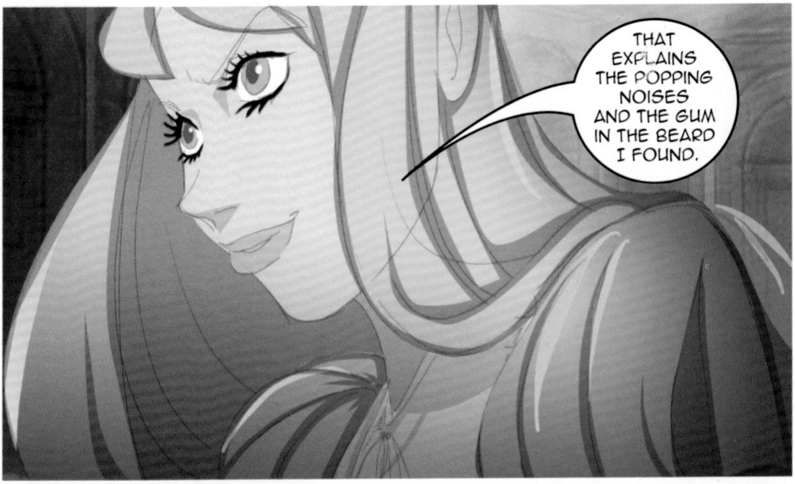
THAT EXPLAINS THE POPPING NOISES AND THE GUM IN THE BEARD I FOUND.

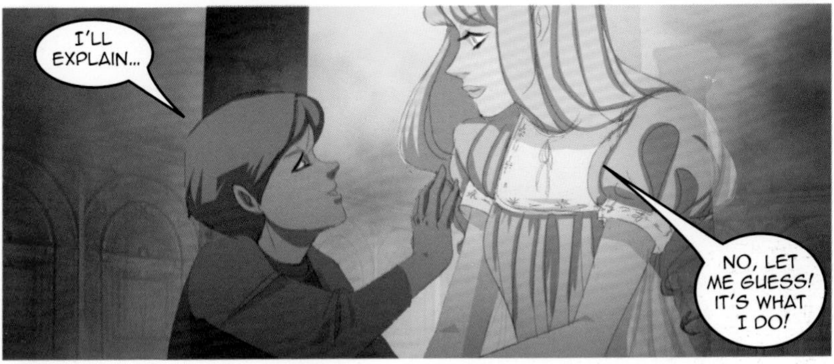
I'LL EXPLAIN...
NO, LET ME GUESS! IT'S WHAT I DO!

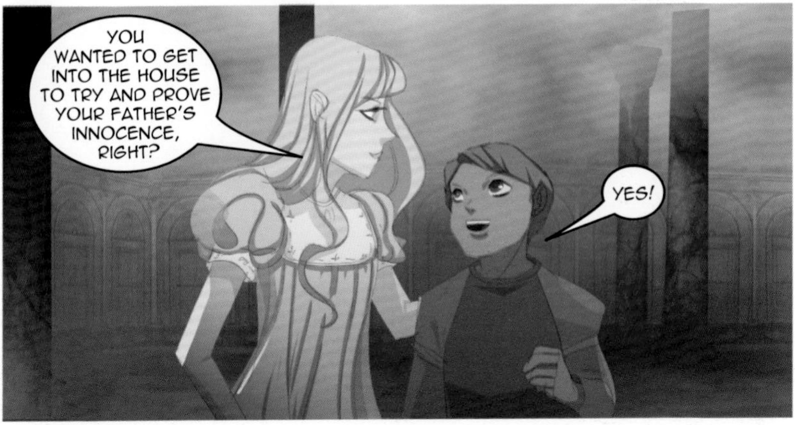
YOU WANTED TO GET INTO THE HOUSE TO TRY AND PROVE YOUR FATHER'S INNOCENCE, RIGHT?
YES!

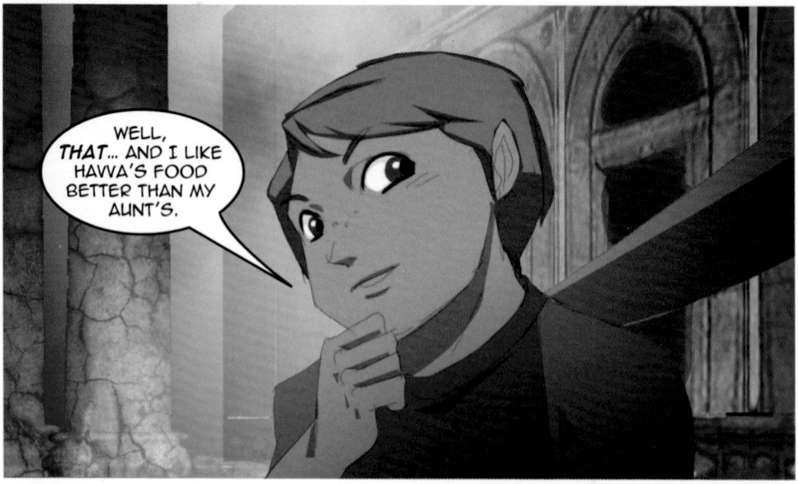
WELL, THAT... AND I LIKE HAVVA'S FOOD BETTER THAN MY AUNT'S.

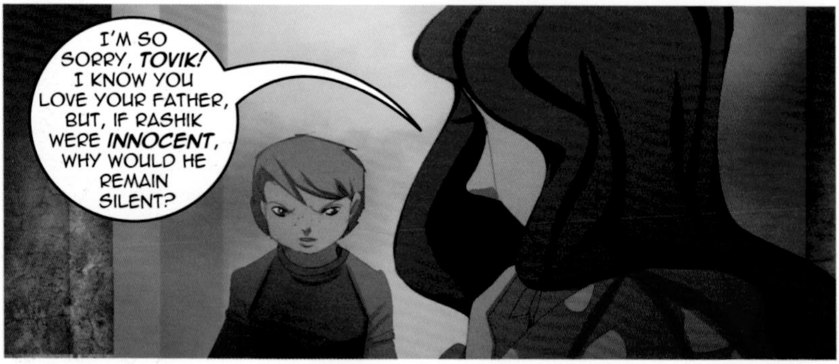
I'M SO SORRY, TOVIK! I KNOW YOU LOVE YOUR FATHER, BUT, IF RASHIK WERE INNOCENT, WHY WOULD HE REMAIN SILENT?

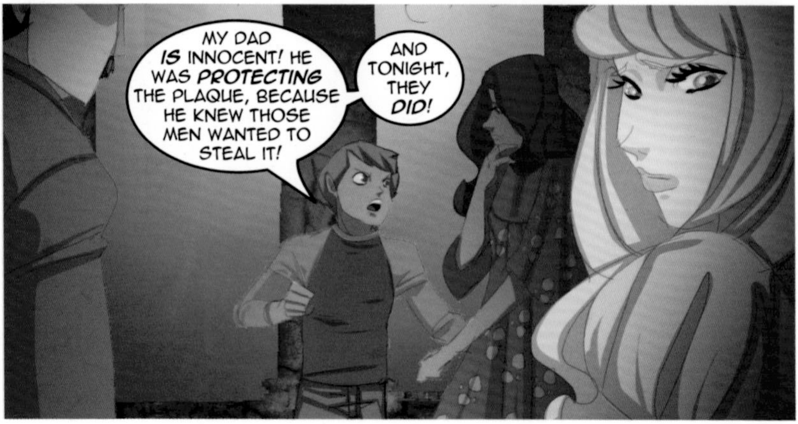
MY DAD IS INNOCENT! HE WAS PROTECTING THE PLAQUE, BECAUSE HE KNEW THOSE MEN WANTED TO STEAL IT!
AND TONIGHT, THEY DID!

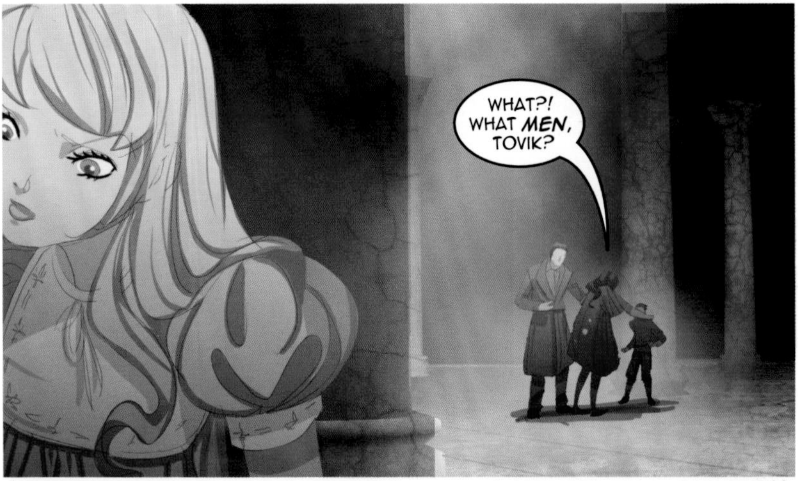
WHAT?! WHAT MEN, TOVIK?

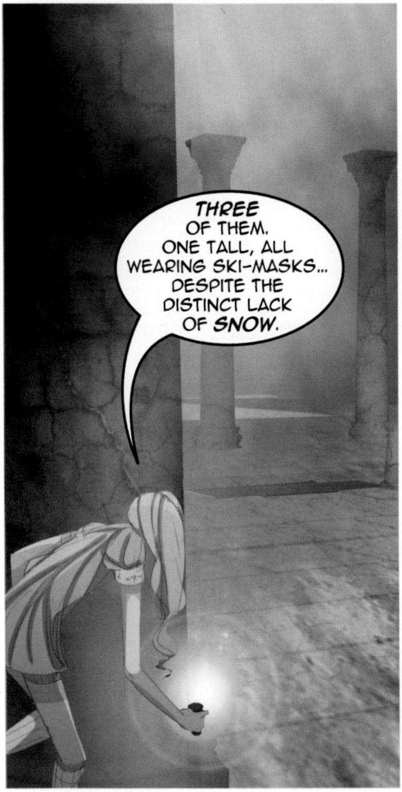
THREE OF THEM. ONE TALL, ALL WEARING SKI-MASKS... DESPITE THE DISTINCT LACK OF SNOW.

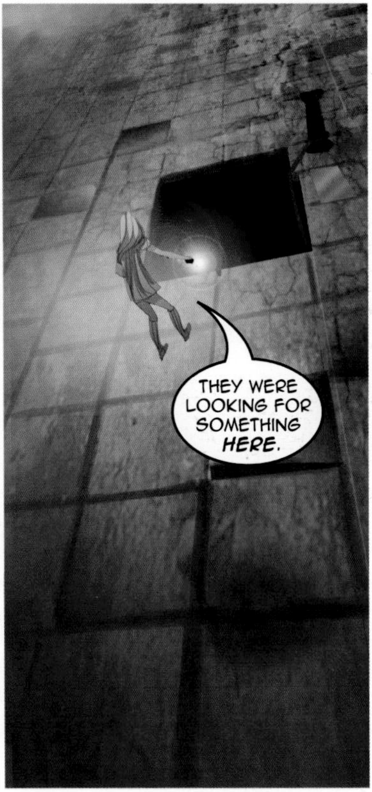
THEY WERE LOOKING FOR SOMETHING HERE.

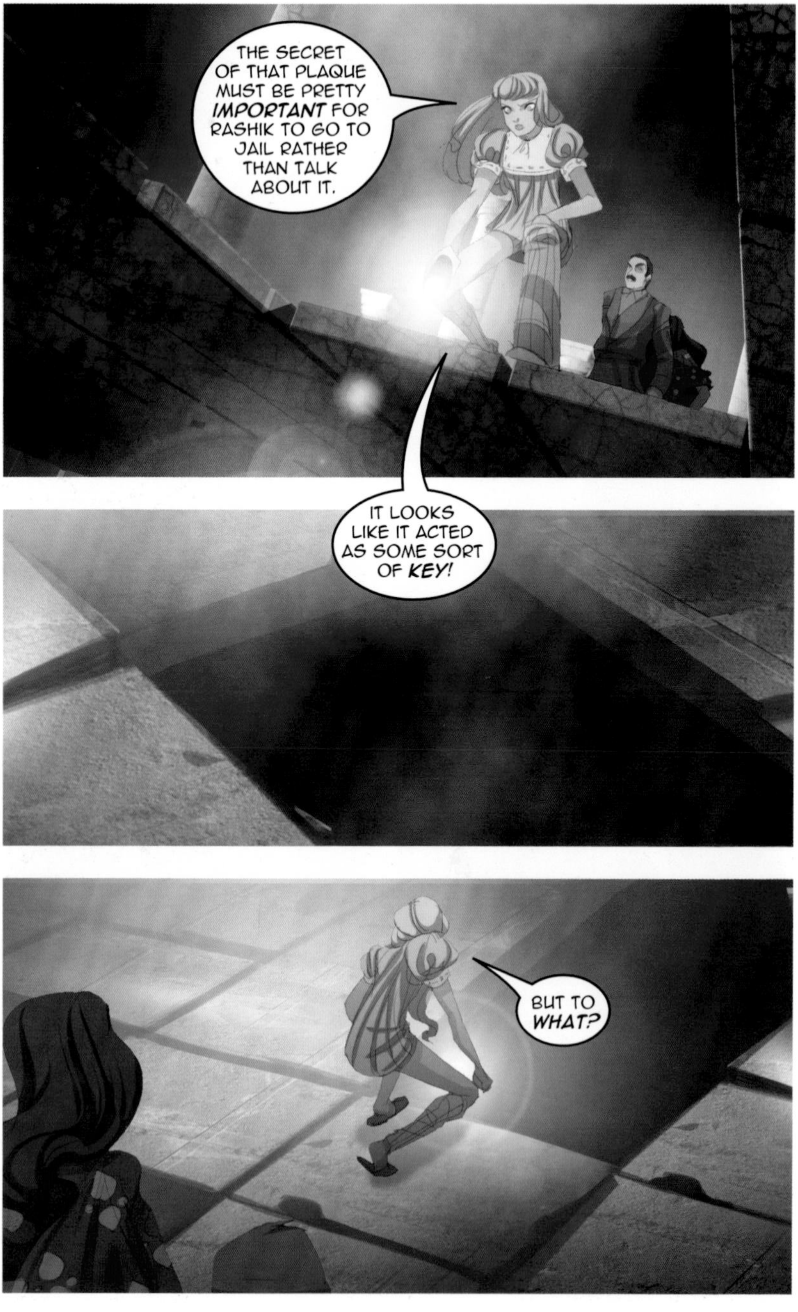
THE SECRET OF THAT PLAQUE MUST BE PRETTY **IMPORTANT** FOR RASHIK TO GO TO JAIL RATHER THAN TALK ABOUT IT.
IT LOOKS LIKE IT ACTED AS SOME SORT OF **KEY**!
BUT TO **WHAT?**

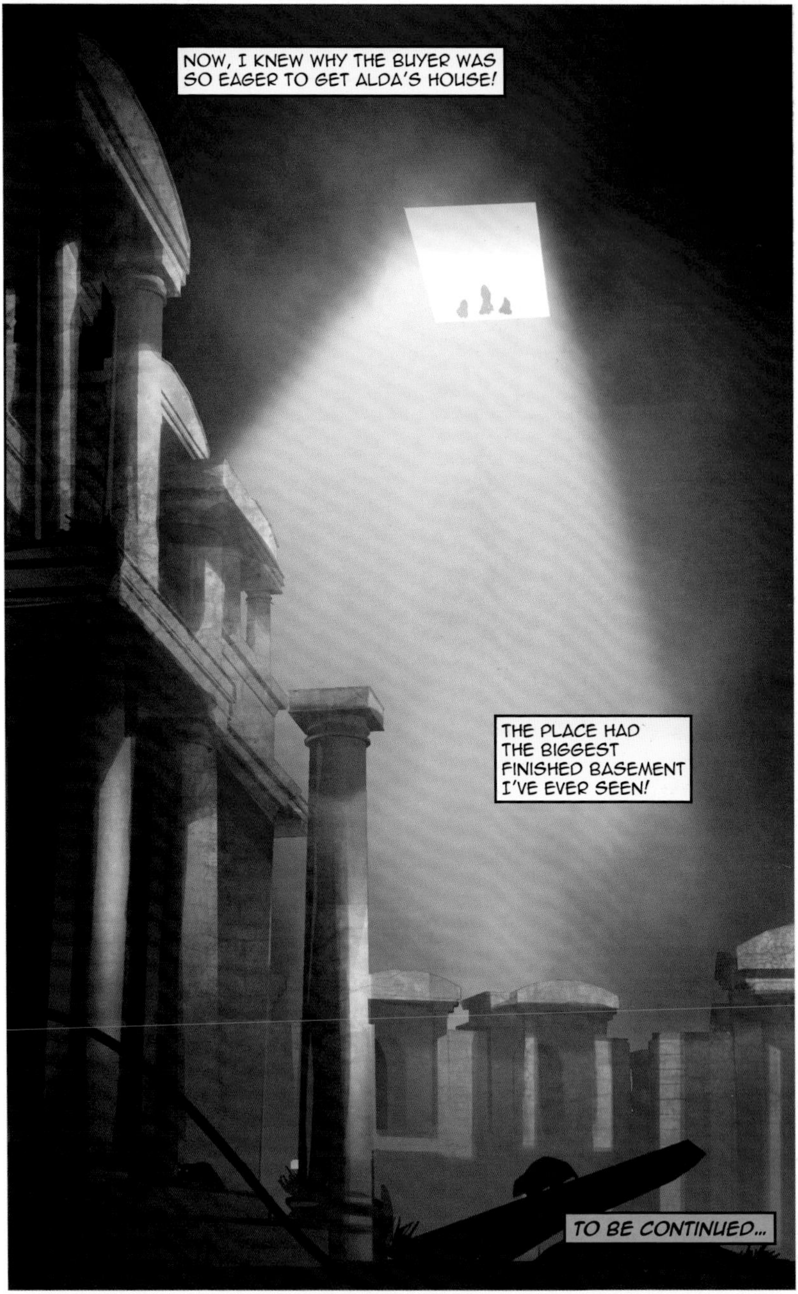
NOW, I KNEW WHY THE BUYER WAS SO EAGER TO GET ALDA'S HOUSE!
THE PLACE HAD THE BIGGEST FINISHED BASEMENT I'VE EVER SEEN!
TO BE CONTINUED...

NANCY DREW GRAPHIC NOVELS AVAILABLE FROM PAPERCUTZ

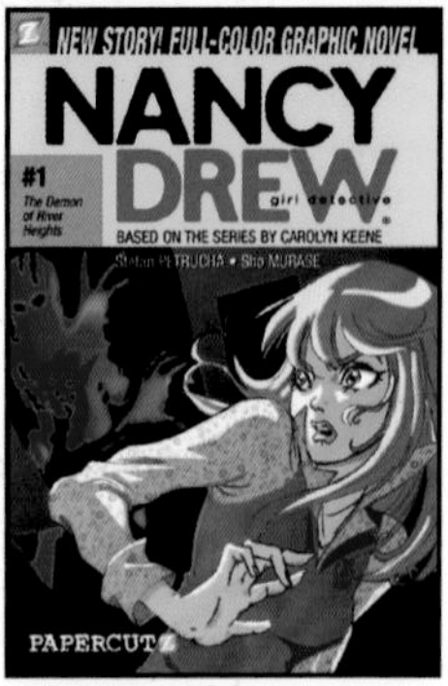
NEW STORY! FULL-COLOR GRAPHIC NOVEL
NANCY DREW
girl detective
#1
BASED ON THE SERIES BY CAROLYN KEENE
Stefan PETRUCHA • Sho MURASE
PAPERCUTZ

#1 "The Demon of River Heights"

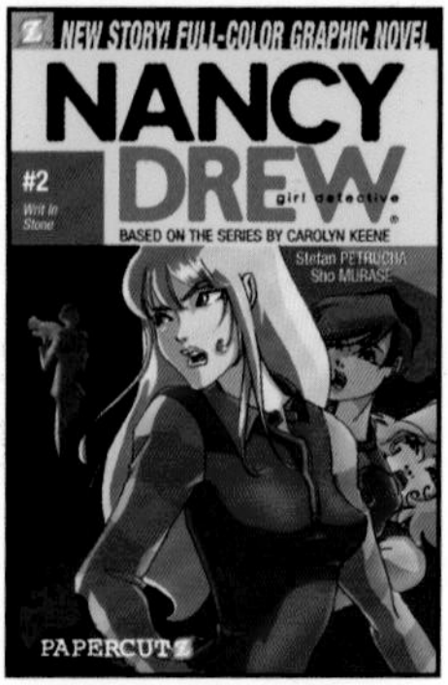
NEW STORY! FULL-COLOR GRAPHIC NOVEL
NANCY DREW
girl detective
#2
Writ In Stone
BASED ON THE SERIES BY CAROLYN KEENE
Stefan PETRUCHA
Sho MURASE
PAPERCUTZ

#2 "Writ In Stone"

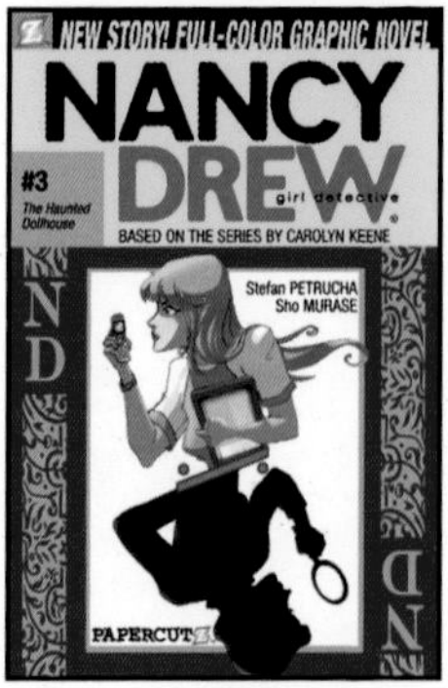
NEW STORY! FULL-COLOR GRAPHIC NOVEL
NANCY DREW
girl detective
#3
The Haunted Dollhouse
BASED ON THE SERIES BY CAROLYN KEENE
Stefan PETRUCHA
Sho MURASE
PAPERCUTZ

#3 "The Haunted Dollhouse"

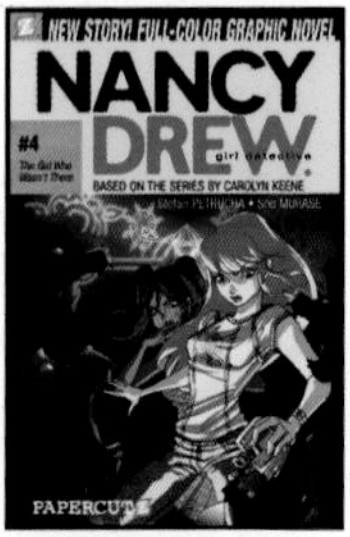
NEW STORY! FULL-COLOR GRAPHIC NOVEL
NANCY DREW
#4
BASED ON THE SERIES BY CAROLYN KEENE
PAPERCUTZ

#4 "The Girl Who Wasn't There"

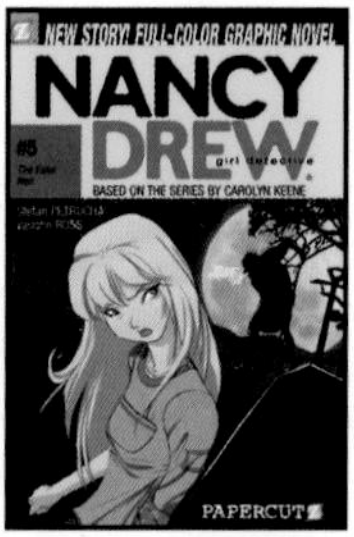
NEW STORY! FULL-COLOR GRAPHIC NOVEL
NANCY DREW
#5
BASED ON THE SERIES BY CAROLYN KEENE
PAPERCUTZ

#5 "The Fake Heir"

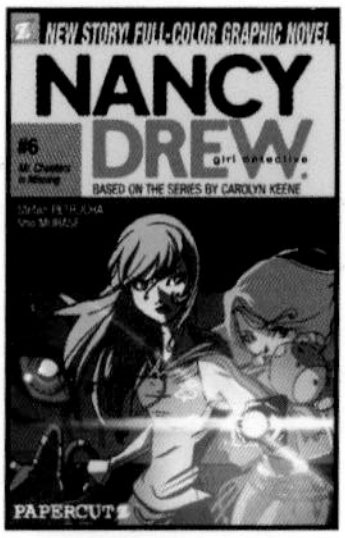
NEW STORY! FULL-COLOR GRAPHIC NOVEL
NANCY DREW
#6
BASED ON THE SERIES BY CAROLYN KEENE
PAPERCUTZ

#6 "Mr. Cheeters Is Missing"

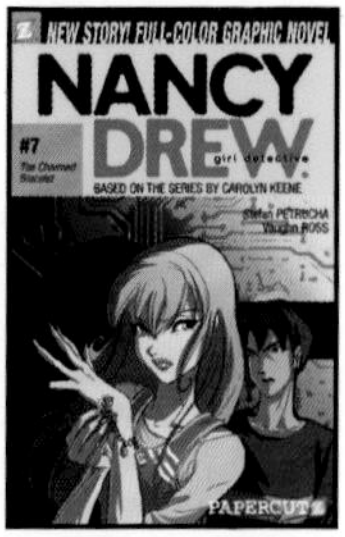
NEW STORY! FULL-COLOR GRAPHIC NOVEL
NANCY DREW
#7
BASED ON THE SERIES BY CAROLYN KEENE
Stefan PETRUCHA
Vaughn ROSS
PAPERCUTZ

#7 "The Charmed Bracelet"

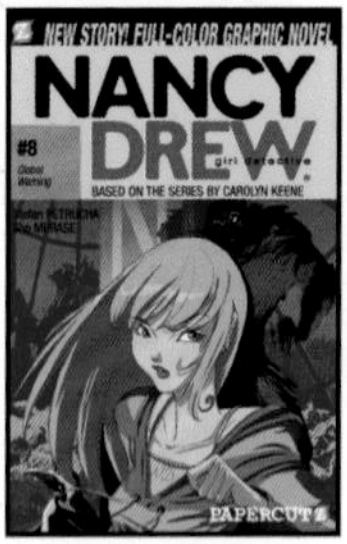
NEW STORY! FULL-COLOR GRAPHIC NOVEL
NANCY DREW
#8
BASED ON THE SERIES BY CAROLYN KEENE
PAPERCUTZ

#8 "Global Warning"

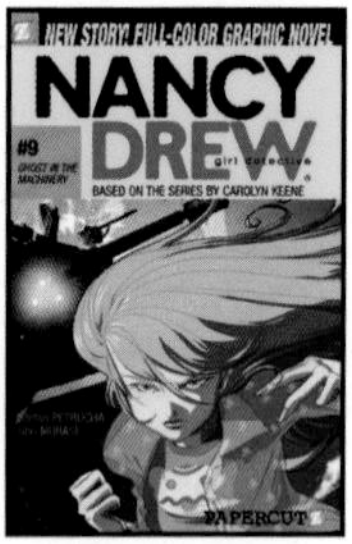
NEW STORY! FULL-COLOR GRAPHIC NOVEL
NANCY DREW
#9
BASED ON THE SERIES BY CAROLYN KEENE
PAPERCUTZ

#9 "Ghost In The Machinery"

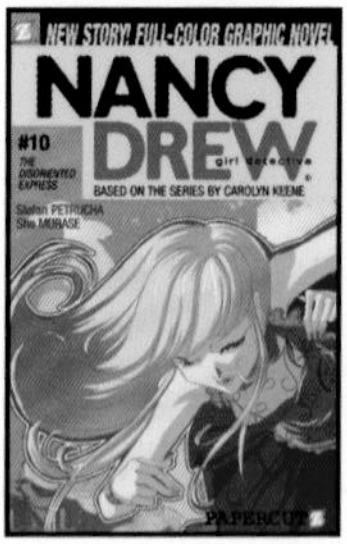
NEW STORY! FULL-COLOR GRAPHIC NOVEL
NANCY DREW
#10
BASED ON THE SERIES BY CAROLYN KEENE
PAPERCUTZ

#10 "The Disoriented Express"

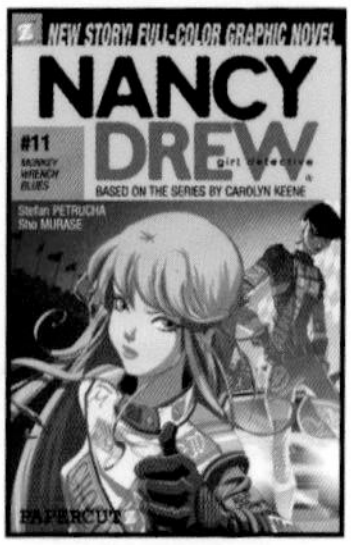
NEW STORY! FULL-COLOR GRAPHIC NOVEL
NANCY DREW
#11
BASED ON THE SERIES BY CAROLYN KEENE
PAPERCUTZ

#11 "Monkey Wrench Blues"

See page 175 for more NANCY DREW graphic novels!

NANCY DREW graphic novels are available at booksellers everywhere.

NANCY DREW graphic novels are $7.95 each in paperback and $12.95 each in hardcover. NANCY DREW DIARIES graphic novels are $9.99 each and available only in paperback. You may also order online at www.papercutz.com. Or call 1-800-886-1223, Monday through Friday, 9 – 5 EST. MC, Visa, and AmEx accepted. To order by mail, please add $4.00 for postage and handling for first book ordered, $1.00 for each additional book and make check payable to NBM Publishing. Send to: Papercutz, 160 Broadway, Suite 700, East Wing, New York, NY 10038.

NANCY DREW and NANCY DREW DIARIES graphic novels are also available digitally wherever e-books are sold.

papercutz.com

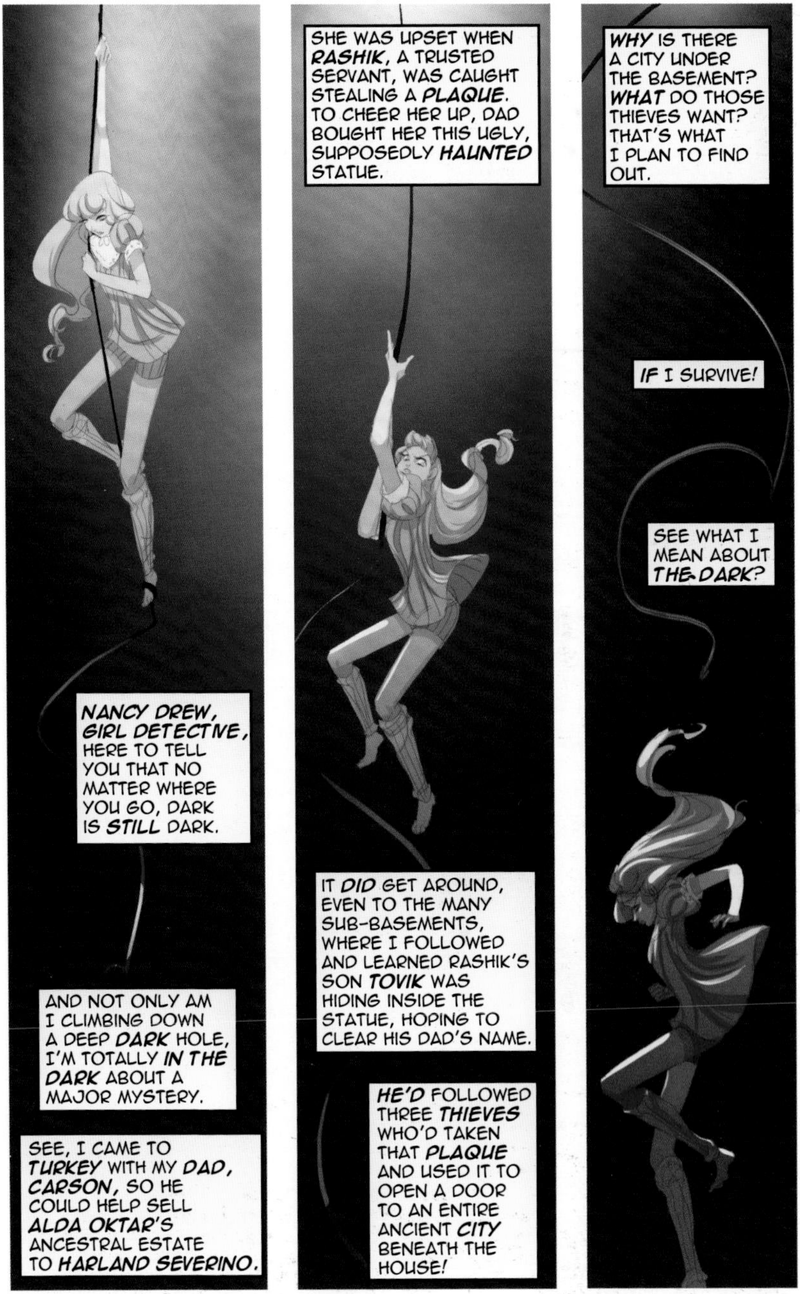
NANCY DREW, GIRL DETECTIVE, HERE TO TELL YOU THAT NO MATTER WHERE YOU GO, DARK IS STILL DARK.
AND NOT ONLY AM I CLIMBING DOWN A DEEP DARK HOLE, I'M TOTALLY IN THE DARK ABOUT A MAJOR MYSTERY.
SEE, I CAME TO TURKEY WITH MY DAD, CARSON, SO HE COULD HELP SELL ALDA OKTAR'S ANCESTRAL ESTATE TO HARLAND SEVERINO.
SHE WAS UPSET WHEN RASHIK, A TRUSTED SERVANT, WAS CAUGHT STEALING A PLAQUE. TO CHEER HER UP, DAD BOUGHT HER THIS UGLY, SUPPOSEDLY HAUNTED STATUE.
IT DID GET AROUND, EVEN TO THE MANY SUB-BASEMENTS, WHERE I FOLLOWED AND LEARNED RASHIK'S SON TOVIK WAS HIDING INSIDE THE STATUE, HOPING TO CLEAR HIS DAD'S NAME.
HE'D FOLLOWED THREE THIEVES WHO'D TAKEN THAT PLAQUE AND USED IT TO OPEN A DOOR TO AN ENTIRE ANCIENT CITY BENEATH THE HOUSE!
WHY IS THERE A CITY UNDER THE BASEMENT? WHAT DO THOSE THIEVES WANT? THAT'S WHAT I PLAN TO FIND OUT.
IF I SURVIVE!
SEE WHAT I MEAN ABOUT THE DARK?

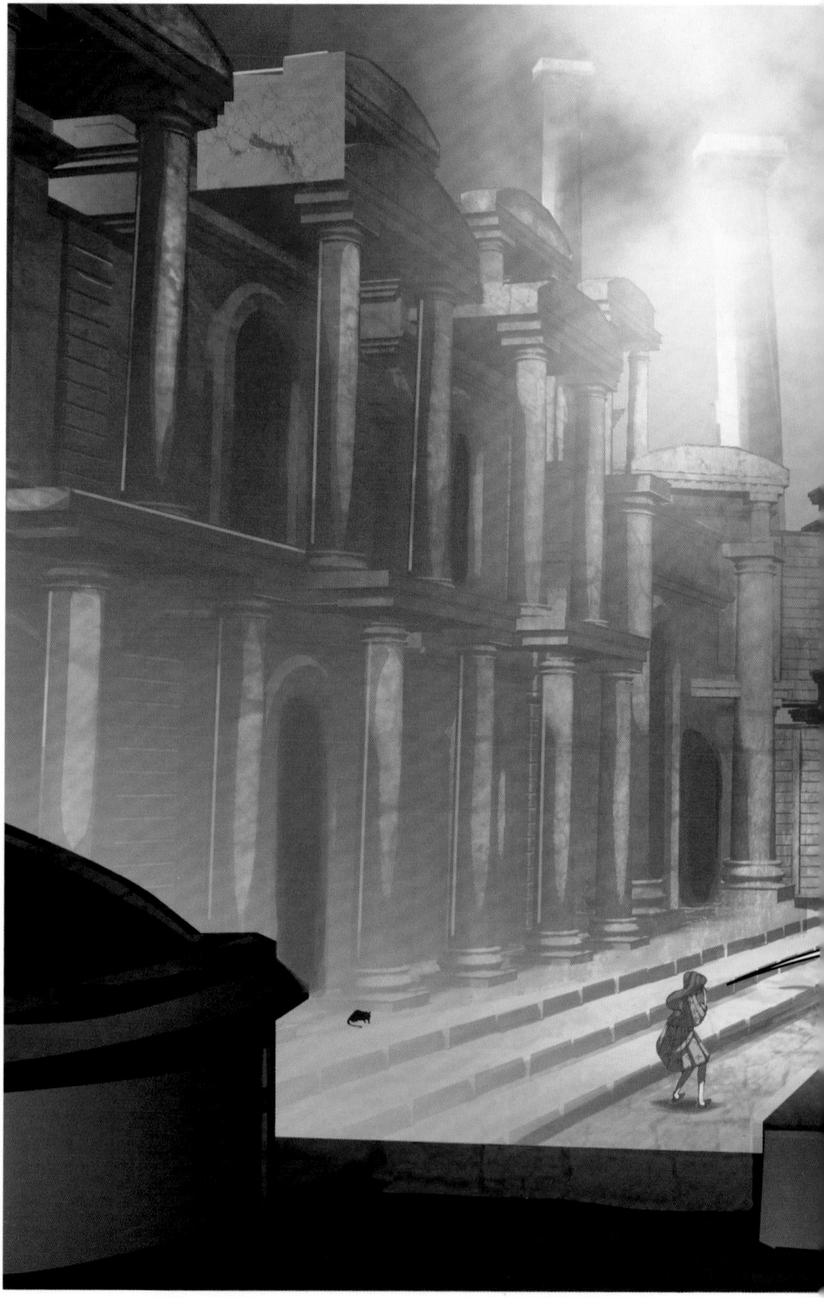

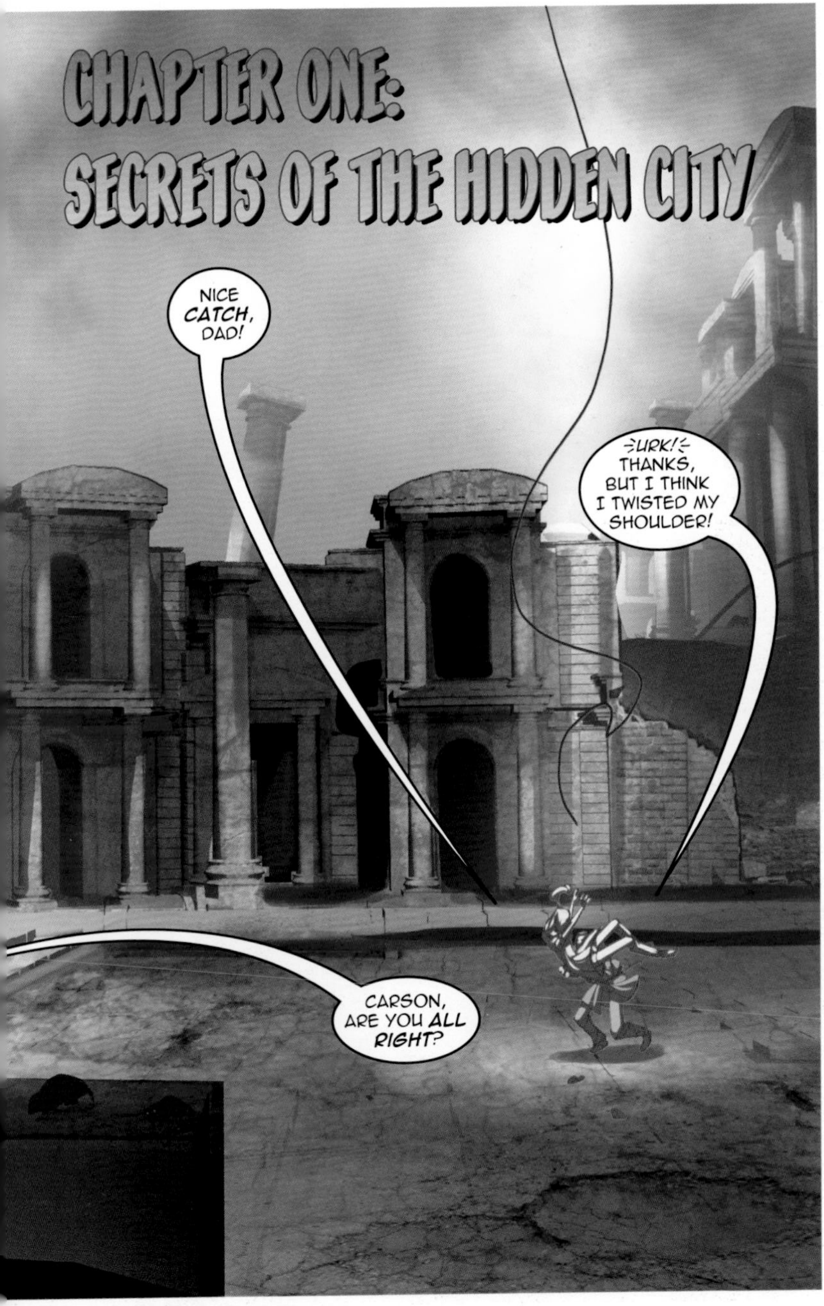
CHAPTER ONE:
SECRETS OF THE HIDDEN CITY
NICE CATCH, DAD!
URK! THANKS, BUT I THINK I TWISTED MY SHOULDER!
CARSON, ARE YOU ALL RIGHT?

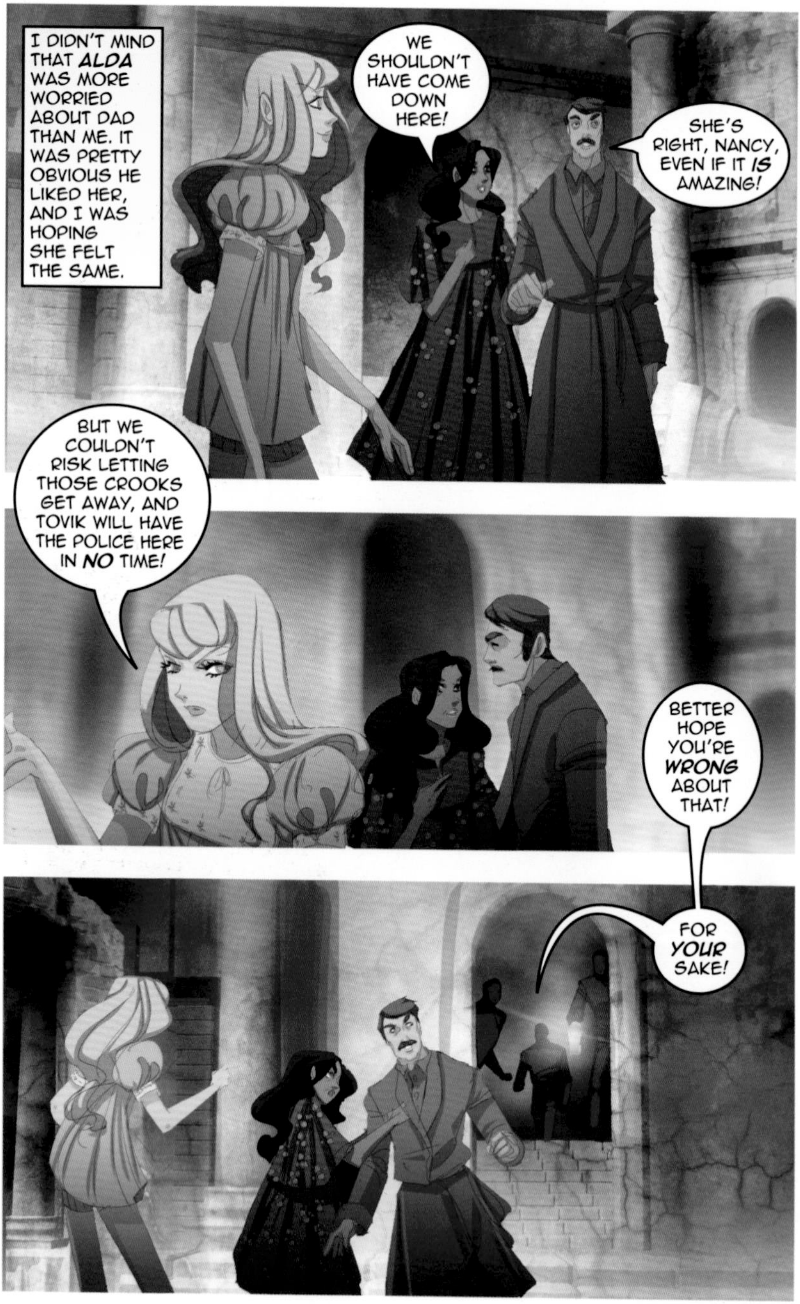
I DIDN'T MIND THAT ALDA WAS MORE WORRIED ABOUT DAD THAN ME. IT WAS PRETTY OBVIOUS HE LIKED HER, AND I WAS HOPING SHE FELT THE SAME.
WE SHOULDN'T HAVE COME DOWN HERE!
SHE'S RIGHT, NANCY, EVEN IF IT IS AMAZING!
BUT WE COULDN'T RISK LETTING THOSE CROOKS GET AWAY, AND TOVIK WILL HAVE THE POLICE HERE IN NO TIME!
BETTER HOPE YOU'RE WRONG ABOUT THAT!
FOR YOUR SAKE!

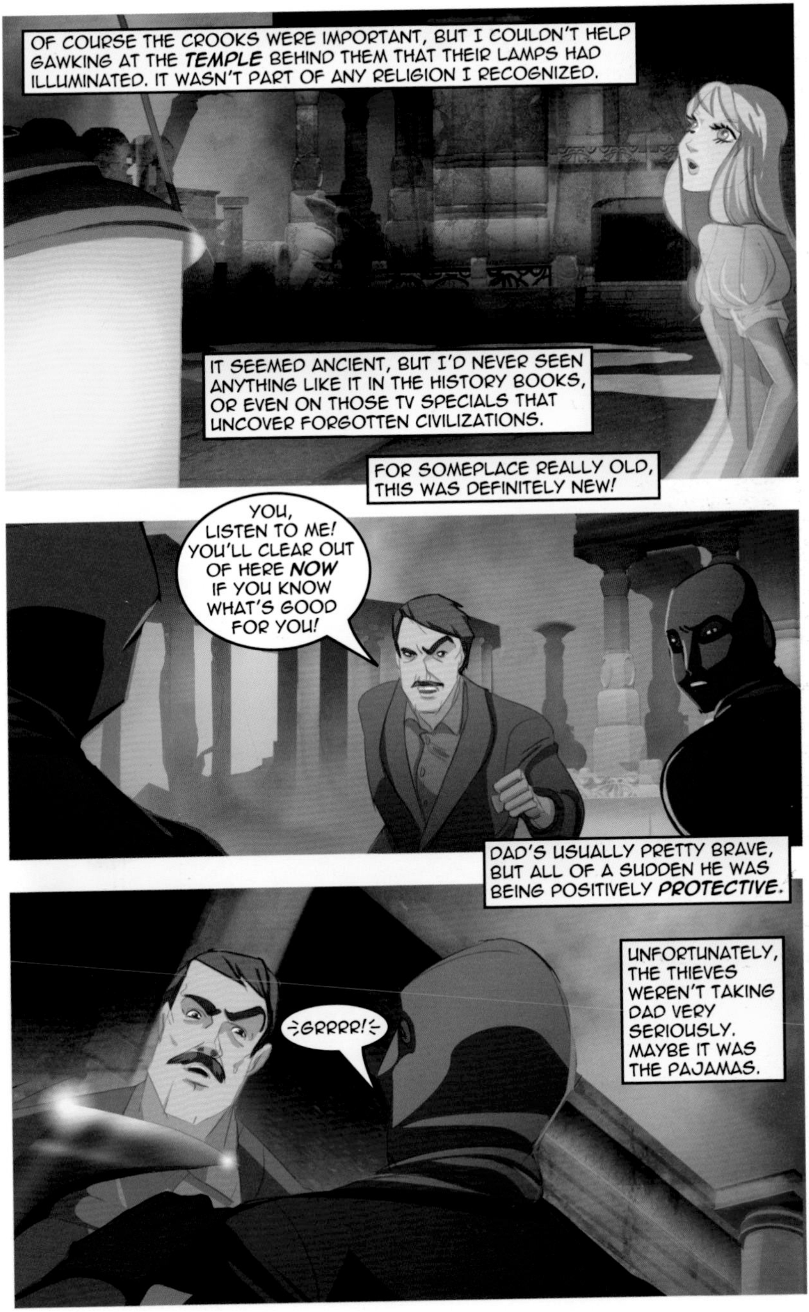
OF COURSE THE CROOKS WERE IMPORTANT, BUT I COULDN'T HELP GAWKING AT THE *TEMPLE* BEHIND THEM THAT THEIR LAMPS HAD ILLUMINATED. IT WASN'T PART OF ANY RELIGION I RECOGNIZED.
IT SEEMED ANCIENT, BUT I'D NEVER SEEN ANYTHING LIKE IT IN THE HISTORY BOOKS, OR EVEN ON THOSE TV SPECIALS THAT UNCOVER FORGOTTEN CIVILIZATIONS.
FOR SOMEPLACE REALLY OLD, THIS WAS DEFINITELY NEW!
YOU, LISTEN TO ME! YOU'LL CLEAR OUT OF HERE *NOW* IF YOU KNOW WHAT'S GOOD FOR YOU!
DAD'S USUALLY PRETTY BRAVE, BUT ALL OF A SUDDEN HE WAS BEING POSITIVELY *PROTECTIVE*.
UNFORTUNATELY, THE THIEVES WEREN'T TAKING DAD VERY SERIOUSLY. MAYBE IT WAS THE PAJAMAS.
GRRRR!

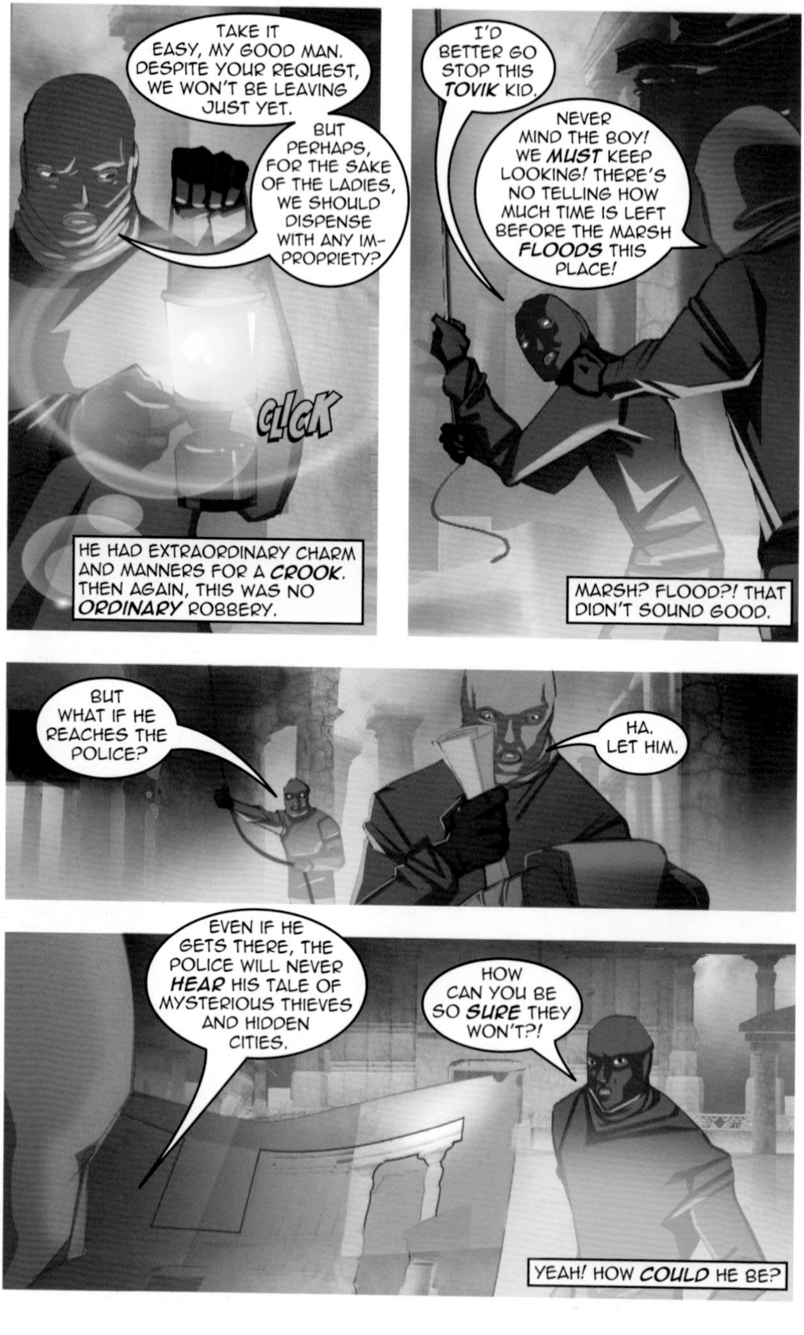
TAKE IT EASY, MY GOOD MAN. DESPITE YOUR REQUEST, WE WON'T BE LEAVING JUST YET.
BUT PERHAPS, FOR THE SAKE OF THE LADIES, WE SHOULD DISPENSE WITH ANY IMPROPRIETY?
CLICK
HE HAD EXTRAORDINARY CHARM AND MANNERS FOR A CROOK. THEN AGAIN, THIS WAS NO ORDINARY ROBBERY.
I'D BETTER GO STOP THIS TOVIK KID.
NEVER MIND THE BOY! WE MUST KEEP LOOKING! THERE'S NO TELLING HOW MUCH TIME IS LEFT BEFORE THE MARSH FLOODS THIS PLACE!
MARSH? FLOOD?! THAT DIDN'T SOUND GOOD.
BUT WHAT IF HE REACHES THE POLICE?
HA. LET HIM.
EVEN IF HE GETS THERE, THE POLICE WILL NEVER HEAR HIS TALE OF MYSTERIOUS THIEVES AND HIDDEN CITIES.
HOW CAN YOU BE SO SURE THEY WON'T?!
YEAH! HOW COULD HE BE?

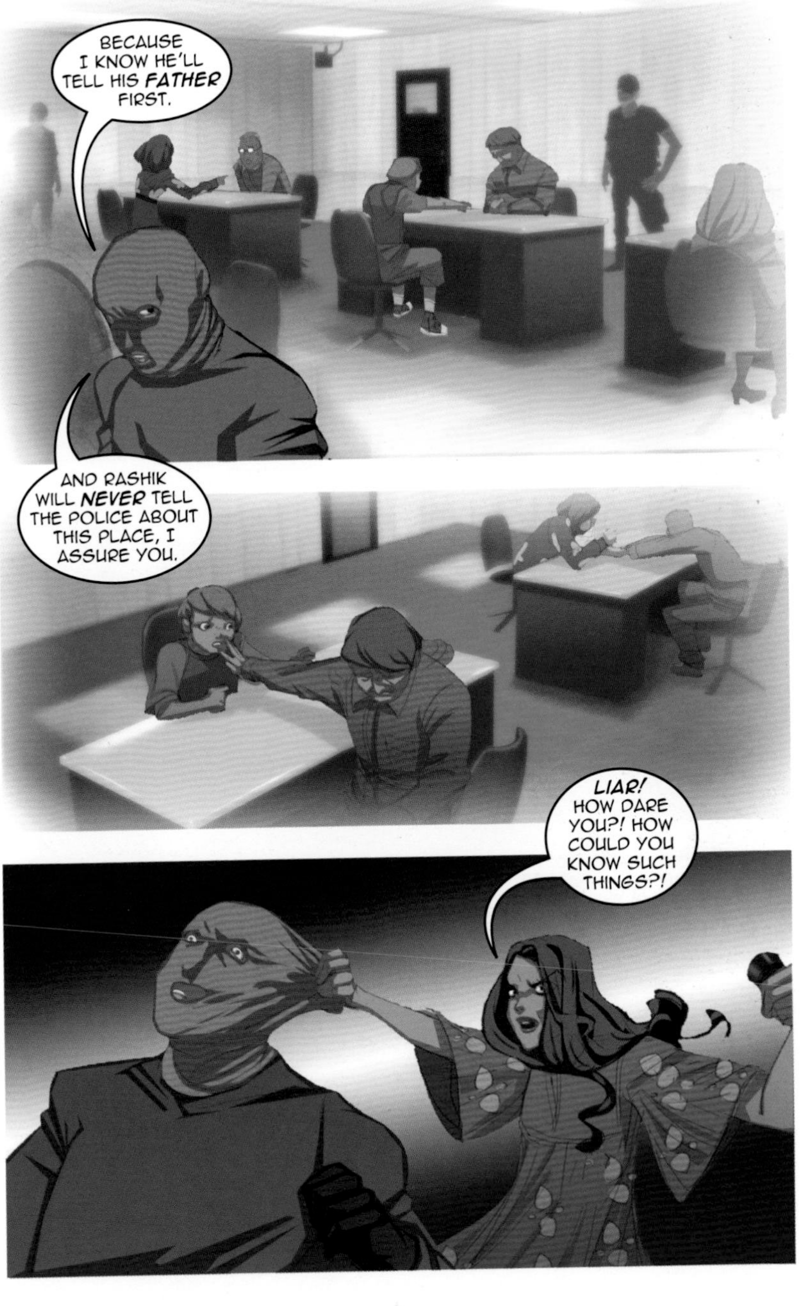
BECAUSE I KNOW HE'LL TELL HIS FATHER FIRST.
AND RASHIK WILL NEVER TELL THE POLICE ABOUT THIS PLACE, I ASSURE YOU.
LIAR! HOW DARE YOU?! HOW COULD YOU KNOW SUCH THINGS?!

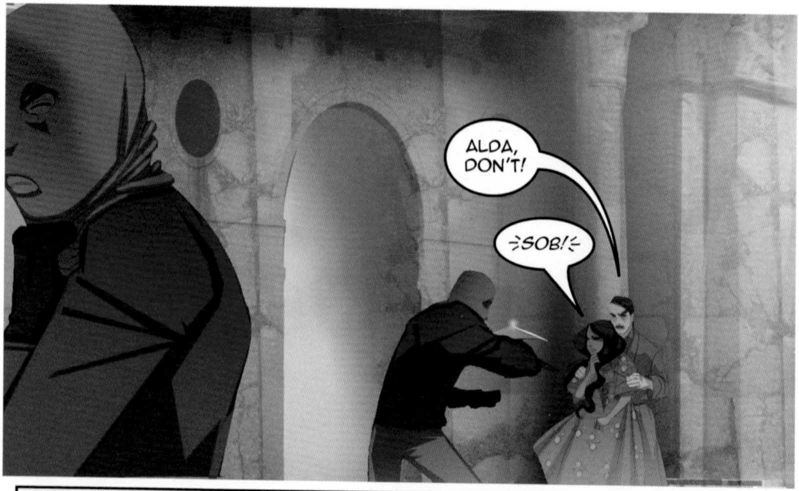
ALDA, DON'T!
-SOB!-

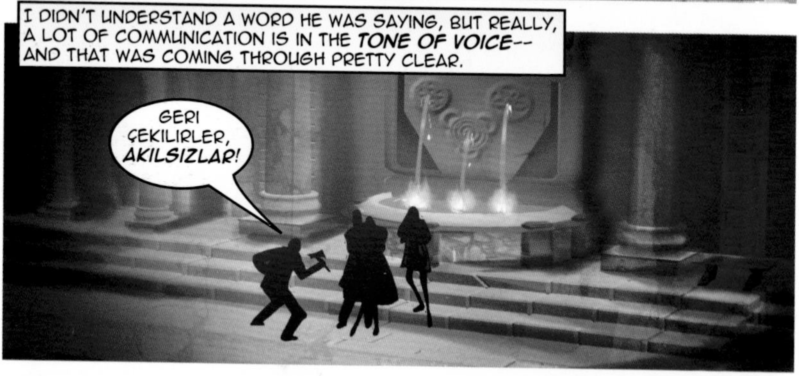
I DIDN'T UNDERSTAND A WORD HE WAS SAYING, BUT REALLY, A LOT OF COMMUNICATION IS IN THE *TONE OF VOICE*-- AND THAT WAS COMING THROUGH PRETTY CLEAR.
GERI ÇEKILIRLER, **AKILSIZLAR!**

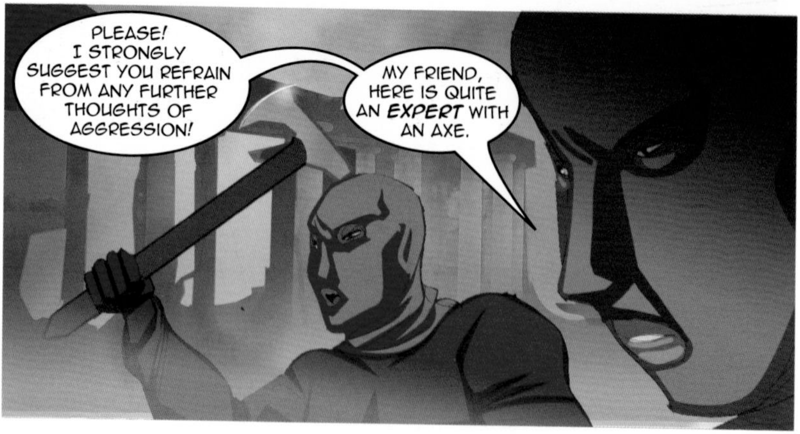
PLEASE! I STRONGLY SUGGEST YOU REFRAIN FROM ANY FURTHER THOUGHTS OF AGGRESSION!
MY FRIEND, HERE IS QUITE AN *EXPERT* WITH AN AXE.

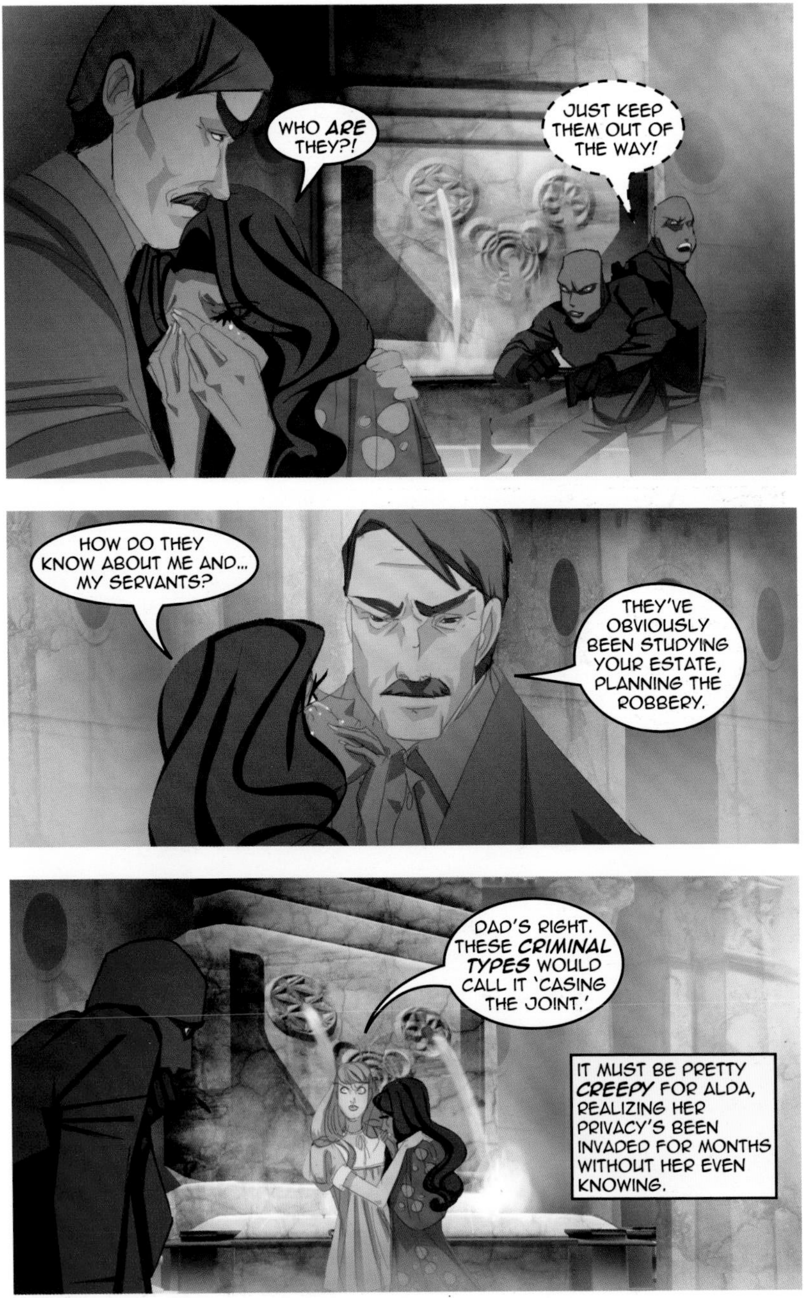
WHO *ARE* THEY?!
JUST KEEP THEM OUT OF THE WAY!
HOW DO THEY KNOW ABOUT ME AND... MY SERVANTS?
THEY'VE OBVIOUSLY BEEN STUDYING YOUR ESTATE, PLANNING THE ROBBERY.
DAD'S RIGHT. THESE *CRIMINAL TYPES* WOULD CALL IT 'CASING THE JOINT.'
IT MUST BE PRETTY *CREEPY* FOR ALDA, REALIZING HER PRIVACY'S BEEN INVADED FOR MONTHS WITHOUT HER EVEN KNOWING.

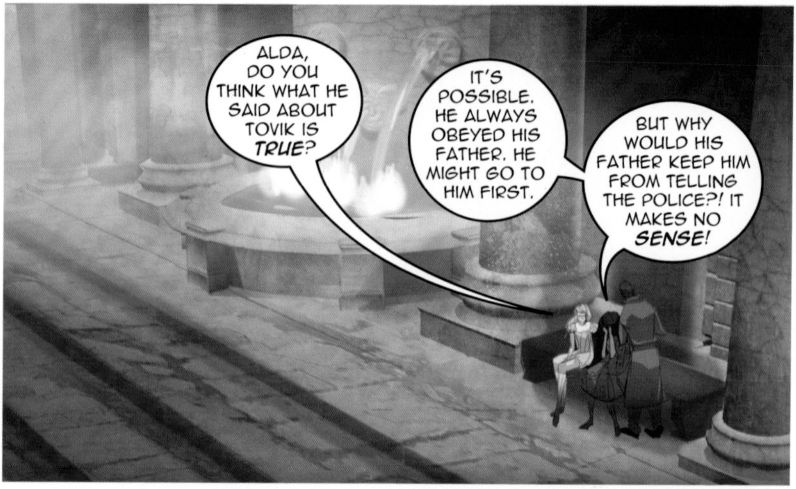
ALDA, DO YOU THINK WHAT HE SAID ABOUT TOVIK IS TRUE?
IT'S POSSIBLE. HE ALWAYS OBEYED HIS FATHER. HE MIGHT GO TO HIM FIRST.
BUT WHY WOULD HIS FATHER KEEP HIM FROM TELLING THE POLICE?! IT MAKES NO SENSE!

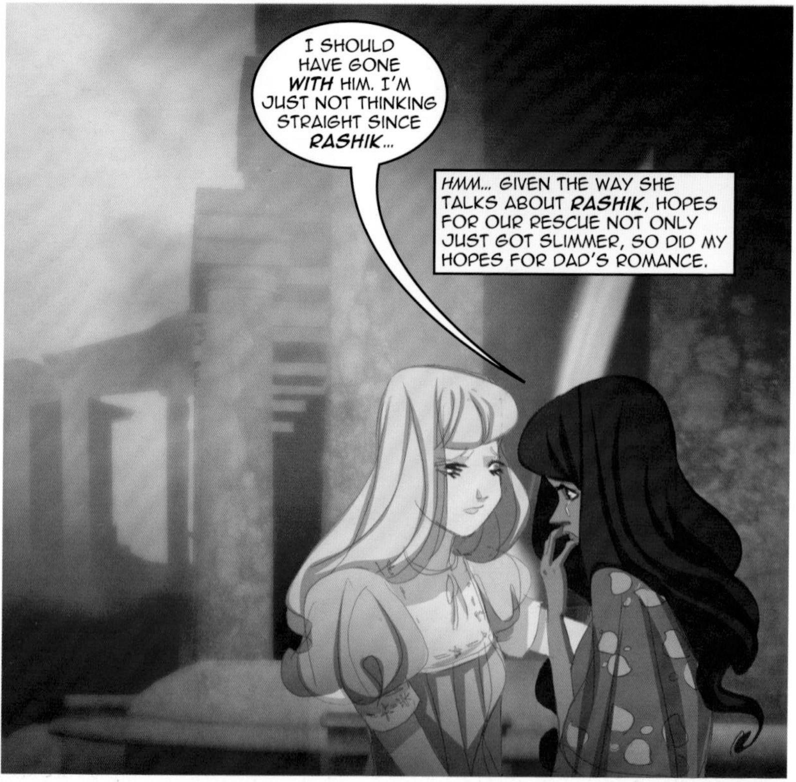
I SHOULD HAVE GONE WITH HIM. I'M JUST NOT THINKING STRAIGHT SINCE RASHIK...
HMM... GIVEN THE WAY SHE TALKS ABOUT RASHIK, HOPES FOR OUR RESCUE NOT ONLY JUST GOT SLIMMER, SO DID MY HOPES FOR DAD'S ROMANCE.

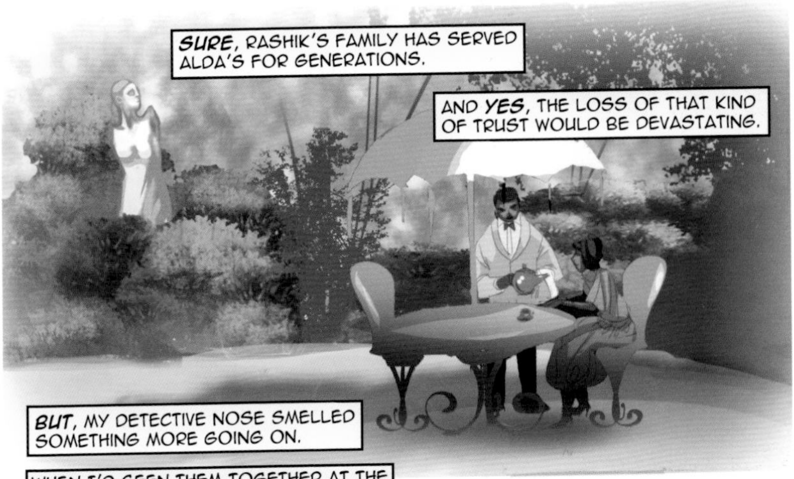
SURE, RASHIK'S FAMILY HAS SERVED ALDA'S FOR GENERATIONS.
AND YES, THE LOSS OF THAT KIND OF TRUST WOULD BE DEVASTATING.
BUT, MY DETECTIVE NOSE SMELLED SOMETHING MORE GOING ON.

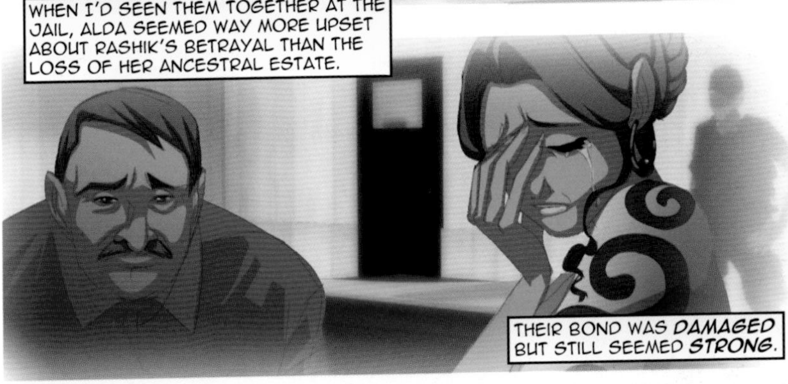
WHEN I'D SEEN THEM TOGETHER AT THE JAIL, ALDA SEEMED WAY MORE UPSET ABOUT RASHIK'S BETRAYAL THAN THE LOSS OF HER ANCESTRAL ESTATE.
THEIR BOND WAS DAMAGED BUT STILL SEEMED STRONG.

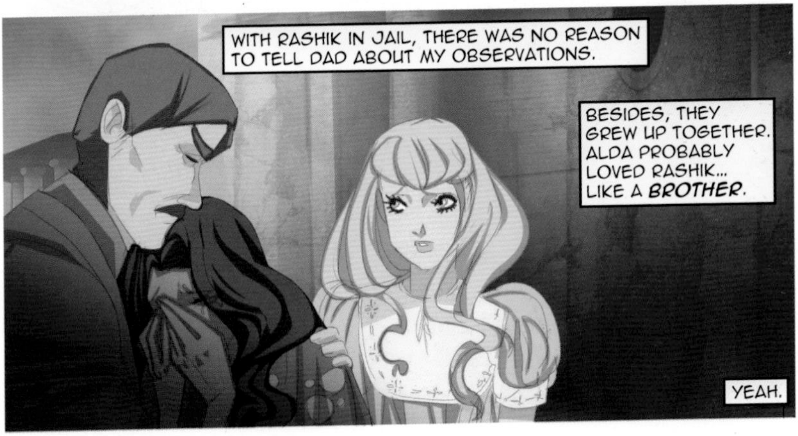
WITH RASHIK IN JAIL, THERE WAS NO REASON TO TELL DAD ABOUT MY OBSERVATIONS.
BESIDES, THEY GREW UP TOGETHER. ALDA PROBABLY LOVED RASHIK... LIKE A BROTHER.
YEAH.

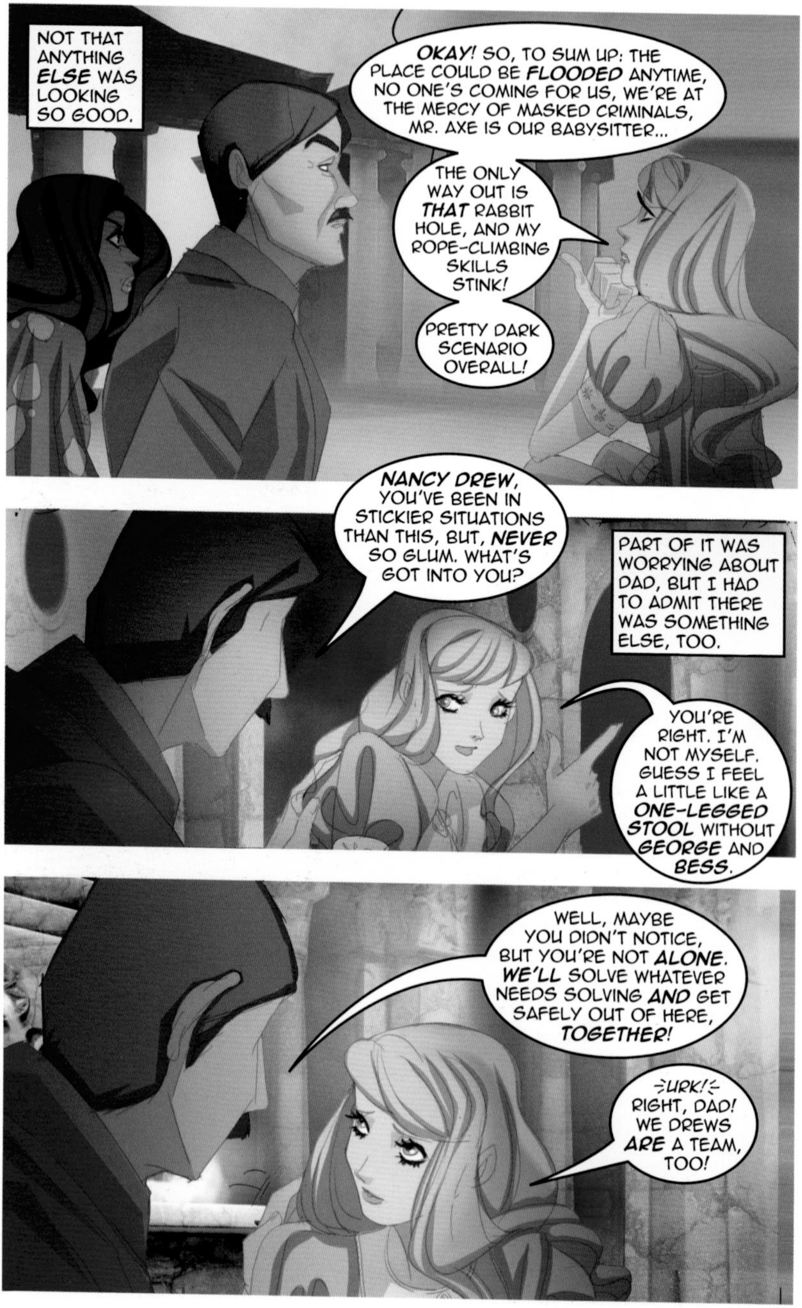
NOT THAT ANYTHING ELSE WAS LOOKING SO GOOD.
OKAY! SO, TO SUM UP: THE PLACE COULD BE FLOODED ANYTIME, NO ONE'S COMING FOR US, WE'RE AT THE MERCY OF MASKED CRIMINALS, MR. AXE IS OUR BABYSITTER...
THE ONLY WAY OUT IS THAT RABBIT HOLE, AND MY ROPE-CLIMBING SKILLS STINK!
PRETTY DARK SCENARIO OVERALL!
NANCY DREW, YOU'VE BEEN IN STICKIER SITUATIONS THAN THIS, BUT, NEVER SO GLUM. WHAT'S GOT INTO YOU?
PART OF IT WAS WORRYING ABOUT DAD, BUT I HAD TO ADMIT THERE WAS SOMETHING ELSE, TOO.
YOU'RE RIGHT. I'M NOT MYSELF. GUESS I FEEL A LITTLE LIKE A ONE-LEGGED STOOL WITHOUT GEORGE AND BESS.
WELL, MAYBE YOU DIDN'T NOTICE, BUT YOU'RE NOT ALONE. WE'LL SOLVE WHATEVER NEEDS SOLVING AND GET SAFELY OUT OF HERE, TOGETHER!
URK!
RIGHT, DAD! WE DREWS ARE A TEAM, TOO!

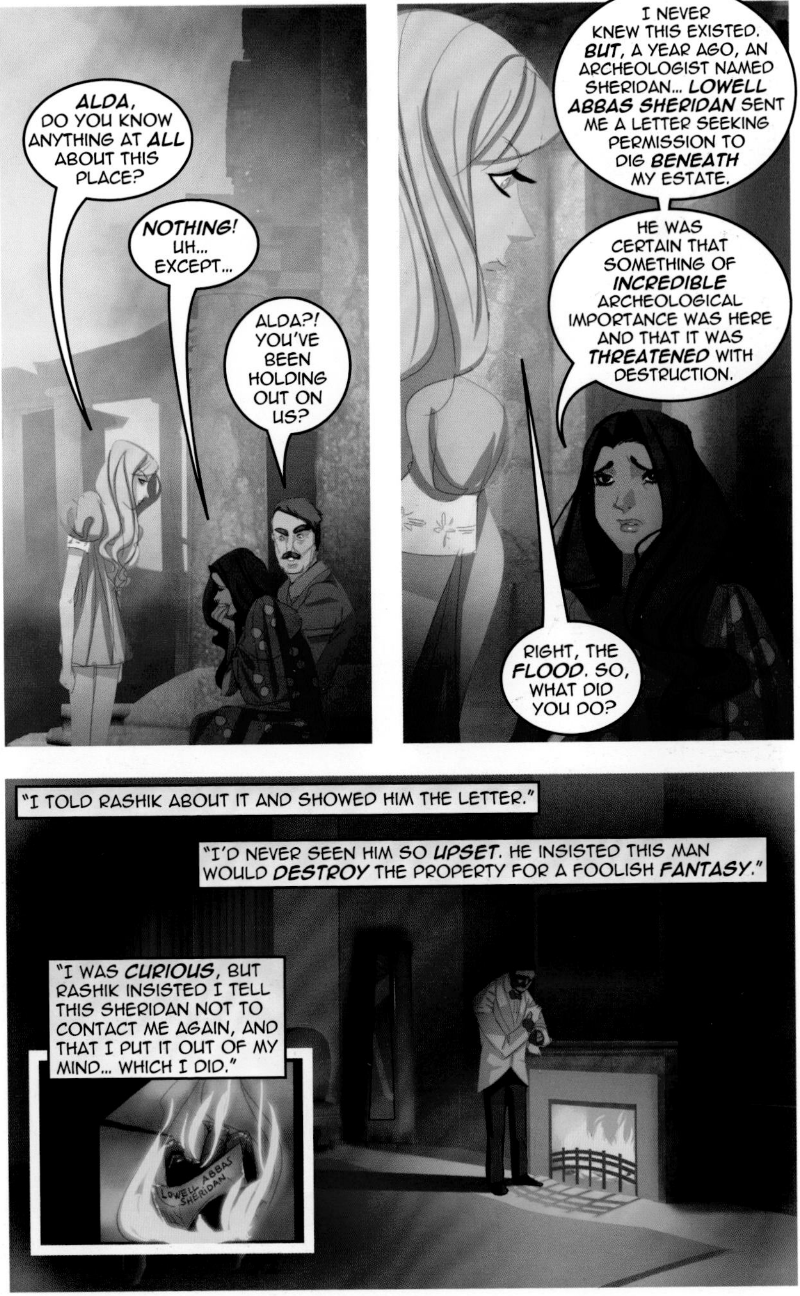
ALDA, DO YOU KNOW ANYTHING AT ALL ABOUT THIS PLACE?
NOTHING! UH... EXCEPT...
ALDA?! YOU'VE BEEN HOLDING OUT ON US?
I NEVER KNEW THIS EXISTED. BUT, A YEAR AGO, AN ARCHEOLOGIST NAMED SHERIDAN... LOWELL ABBAS SHERIDAN SENT ME A LETTER SEEKING PERMISSION TO DIG BENEATH MY ESTATE.
HE WAS CERTAIN THAT SOMETHING OF INCREDIBLE ARCHEOLOGICAL IMPORTANCE WAS HERE AND THAT IT WAS THREATENED WITH DESTRUCTION.
RIGHT, THE FLOOD. SO, WHAT DID YOU DO?
"I TOLD RASHIK ABOUT IT AND SHOWED HIM THE LETTER."
"I'D NEVER SEEN HIM SO UPSET. HE INSISTED THIS MAN WOULD DESTROY THE PROPERTY FOR A FOOLISH FANTASY."
"I WAS CURIOUS, BUT RASHIK INSISTED I TELL THIS SHERIDAN NOT TO CONTACT ME AGAIN, AND THAT I PUT IT OUT OF MY MIND... WHICH I DID."
LOWELL ABBAS SHERIDAN

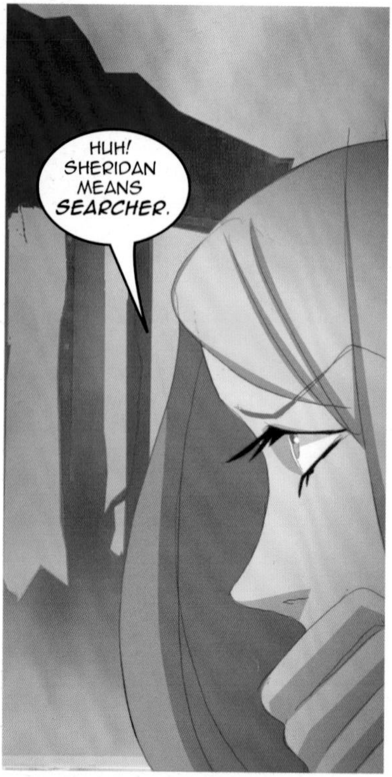
HUH! SHERIDAN MEANS SEARCHER.

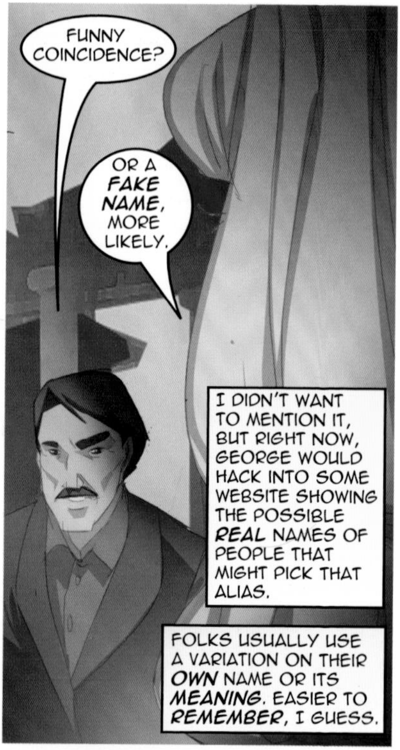
FUNNY COINCIDENCE?
OR A FAKE NAME, MORE LIKELY.
I DIDN'T WANT TO MENTION IT, BUT RIGHT NOW, GEORGE WOULD HACK INTO SOME WEBSITE SHOWING THE POSSIBLE REAL NAMES OF PEOPLE THAT MIGHT PICK THAT ALIAS.
FOLKS USUALLY USE A VARIATION ON THEIR OWN NAME OR ITS MEANING. EASIER TO REMEMBER, I GUESS.

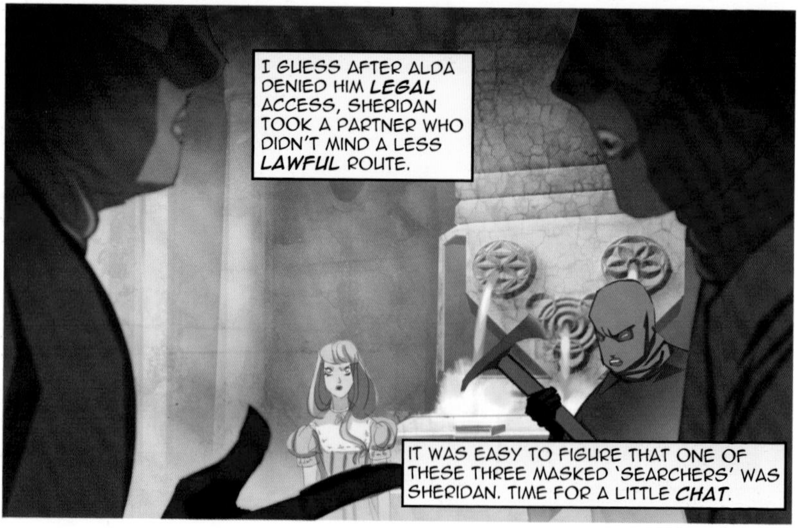
I GUESS AFTER ALDA DENIED HIM LEGAL ACCESS, SHERIDAN TOOK A PARTNER WHO DIDN'T MIND A LESS LAWFUL ROUTE.
IT WAS EASY TO FIGURE THAT ONE OF THESE THREE MASKED 'SEARCHERS' WAS SHERIDAN. TIME FOR A LITTLE CHAT.

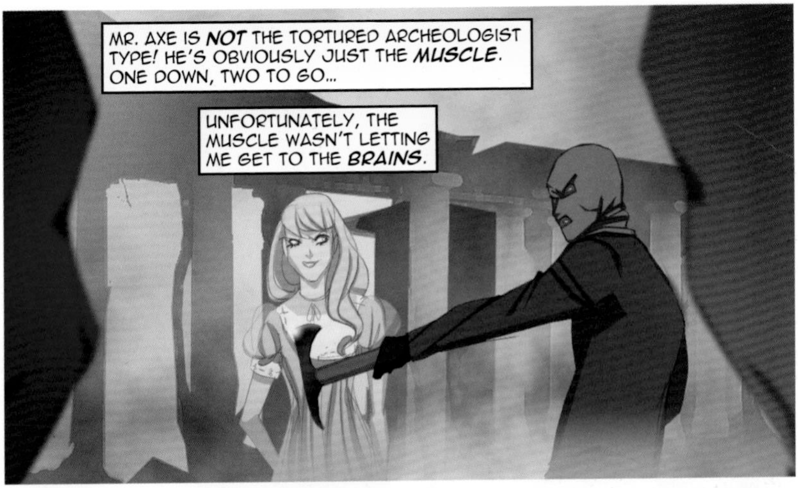
MR. AXE IS NOT THE TORTURED ARCHEOLOGIST TYPE! HE'S OBVIOUSLY JUST THE MUSCLE. ONE DOWN, TWO TO GO...
UNFORTUNATELY, THE MUSCLE WASN'T LETTING ME GET TO THE BRAINS.

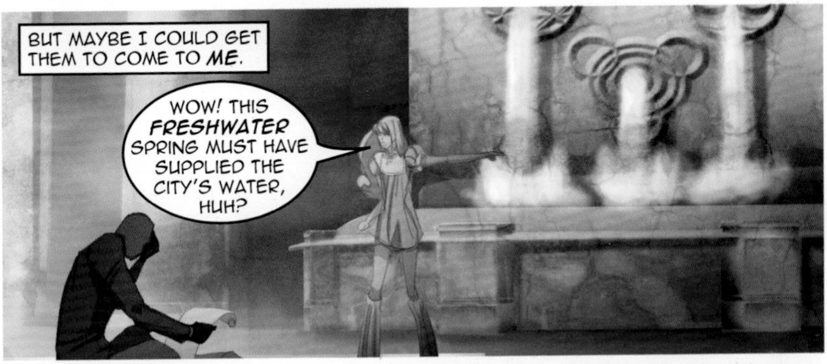
BUT MAYBE I COULD GET THEM TO COME TO ME.
WOW! THIS FRESHWATER SPRING MUST HAVE SUPPLIED THE CITY'S WATER, HUH?

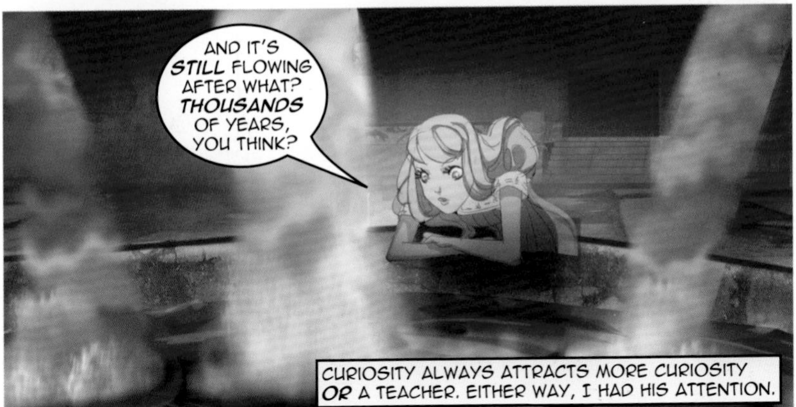
AND IT'S STILL FLOWING AFTER WHAT? THOUSANDS OF YEARS, YOU THINK?
CURIOSITY ALWAYS ATTRACTS MORE CURIOSITY OR A TEACHER. EITHER WAY, I HAD HIS ATTENTION.

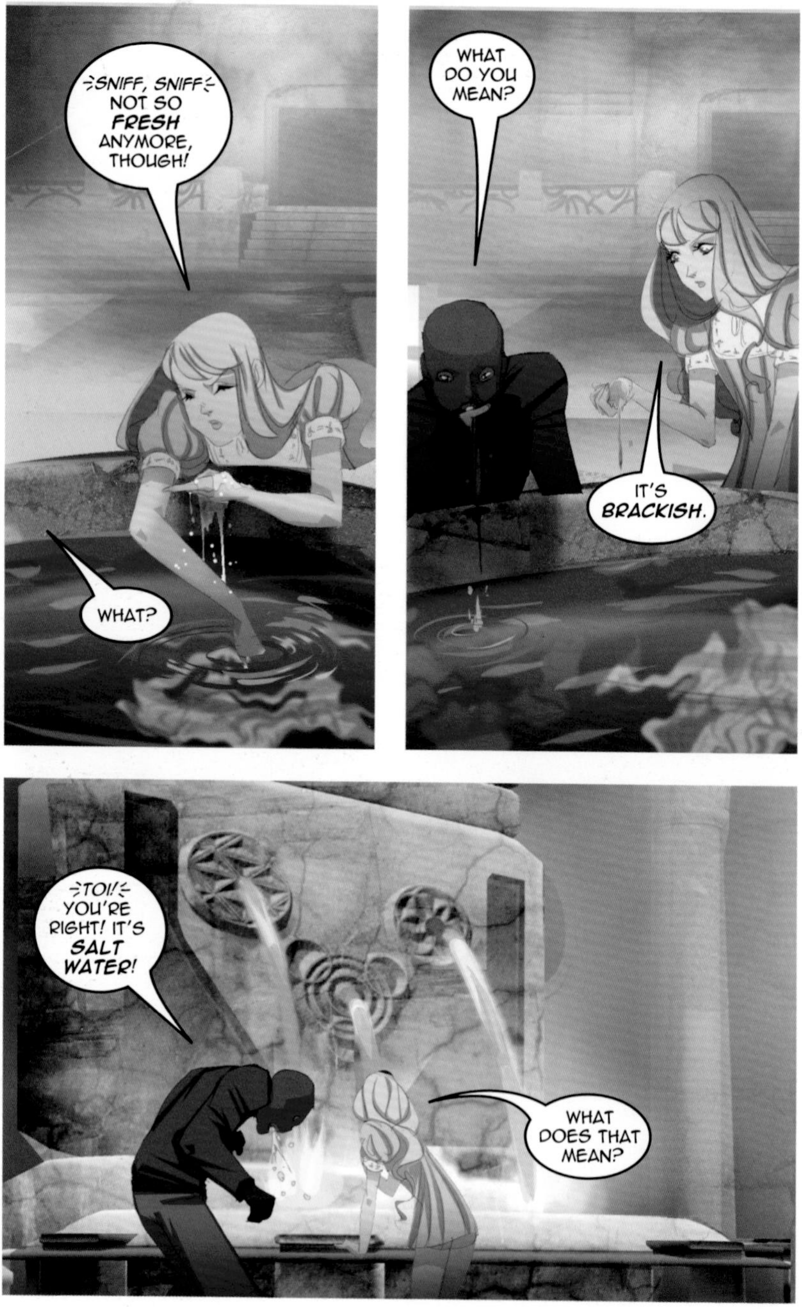

=SNIFF, SNIFF= NOT SO FRESH ANYMORE, THOUGH!
WHAT?
WHAT DO YOU MEAN?
IT'S BRACKISH.
=TOI!= YOU'RE RIGHT! IT'S SALT WATER!
WHAT DOES THAT MEAN?

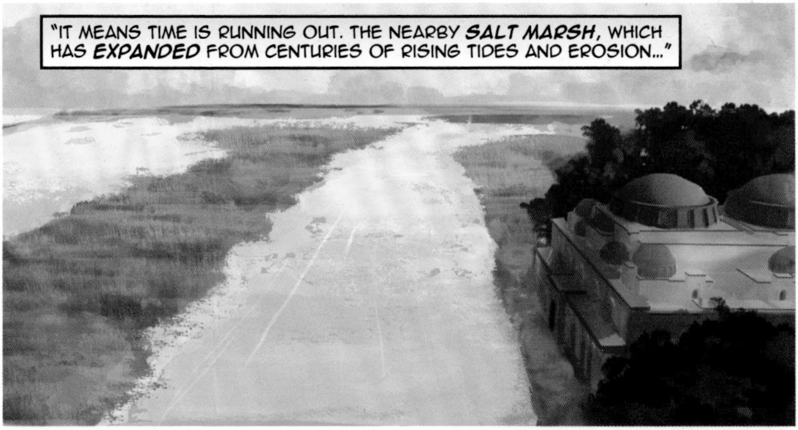
"IT MEANS TIME IS RUNNING OUT. THE NEARBY ***SALT MARSH***, WHICH HAS ***EXPANDED*** FROM CENTURIES OF RISING TIDES AND EROSION..."

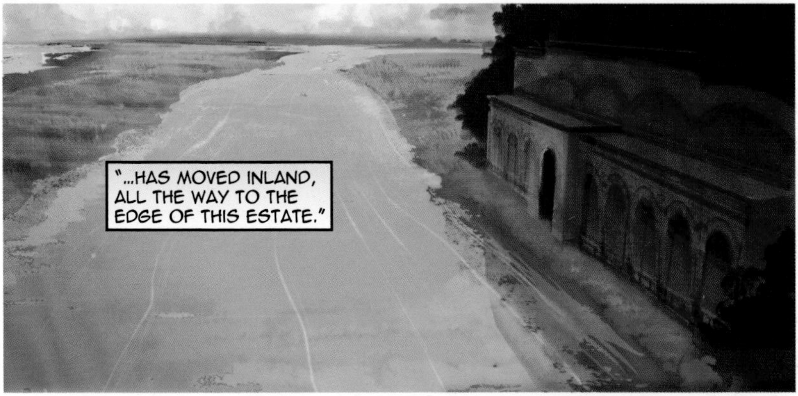
"...HAS MOVED INLAND, ALL THE WAY TO THE EDGE OF THIS ESTATE."

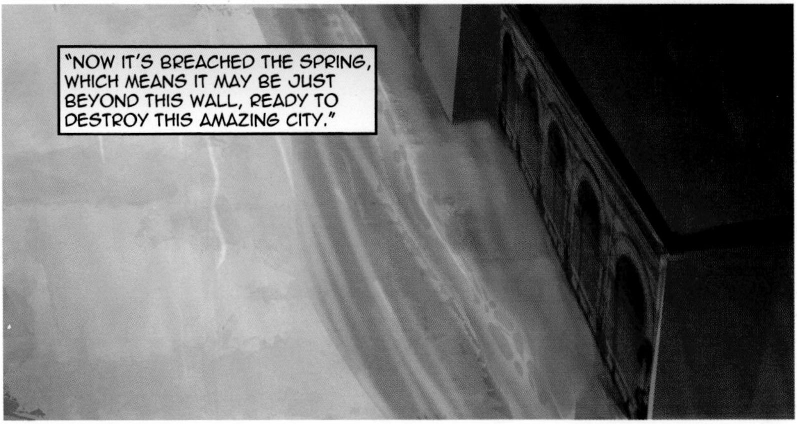
"NOW IT'S BREACHED THE SPRING, WHICH MEANS IT MAY BE JUST BEYOND THIS WALL, READY TO DESTROY THIS AMAZING CITY."

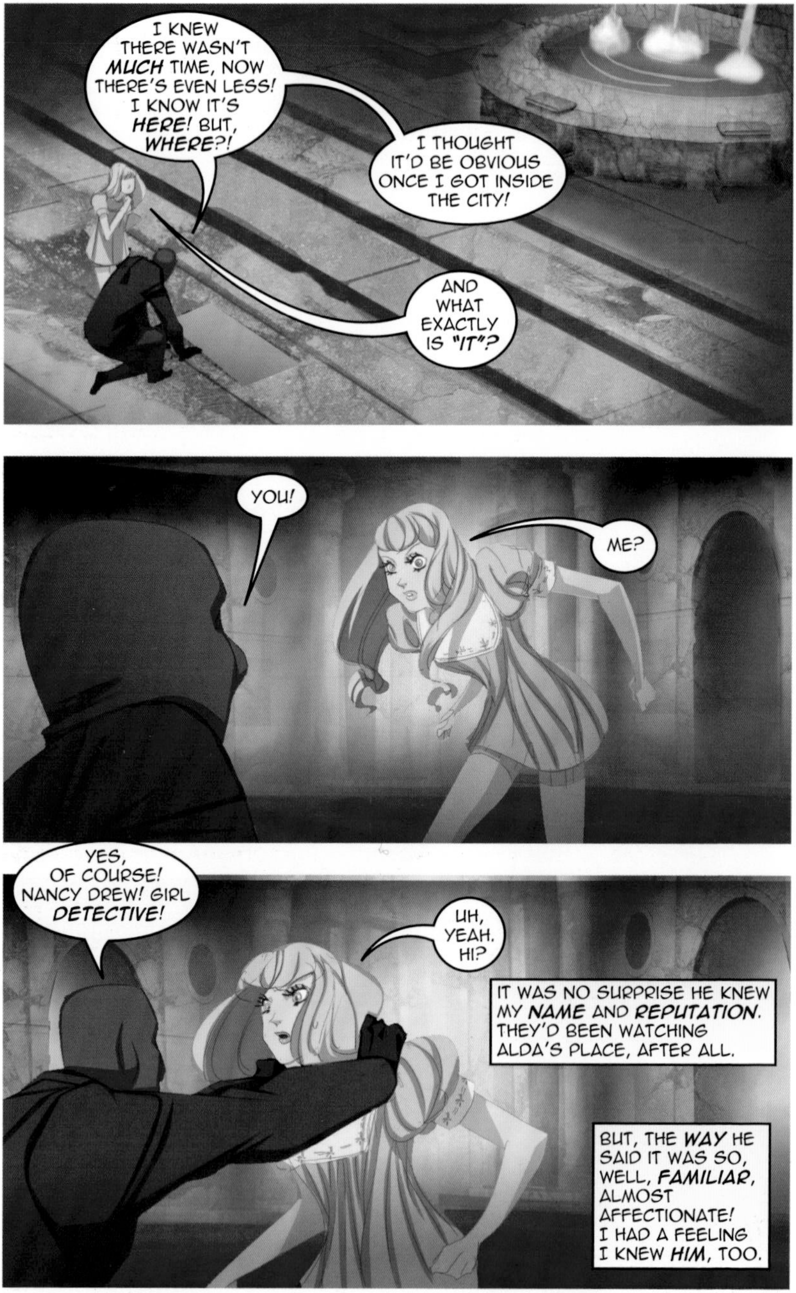
I KNEW THERE WASN'T MUCH TIME, NOW THERE'S EVEN LESS! I KNOW IT'S HERE! BUT, WHERE?!
I THOUGHT IT'D BE OBVIOUS ONCE I GOT INSIDE THE CITY!
AND WHAT EXACTLY IS "IT"?
YOU!
ME?
YES, OF COURSE! NANCY DREW! GIRL DETECTIVE!
UH, YEAH. HI?
IT WAS NO SURPRISE HE KNEW MY NAME AND REPUTATION. THEY'D BEEN WATCHING ALDA'S PLACE, AFTER ALL.
BUT, THE WAY HE SAID IT WAS SO, WELL, FAMILIAR, ALMOST AFFECTIONATE! I HAD A FEELING I KNEW HIM, TOO.

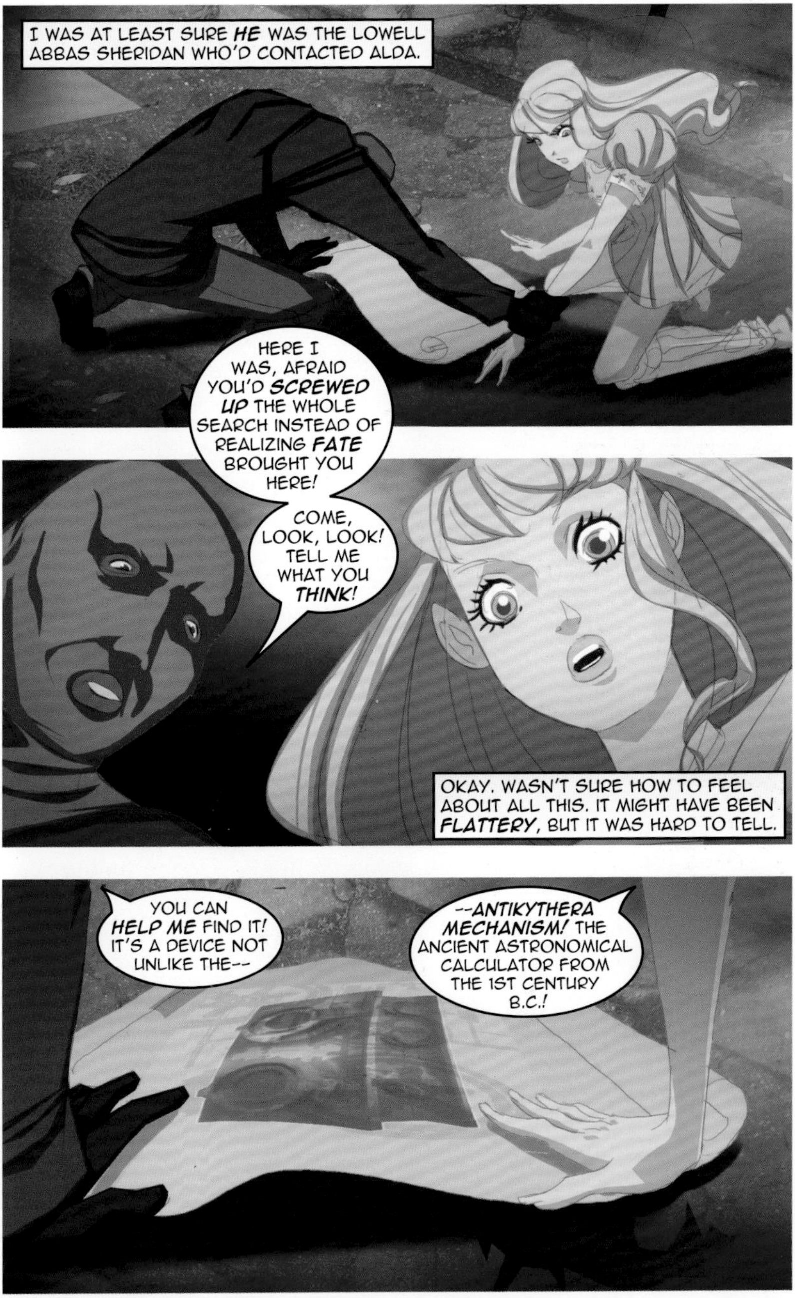
I WAS AT LEAST SURE HE WAS THE LOWELL ABBAS SHERIDAN WHO'D CONTACTED ALDA.
HERE I WAS, AFRAID YOU'D SCREWED UP THE WHOLE SEARCH INSTEAD OF REALIZING FATE BROUGHT YOU HERE!
COME, LOOK, LOOK! TELL ME WHAT YOU THINK!
OKAY. WASN'T SURE HOW TO FEEL ABOUT ALL THIS. IT MIGHT HAVE BEEN FLATTERY, BUT IT WAS HARD TO TELL.
YOU CAN HELP ME FIND IT! IT'S A DEVICE NOT UNLIKE THE--
--ANTIKYTHERA MECHANISM! THE ANCIENT ASTRONOMICAL CALCULATOR FROM THE 1ST CENTURY B.C.!

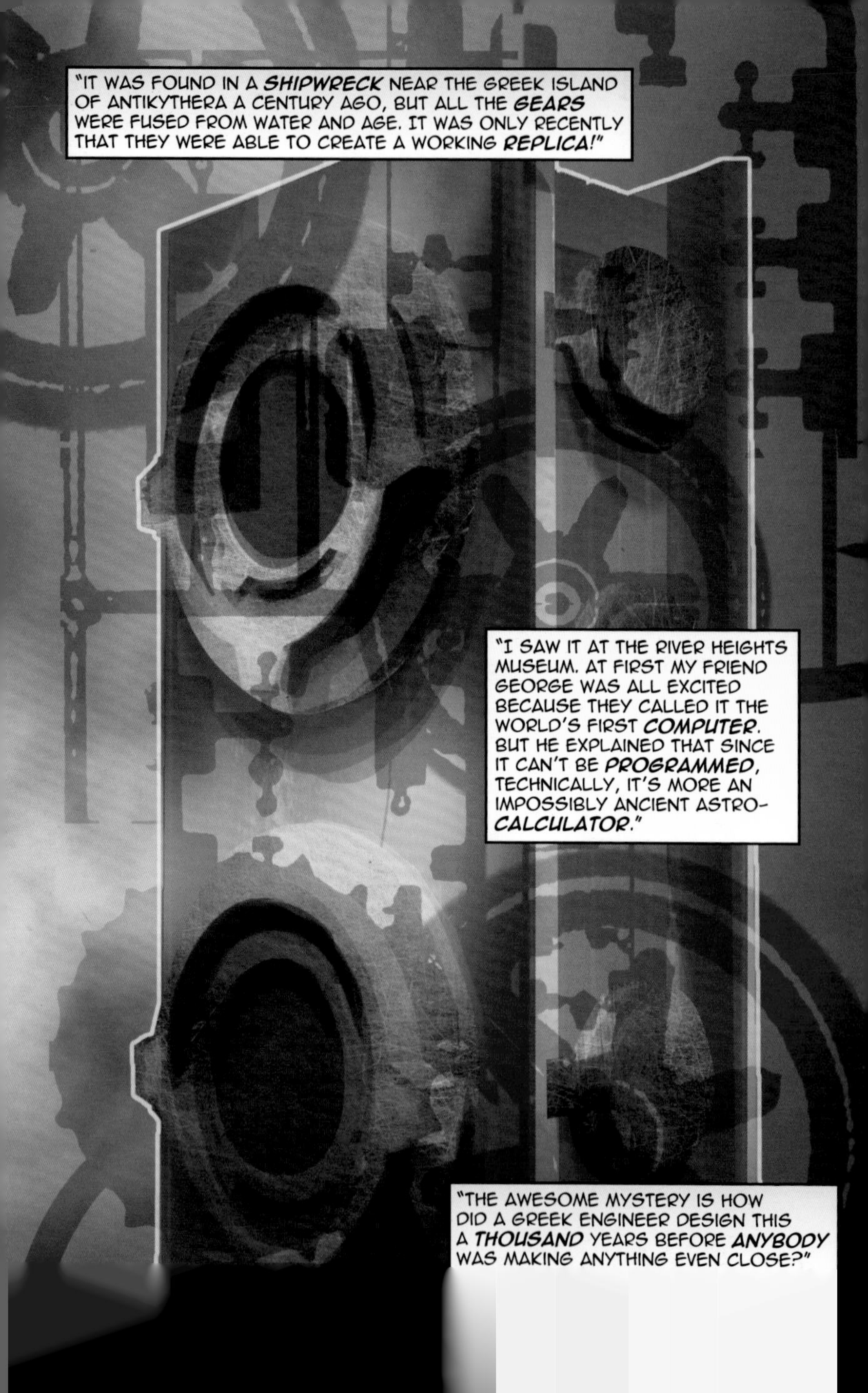
"IT WAS FOUND IN A SHIPWRECK NEAR THE GREEK ISLAND OF ANTIKYTHERA A CENTURY AGO, BUT ALL THE GEARS WERE FUSED FROM WATER AND AGE. IT WAS ONLY RECENTLY THAT THEY WERE ABLE TO CREATE A WORKING REPLICA!"
"I SAW IT AT THE RIVER HEIGHTS MUSEUM. AT FIRST MY FRIEND GEORGE WAS ALL EXCITED BECAUSE THEY CALLED IT THE WORLD'S FIRST COMPUTER. BUT HE EXPLAINED THAT SINCE IT CAN'T BE PROGRAMMED, TECHNICALLY, IT'S MORE AN IMPOSSIBLY ANCIENT ASTRO-CALCULATOR."
"THE AWESOME MYSTERY IS HOW DID A GREEK ENGINEER DESIGN THIS A THOUSAND YEARS BEFORE ANYBODY WAS MAKING ANYTHING EVEN CLOSE?"

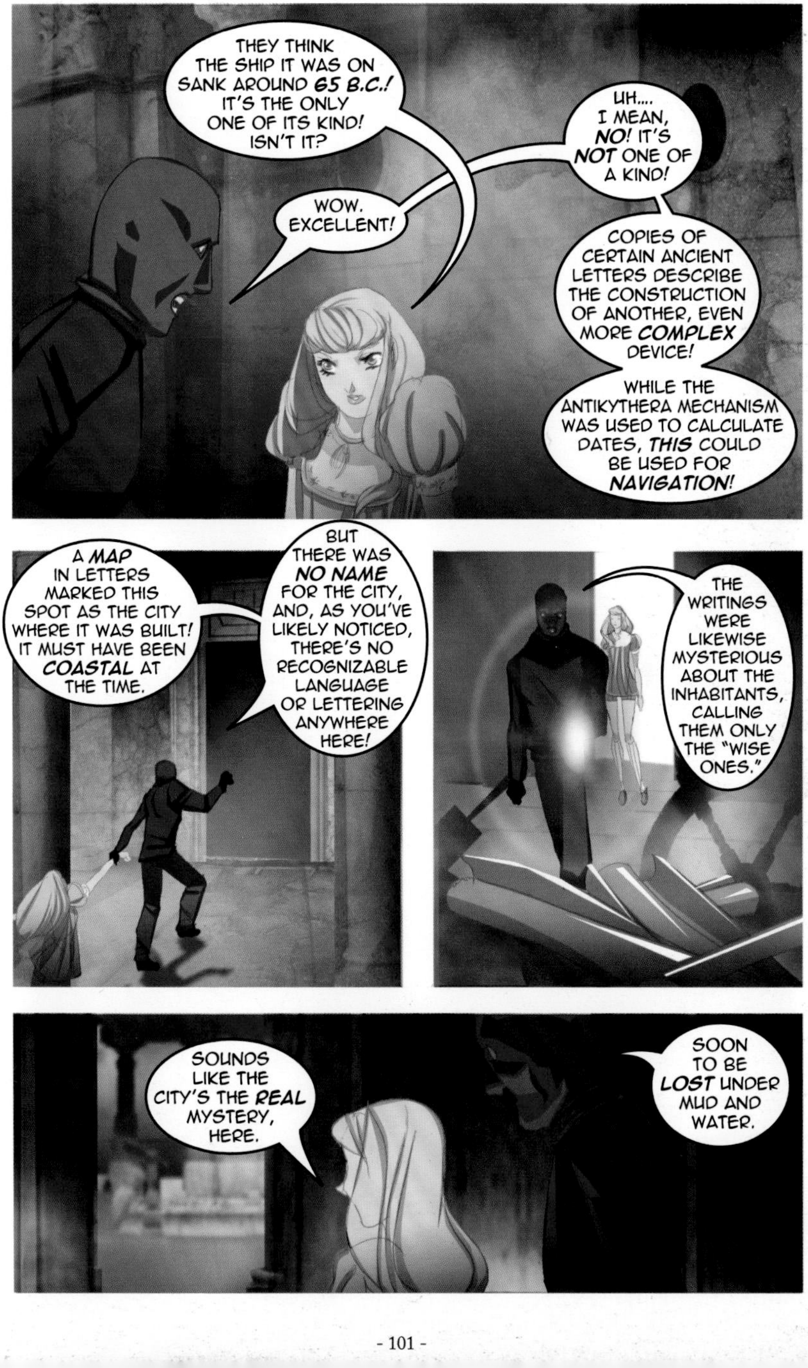
THEY THINK THE SHIP IT WAS ON SANK AROUND 65 B.C.! IT'S THE ONLY ONE OF ITS KIND! ISN'T IT?
WOW. EXCELLENT!
UH.... I MEAN, NO! IT'S NOT ONE OF A KIND!
COPIES OF CERTAIN ANCIENT LETTERS DESCRIBE THE CONSTRUCTION OF ANOTHER, EVEN MORE COMPLEX DEVICE!
WHILE THE ANTIKYTHERA MECHANISM WAS USED TO CALCULATE DATES, THIS COULD BE USED FOR NAVIGATION!
A MAP IN LETTERS MARKED THIS SPOT AS THE CITY WHERE IT WAS BUILT! IT MUST HAVE BEEN COASTAL AT THE TIME.
BUT THERE WAS NO NAME FOR THE CITY, AND, AS YOU'VE LIKELY NOTICED, THERE'S NO RECOGNIZABLE LANGUAGE OR LETTERING ANYWHERE HERE!
THE WRITINGS WERE LIKEWISE MYSTERIOUS ABOUT THE INHABITANTS, CALLING THEM ONLY THE "WISE ONES."
SOUNDS LIKE THE CITY'S THE REAL MYSTERY, HERE.
SOON TO BE LOST UNDER MUD AND WATER.

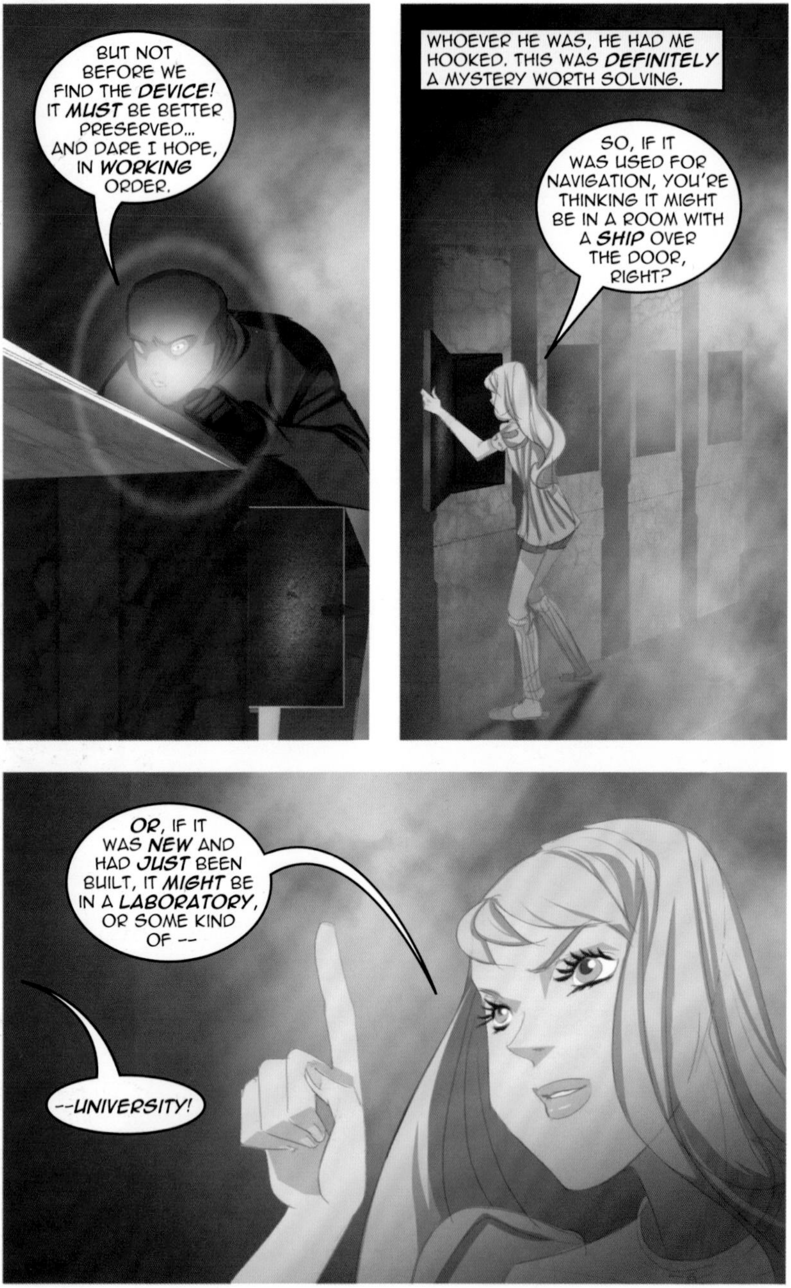
BUT NOT BEFORE WE FIND THE DEVICE! IT MUST BE BETTER PRESERVED... AND DARE I HOPE, IN WORKING ORDER.
WHOEVER HE WAS, HE HAD ME HOOKED. THIS WAS DEFINITELY A MYSTERY WORTH SOLVING.
SO, IF IT WAS USED FOR NAVIGATION, YOU'RE THINKING IT MIGHT BE IN A ROOM WITH A SHIP OVER THE DOOR, RIGHT?
OR, IF IT WAS NEW AND HAD JUST BEEN BUILT, IT MIGHT BE IN A LABORATORY, OR SOME KIND OF --
--UNIVERSITY!

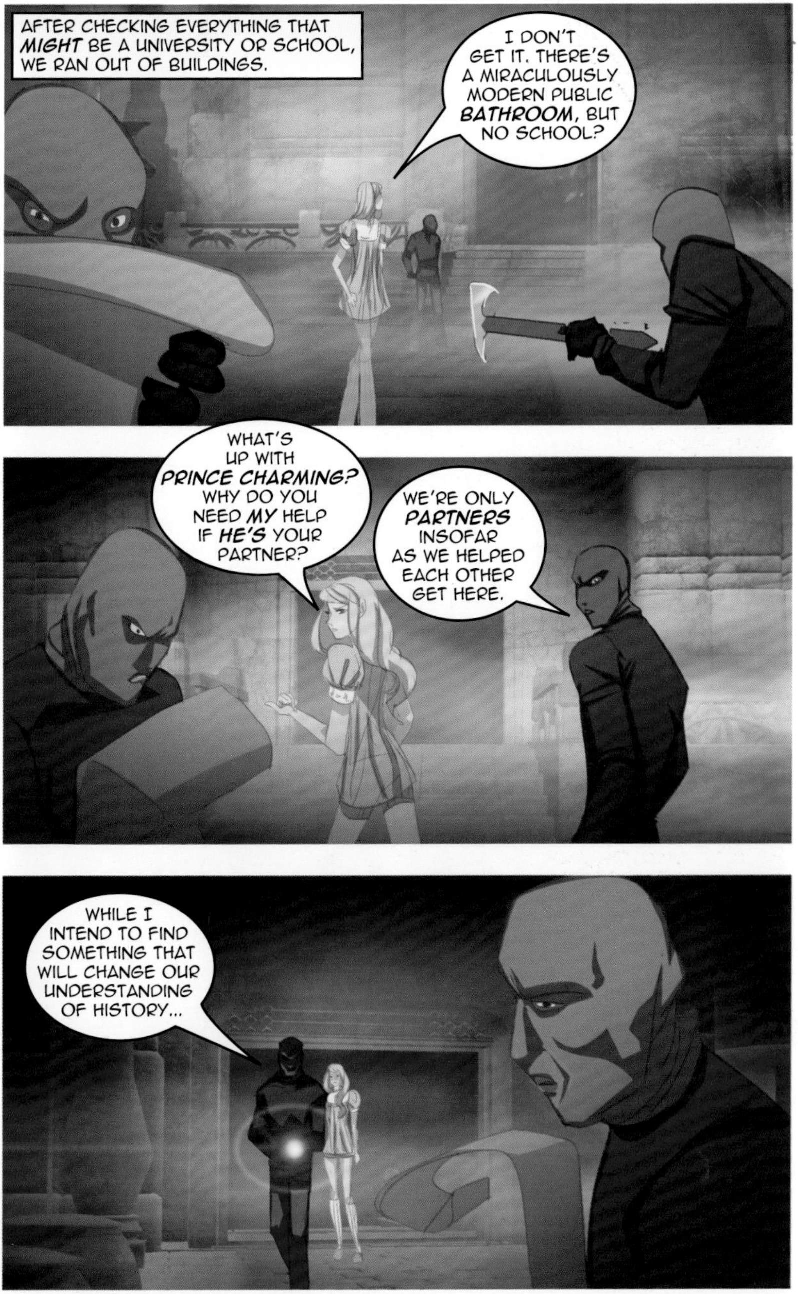
AFTER CHECKING EVERYTHING THAT *MIGHT* BE A UNIVERSITY OR SCHOOL, WE RAN OUT OF BUILDINGS.
I DON'T GET IT. THERE'S A MIRACULOUSLY MODERN PUBLIC *BATHROOM*, BUT NO SCHOOL?
WHAT'S UP WITH *PRINCE CHARMING?* WHY DO YOU NEED *MY* HELP IF *HE'S* YOUR PARTNER?
WE'RE ONLY *PARTNERS* INSOFAR AS WE HELPED EACH OTHER GET HERE.
WHILE I INTEND TO FIND SOMETHING THAT WILL CHANGE OUR UNDERSTANDING OF HISTORY...

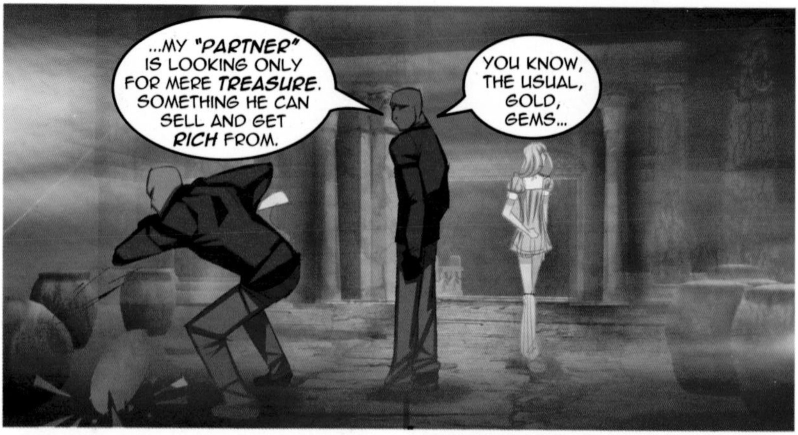
...MY "PARTNER" IS LOOKING ONLY FOR MERE TREASURE. SOMETHING HE CAN SELL AND GET RICH FROM.
YOU KNOW, THE USUAL, GOLD, GEMS...

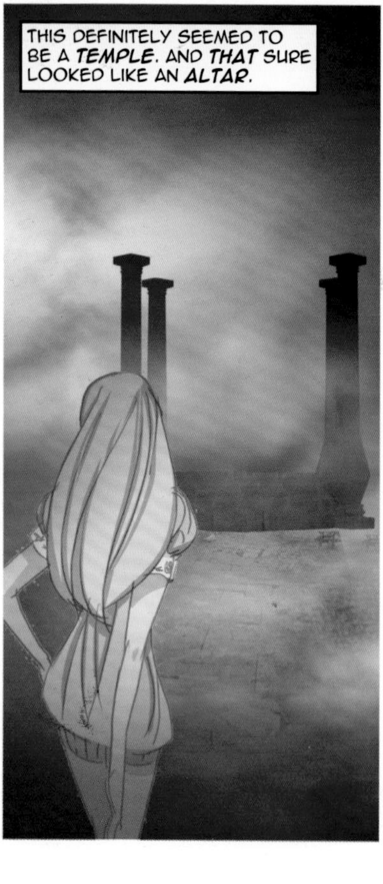
THIS DEFINITELY SEEMED TO BE A TEMPLE. AND THAT SURE LOOKED LIKE AN ALTAR.

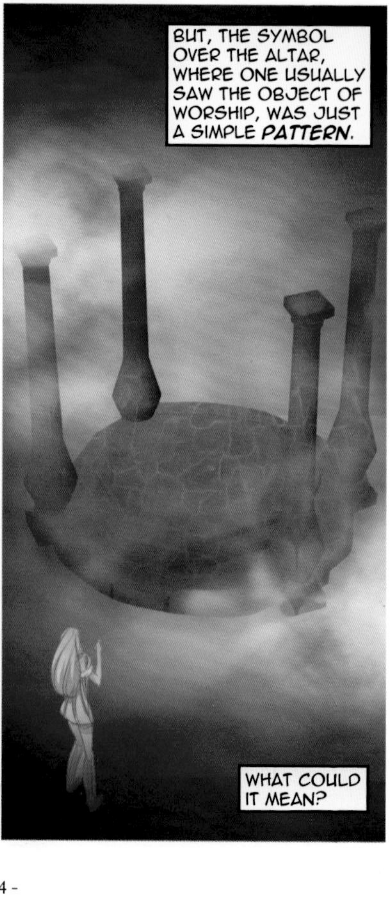
BUT, THE SYMBOL OVER THE ALTAR, WHERE ONE USUALLY SAW THE OBJECT OF WORSHIP, WAS JUST A SIMPLE PATTERN.
WHAT COULD IT MEAN?

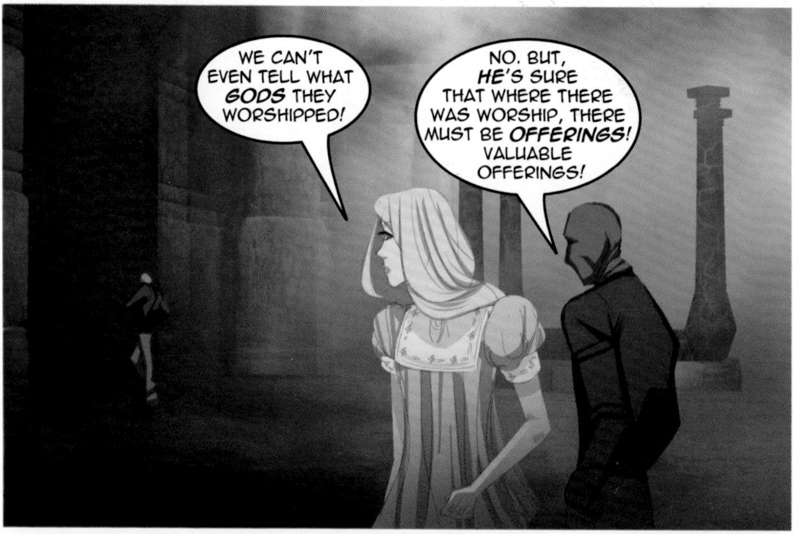
WE CAN'T EVEN TELL WHAT GODS THEY WORSHIPPED!
NO. BUT, HE'S SURE THAT WHERE THERE WAS WORSHIP, THERE MUST BE OFFERINGS! VALUABLE OFFERINGS!

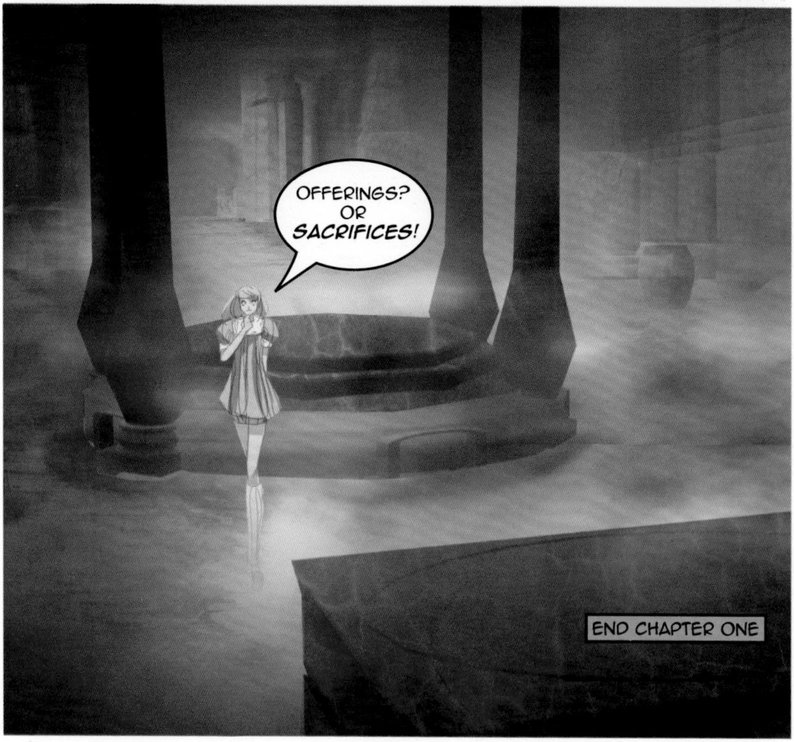
OFFERINGS? OR SACRIFICES!
END CHAPTER ONE

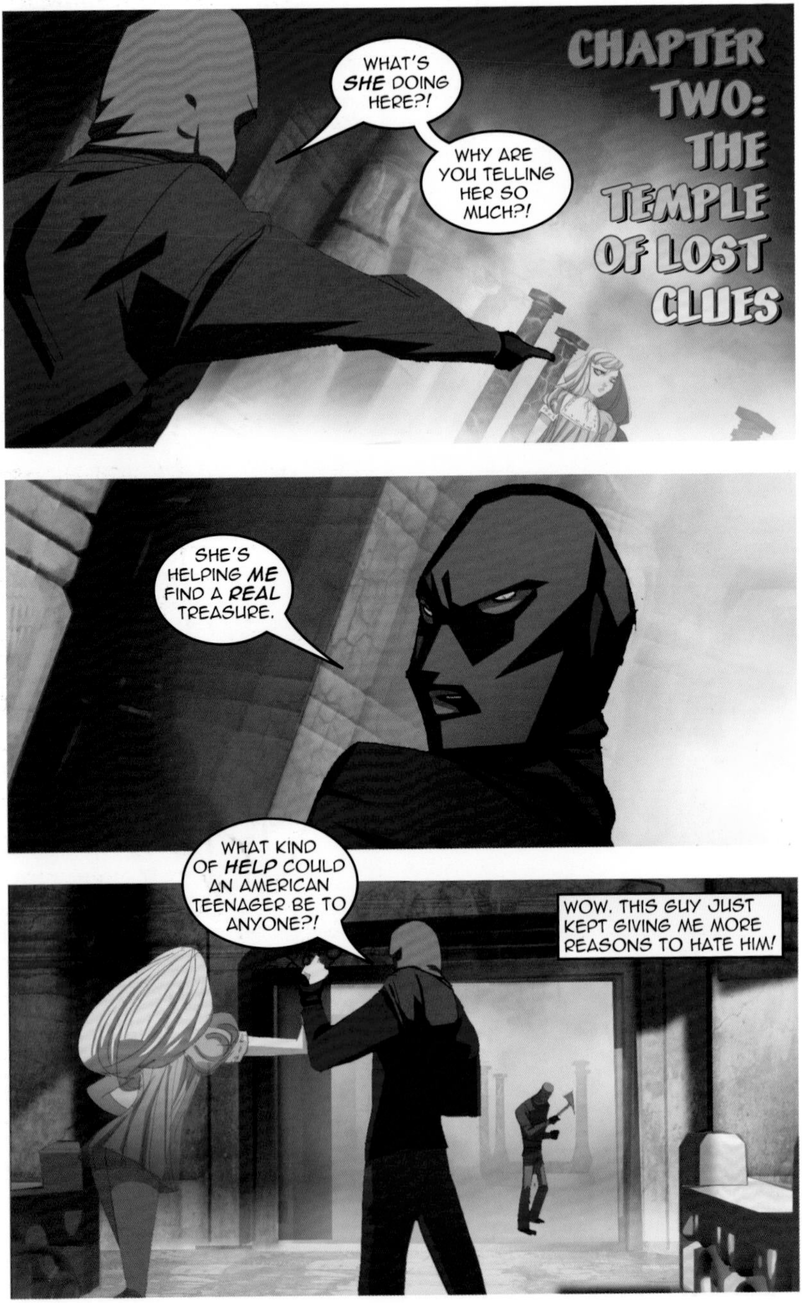
CHAPTER TWO: THE TEMPLE OF LOST CLUES
WHAT'S SHE DOING HERE?!
WHY ARE YOU TELLING HER SO MUCH?!
SHE'S HELPING ME FIND A REAL TREASURE.
WHAT KIND OF HELP COULD AN AMERICAN TEENAGER BE TO ANYONE?!
WOW. THIS GUY JUST KEPT GIVING ME MORE REASONS TO HATE HIM!

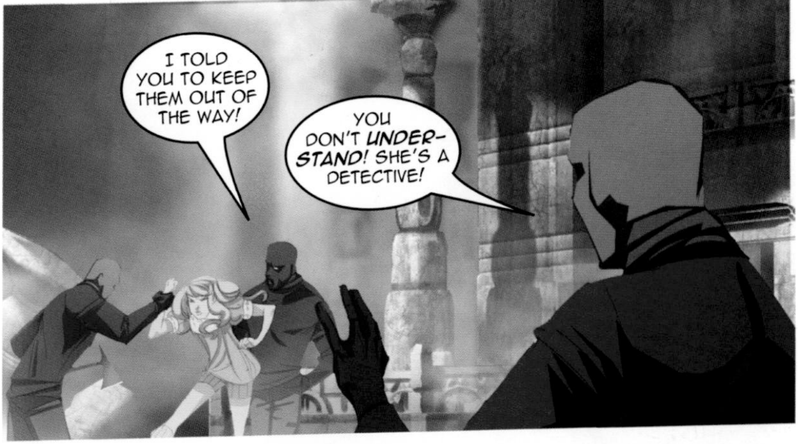
I TOLD YOU TO KEEP THEM OUT OF THE WAY!
YOU DON'T **UNDER-STAND**! SHE'S A DETECTIVE!

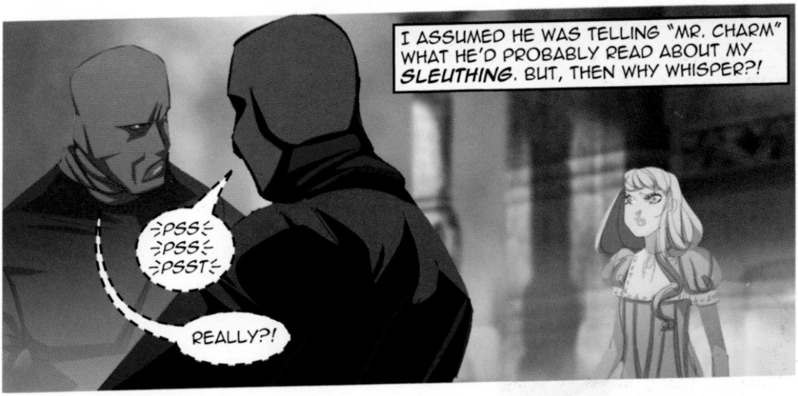
I ASSUMED HE WAS TELLING "MR. CHARM" WHAT HE'D PROBABLY READ ABOUT MY **SLEUTHING**. BUT, THEN WHY WHISPER?!
PSS PSS PSST
REALLY?!

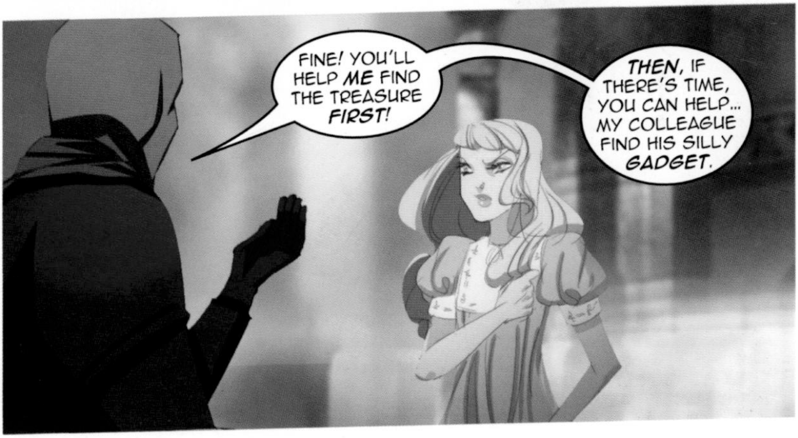
FINE! YOU'LL HELP **ME** FIND THE TREASURE **FIRST**!
THEN, IF THERE'S TIME, YOU CAN HELP... MY COLLEAGUE FIND HIS SILLY **GADGET**.

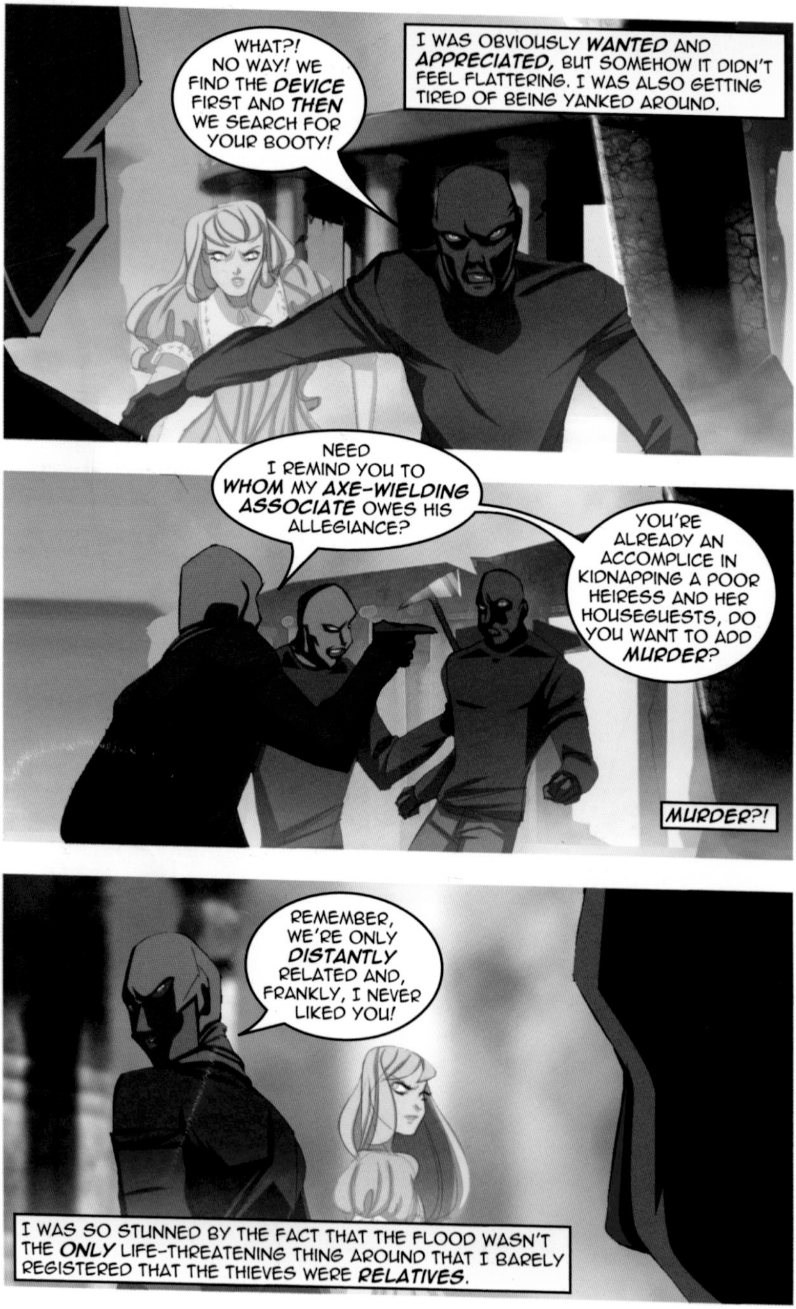
WHAT?! NO WAY! WE FIND THE DEVICE FIRST AND THEN WE SEARCH FOR YOUR BOOTY!
I WAS OBVIOUSLY WANTED AND APPRECIATED, BUT SOMEHOW IT DIDN'T FEEL FLATTERING. I WAS ALSO GETTING TIRED OF BEING YANKED AROUND.
NEED I REMIND YOU TO WHOM MY AXE-WIELDING ASSOCIATE OWES HIS ALLEGIANCE?
YOU'RE ALREADY AN ACCOMPLICE IN KIDNAPPING A POOR HEIRESS AND HER HOUSEGUESTS, DO YOU WANT TO ADD MURDER?
MURDER?!
REMEMBER, WE'RE ONLY DISTANTLY RELATED AND, FRANKLY, I NEVER LIKED YOU!
I WAS SO STUNNED BY THE FACT THAT THE FLOOD WASN'T THE ONLY LIFE-THREATENING THING AROUND THAT I BARELY REGISTERED THAT THE THIEVES WERE RELATIVES.

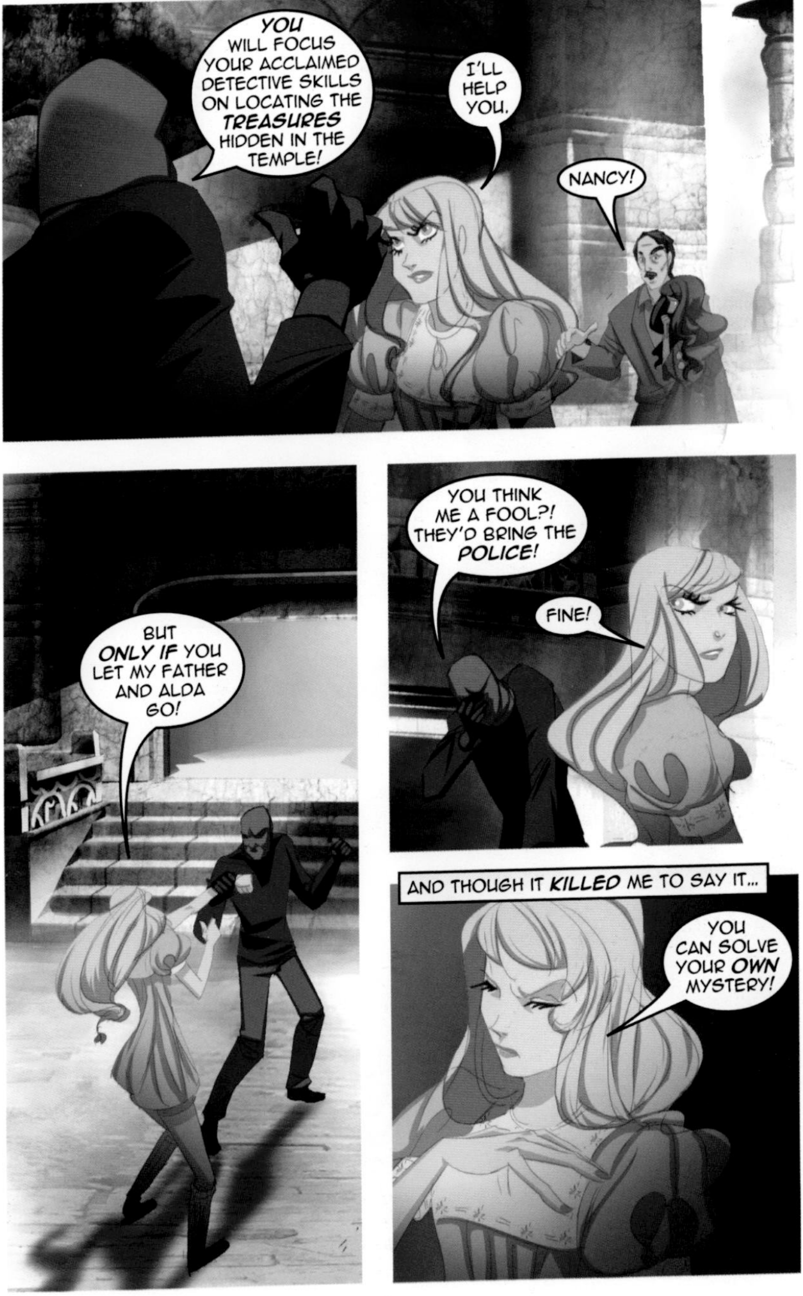
YOU WILL FOCUS YOUR ACCLAIMED DETECTIVE SKILLS ON LOCATING THE TREASURES HIDDEN IN THE TEMPLE!
I'LL HELP YOU,
NANCY!
BUT ONLY IF YOU LET MY FATHER AND ALDA GO!
YOU THINK ME A FOOL?! THEY'D BRING THE POLICE!
FINE!
AND THOUGH IT KILLED ME TO SAY IT...
YOU CAN SOLVE YOUR OWN MYSTERY!

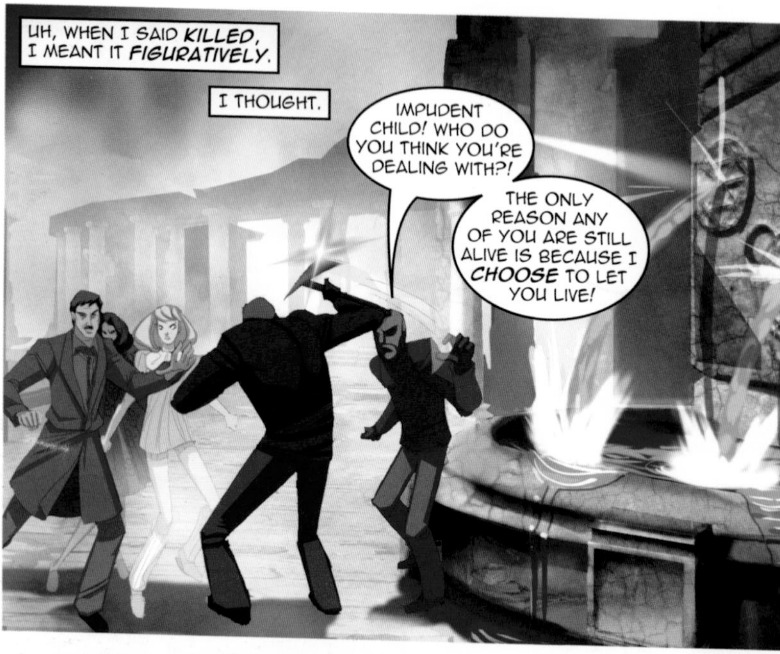
UH, WHEN I SAID KILLED, I MEANT IT FIGURATIVELY.
I THOUGHT.
IMPUDENT CHILD! WHO DO YOU THINK YOU'RE DEALING WITH?!
THE ONLY REASON ANY OF YOU ARE STILL ALIVE IS BECAUSE I CHOOSE TO LET YOU LIVE!

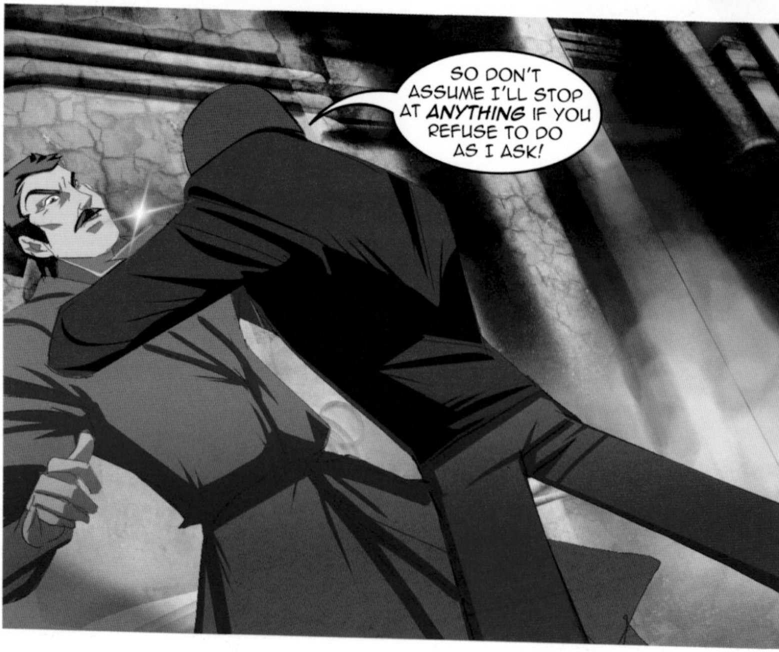
SO DON'T ASSUME I'LL STOP AT ANYTHING IF YOU REFUSE TO DO AS I ASK!

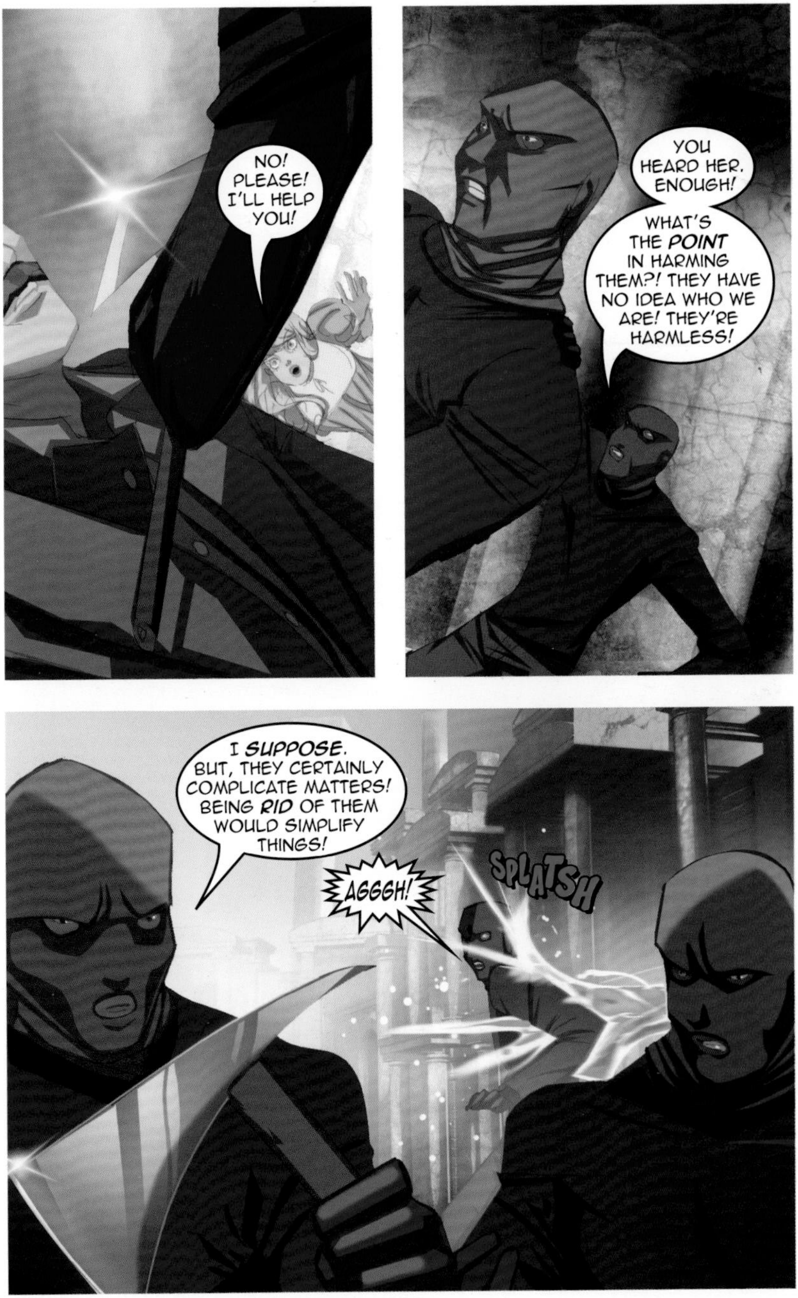
NO! PLEASE! I'LL HELP YOU!
YOU HEARD HER. ENOUGH!
WHAT'S THE ***POINT*** IN HARMING THEM?! THEY HAVE NO IDEA WHO WE ARE! THEY'RE HARMLESS!
I ***SUPPOSE***. BUT, THEY CERTAINLY COMPLICATE MATTERS! BEING ***RID*** OF THEM WOULD SIMPLIFY THINGS!
AGGGH!
SPLATSH

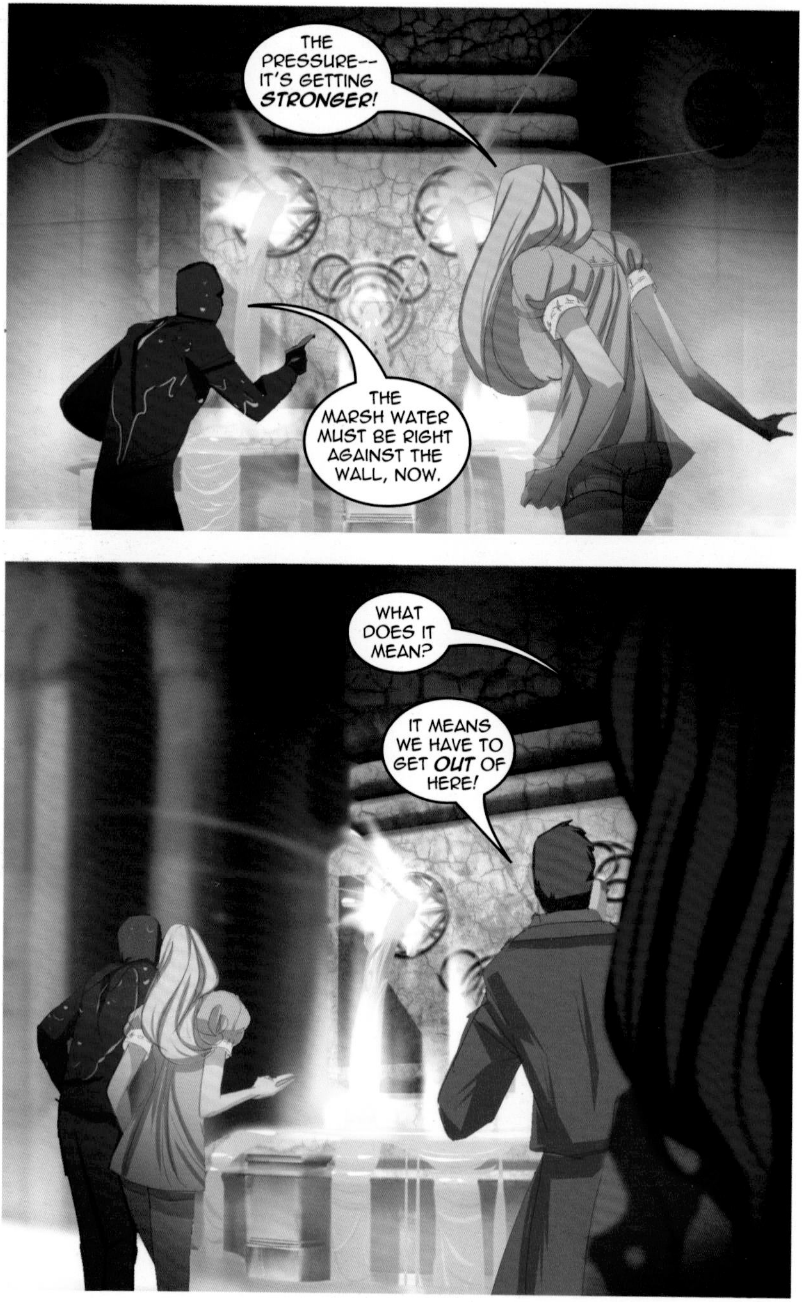
THE PRESSURE-- IT'S GETTING STRONGER!
THE MARSH WATER MUST BE RIGHT AGAINST THE WALL, NOW.
WHAT DOES IT MEAN?
IT MEANS WE HAVE TO GET OUT OF HERE!

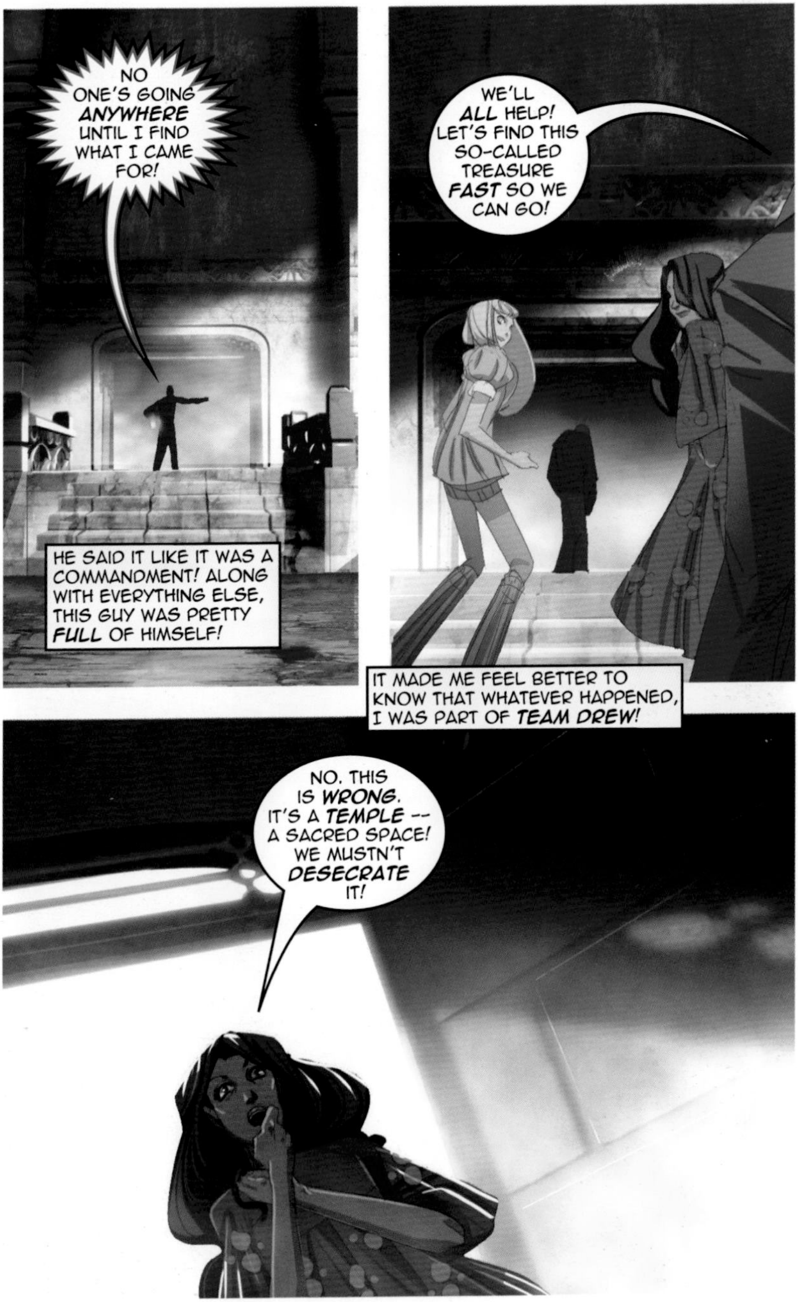
NO ONE'S GOING ANYWHERE UNTIL I FIND WHAT I CAME FOR!
HE SAID IT LIKE IT WAS A COMMANDMENT! ALONG WITH EVERYTHING ELSE, THIS GUY WAS PRETTY FULL OF HIMSELF!
WE'LL ALL HELP! LET'S FIND THIS SO-CALLED TREASURE FAST SO WE CAN GO!
IT MADE ME FEEL BETTER TO KNOW THAT WHATEVER HAPPENED, I WAS PART OF TEAM DREW!
NO. THIS IS WRONG. IT'S A TEMPLE -- A SACRED SPACE! WE MUSTN'T DESECRATE IT!

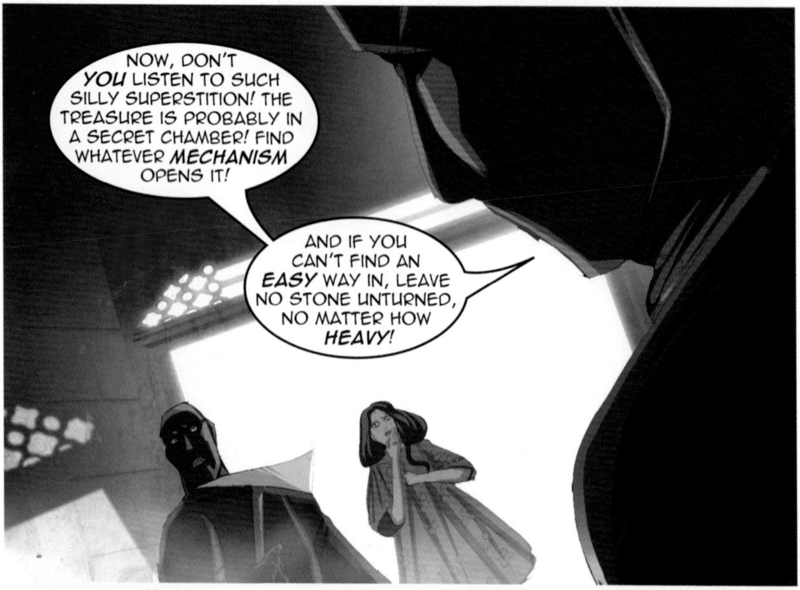
NOW, DON'T YOU LISTEN TO SUCH SILLY SUPERSTITION! THE TREASURE IS PROBABLY IN A SECRET CHAMBER! FIND WHATEVER MECHANISM OPENS IT!
AND IF YOU CAN'T FIND AN EASY WAY IN, LEAVE NO STONE UNTURNED, NO MATTER HOW HEAVY!

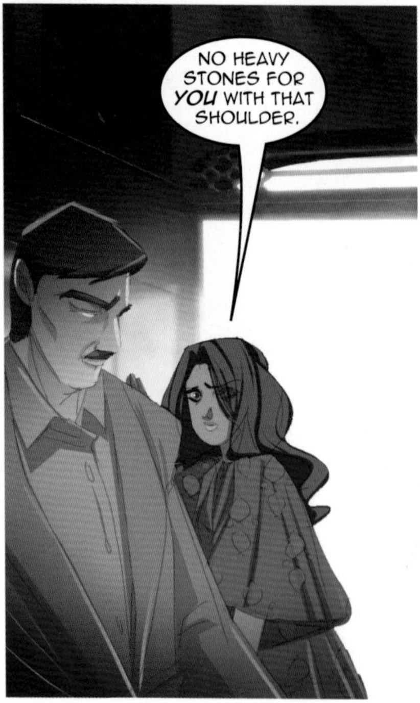
NO HEAVY STONES FOR YOU WITH THAT SHOULDER.

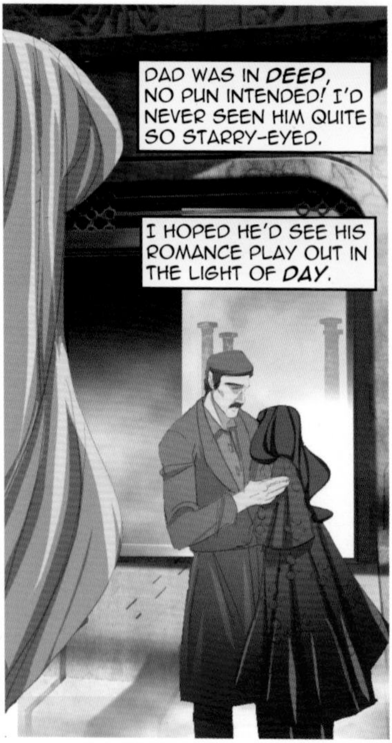
DAD WAS IN DEEP, NO PUN INTENDED! I'D NEVER SEEN HIM QUITE SO STARRY-EYED.
I HOPED HE'D SEE HIS ROMANCE PLAY OUT IN THE LIGHT OF DAY.

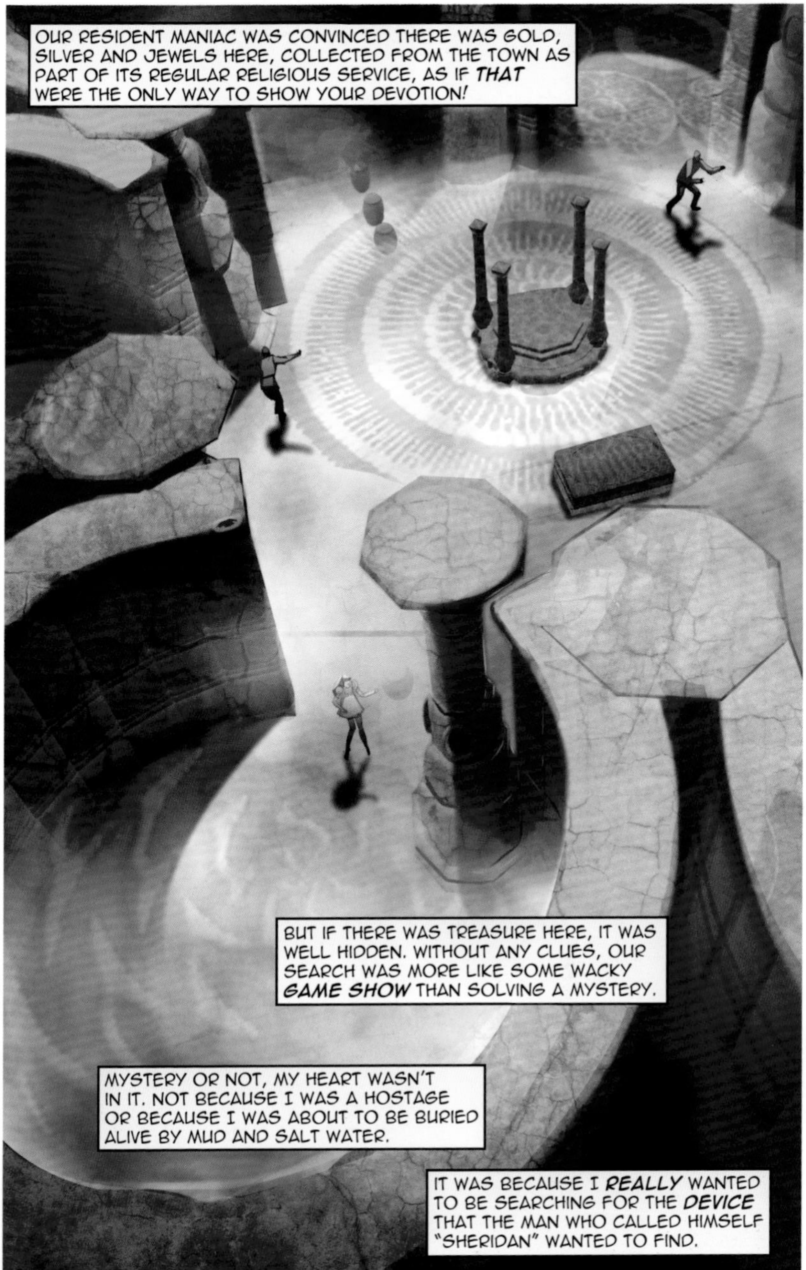
OUR RESIDENT MANIAC WAS CONVINCED THERE WAS GOLD, SILVER AND JEWELS HERE, COLLECTED FROM THE TOWN AS PART OF ITS REGULAR RELIGIOUS SERVICE, AS IF *THAT* WERE THE ONLY WAY TO SHOW YOUR DEVOTION!
BUT IF THERE WAS TREASURE HERE, IT WAS WELL HIDDEN. WITHOUT ANY CLUES, OUR SEARCH WAS MORE LIKE SOME WACKY *GAME SHOW* THAN SOLVING A MYSTERY.
MYSTERY OR NOT, MY HEART WASN'T IN IT. NOT BECAUSE I WAS A HOSTAGE OR BECAUSE I WAS ABOUT TO BE BURIED ALIVE BY MUD AND SALT WATER.
IT WAS BECAUSE I *REALLY* WANTED TO BE SEARCHING FOR THE *DEVICE* THAT THE MAN WHO CALLED HIMSELF "SHERIDAN" WANTED TO FIND.

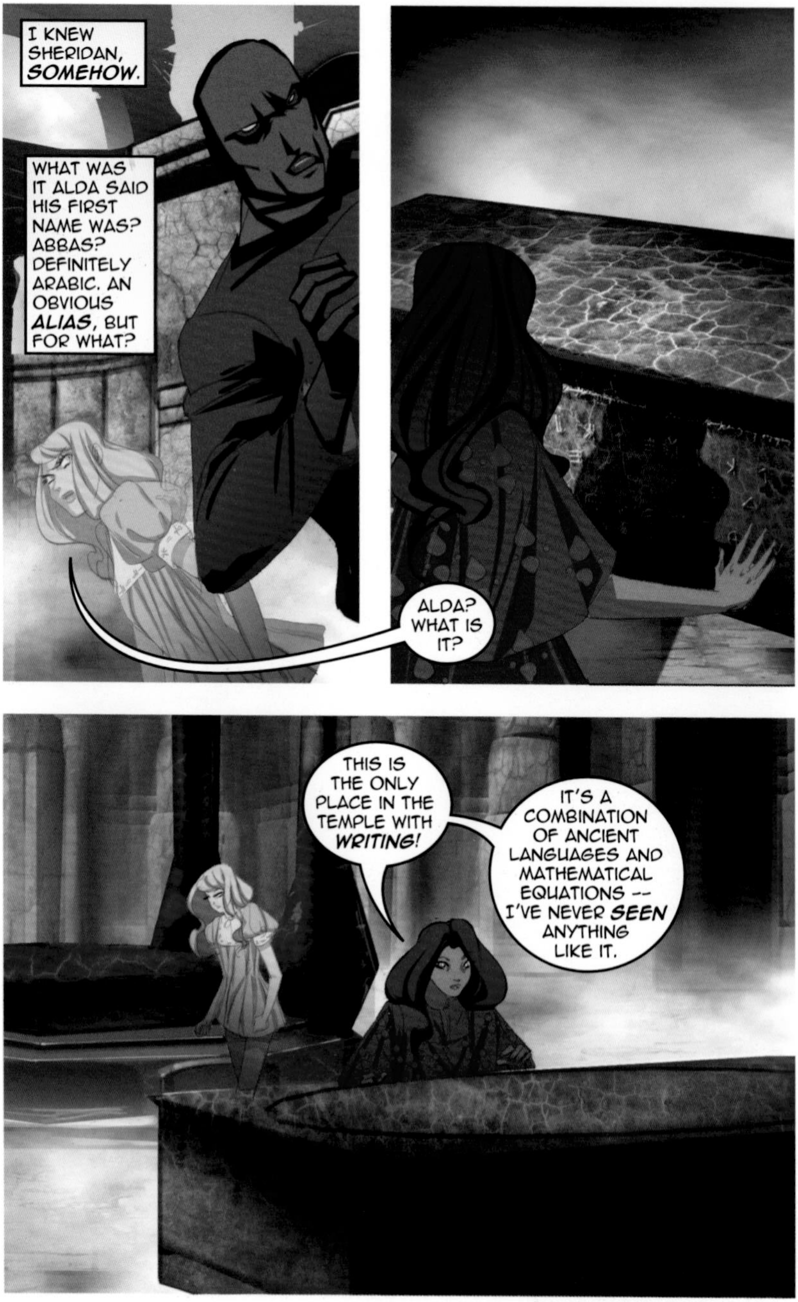
I KNEW SHERIDAN, SOMEHOW.
WHAT WAS IT ALDA SAID HIS FIRST NAME WAS? ABBAS? DEFINITELY ARABIC. AN OBVIOUS ALIAS, BUT FOR WHAT?
ALDA? WHAT IS IT?
THIS IS THE ONLY PLACE IN THE TEMPLE WITH WRITING!
IT'S A COMBINATION OF ANCIENT LANGUAGES AND MATHEMATICAL EQUATIONS -- I'VE NEVER SEEN ANYTHING LIKE IT.

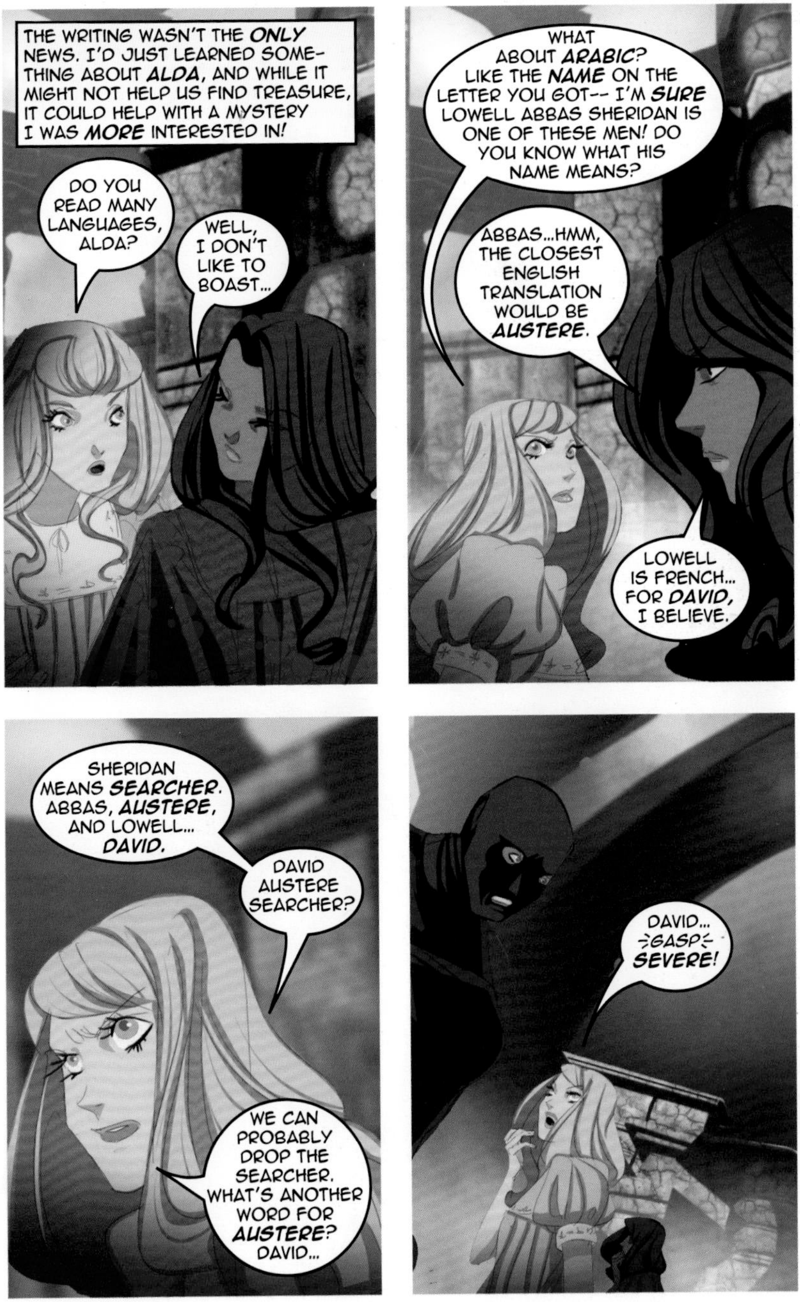
THE WRITING WASN'T THE ONLY NEWS. I'D JUST LEARNED SOMETHING ABOUT ALDA, AND WHILE IT MIGHT NOT HELP US FIND TREASURE, IT COULD HELP WITH A MYSTERY I WAS MORE INTERESTED IN!
DO YOU READ MANY LANGUAGES, ALDA?
WELL, I DON'T LIKE TO BOAST...
WHAT ABOUT ARABIC? LIKE THE NAME ON THE LETTER YOU GOT-- I'M SURE LOWELL ABBAS SHERIDAN IS ONE OF THESE MEN! DO YOU KNOW WHAT HIS NAME MEANS?
ABBAS...HMM, THE CLOSEST ENGLISH TRANSLATION WOULD BE AUSTERE.
LOWELL IS FRENCH... FOR DAVID, I BELIEVE.
SHERIDAN MEANS SEARCHER. ABBAS, AUSTERE, AND LOWELL... DAVID.
DAVID AUSTERE SEARCHER?
WE CAN PROBABLY DROP THE SEARCHER. WHAT'S ANOTHER WORD FOR AUSTERE? DAVID...
DAVID... GASP SEVERE!

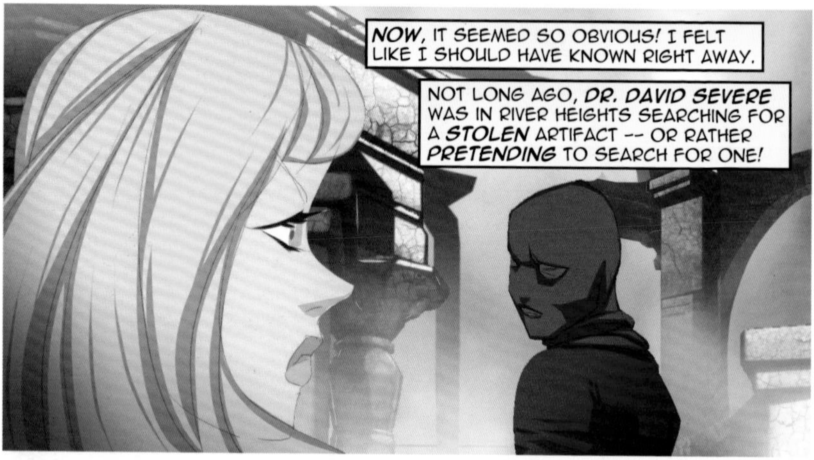
NOW, IT SEEMED SO OBVIOUS! I FELT LIKE I SHOULD HAVE KNOWN RIGHT AWAY.
NOT LONG AGO, DR. DAVID SEVERE WAS IN RIVER HEIGHTS SEARCHING FOR A STOLEN ARTIFACT -- OR RATHER PRETENDING TO SEARCH FOR ONE!

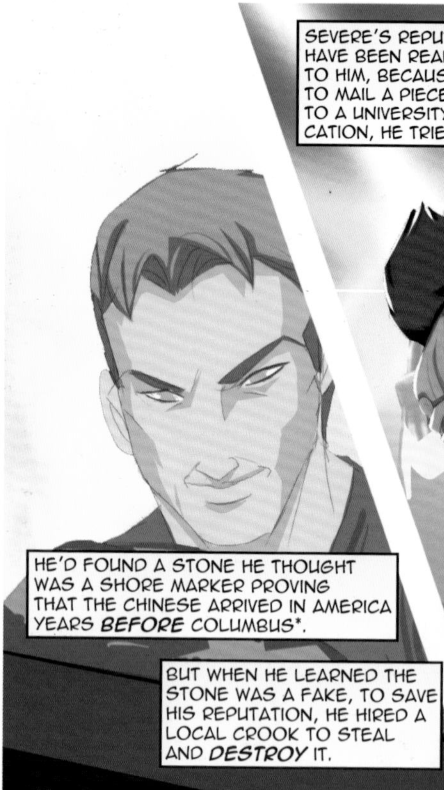
HE'D FOUND A STONE HE THOUGHT WAS A SHORE MARKER PROVING THAT THE CHINESE ARRIVED IN AMERICA YEARS BEFORE COLUMBUS*.
BUT WHEN HE LEARNED THE STONE WAS A FAKE, TO SAVE HIS REPUTATION, HE HIRED A LOCAL CROOK TO STEAL AND DESTROY IT.

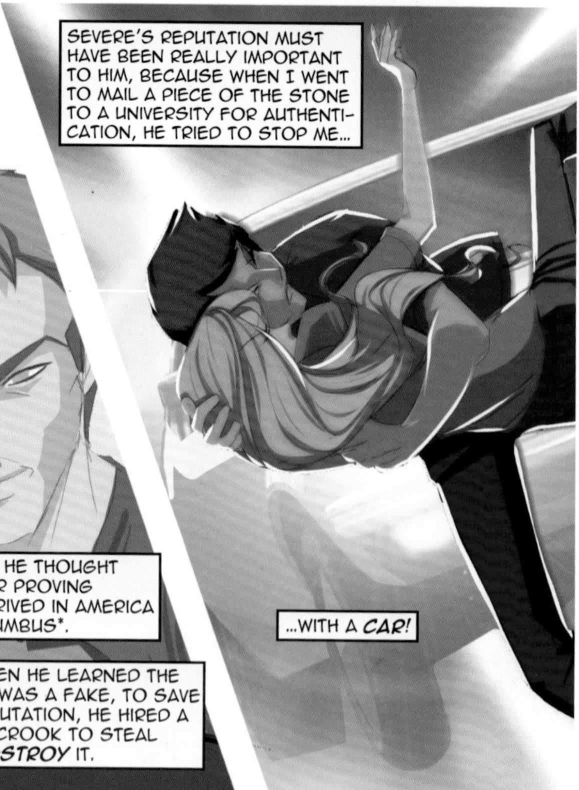
SEVERE'S REPUTATION MUST HAVE BEEN REALLY IMPORTANT TO HIM, BECAUSE WHEN I WENT TO MAIL A PIECE OF THE STONE TO A UNIVERSITY FOR AUTHENTICATION, HE TRIED TO STOP ME...
...WITH A CAR!

*See NANCY DREW DIARIES Volume 1 "Writ in Stone"

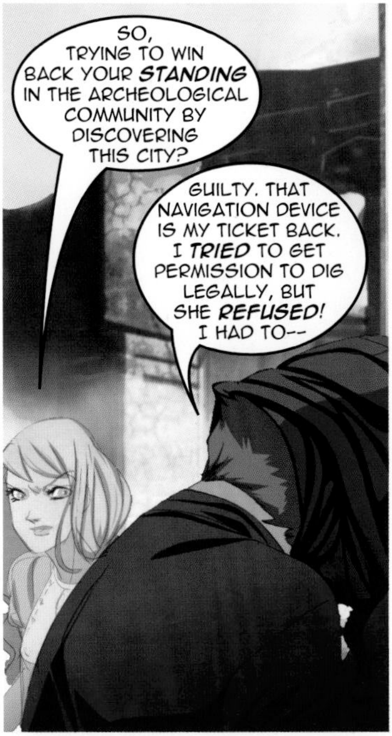
SO, TRYING TO WIN BACK YOUR STANDING IN THE ARCHEOLOGICAL COMMUNITY BY DISCOVERING THIS CITY?
GUILTY. THAT NAVIGATION DEVICE IS MY TICKET BACK. I TRIED TO GET PERMISSION TO DIG LEGALLY, BUT SHE REFUSED! I HAD TO--

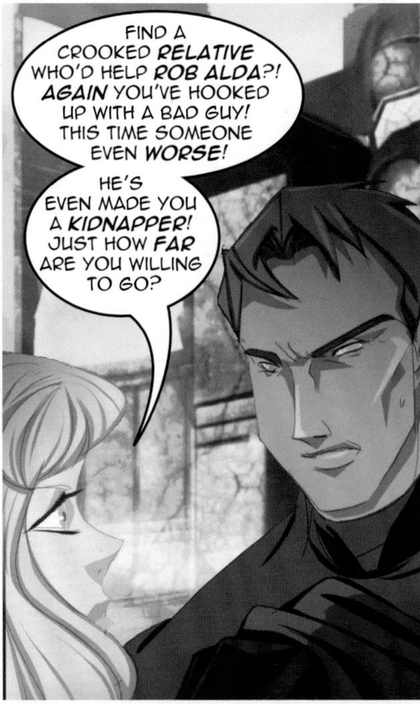
FIND A CROOKED RELATIVE WHO'D HELP ROB ALDA?! AGAIN YOU'VE HOOKED UP WITH A BAD GUY! THIS TIME SOMEONE EVEN WORSE!
HE'S EVEN MADE YOU A KIDNAPPER! JUST HOW FAR ARE YOU WILLING TO GO?

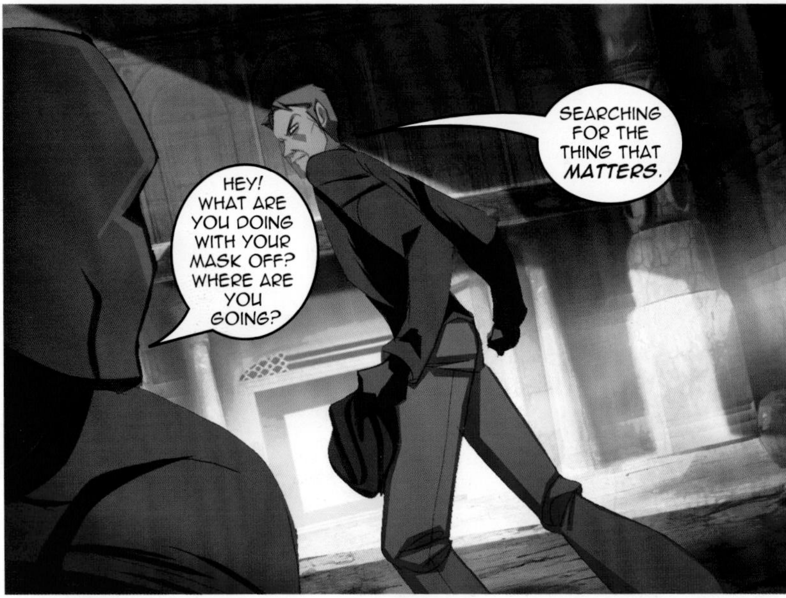
SEARCHING FOR THE THING THAT MATTERS.
HEY! WHAT ARE YOU DOING WITH YOUR MASK OFF? WHERE ARE YOU GOING?

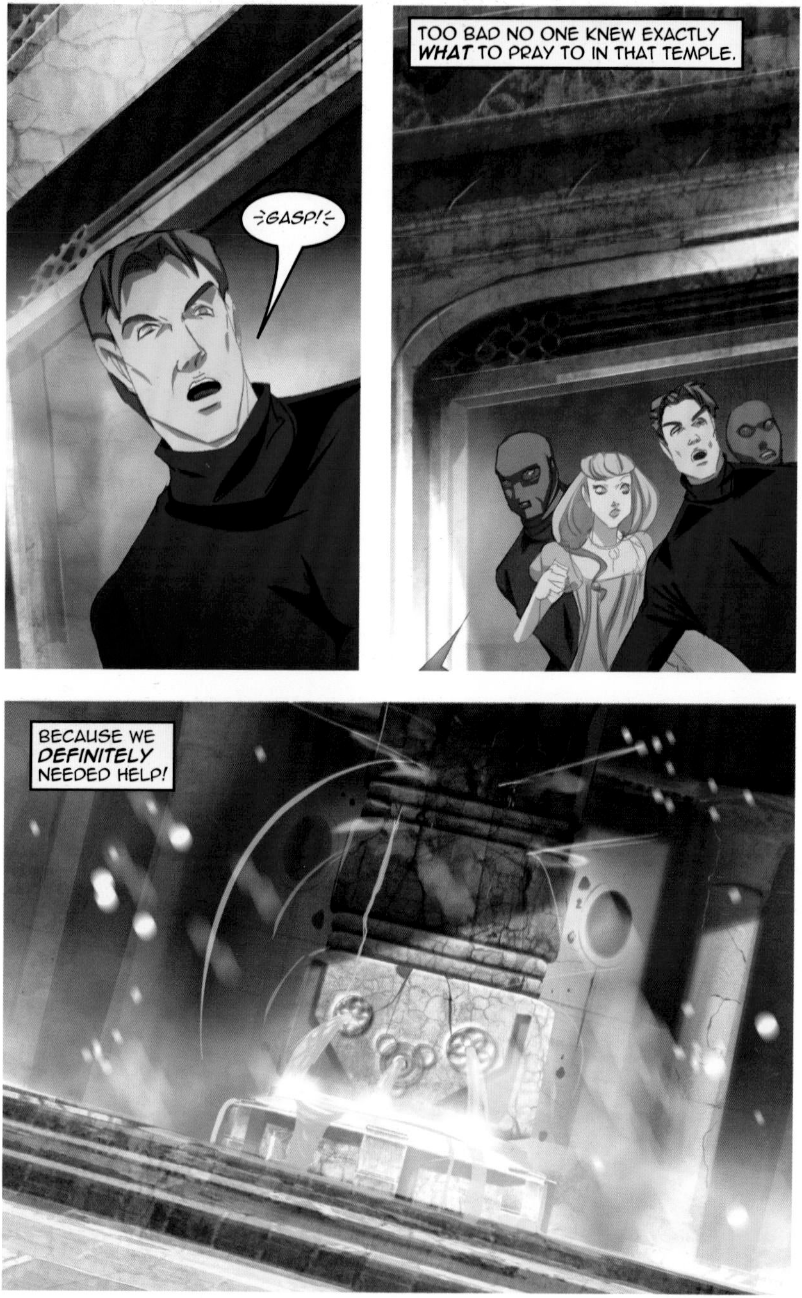

=GASP!=
TOO BAD NO ONE KNEW EXACTLY WHAT TO PRAY TO IN THAT TEMPLE.
BECAUSE WE DEFINITELY NEEDED HELP!

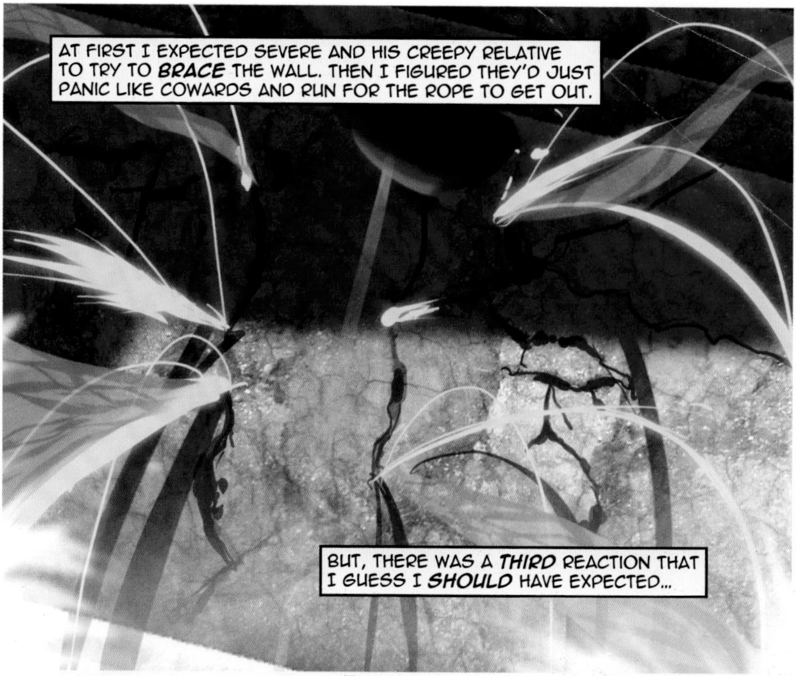
AT FIRST I EXPECTED SEVERE AND HIS CREEPY RELATIVE TO TRY TO BRACE THE WALL. THEN I FIGURED THEY'D JUST PANIC LIKE COWARDS AND RUN FOR THE ROPE TO GET OUT.
BUT, THERE WAS A THIRD REACTION THAT I GUESS I SHOULD HAVE EXPECTED...

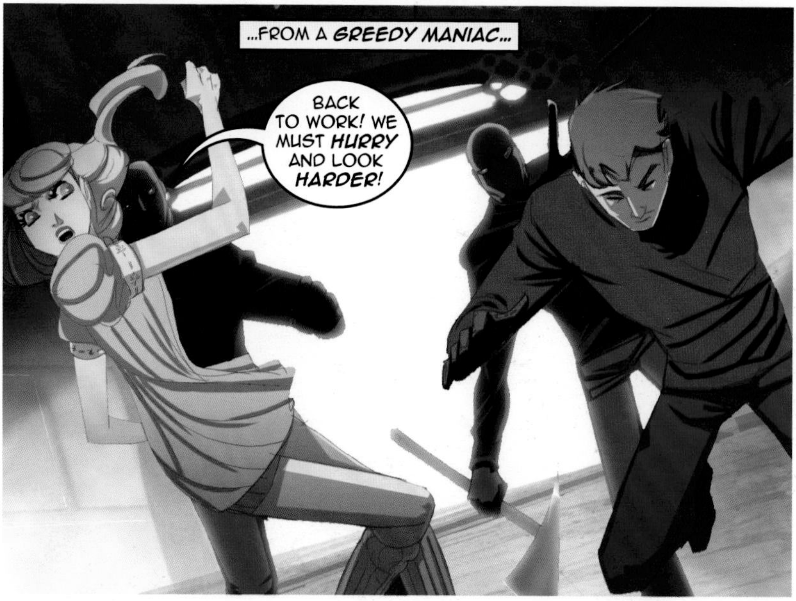
...FROM A GREEDY MANIAC...
BACK TO WORK! WE MUST HURRY AND LOOK HARDER!

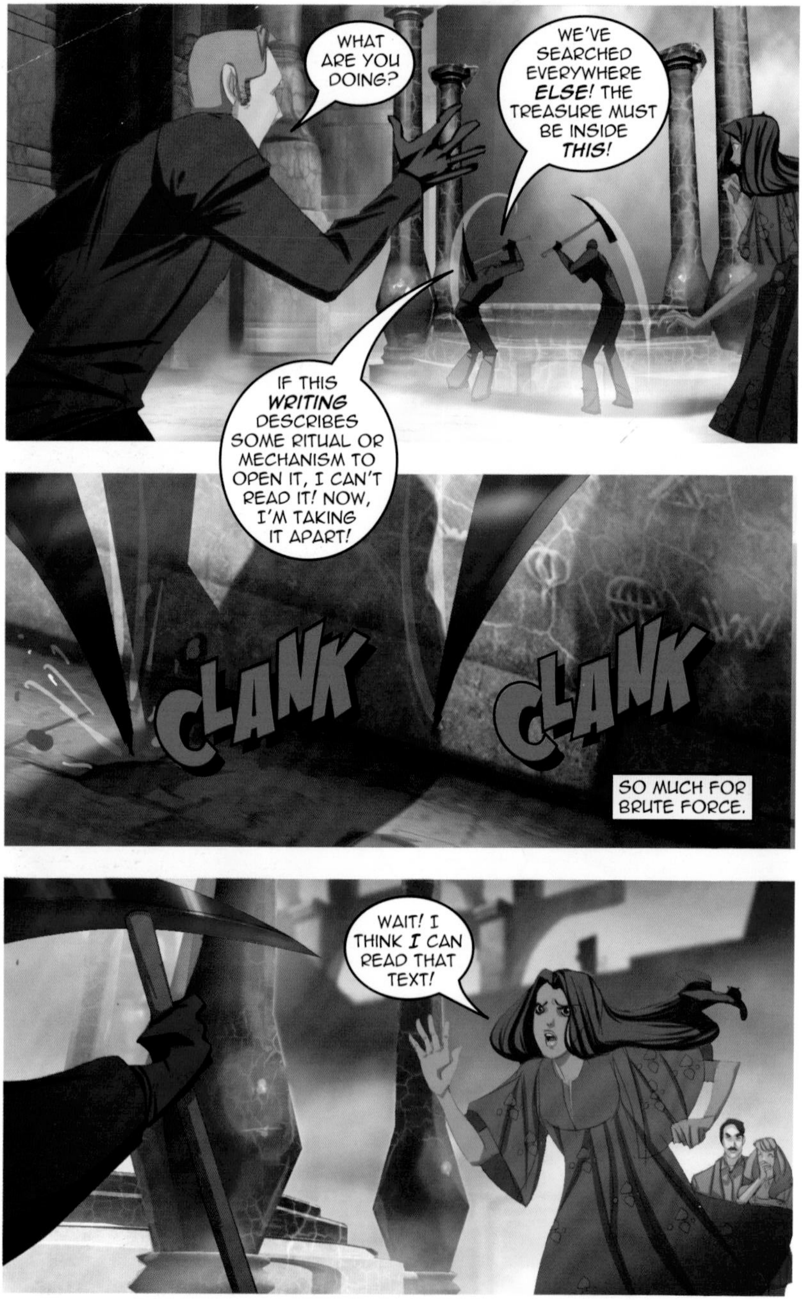
WHAT ARE YOU DOING?
WE'VE SEARCHED EVERYWHERE ELSE! THE TREASURE MUST BE INSIDE THIS!
IF THIS WRITING DESCRIBES SOME RITUAL OR MECHANISM TO OPEN IT, I CAN'T READ IT! NOW, I'M TAKING IT APART!
CLANK
CLANK
SO MUCH FOR BRUTE FORCE.
WAIT! I THINK I CAN READ THAT TEXT!

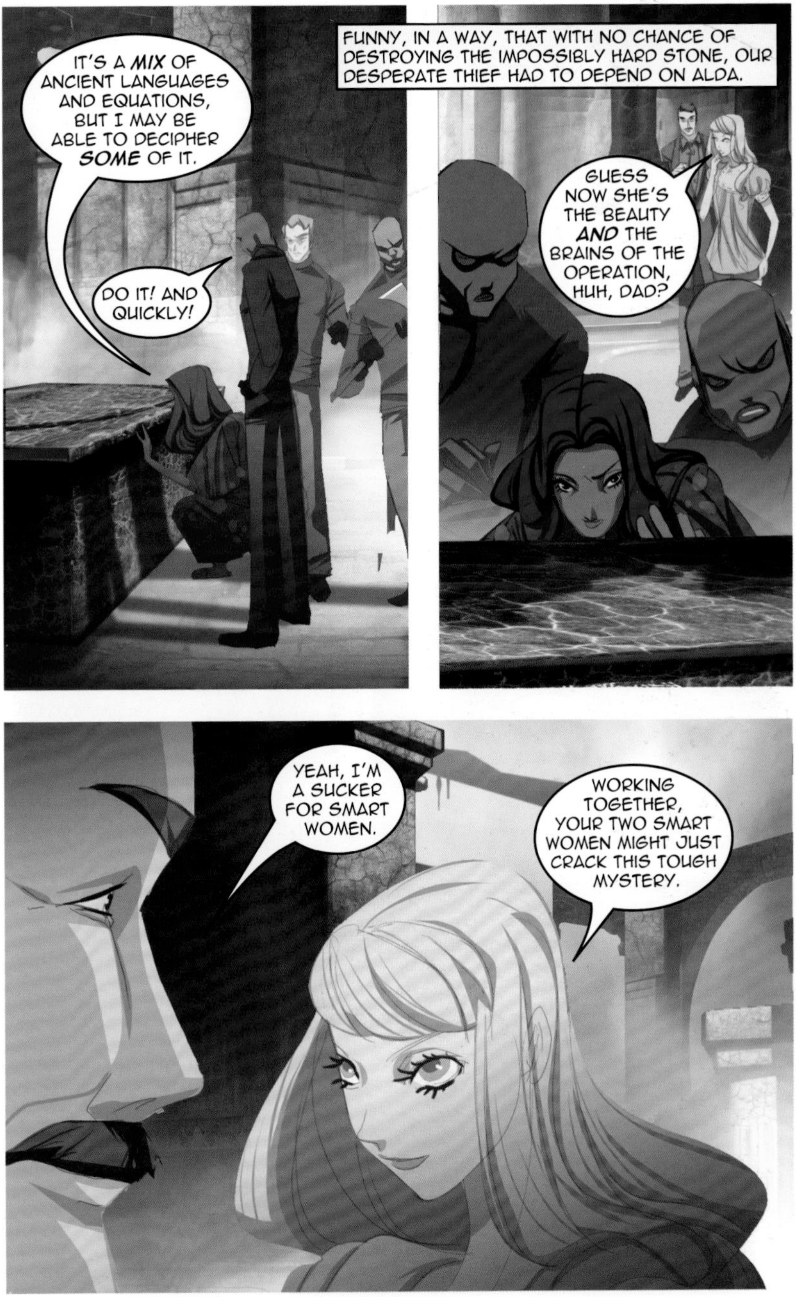
IT'S A MIX OF ANCIENT LANGUAGES AND EQUATIONS, BUT I MAY BE ABLE TO DECIPHER SOME OF IT.
DO IT! AND QUICKLY!
FUNNY, IN A WAY, THAT WITH NO CHANCE OF DESTROYING THE IMPOSSIBLY HARD STONE, OUR DESPERATE THIEF HAD TO DEPEND ON ALDA.
GUESS NOW SHE'S THE BEAUTY AND THE BRAINS OF THE OPERATION, HUH, DAD?
YEAH, I'M A SUCKER FOR SMART WOMEN.
WORKING TOGETHER, YOUR TWO SMART WOMEN MIGHT JUST CRACK THIS TOUGH MYSTERY.

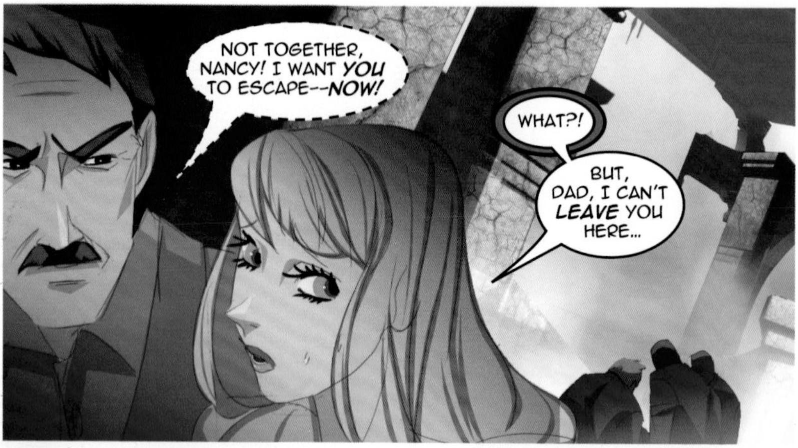
NOT TOGETHER, NANCY! I WANT YOU TO ESCAPE--NOW!
WHAT?!
BUT, DAD, I CAN'T LEAVE YOU HERE...

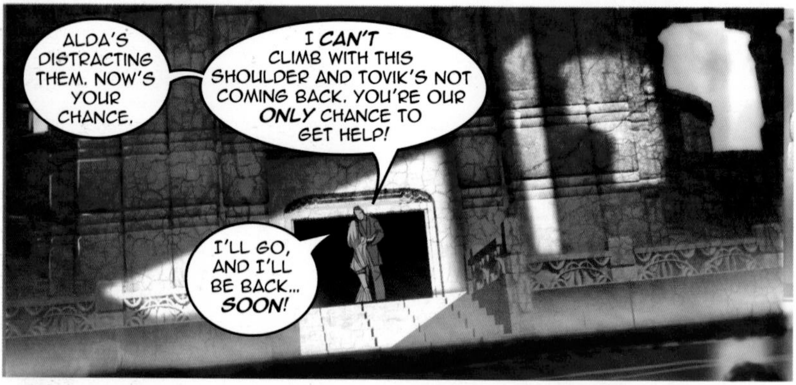
ALDA'S DISTRACTING THEM. NOW'S YOUR CHANCE.
I CAN'T CLIMB WITH THIS SHOULDER AND TOVIK'S NOT COMING BACK. YOU'RE OUR ONLY CHANCE TO GET HELP!
I'LL GO, AND I'LL BE BACK... SOON!

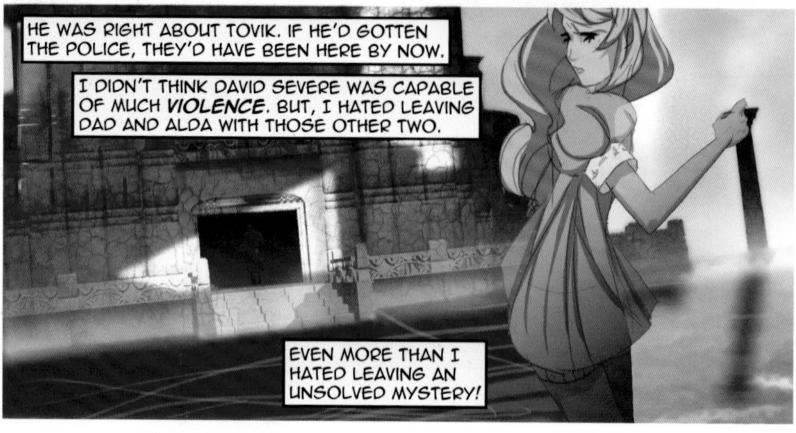
HE WAS RIGHT ABOUT TOVIK. IF HE'D GOTTEN THE POLICE, THEY'D HAVE BEEN HERE BY NOW.
I DIDN'T THINK DAVID SEVERE WAS CAPABLE OF MUCH VIOLENCE. BUT, I HATED LEAVING DAD AND ALDA WITH THOSE OTHER TWO.
EVEN MORE THAN I HATED LEAVING AN UNSOLVED MYSTERY!

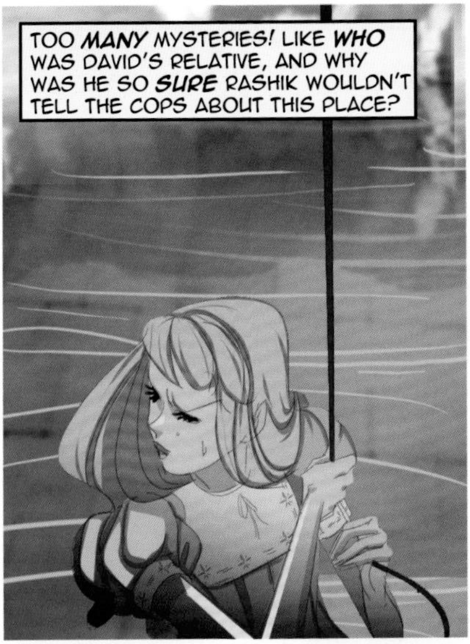
TOO MANY MYSTERIES! LIKE WHO WAS DAVID'S RELATIVE, AND WHY WAS HE SO SURE RASHIK WOULDN'T TELL THE COPS ABOUT THIS PLACE?

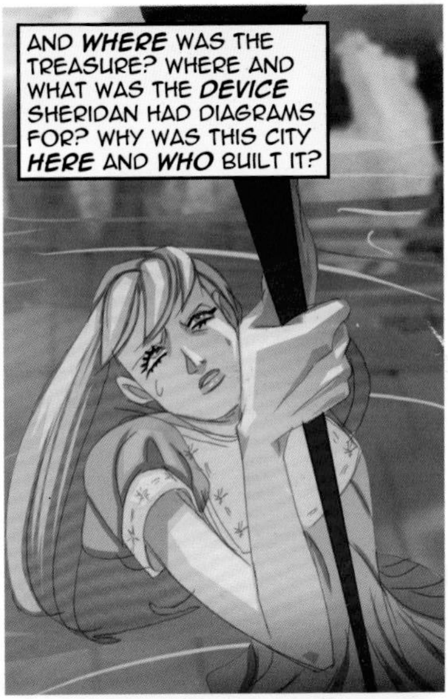
AND WHERE WAS THE TREASURE? WHERE AND WHAT WAS THE DEVICE SHERIDAN HAD DIAGRAMS FOR? WHY WAS THIS CITY HERE AND WHO BUILT IT?

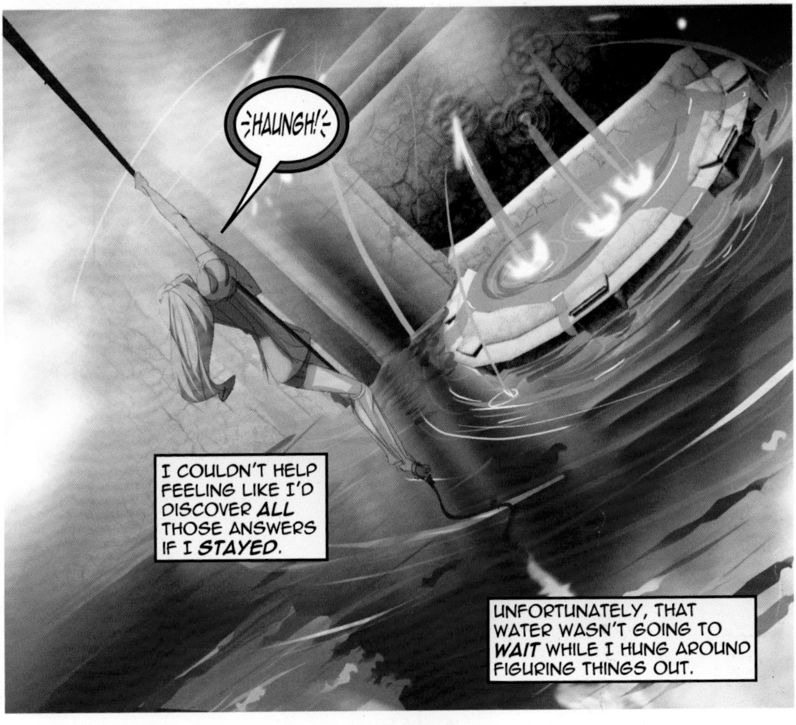
HAUNGH!
I COULDN'T HELP FEELING LIKE I'D DISCOVER ALL THOSE ANSWERS IF I STAYED.
UNFORTUNATELY, THAT WATER WASN'T GOING TO WAIT WHILE I HUNG AROUND FIGURING THINGS OUT.

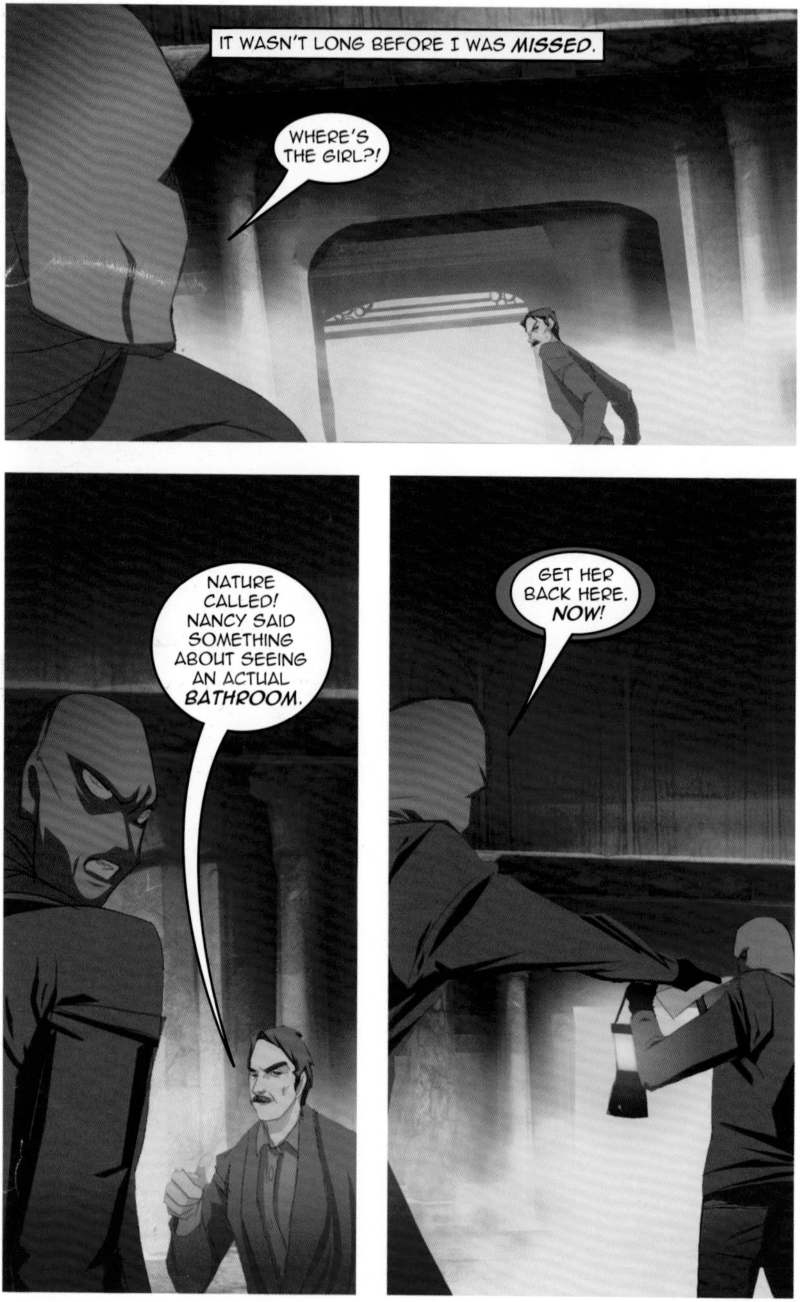
IT WASN'T LONG BEFORE I WAS MISSED.
WHERE'S THE GIRL?!
NATURE CALLED! NANCY SAID SOMETHING ABOUT SEEING AN ACTUAL BATHROOM.
GET HER BACK HERE. NOW!

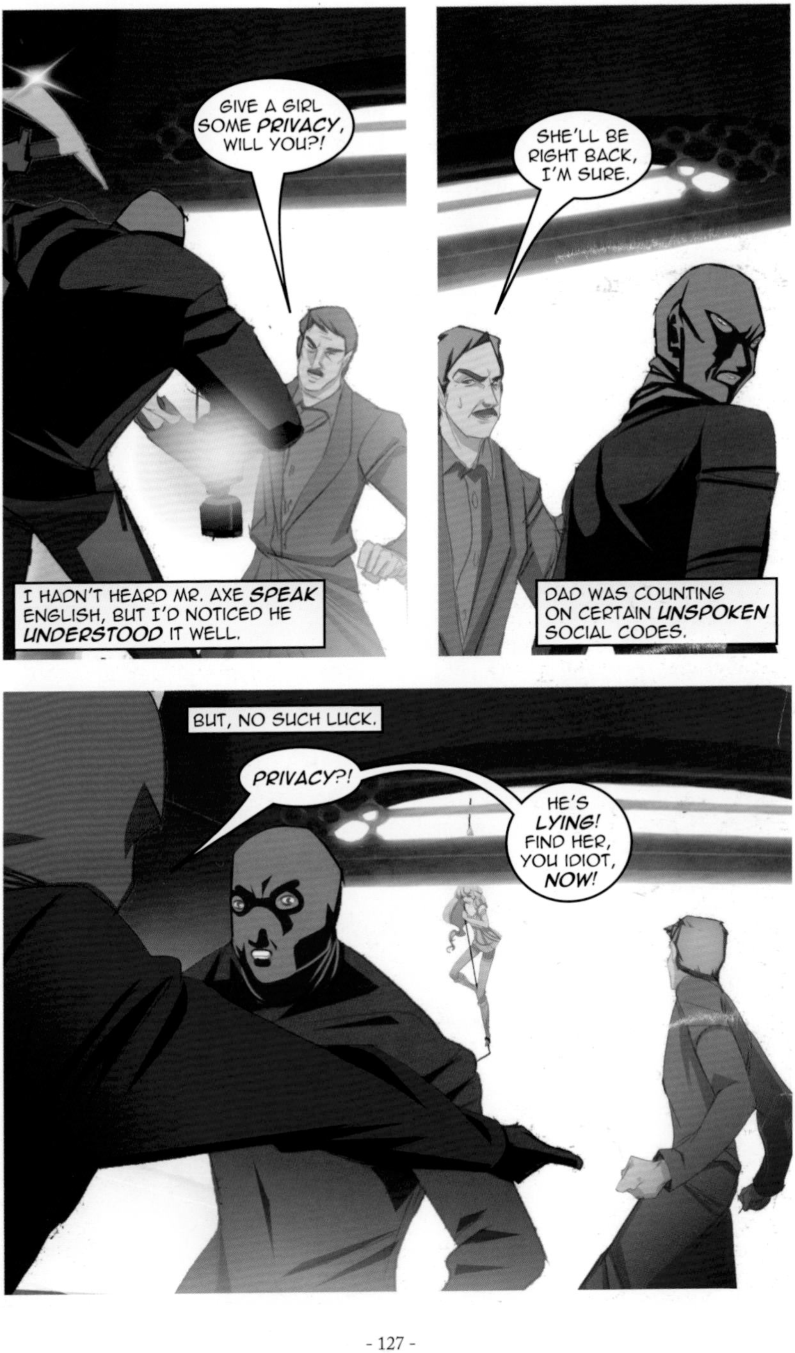
GIVE A GIRL SOME PRIVACY, WILL YOU?!
I HADN'T HEARD MR. AXE SPEAK ENGLISH, BUT I'D NOTICED HE UNDERSTOOD IT WELL.
SHE'LL BE RIGHT BACK, I'M SURE.
DAD WAS COUNTING ON CERTAIN UNSPOKEN SOCIAL CODES.
BUT, NO SUCH LUCK.
PRIVACY?!
HE'S LYING! FIND HER, YOU IDIOT, NOW!

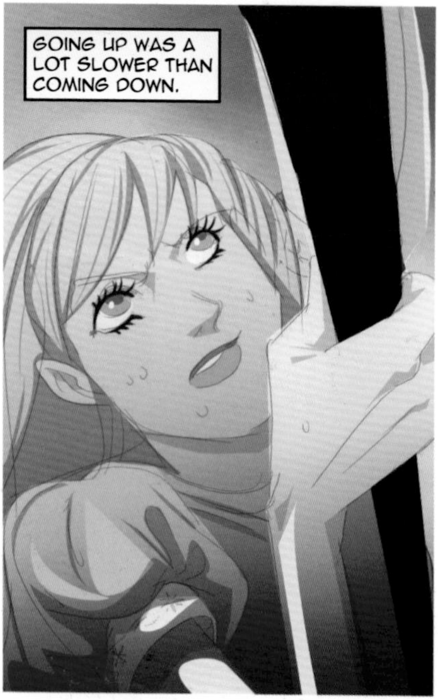
GOING UP WAS A LOT SLOWER THAN COMING DOWN.

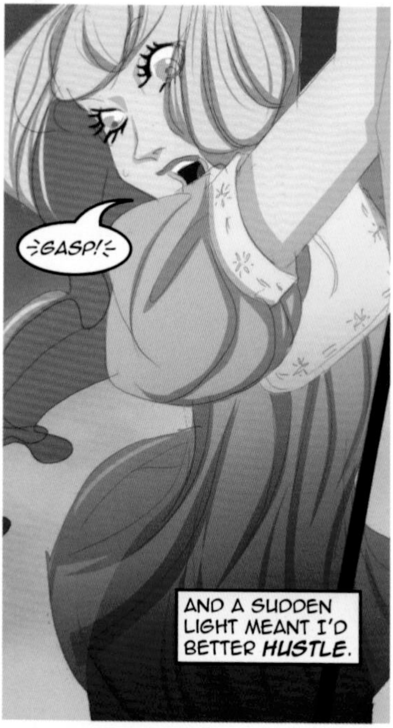
GASP!
AND A SUDDEN LIGHT MEANT I'D BETTER HUSTLE.

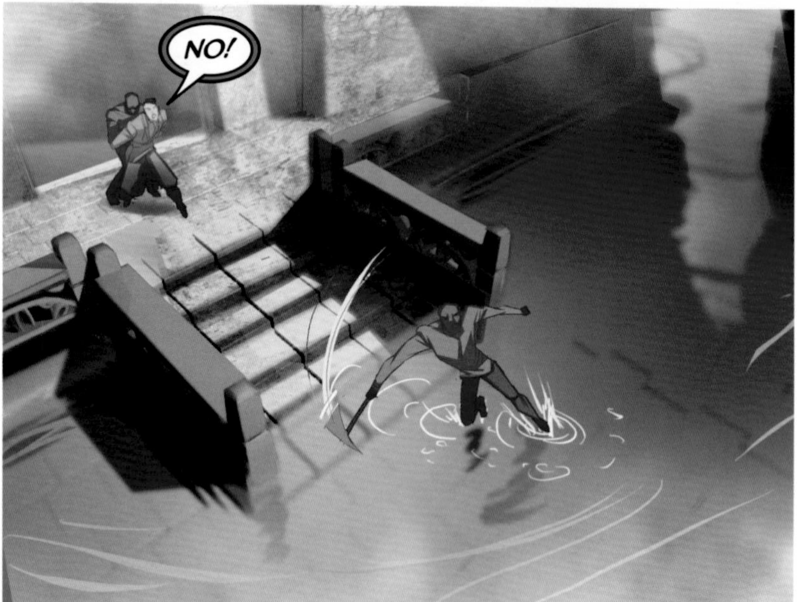
NO!

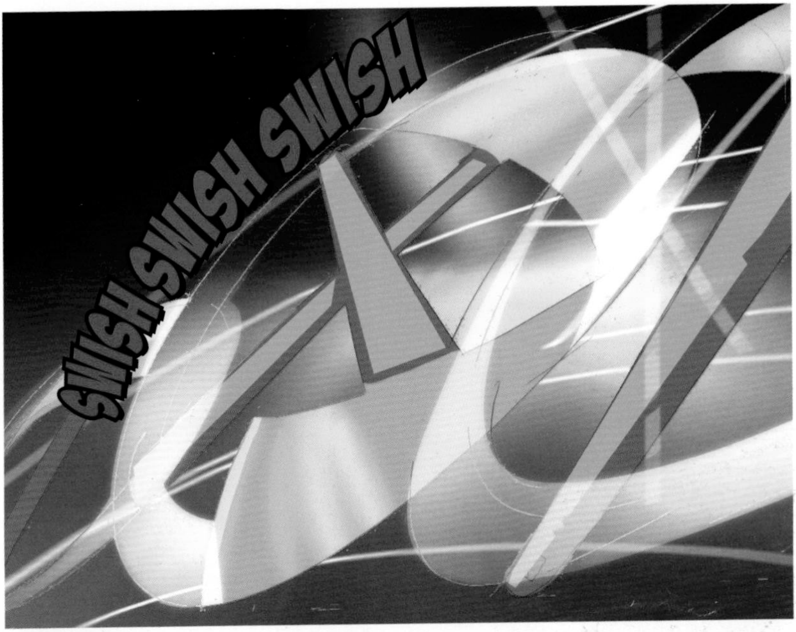
SWISH SWISH SWISH

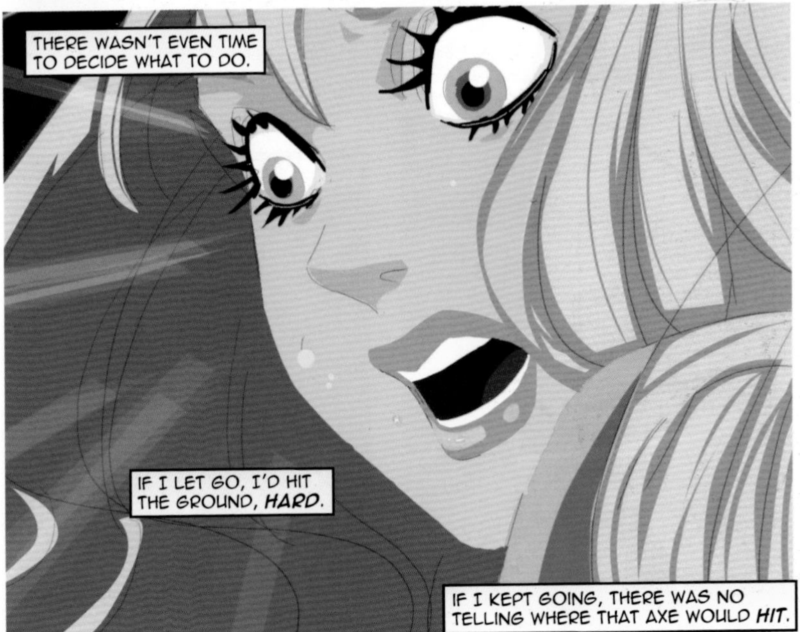
THERE WASN'T EVEN TIME TO DECIDE WHAT TO DO.
IF I LET GO, I'D HIT THE GROUND, *HARD*.
IF I KEPT GOING, THERE WAS NO TELLING WHERE THAT AXE WOULD *HIT*.

SLEEECCHH

THE LAST THING I SAW WAS A LIGHT COMING DOWN THROUGH THE HOLE ABOVE. FOR A SINGLE SECOND, I WONDERED WHERE IT COULD BE COMING FROM.

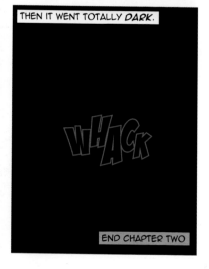

THEN IT WENT TOTALLY *DARK*.

WHACK

END CHAPTER TWO

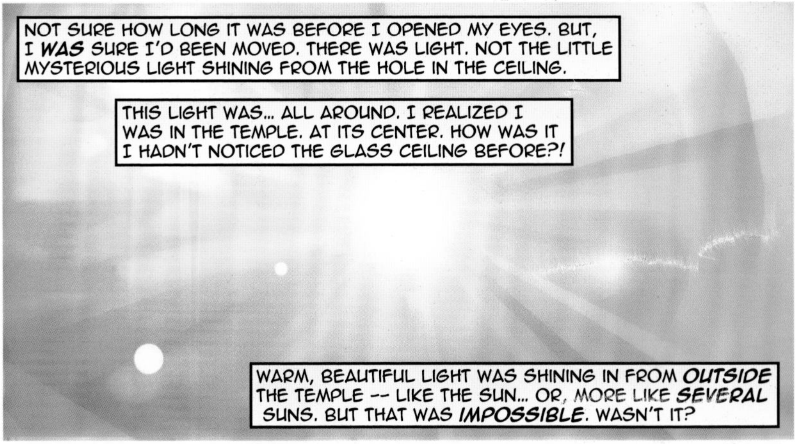
NOT SURE HOW LONG IT WAS BEFORE I OPENED MY EYES. BUT, I *WAS* SURE I'D BEEN MOVED. THERE WAS LIGHT. NOT THE LITTLE MYSTERIOUS LIGHT SHINING FROM THE HOLE IN THE CEILING.
THIS LIGHT WAS... ALL AROUND. I REALIZED I WAS IN THE TEMPLE. AT ITS CENTER. HOW WAS IT I HADN'T NOTICED THE GLASS CEILING BEFORE?!
WARM, BEAUTIFUL LIGHT WAS SHINING IN FROM *OUTSIDE* THE TEMPLE -- LIKE THE SUN... OR, MORE LIKE *SEVERAL* SUNS. BUT THAT WAS *IMPOSSIBLE*. WASN'T IT?

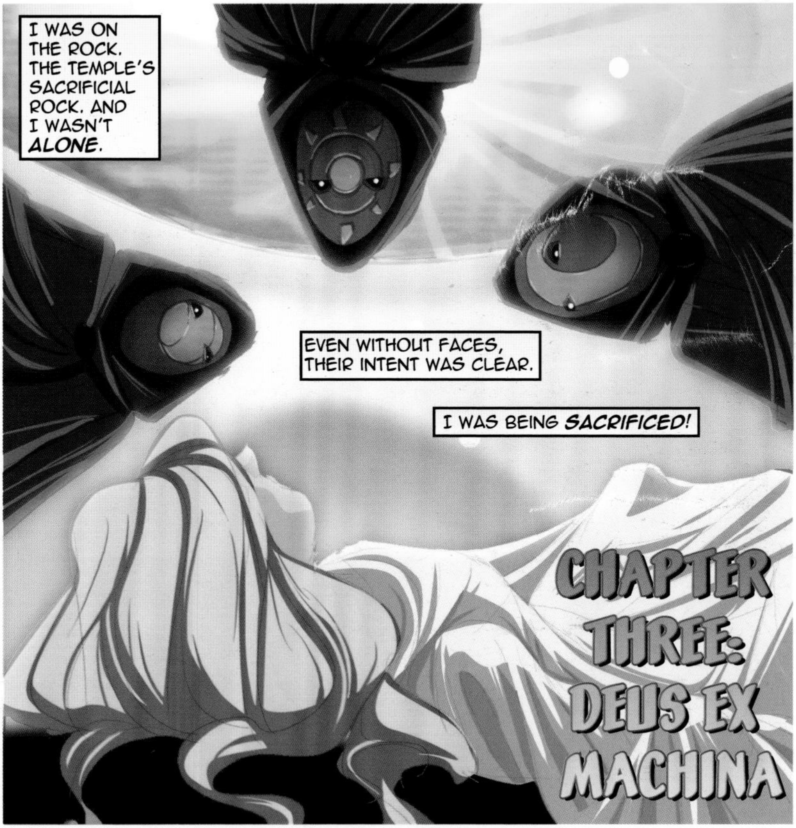
I WAS ON THE ROCK. THE TEMPLE'S SACRIFICIAL ROCK. AND I WASN'T *ALONE*.
EVEN WITHOUT FACES, THEIR INTENT WAS CLEAR.
I WAS BEING *SACRIFICED*!
CHAPTER THREE: DEUS EX MACHINA

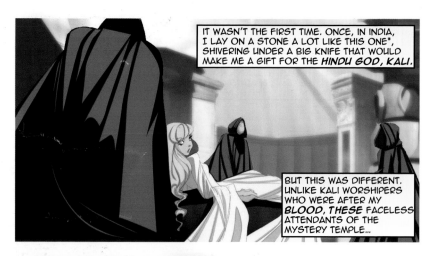

IT WASN'T THE FIRST TIME. ONCE, IN INDIA, I LAY ON A STONE A LOT LIKE THIS ONE*, SHIVERING UNDER A BIG KNIFE THAT WOULD MAKE ME A GIFT FOR THE *HINDU GOD, KALI.*

BUT THIS WAS DIFFERENT. UNLIKE KALI WORSHIPERS WHO WERE AFTER MY *BLOOD, THESE* FACELESS ATTENDANTS OF THE MYSTERY TEMPLE...

...WERE MORE INTO MY *BRAIN!*

BOY, I'D HAD SOME *STRANGE* DREAMS IN TURKEY.

"WAKE UP, NANCY!"

★ *See NANCY DREW DIARIES Volume 2 "The Girl Who Wasn't There."*

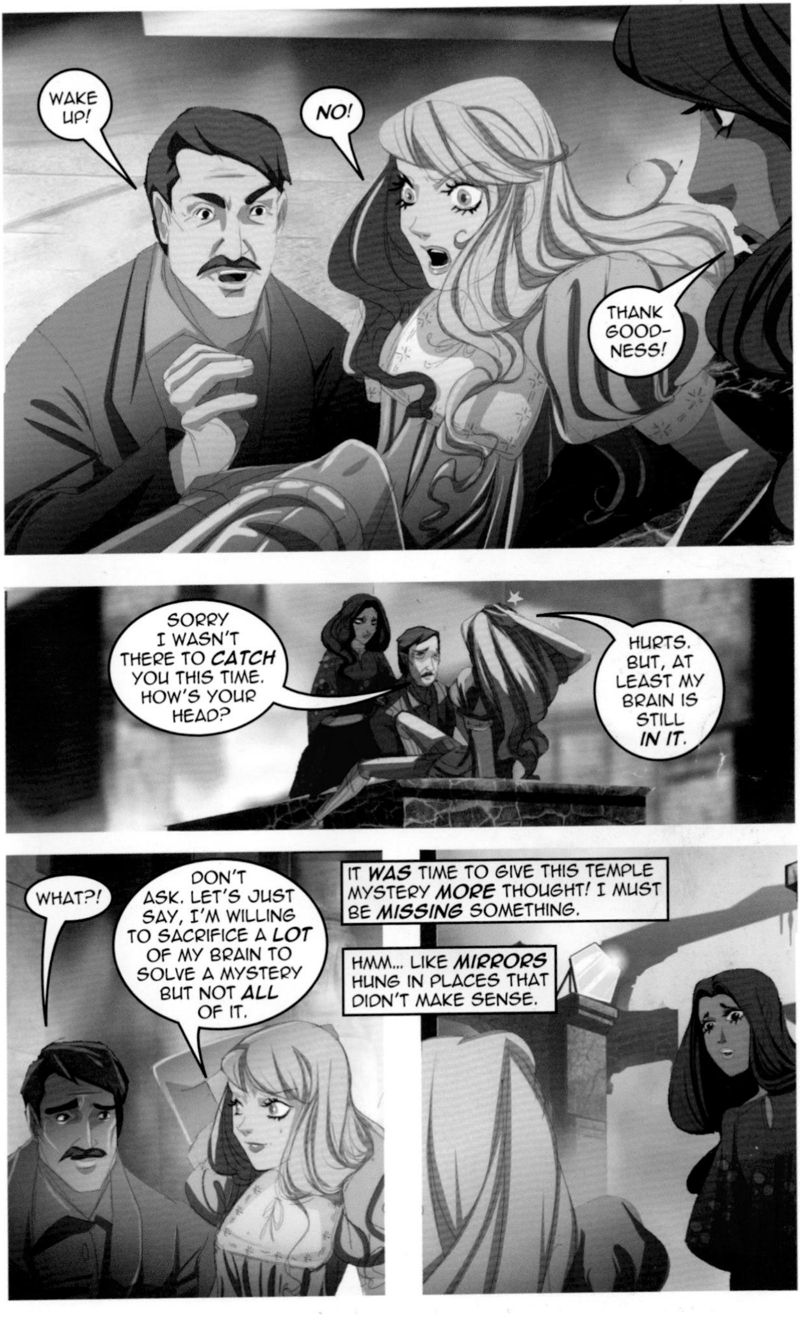
WAKE UP!
NO!
THANK GOOD-NESS!
SORRY I WASN'T THERE TO CATCH YOU THIS TIME. HOW'S YOUR HEAD?
HURTS. BUT, AT LEAST MY BRAIN IS STILL IN IT.
WHAT?!
DON'T ASK. LET'S JUST SAY, I'M WILLING TO SACRIFICE A LOT OF MY BRAIN TO SOLVE A MYSTERY BUT NOT ALL OF IT.
IT WAS TIME TO GIVE THIS TEMPLE MYSTERY MORE THOUGHT! I MUST BE MISSING SOMETHING.
HMM... LIKE MIRRORS HUNG IN PLACES THAT DIDN'T MAKE SENSE.

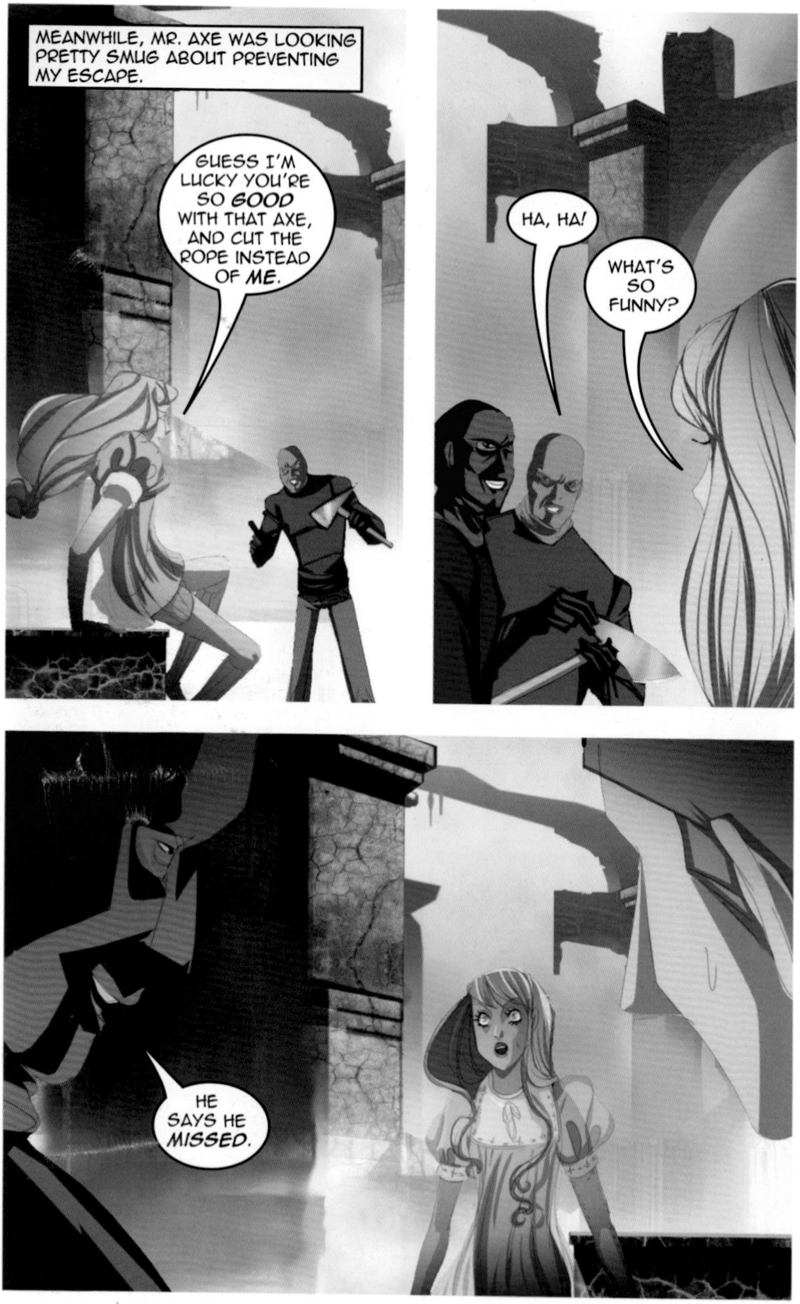
MEANWHILE, MR. AXE WAS LOOKING PRETTY SMUG ABOUT PREVENTING MY ESCAPE.
GUESS I'M LUCKY YOU'RE SO GOOD WITH THAT AXE, AND CUT THE ROPE INSTEAD OF ME.
HA, HA!
WHAT'S SO FUNNY?
HE SAYS HE MISSED.

HE MAY HAVE THOUGHT IT *FUNNY* THAT HE DIDN'T REMOVE MY HEAD...

...BUT THERE WAS NO LAUGHING AT THE FACT THAT THE BLADE HAD CUT SHORT THE *ONLY* ESCAPE FROM WHAT WAS RAPIDLY BECOMING A WATERY *GRAVE*. THE ROPE WAS NOW TOO SHORT FOR ANYONE TO REACH.

AND THE HOPEFUL LITTLE LIGHT IN THE HOLE HAD GONE *DARK*. OR HAD I DREAMT THAT, TOO?

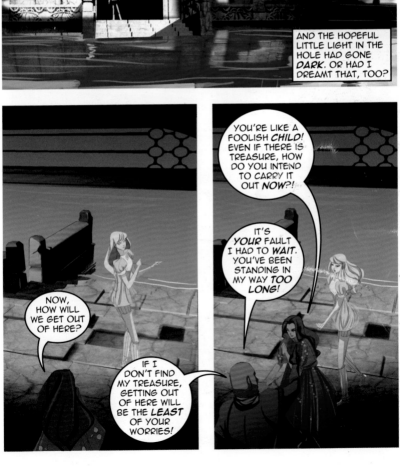

YOU'RE LIKE A FOOLISH *CHILD!* EVEN IF THERE IS TREASURE, HOW DO YOU INTEND TO *CARRY* IT OUT *NOW?!*

IT'S *YOUR* FAULT I HAD TO *WAIT*. YOU'VE BEEN STANDING IN MY WAY *TOO LONG!*

NOW, HOW WILL WE GET OUT OF HERE?

IF I DON'T FIND MY TREASURE, GETTING OUT OF HERE WILL BE THE *LEAST* OF YOUR WORRIES!

- 135 -

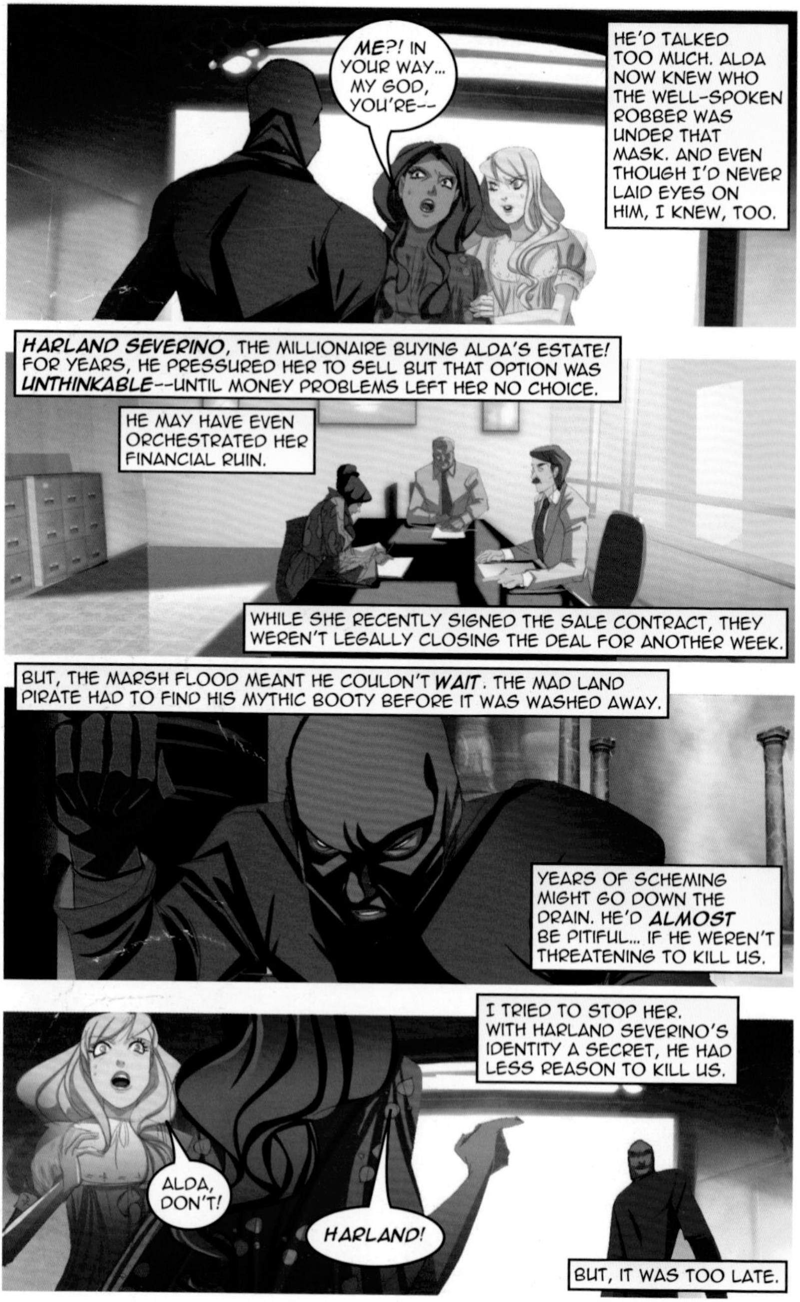
ME?! IN YOUR WAY... MY GOD, YOU'RE--
HE'D TALKED TOO MUCH. ALDA NOW KNEW WHO THE WELL-SPOKEN ROBBER WAS UNDER THAT MASK. AND EVEN THOUGH I'D NEVER LAID EYES ON HIM, I KNEW, TOO.
HARLAND SEVERINO, THE MILLIONAIRE BUYING ALDA'S ESTATE! FOR YEARS, HE PRESSURED HER TO SELL BUT THAT OPTION WAS UNTHINKABLE--UNTIL MONEY PROBLEMS LEFT HER NO CHOICE.
HE MAY HAVE EVEN ORCHESTRATED HER FINANCIAL RUIN.
WHILE SHE RECENTLY SIGNED THE SALE CONTRACT, THEY WEREN'T LEGALLY CLOSING THE DEAL FOR ANOTHER WEEK.
BUT, THE MARSH FLOOD MEANT HE COULDN'T WAIT. THE MAD LAND PIRATE HAD TO FIND HIS MYTHIC BOOTY BEFORE IT WAS WASHED AWAY.
YEARS OF SCHEMING MIGHT GO DOWN THE DRAIN. HE'D ALMOST BE PITIFUL... IF HE WEREN'T THREATENING TO KILL US.
I TRIED TO STOP HER. WITH HARLAND SEVERINO'S IDENTITY A SECRET, HE HAD LESS REASON TO KILL US.
ALDA, DON'T!
HARLAND!
BUT, IT WAS TOO LATE.

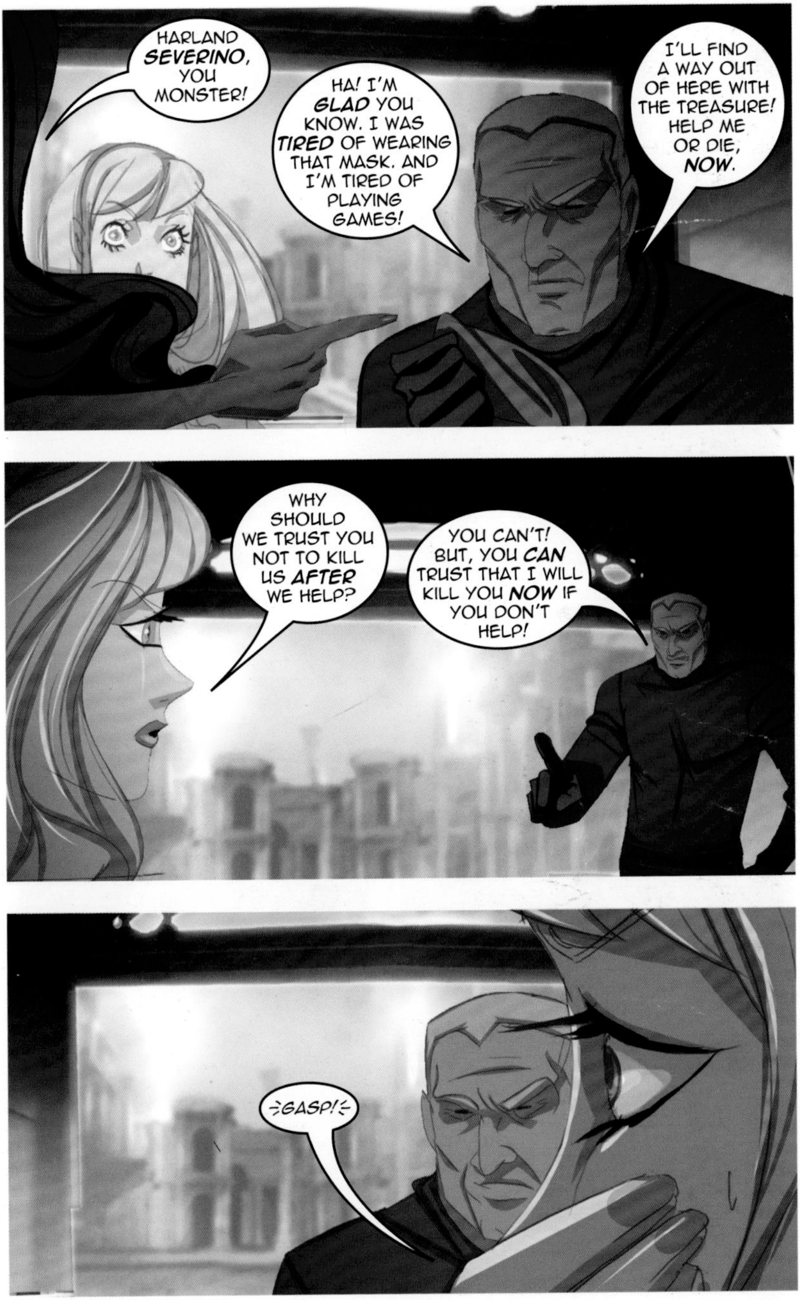
HARLAND SEVERINO, YOU MONSTER!
HA! I'M GLAD YOU KNOW. I WAS TIRED OF WEARING THAT MASK. AND I'M TIRED OF PLAYING GAMES!
I'LL FIND A WAY OUT OF HERE WITH THE TREASURE! HELP ME OR DIE, NOW.
WHY SHOULD WE TRUST YOU NOT TO KILL US AFTER WE HELP?
YOU CAN'T! BUT, YOU CAN TRUST THAT I WILL KILL YOU NOW IF YOU DON'T HELP!
GASP!

TOVIK!

THAT ROPE SEEMED GOOD FOR NOTHING BUT FALLING FROM.

LUCKILY, *WATER* WOULDN'T HURT AS MUCH AS *STONE*.

ASSUMING TOVIK COULD *SWIM!*

I'M COMING, TOVIK!

NO. I'LL GO!

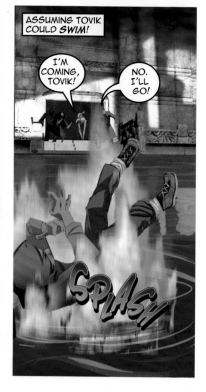

SPLASH

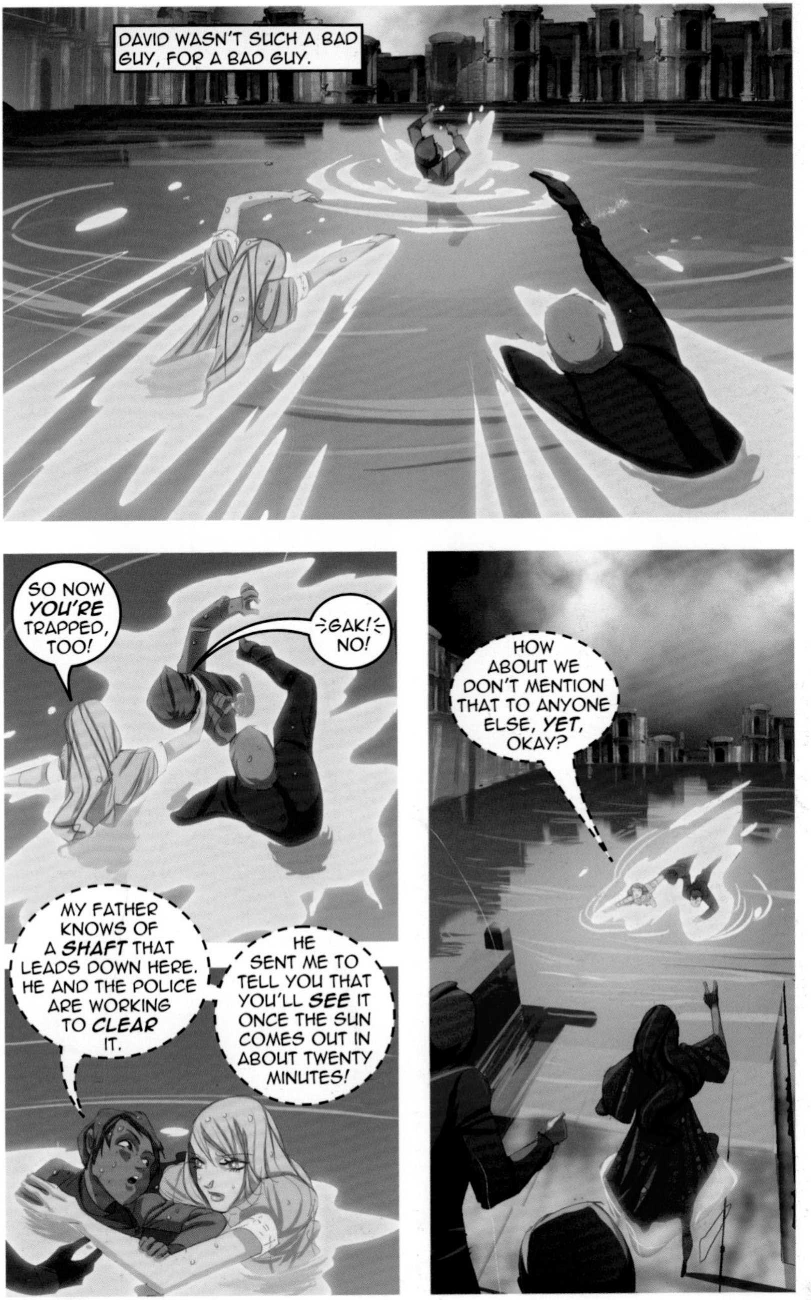
DAVID WASN'T SUCH A BAD GUY, FOR A BAD GUY.
SO NOW YOU'RE TRAPPED, TOO!
GAK! NO!
MY FATHER KNOWS OF A SHAFT THAT LEADS DOWN HERE. HE AND THE POLICE ARE WORKING TO CLEAR IT.
HE SENT ME TO TELL YOU THAT YOU'LL SEE IT ONCE THE SUN COMES OUT IN ABOUT TWENTY MINUTES!
HOW ABOUT WE DON'T MENTION THAT TO ANYONE ELSE, YET, OKAY?

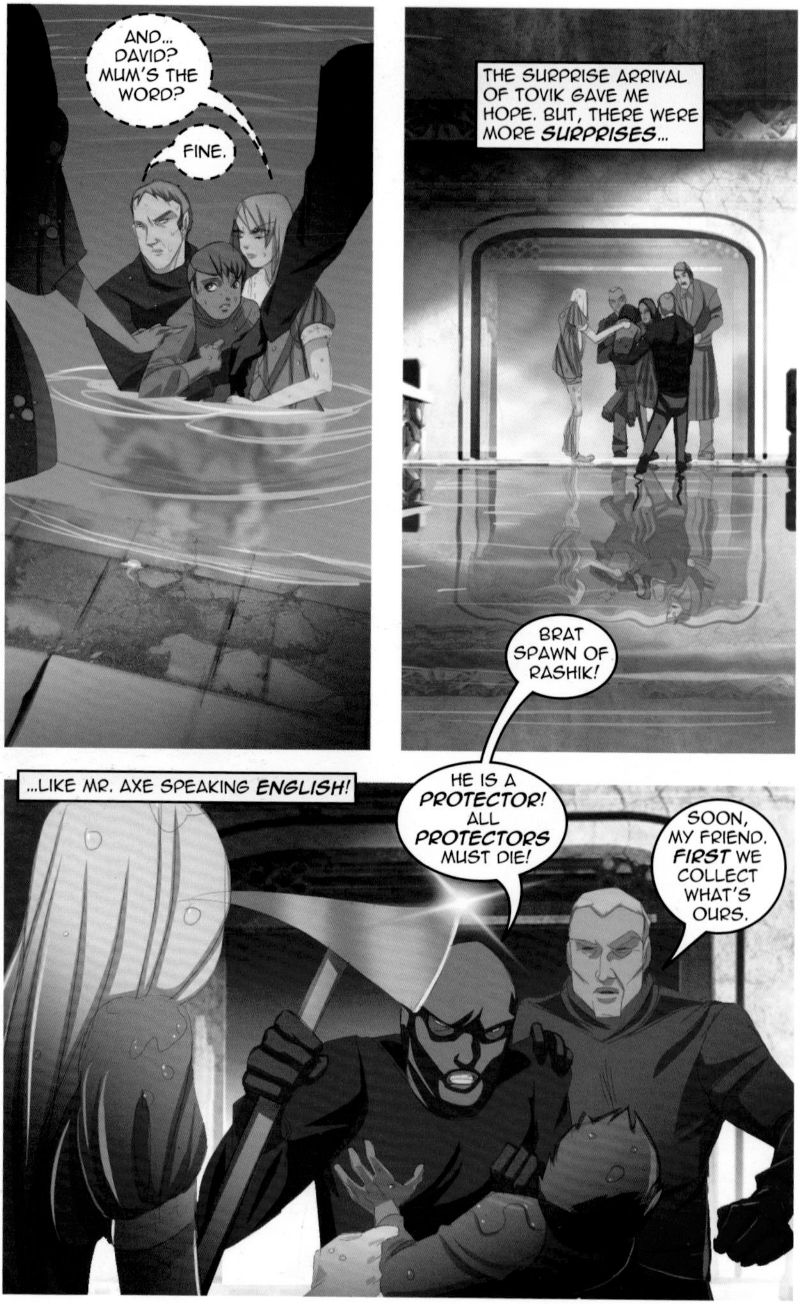
AND... DAVID? MUM'S THE WORD?
FINE.
THE SURPRISE ARRIVAL OF TOVIK GAVE ME HOPE. BUT, THERE WERE MORE **SURPRISES**...
BRAT SPAWN OF RASHIK!
...LIKE MR. AXE SPEAKING **ENGLISH**!
HE IS A **PROTECTOR**! ALL **PROTECTORS** MUST DIE!
SOON, MY FRIEND. **FIRST** WE COLLECT WHAT'S OURS.

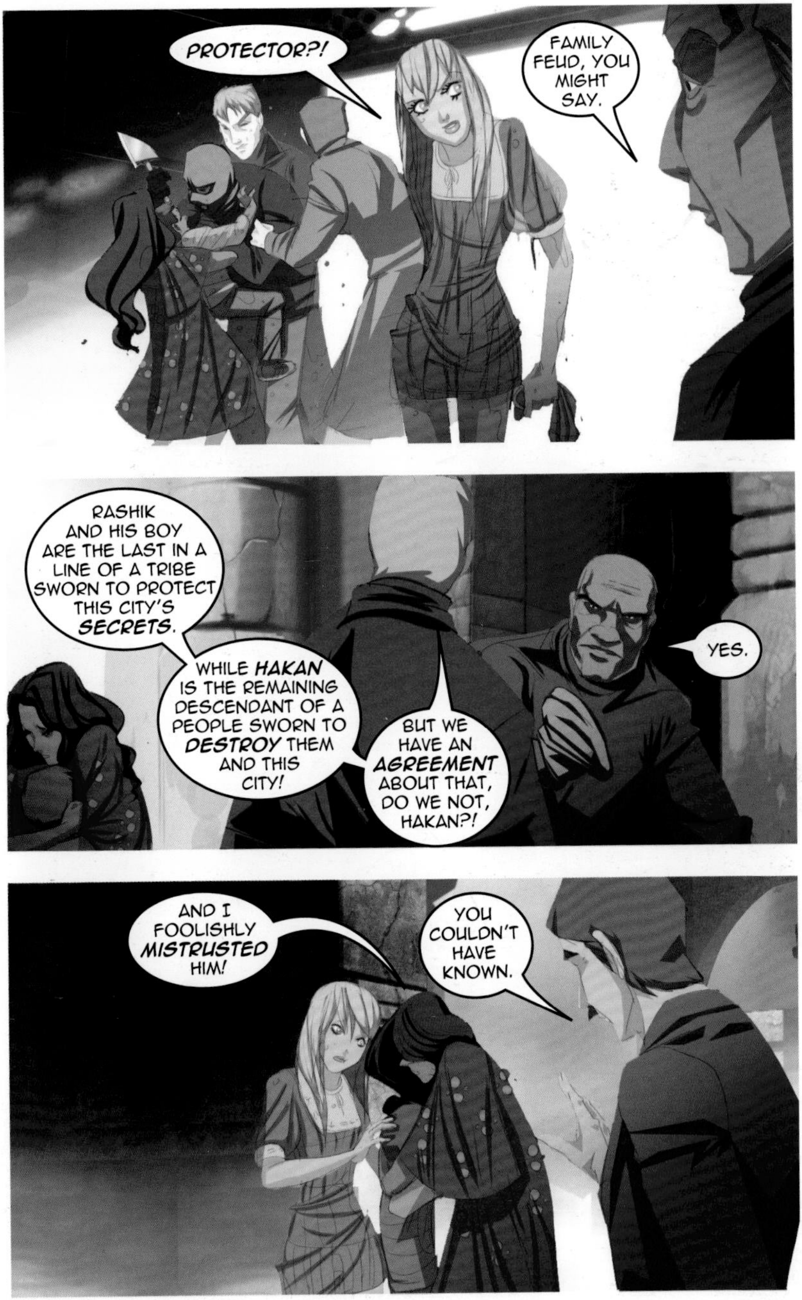
PROTECTOR?!
FAMILY FEUD, YOU MIGHT SAY.
RASHIK AND HIS BOY ARE THE LAST IN A LINE OF A TRIBE SWORN TO PROTECT THIS CITY'S SECRETS.
WHILE HAKAN IS THE REMAINING DESCENDANT OF A PEOPLE SWORN TO DESTROY THEM AND THIS CITY!
BUT WE HAVE AN AGREEMENT ABOUT THAT, DO WE NOT, HAKAN?!
YES.
AND I FOOLISHLY MISTRUSTED HIM!
YOU COULDN'T HAVE KNOWN.

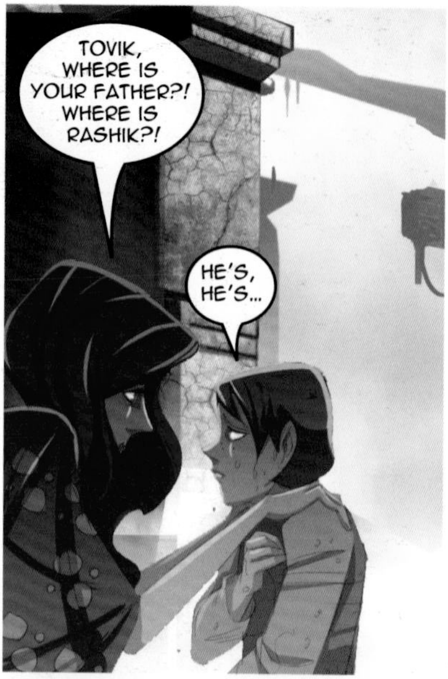
TOVIK, WHERE IS YOUR FATHER?! WHERE IS RASHIK?!
HE'S, HE'S...

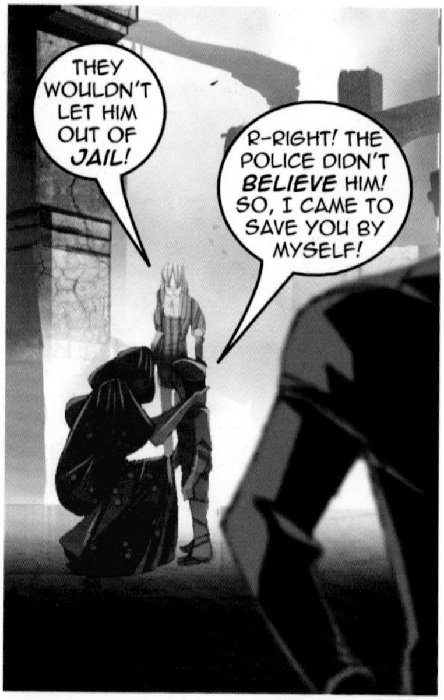
THEY WOULDN'T LET HIM OUT OF JAIL!
R-RIGHT! THE POLICE DIDN'T BELIEVE HIM! SO, I CAME TO SAVE YOU BY MYSELF!

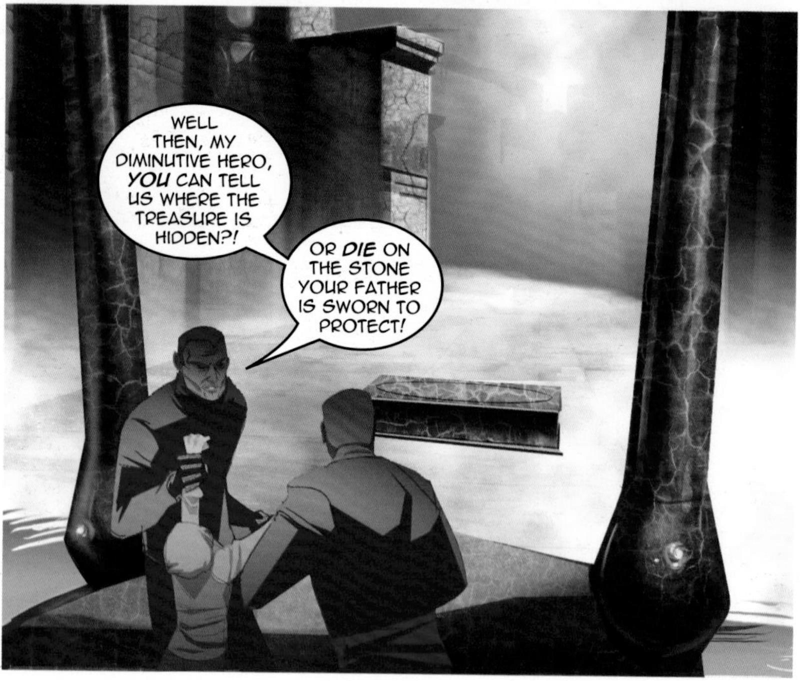
WELL THEN, MY DIMINUTIVE HERO, YOU CAN TELL US WHERE THE TREASURE IS HIDDEN?!
OR DIE ON THE STONE YOUR FATHER IS SWORN TO PROTECT!

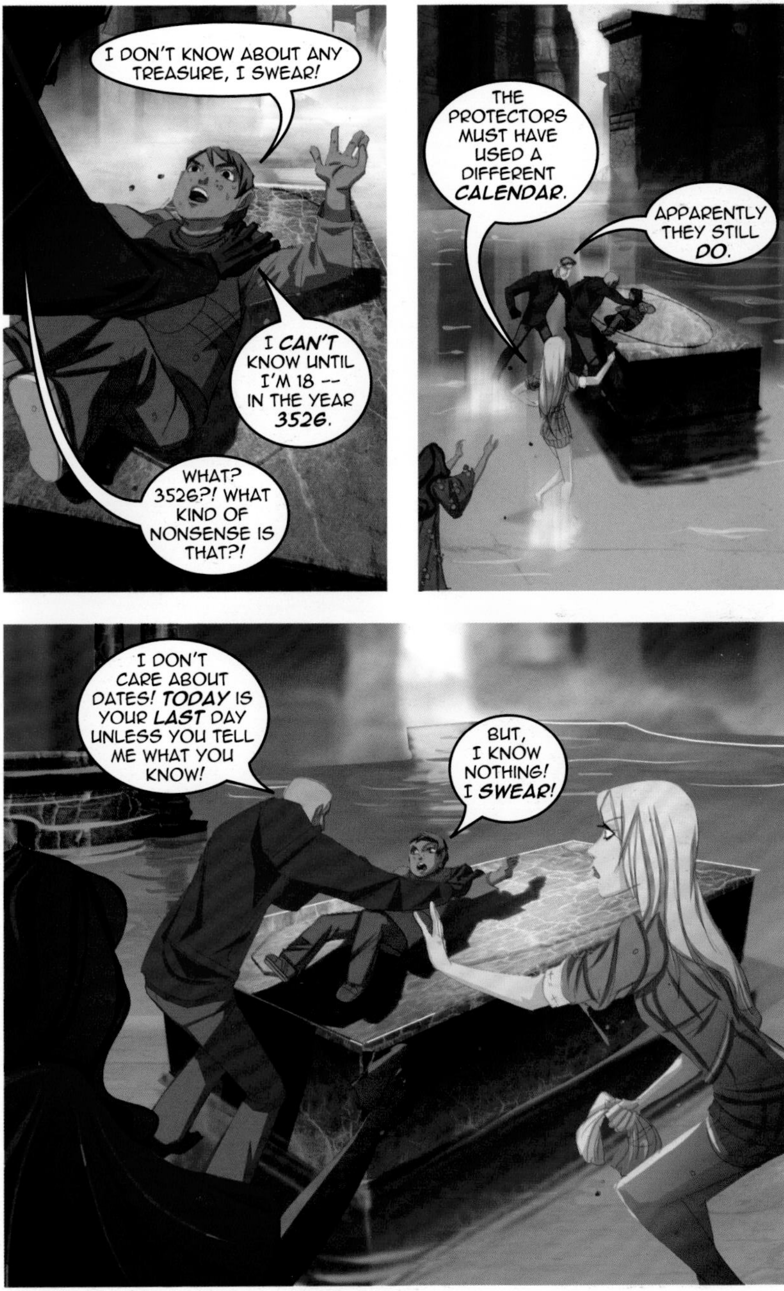
I DON'T KNOW ABOUT ANY TREASURE, I SWEAR!
I CAN'T KNOW UNTIL I'M 18 -- IN THE YEAR 3526.
WHAT? 3526?! WHAT KIND OF NONSENSE IS THAT?!
THE PROTECTORS MUST HAVE USED A DIFFERENT CALENDAR.
APPARENTLY THEY STILL DO.
I DON'T CARE ABOUT DATES! TODAY IS YOUR LAST DAY UNLESS YOU TELL ME WHAT YOU KNOW!
BUT, I KNOW NOTHING! I SWEAR!

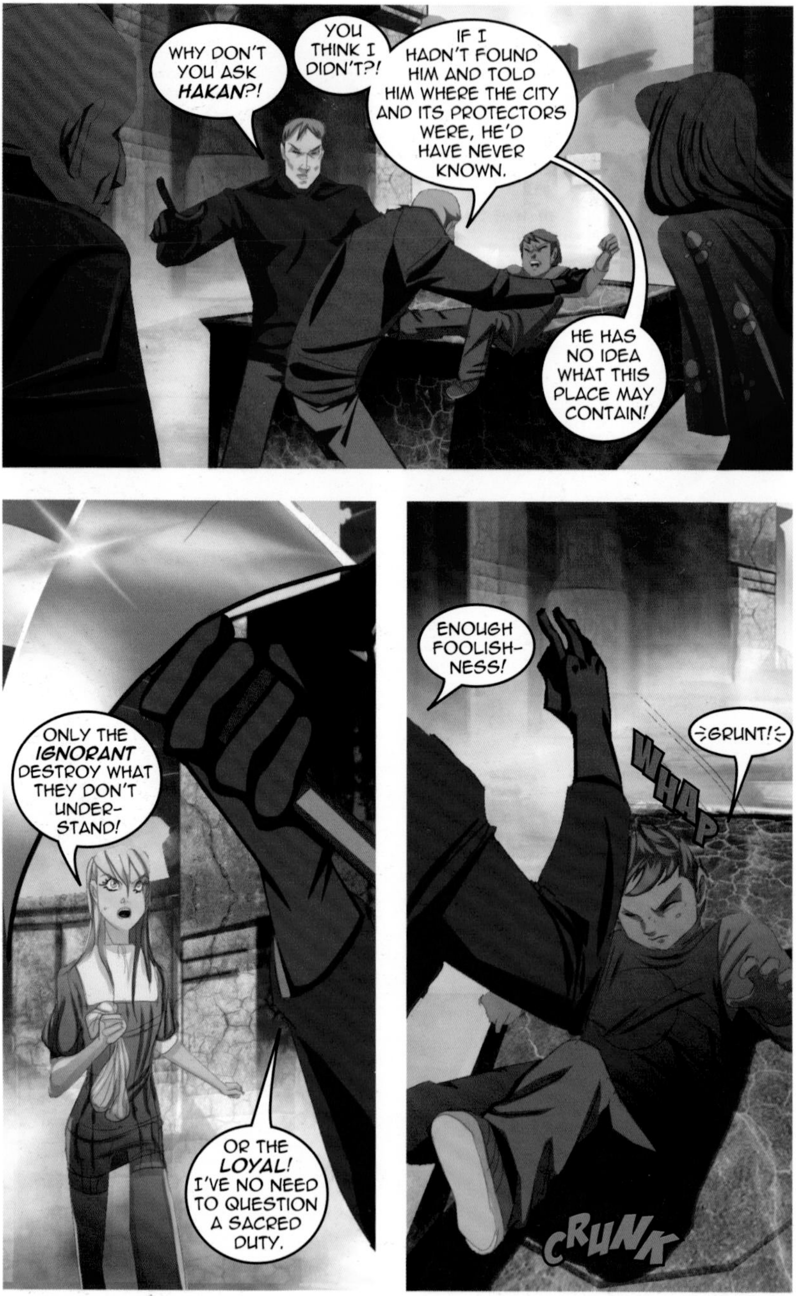
WHY DON'T YOU ASK *HAKAN*?!
YOU THINK I DIDN'T?!
IF I HADN'T FOUND HIM AND TOLD HIM WHERE THE CITY AND ITS PROTECTORS WERE, HE'D HAVE NEVER KNOWN.
HE HAS NO IDEA WHAT THIS PLACE MAY CONTAIN!
ONLY THE *IGNORANT* DESTROY WHAT THEY DON'T UNDER-STAND!
OR THE *LOYAL*! I'VE NO NEED TO QUESTION A SACRED DUTY.
ENOUGH FOOLISH-NESS!
WHAP
GRUNT!
CRUNK

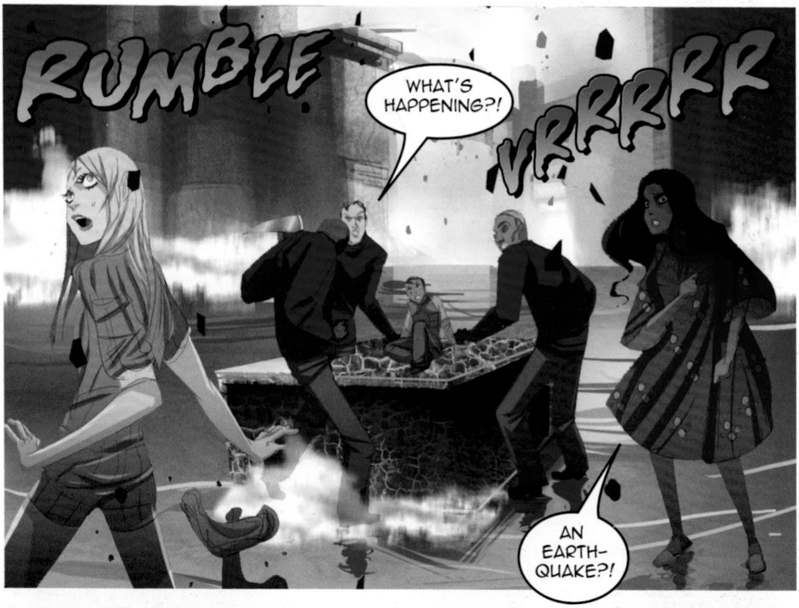
RUMBLE
WHAT'S HAPPENING?!
VRRRRR
AN EARTH-QUAKE?!

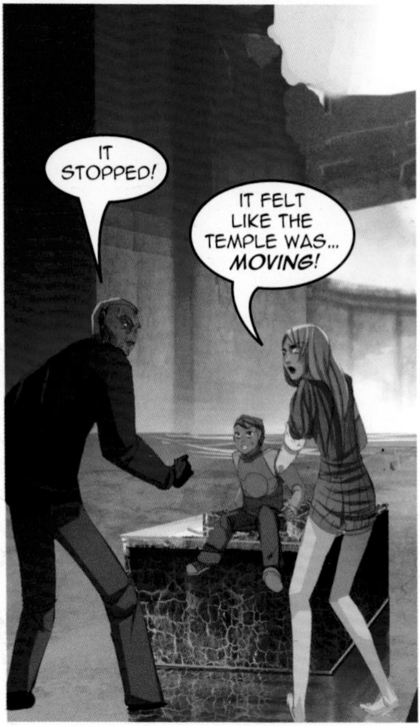
IT STOPPED!
IT FELT LIKE THE TEMPLE WAS... *MOVING*!

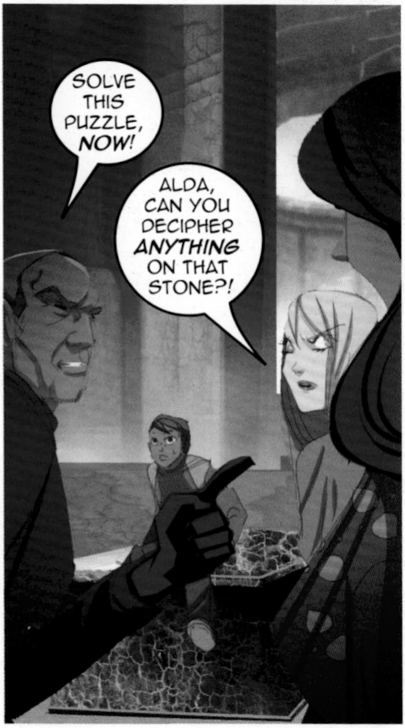
SOLVE THIS PUZZLE, *NOW*!
ALDA, CAN YOU DECIPHER *ANYTHING* ON THAT STONE?!

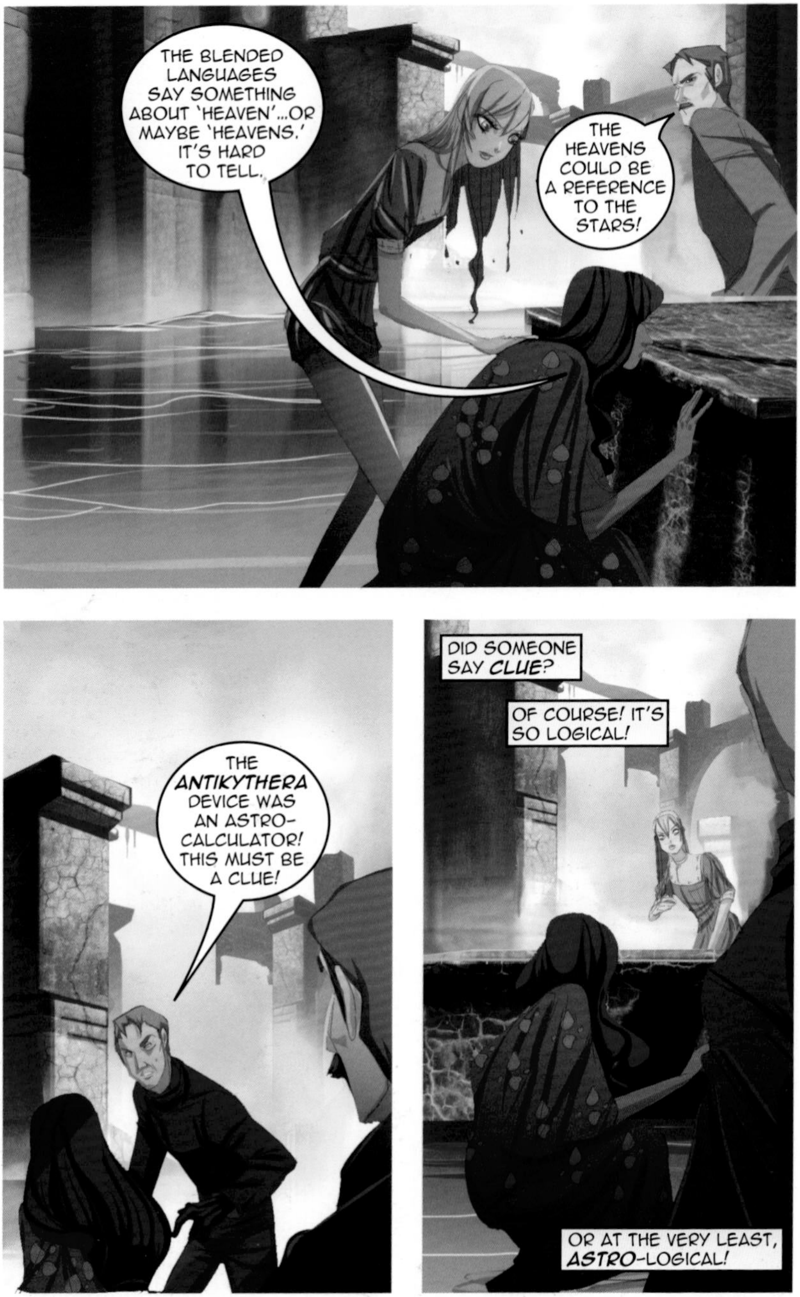
THE BLENDED LANGUAGES SAY SOMETHING ABOUT 'HEAVEN'...OR MAYBE 'HEAVENS.' IT'S HARD TO TELL.
THE HEAVENS COULD BE A REFERENCE TO THE STARS!
THE ANTIKYTHERA DEVICE WAS AN ASTRO-CALCULATOR! THIS MUST BE A CLUE!
DID SOMEONE SAY CLUE?
OF COURSE! IT'S SO LOGICAL!
OR AT THE VERY LEAST, ASTRO-LOGICAL!

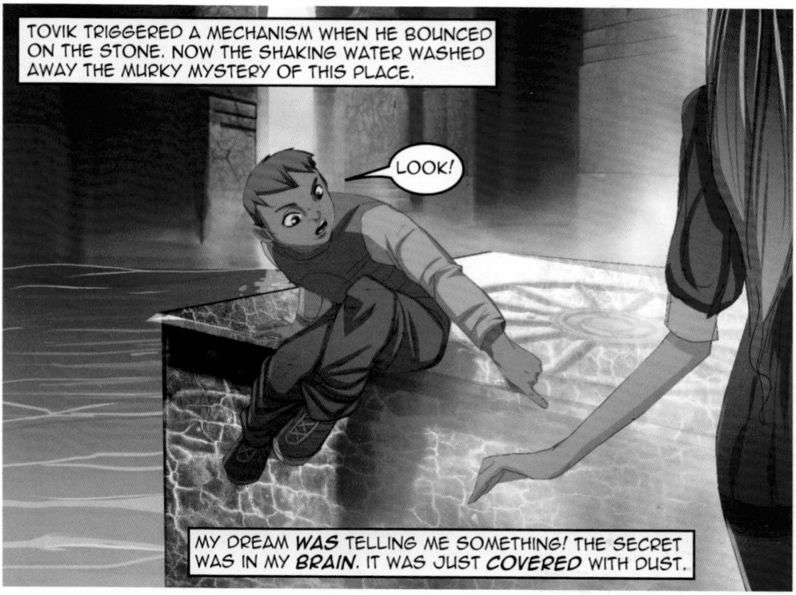
TOVIK TRIGGERED A MECHANISM WHEN HE BOUNCED ON THE STONE. NOW THE SHAKING WATER WASHED AWAY THE MURKY MYSTERY OF THIS PLACE.
LOOK!
MY DREAM WAS TELLING ME SOMETHING! THE SECRET WAS IN MY BRAIN. IT WAS JUST COVERED WITH DUST.

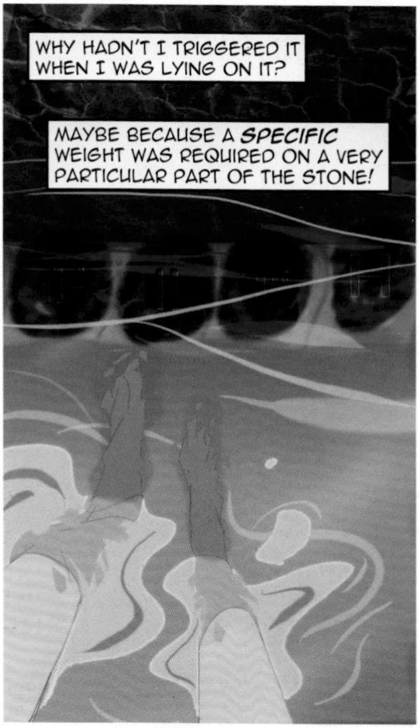
WHY HADN'T I TRIGGERED IT WHEN I WAS LYING ON IT?
MAYBE BECAUSE A SPECIFIC WEIGHT WAS REQUIRED ON A VERY PARTICULAR PART OF THE STONE!

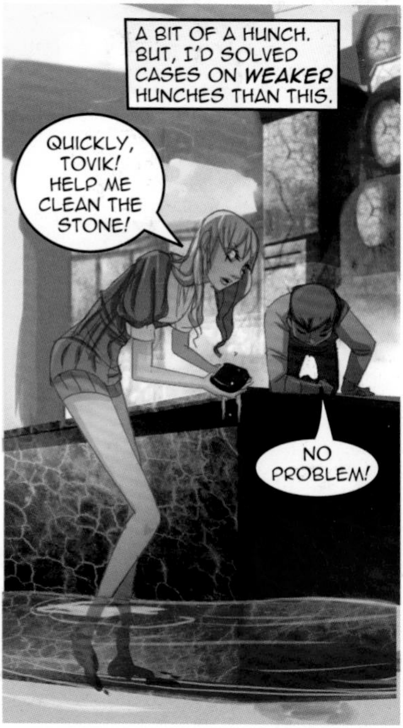
A BIT OF A HUNCH. BUT, I'D SOLVED CASES ON WEAKER HUNCHES THAN THIS.
QUICKLY, TOVIK! HELP ME CLEAN THE STONE!
NO PROBLEM!

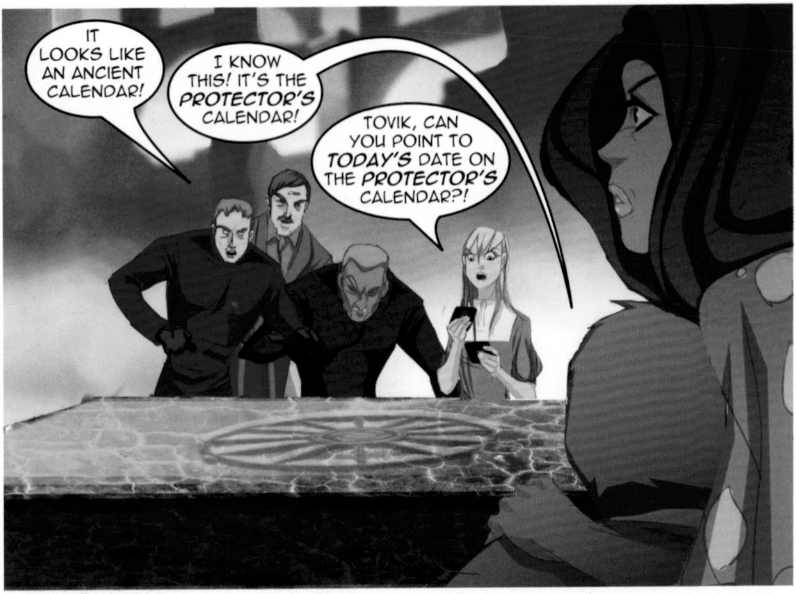
IT LOOKS LIKE AN ANCIENT CALENDAR!
I KNOW THIS! IT'S THE PROTECTOR'S CALENDAR!
TOVIK, CAN YOU POINT TO TODAY'S DATE ON THE PROTECTOR'S CALENDAR?!

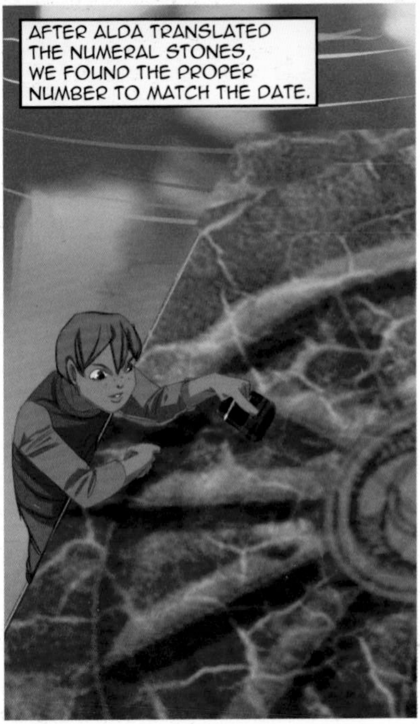
AFTER ALDA TRANSLATED THE NUMERAL STONES, WE FOUND THE PROPER NUMBER TO MATCH THE DATE.

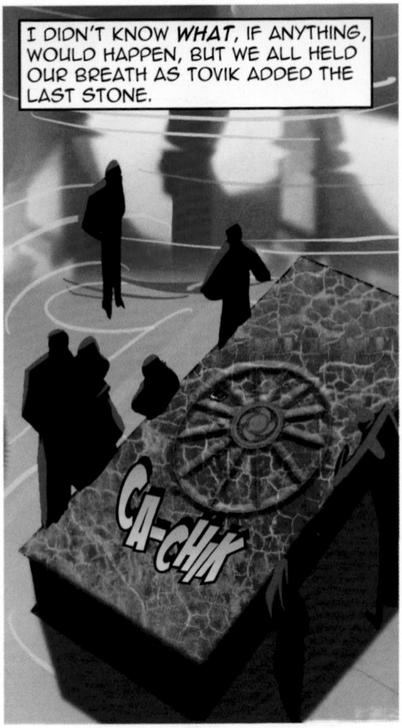
I DIDN'T KNOW WHAT, IF ANYTHING, WOULD HAPPEN, BUT WE ALL HELD OUR BREATH AS TOVIK ADDED THE LAST STONE.
CA-CHIK

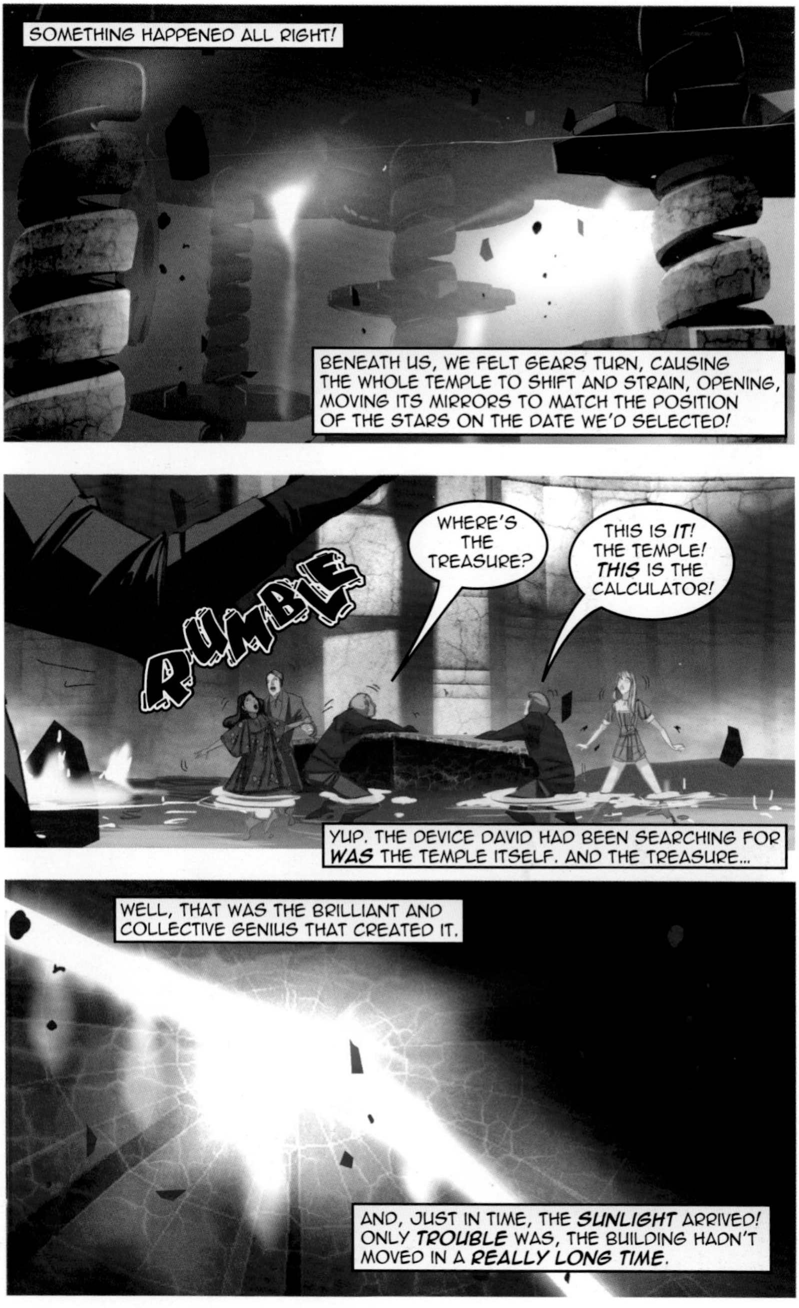
SOMETHING HAPPENED ALL RIGHT!
BENEATH US, WE FELT GEARS TURN, CAUSING THE WHOLE TEMPLE TO SHIFT AND STRAIN, OPENING, MOVING ITS MIRRORS TO MATCH THE POSITION OF THE STARS ON THE DATE WE'D SELECTED!
RUMBLE
WHERE'S THE TREASURE?
THIS IS IT! THE TEMPLE! THIS IS THE CALCULATOR!
YUP. THE DEVICE DAVID HAD BEEN SEARCHING FOR WAS THE TEMPLE ITSELF. AND THE TREASURE...
WELL, THAT WAS THE BRILLIANT AND COLLECTIVE GENIUS THAT CREATED IT.
AND, JUST IN TIME, THE SUNLIGHT ARRIVED! ONLY TROUBLE WAS, THE BUILDING HADN'T MOVED IN A REALLY LONG TIME.

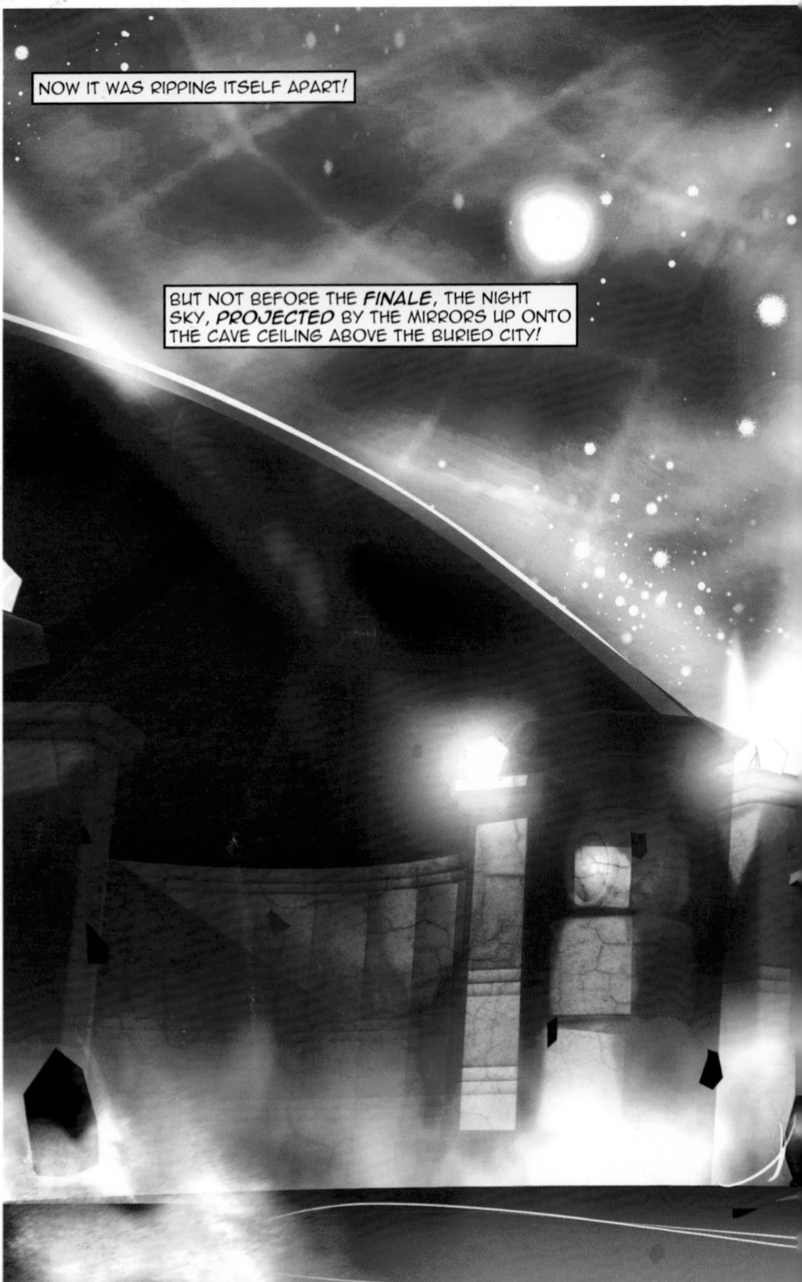
NOW IT WAS RIPPING ITSELF APART!
BUT NOT BEFORE THE FINALE, THE NIGHT SKY, PROJECTED BY THE MIRRORS UP ONTO THE CAVE CEILING ABOVE THE BURIED CITY!

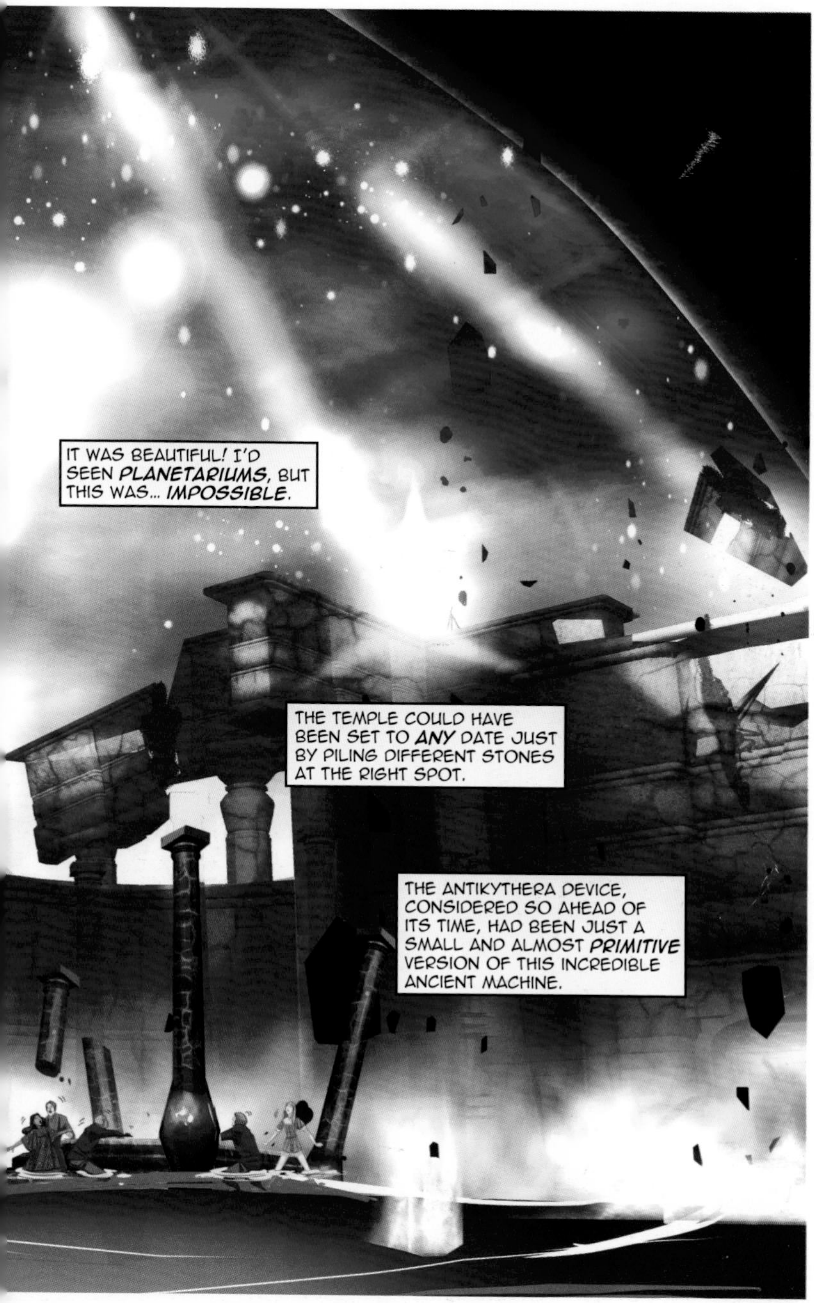
IT WAS BEAUTIFUL! I'D SEEN PLANETARIUMS, BUT THIS WAS... IMPOSSIBLE.
THE TEMPLE COULD HAVE BEEN SET TO ANY DATE JUST BY PILING DIFFERENT STONES AT THE RIGHT SPOT.
THE ANTIKYTHERA DEVICE, CONSIDERED SO AHEAD OF ITS TIME, HAD BEEN JUST A SMALL AND ALMOST PRIMITIVE VERSION OF THIS INCREDIBLE ANCIENT MACHINE.

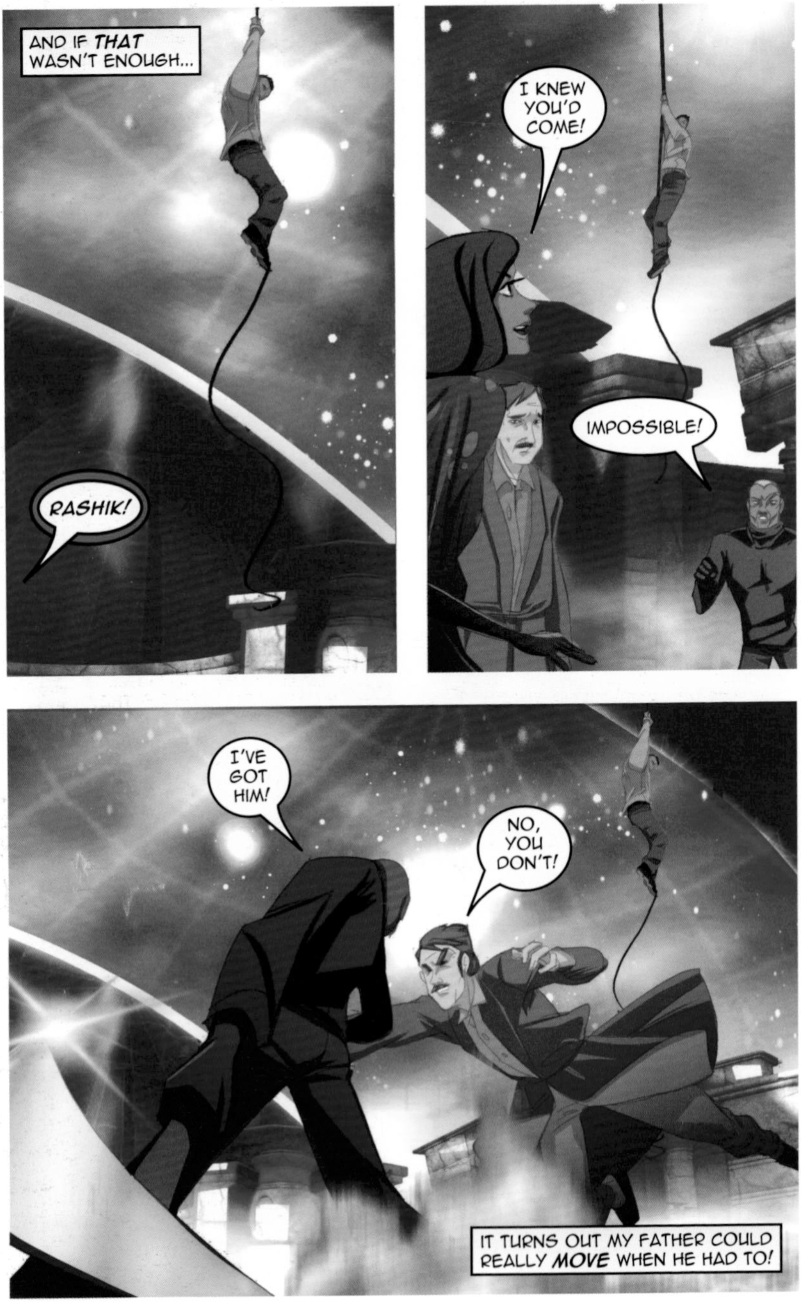
AND IF THAT WASN'T ENOUGH...
RASHIK!
I KNEW YOU'D COME!
IMPOSSIBLE!
I'VE GOT HIM!
NO, YOU DON'T!
IT TURNS OUT MY FATHER COULD REALLY MOVE WHEN HE HAD TO!

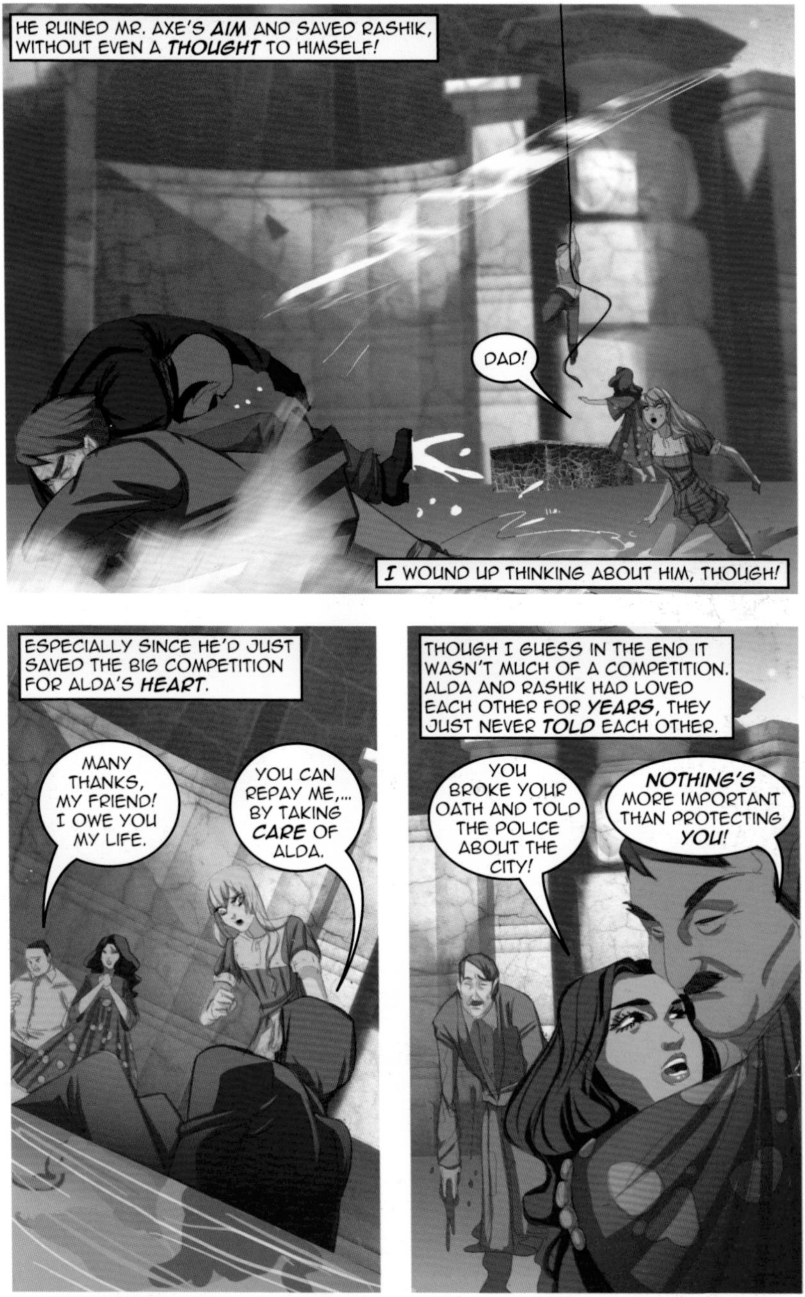
HE RUINED MR. AXE'S AIM AND SAVED RASHIK, WITHOUT EVEN A THOUGHT TO HIMSELF!
DAD!
I WOUND UP THINKING ABOUT HIM, THOUGH!
ESPECIALLY SINCE HE'D JUST SAVED THE BIG COMPETITION FOR ALDA'S HEART.
MANY THANKS, MY FRIEND! I OWE YOU MY LIFE.
YOU CAN REPAY ME,... BY TAKING CARE OF ALDA.
THOUGH I GUESS IN THE END IT WASN'T MUCH OF A COMPETITION. ALDA AND RASHIK HAD LOVED EACH OTHER FOR YEARS, THEY JUST NEVER TOLD EACH OTHER.
YOU BROKE YOUR OATH AND TOLD THE POLICE ABOUT THE CITY!
NOTHING'S MORE IMPORTANT THAN PROTECTING YOU!

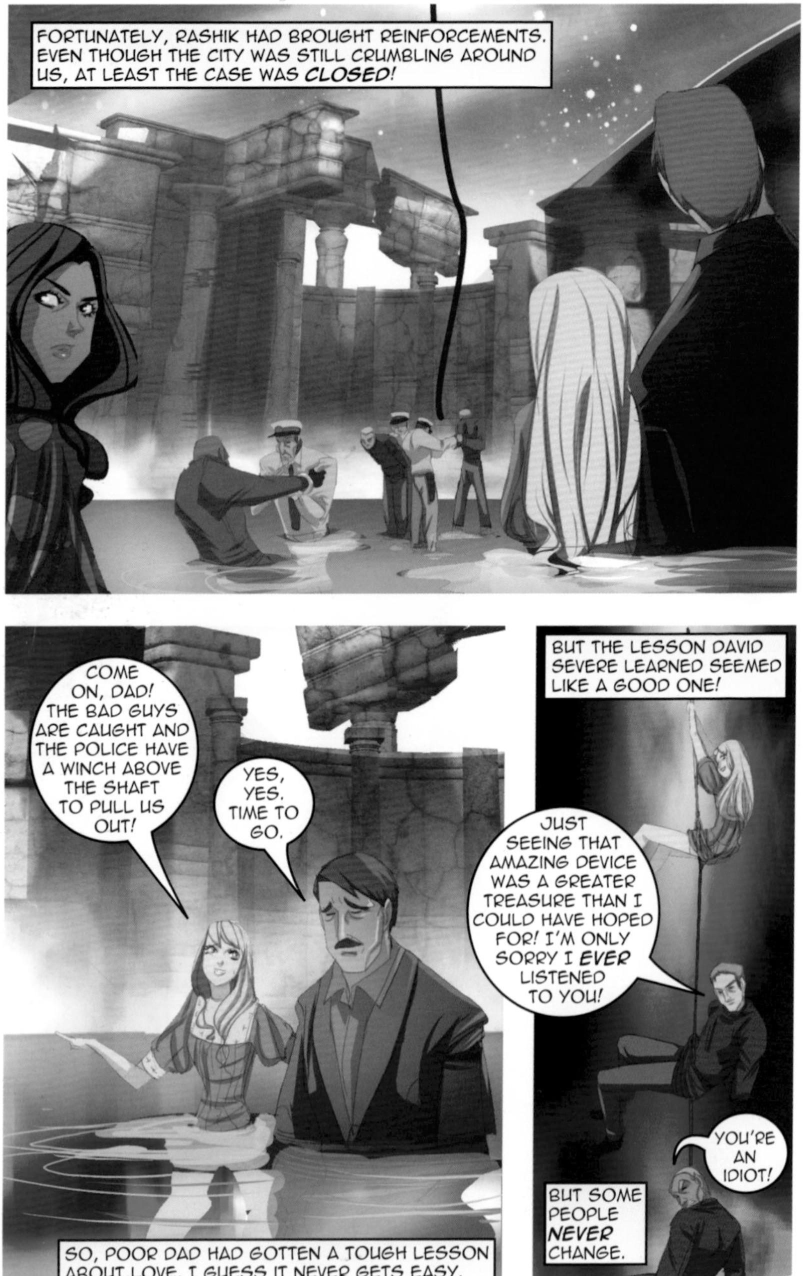
FORTUNATELY, RASHIK HAD BROUGHT REINFORCEMENTS. EVEN THOUGH THE CITY WAS STILL CRUMBLING AROUND US, AT LEAST THE CASE WAS *CLOSED*!
COME ON, DAD! THE BAD GUYS ARE CAUGHT AND THE POLICE HAVE A WINCH ABOVE THE SHAFT TO PULL US OUT!
YES, YES. TIME TO GO.
SO, POOR DAD HAD GOTTEN A TOUGH LESSON ABOUT LOVE. I GUESS IT NEVER GETS EASY.
BUT THE LESSON DAVID SEVERE LEARNED SEEMED LIKE A GOOD ONE!
JUST SEEING THAT AMAZING DEVICE WAS A GREATER TREASURE THAN I COULD HAVE HOPED FOR! I'M ONLY SORRY I *EVER* LISTENED TO YOU!
YOU'RE AN IDIOT!
BUT SOME PEOPLE *NEVER* CHANGE.

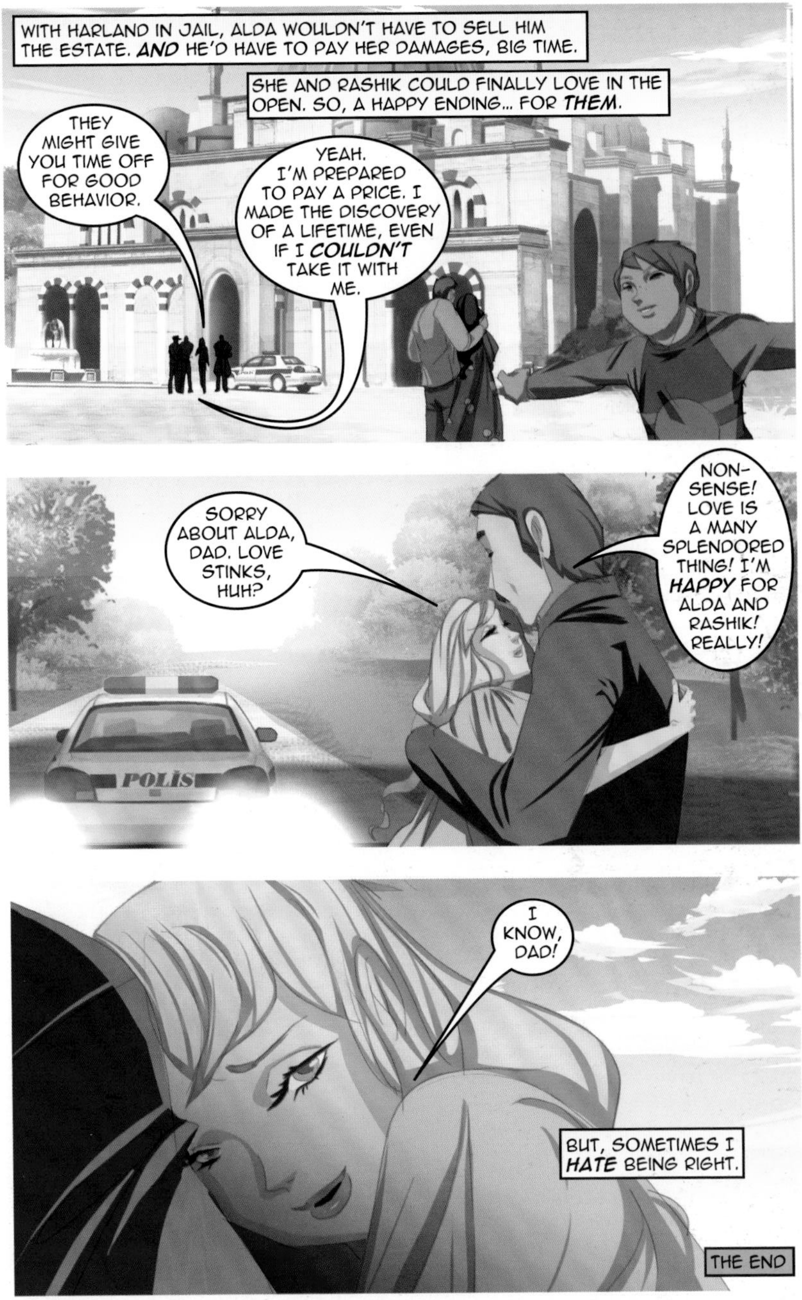
WITH HARLAND IN JAIL, ALDA WOULDN'T HAVE TO SELL HIM THE ESTATE. *AND* HE'D HAVE TO PAY HER DAMAGES, BIG TIME.
SHE AND RASHIK COULD FINALLY LOVE IN THE OPEN. SO, A HAPPY ENDING... FOR *THEM*.
THEY MIGHT GIVE YOU TIME OFF FOR GOOD BEHAVIOR.
YEAH. I'M PREPARED TO PAY A PRICE. I MADE THE DISCOVERY OF A LIFETIME, EVEN IF I *COULDN'T* TAKE IT WITH ME.
SORRY ABOUT ALDA, DAD. LOVE STINKS, HUH?
NON-SENSE! LOVE IS A MANY SPLENDORED THING! I'M *HAPPY* FOR ALDA AND RASHIK! REALLY!
POLIS
I KNOW, DAD!
BUT, SOMETIMES I *HATE* BEING RIGHT.
THE END

WATCH OUT FOR PAPERCUTZ™

Hi, mystery-lovers! Welcome to the ninth NANCY DREW DIARIES graphic novel starring that nighties-wearing, gum-chewing-eschewing-gumshoe Nancy Drew in a special double-length adventure by Stefan Petrucha, Sarah Kinney, Sho Murase, and Carlos Jose Guzman, brought to you by Papercutz—those secretive sorts dedicated to publishing great graphic novels for all ages. I'm Jim Salicrup, the Editor-in-Chief and Hopeless Romantic.

When "Night of the Living Chatchke" and "City Under the Basement" were originally published by Papercutz, it was in two separate volumes – NANCY DREW GIRL DETECTIVE #17 and #18. It's great to finally publish both parts in a single volume. After all, it always seemed like these two stories belonged together. Speaking of which, were Nancy Drew and I the only ones hoping to see Carson Drew and Alda Oktar wind up together? After all, I did say I was a "Hopeless Romantic." But while Nancy does date Ned Nickerson between solving cases, the focus in NANCY DREW DIARIES is on mysteries, not romance. So what's a comics fan looking for romantic adventures to do? Funny I should ask, because Papercutz is about to debut an all-new imprint that embraces just that! It's called Charmz, and here're a few of the titles that'll soon be coming your way...

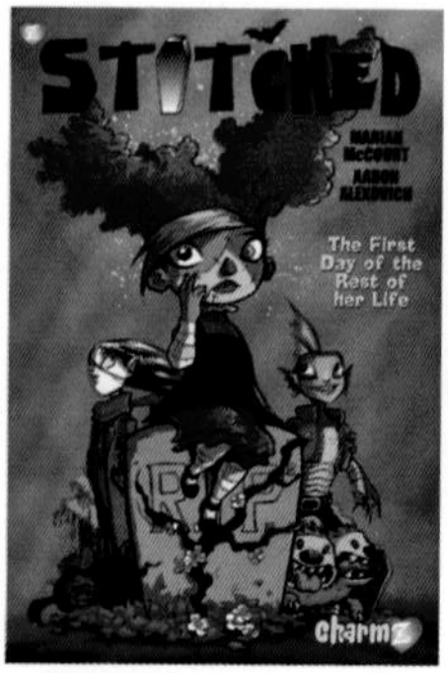
STITCHED
MARIAH McCOURT
AARON ALEXOVICH
The First Day of the Rest of her Life
charmz

First up is STITCHED, by Mariah McCourt, writer (and Charmz Editor), and Aaron Alexovich, artist. STITCHED is a supernatural tale about Crimson Volania Mulch, a rag-doll girl who wakes up in a cemetery, but doesn't know anything except her name. Her first few nights "alive" are a spooky whirlwind of ghosts, werewolves, witches, and weirdly-beautiful boys. Will she find out where she comes from? Do two-headed badger/hedgehogs eat cupcakes? Does Crimson even have time for romance when she doesn't even know who she is? Or does she have to fall apart before she can be whole again?

Next there's SWEETIES, based on Cathy Cassidy's novel *The Chocolate Box Girls*, adapted by Véronique Grisseaux, writer, and Anna Merli, artist, is about blending two families into one. Cherry acquires four half-sisters, Honey, Skye, Summer, and Coco, when her candy-making father Paddy marries their mother, Charlotte. Things get complicated when Cherry falls for Honey's boyfriend and Skye falls in love with the man of her dreams – literally!

Finally (for now) there's CHLOE, by Greg Tessier, writer, and Amandine, co-writer and artist. Chloe Blin is determined to be popular, confident, and in love! Unfortunately she has to deal with mean girl cliques, fashion faux-pas, and trying to impress the cutest boy in school with her sweet moves... only to fall completely flat. Whether it's rocking a party that goes sideways or making the best of a less than ideal vacation, Chloe may not always get it right at first, but she doesn't give up! Charmz editor Mariah McCourt describes what she wants these graphic novels to be like as "the book equivalent of a hot chocolate; sweet, maybe a little dark sometimes, comforting, and made just for you. You can curl up with our tales, settle in, and enjoy falling in love with our characters just like they fall in love with each other."

To get a better idea what these graphic novels are like, check out the special previews of STITCHED, SWEETIES, and CHLOE on the following pages. The graphic novels are available now at booksellers and libraries everywhere.

As for NANCY DREW DIARIES, don't miss the next volume featuring three complete NANCY DREW graphic novels in one – "Cliffhanger," plus parts one and two of "High School Musical Mystery," in which Nancy meets Carolyn Keene's sister-sleuths, the Dana Girls! For romance, we offer Charmz, for mystery, there's always NANCY DREW DIARIES!

Jim

STAY IN TOUCH!

EMAIL:	salicrup@papercutz.com
WEB:	papercutz.com
TWITTER:	@papercutzgn
INSTAGRAM:	@papercutzgn
FACEBOOK:	PAPERCUTZGRAPHICNOVELS
FANMAIL:	Papercutz, 160 Broadway, Suite 700 East Wing, New York, NY 10038

Preview of STITCHED #1 "The First Day of the Rest of her Life," a spooky love story about putting yourself back together!

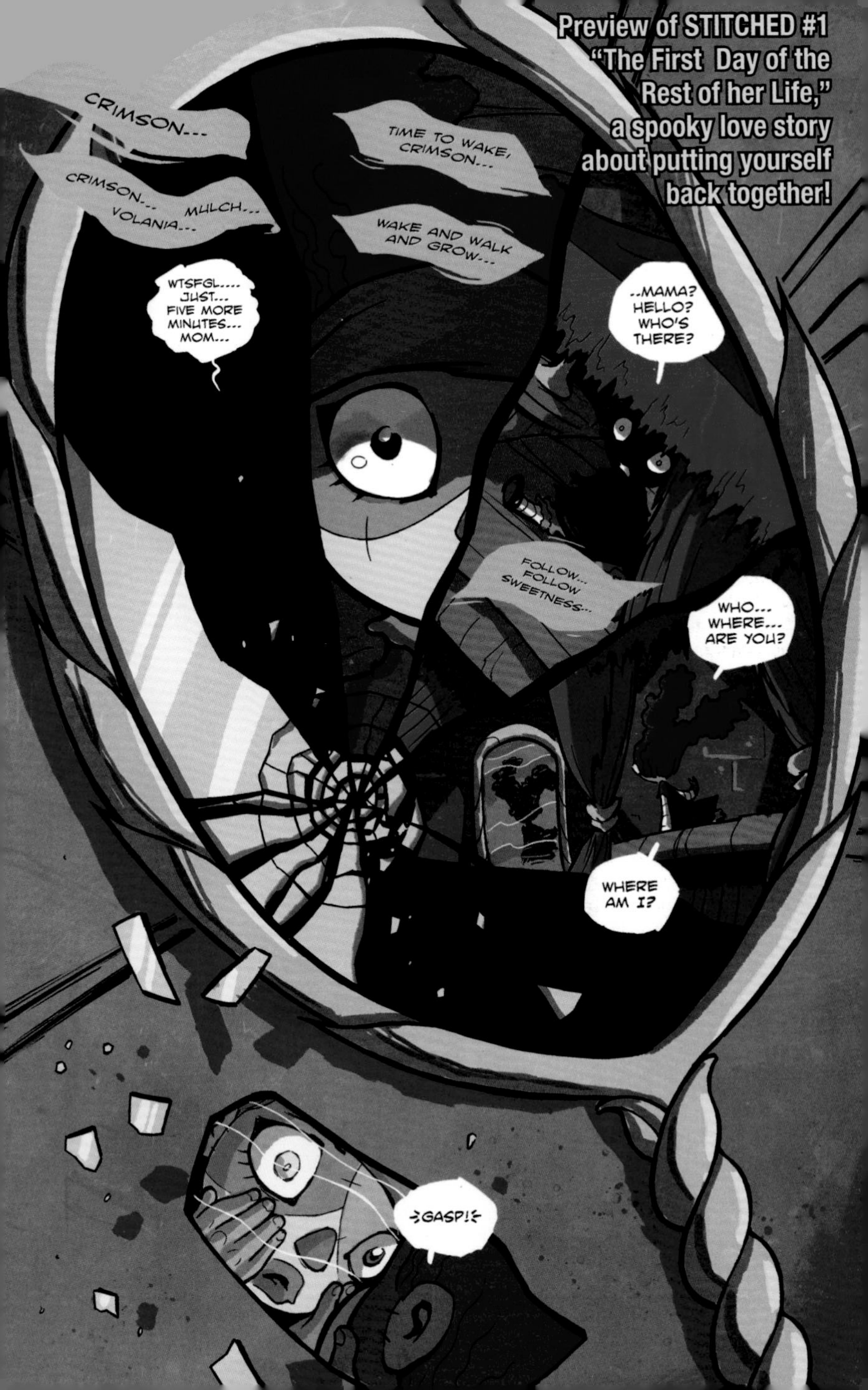

CRIMSON...
CRIMSON... MULCH... VOLANIA...
TIME TO WAKE, CRIMSON...
WAKE AND WALK AND GROW...
WTSFGL.... JUST... FIVE MORE MINUTES... MOM...
..MAMA? HELLO? WHO'S THERE?
FOLLOW... FOLLOW SWEETNESS...
WHO... WHERE... ARE YOU?
WHERE AM I?
≻GASP!≺

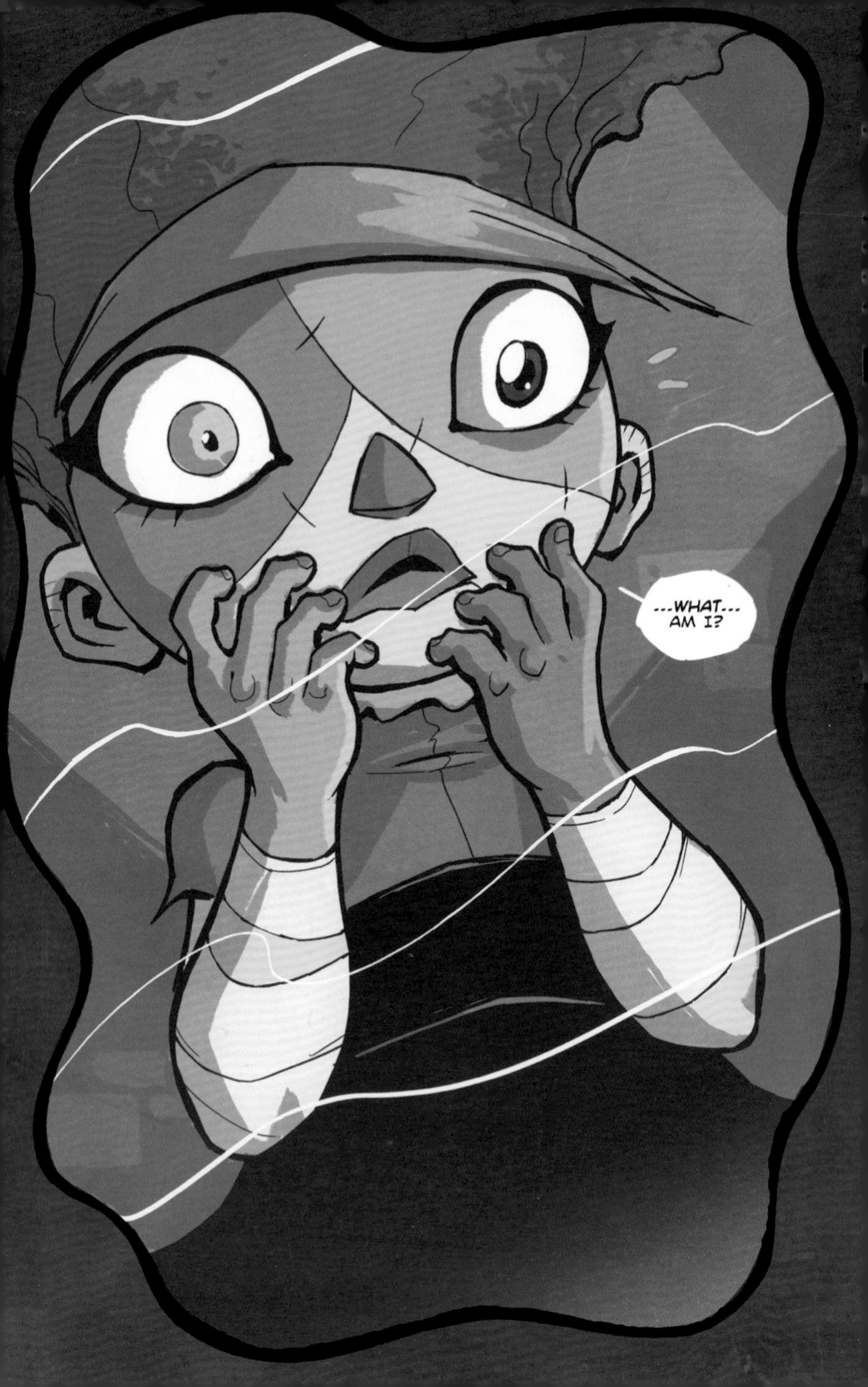
...WHAT... AM I?

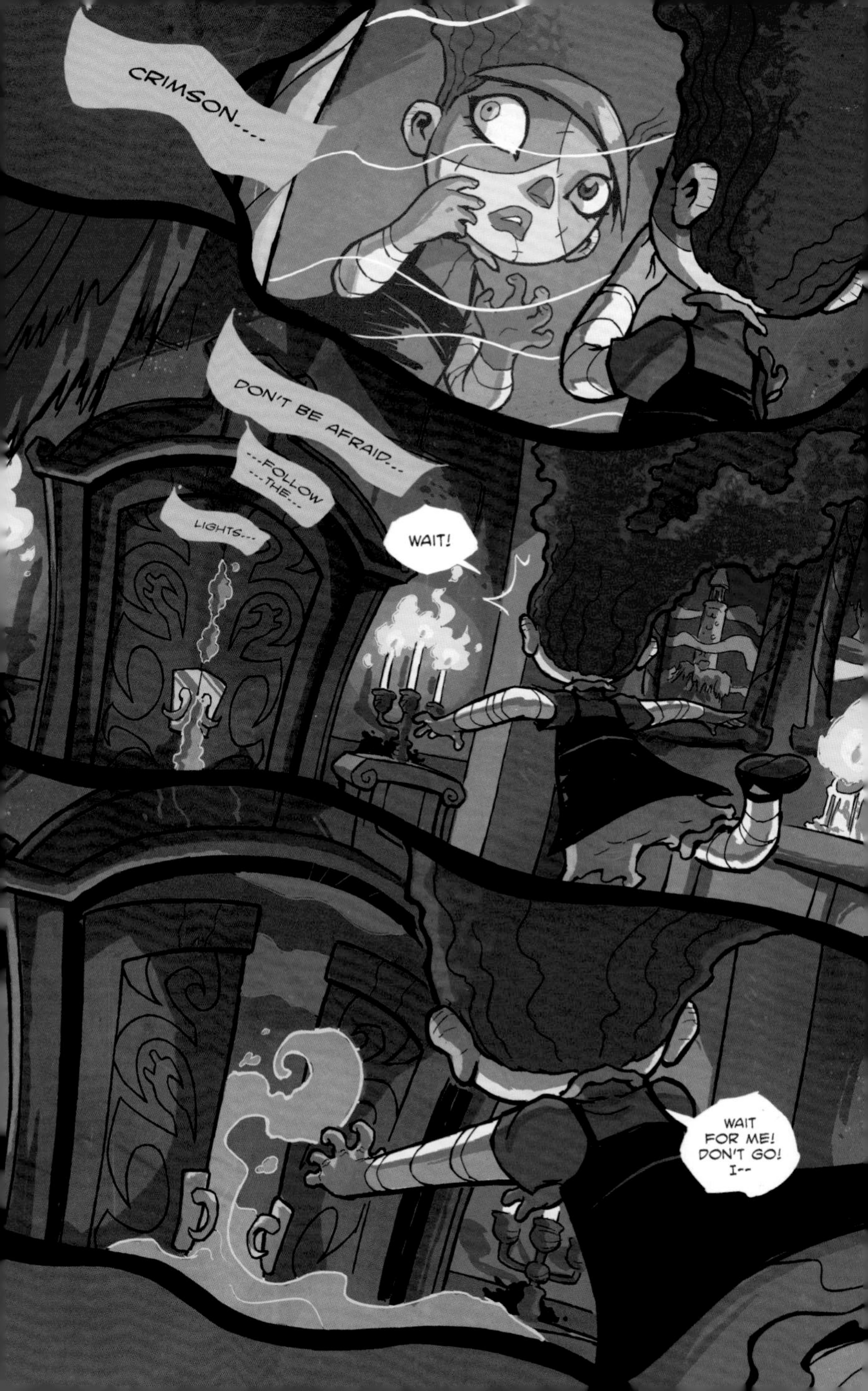
CRIMSON....
DON'T BE AFRAID...
...FOLLOW ...THE...
LIGHTS...
WAIT!
WAIT FOR ME! DON'T GO! I--

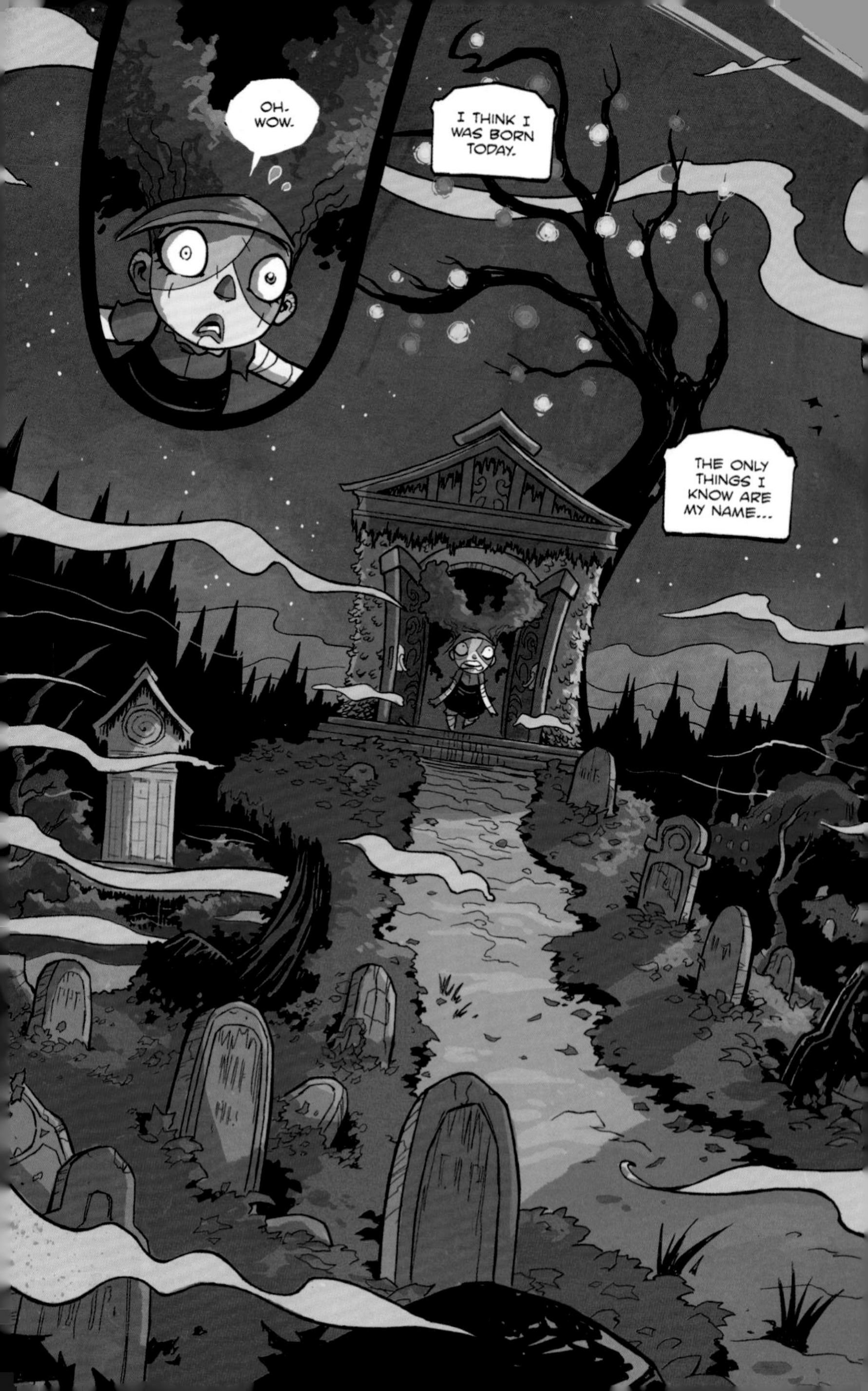
OH. WOW.
I THINK I WAS BORN TODAY.
THE ONLY THINGS I KNOW ARE MY NAME...

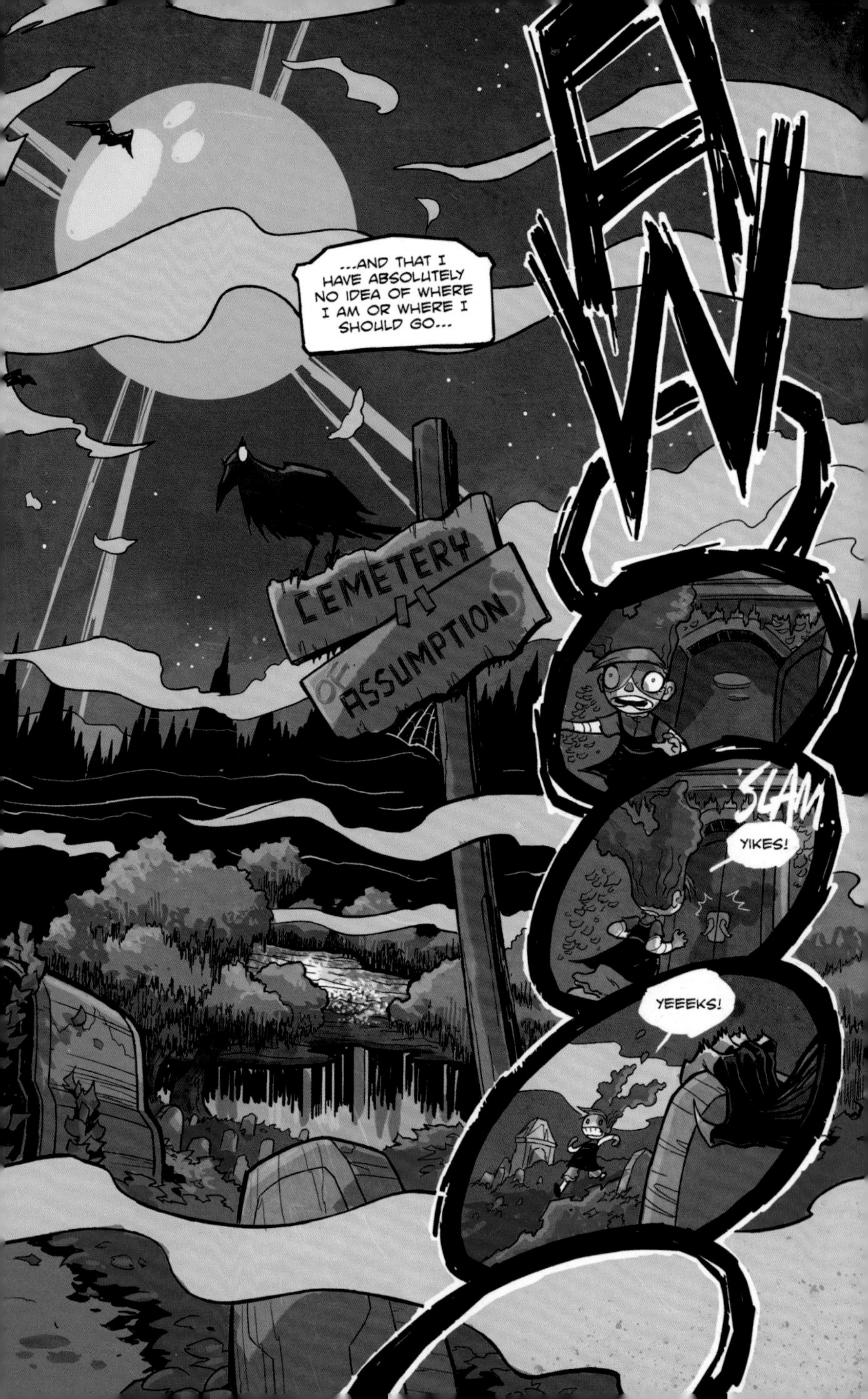
...AND THAT I HAVE ABSOLUTELY NO IDEA OF WHERE I AM OR WHERE I SHOULD GO...
CEMETERY
ASSUMPTIONS
FWW
SLAM
YIKES!
YEEEKS!

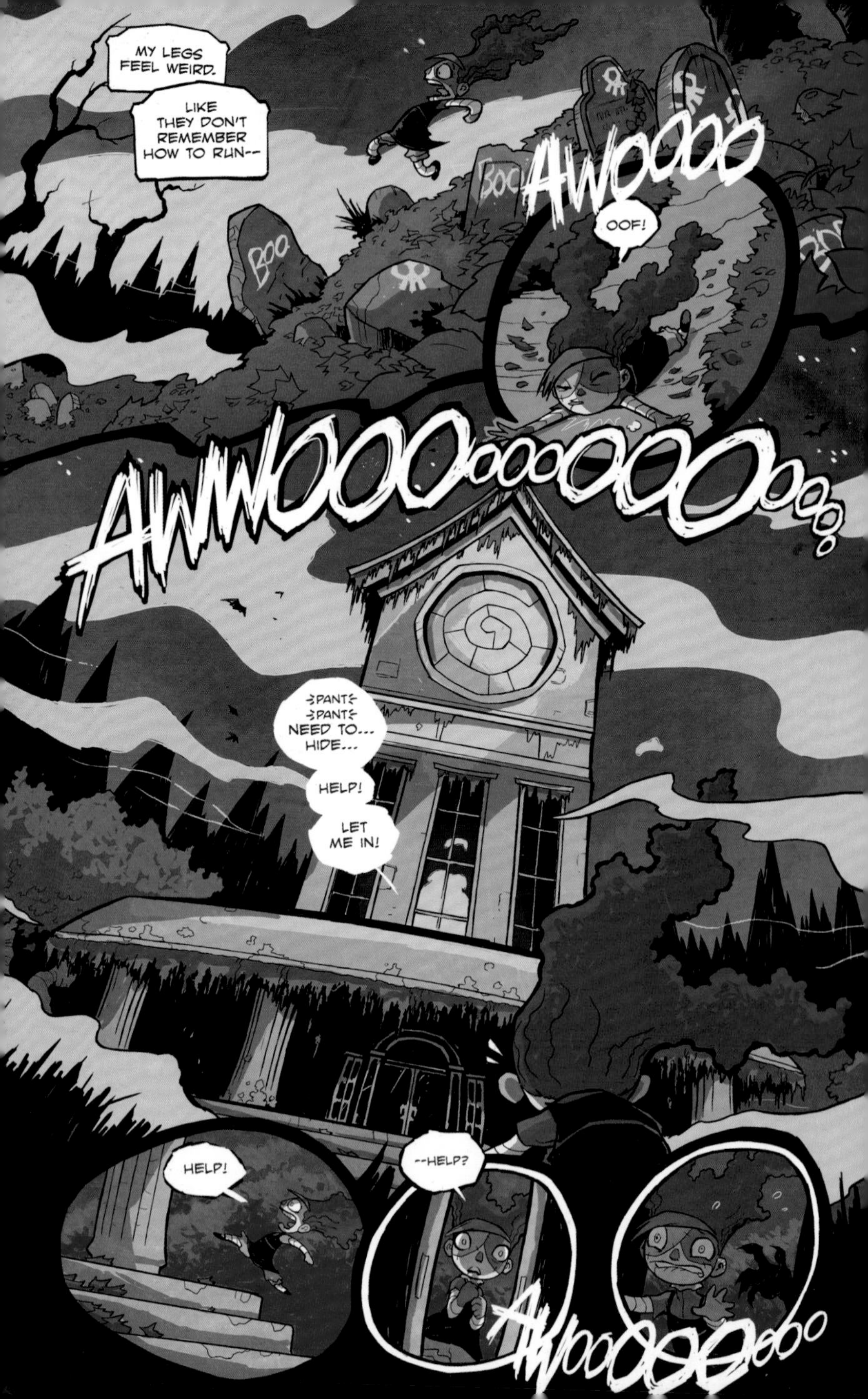
MY LEGS FEEL WEIRD.
LIKE THEY DON'T REMEMBER HOW TO RUN--
AWOOOO
OOF!
AWWOOOOOOOOOOOOOO
PANT PANT NEED TO... HIDE...
HELP!
LET ME IN!
HELP!
--HELP?
AWOOOOOOOOOO

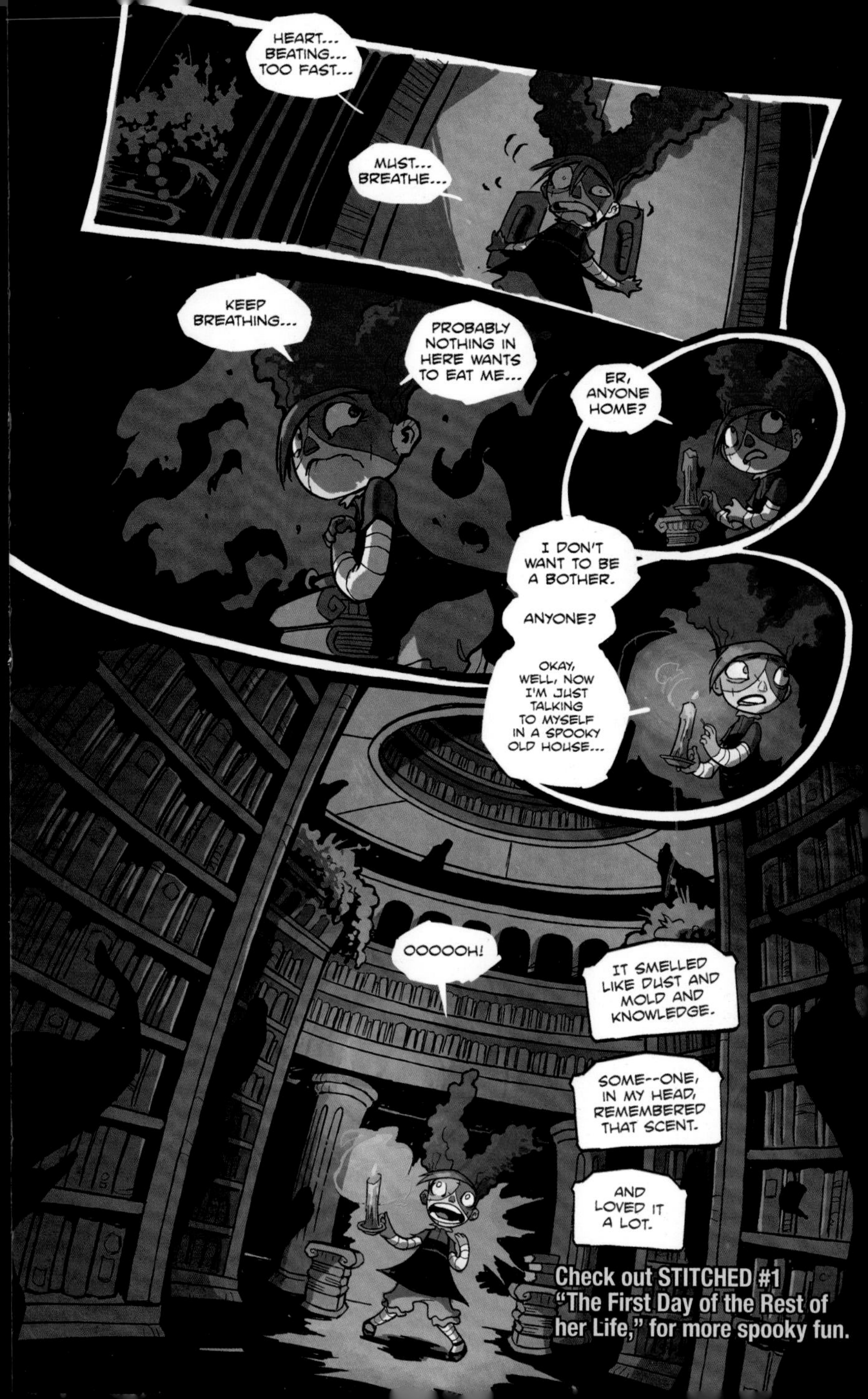
HEART... BEATING... TOO FAST...
MUST... BREATHE...
KEEP BREATHING...
PROBABLY NOTHING IN HERE WANTS TO EAT ME...
ER, ANYONE HOME?
I DON'T WANT TO BE A BOTHER.
ANYONE?
OKAY, WELL, NOW I'M JUST TALKING TO MYSELF IN A SPOOKY OLD HOUSE...
OOOOOH!
IT SMELLED LIKE DUST AND MOLD AND KNOWLEDGE.
SOME--ONE, IN MY HEAD, REMEMBERED THAT SCENT.
AND LOVED IT A LOT.

Preview of SWEETIES #1 "Cherry/Skye." A brand new family, a forbidden love, and all the sweets you can handle!

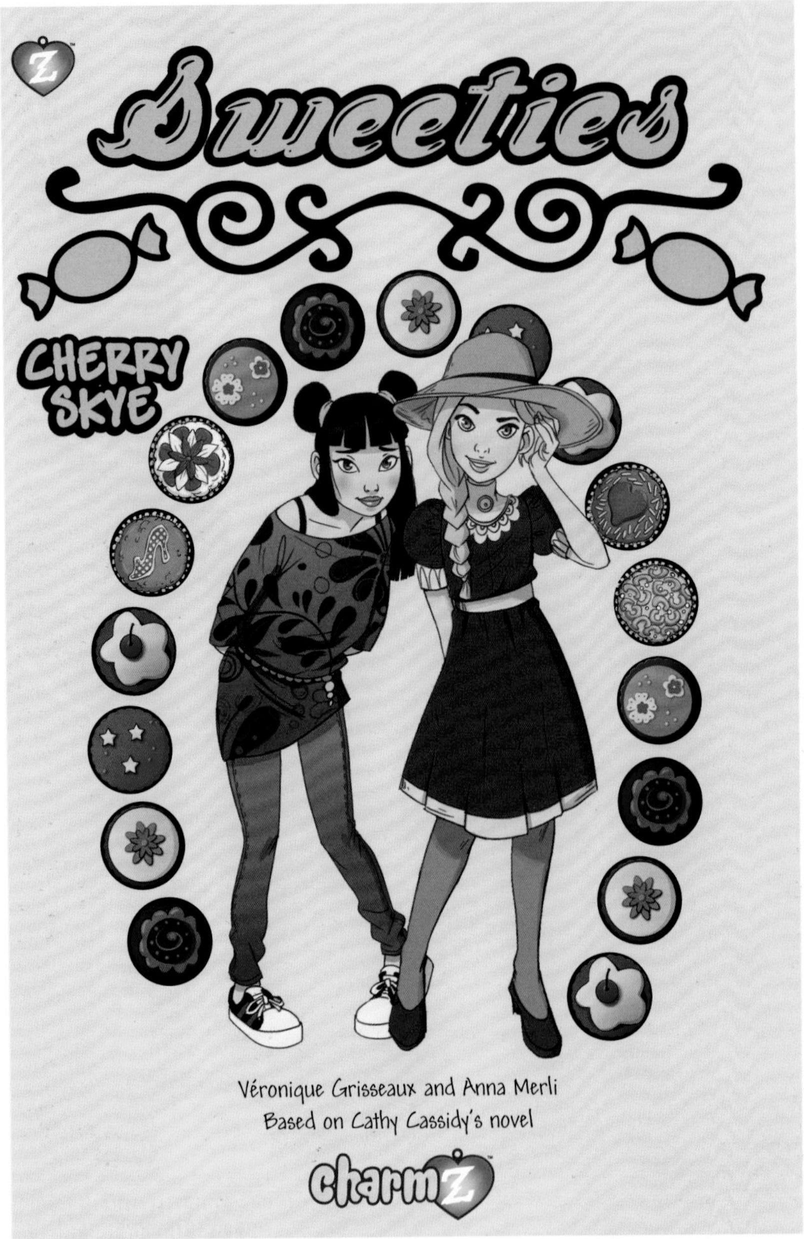
Sweeties
CHERRY
SKYE
Véronique Grisseaux and Anna Merli
Based on Cathy Cassidy's novel
charmz

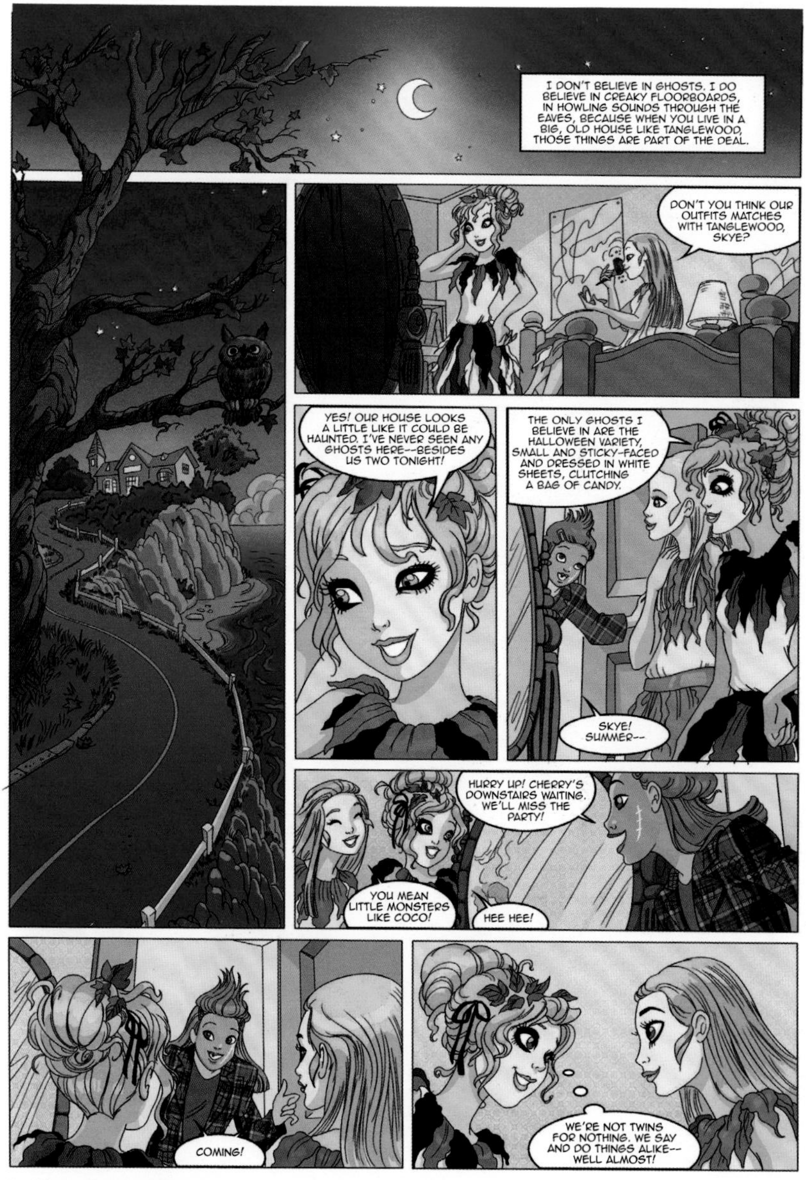
I DON'T BELIEVE IN GHOSTS. I DO BELIEVE IN CREAKY FLOORBOARDS, IN HOWLING SOUNDS THROUGH THE EAVES, BECAUSE WHEN YOU LIVE IN A BIG, OLD HOUSE LIKE TANGLEWOOD, THOSE THINGS ARE PART OF THE DEAL.
DON'T YOU THINK OUR OUTFITS MATCHES WITH TANGLEWOOD, SKYE?
YES! OUR HOUSE LOOKS A LITTLE LIKE IT COULD BE HAUNTED. I'VE NEVER SEEN ANY GHOSTS HERE--BESIDES US TWO TONIGHT!
THE ONLY GHOSTS I BELIEVE IN ARE THE HALLOWEEN VARIETY, SMALL AND STICKY-FACED AND DRESSED IN WHITE SHEETS, CLUTCHING A BAG OF CANDY.
SKYE! SUMMER--
HURRY UP! CHERRY'S DOWNSTAIRS WAITING. WE'LL MISS THE PARTY!
YOU MEAN LITTLE MONSTERS LIKE COCO!
HEE HEE!
COMING!
WE'RE NOT TWINS FOR NOTHING. WE SAY AND DO THINGS ALIKE-- WELL ALMOST!

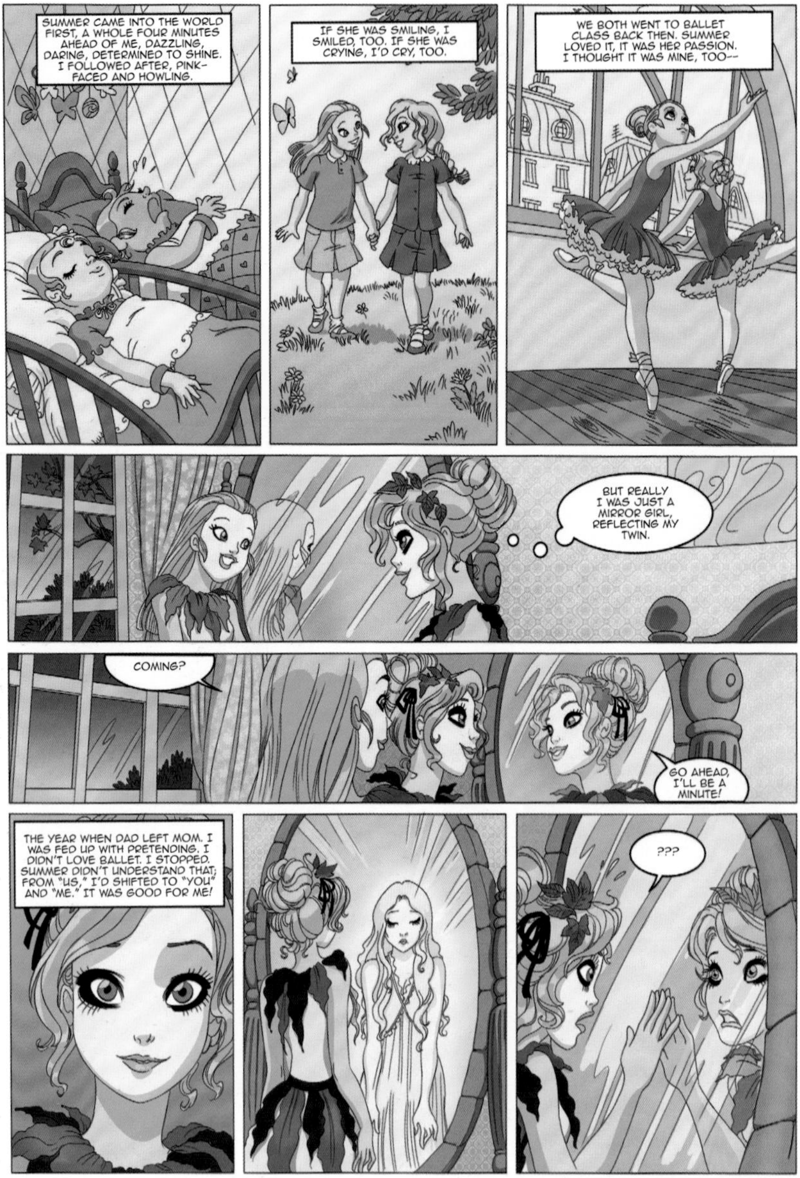
SUMMER CAME INTO THE WORLD FIRST, A WHOLE FOUR MINUTES AHEAD OF ME, DAZZLING, DARING, DETERMINED TO SHINE. I FOLLOWED AFTER, PINK-FACED AND HOWLING.
IF SHE WAS SMILING, I SMILED, TOO. IF SHE WAS CRYING, I'D CRY, TOO.
WE BOTH WENT TO BALLET CLASS BACK THEN. SUMMER LOVED IT, IT WAS HER PASSION. I THOUGHT IT WAS MINE, TOO--
BUT REALLY I WAS JUST A MIRROR GIRL, REFLECTING MY TWIN.
COMING?
GO AHEAD, I'LL BE A MINUTE!
THE YEAR WHEN DAD LEFT MOM. I WAS FED UP WITH PRETENDING. I DIDN'T LOVE BALLET. I STOPPED. SUMMER DIDN'T UNDERSTAND THAT; FROM "US," I'D SHIFTED TO "YOU" AND "ME." IT WAS GOOD FOR ME!
???

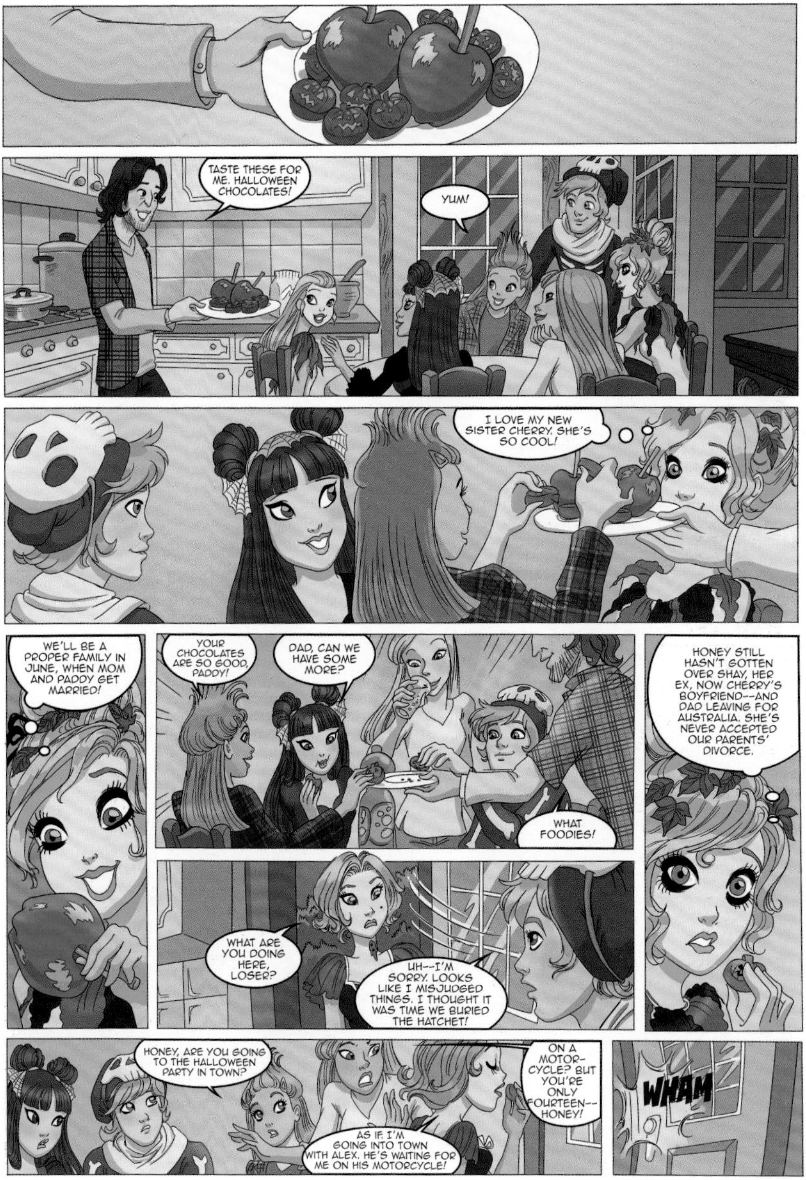
TASTE THESE FOR ME. HALLOWEEN CHOCOLATES!
YUM!
I LOVE MY NEW SISTER CHERRY. SHE'S SO COOL!
WE'LL BE A PROPER FAMILY IN JUNE, WHEN MOM AND PADDY GET MARRIED!
YOUR CHOCOLATES ARE SO GOOD, PADDY!
DAD, CAN WE HAVE SOME MORE?
WHAT FOODIES!
HONEY STILL HASN'T GOTTEN OVER SHAY, HER EX, NOW CHERRY'S BOYFRIEND--AND DAD LEAVING FOR AUSTRALIA. SHE'S NEVER ACCEPTED OUR PARENTS' DIVORCE.
WHAT ARE YOU DOING HERE, LOSER?
UH--I'M SORRY. LOOKS LIKE I MISJUDGED THINGS. I THOUGHT IT WAS TIME WE BURIED THE HATCHET!
HONEY, ARE YOU GOING TO THE HALLOWEEN PARTY IN TOWN?
AS IF. I'M GOING INTO TOWN WITH ALEX. HE'S WAITING FOR ME ON HIS MOTORCYCLE!
ON A MOTOR-CYCLE? BUT YOU'RE ONLY FOURTEEN--HONEY!
WHAM

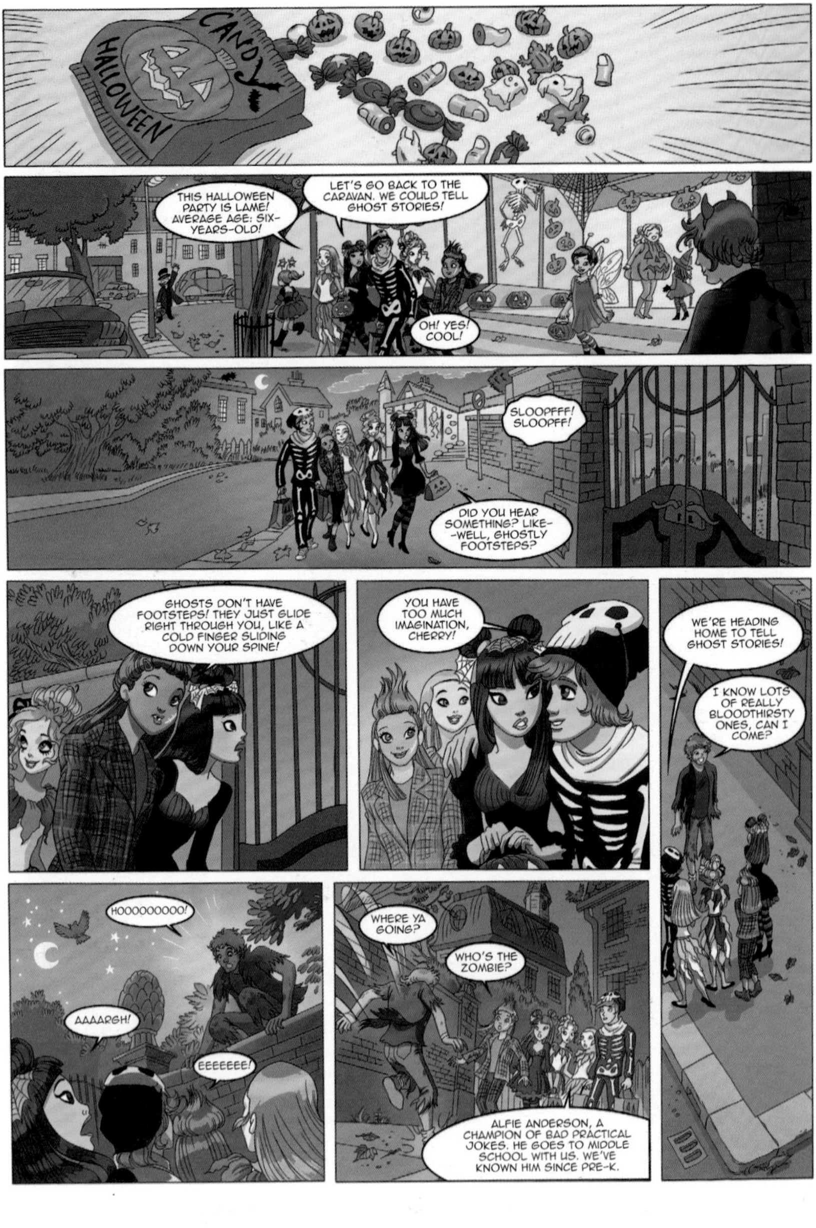
CANDY
HALLOWEEN
THIS HALLOWEEN PARTY IS LAME! AVERAGE AGE: SIX-YEARS-OLD!
LET'S GO BACK TO THE CARAVAN. WE COULD TELL GHOST STORIES!
OH! YES! COOL!
SLOOPFFF! SLOOPFF!
DID YOU HEAR SOMETHING? LIKE--WELL, GHOSTLY FOOTSTEPS?
GHOSTS DON'T HAVE FOOTSTEPS! THEY JUST GLIDE RIGHT THROUGH YOU, LIKE A COLD FINGER SLIDING DOWN YOUR SPINE!
YOU HAVE TOO MUCH IMAGINATION, CHERRY!
WE'RE HEADING HOME TO TELL GHOST STORIES!
I KNOW LOTS OF REALLY BLOODTHIRSTY ONES, CAN I COME?
HOOOOOOOOO!
AAAARGH!
EEEEEEE!
WHERE YA GOING?
WHO'S THE ZOMBIE?
ALFIE ANDERSON, A CHAMPION OF BAD PRACTICAL JOKES. HE GOES TO MIDDLE SCHOOL WITH US. WE'VE KNOWN HIM SINCE PRE-K.

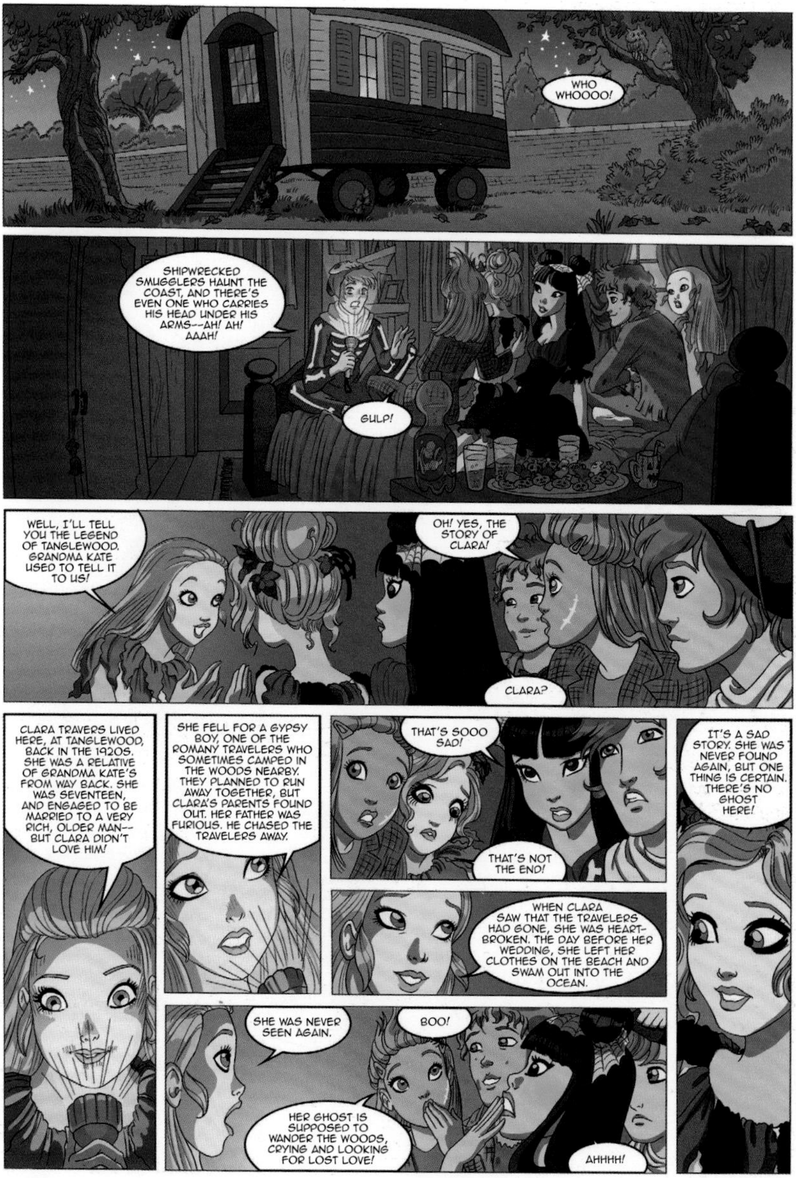
WHO WHOOOO!
SHIPWRECKED SMUGGLERS HAUNT THE COAST, AND THERE'S EVEN ONE WHO CARRIES HIS HEAD UNDER HIS ARMS--AH! AH! AAAH!
GULP!
WELL, I'LL TELL YOU THE LEGEND OF TANGLEWOOD. GRANDMA KATE USED TO TELL IT TO US!
OH! YES, THE STORY OF CLARA!
CLARA?
CLARA TRAVERS LIVED HERE, AT TANGLEWOOD, BACK IN THE 1920S. SHE WAS A RELATIVE OF GRANDMA KATE'S FROM WAY BACK. SHE WAS SEVENTEEN, AND ENGAGED TO BE MARRIED TO A VERY RICH, OLDER MAN-- BUT CLARA DIDN'T LOVE HIM!
SHE FELL FOR A GYPSY BOY, ONE OF THE ROMANY TRAVELERS WHO SOMETIMES CAMPED IN THE WOODS NEARBY. THEY PLANNED TO RUN AWAY TOGETHER, BUT CLARA'S PARENTS FOUND OUT. HER FATHER WAS FURIOUS. HE CHASED THE TRAVELERS AWAY.
THAT'S SOOO SAD!
THAT'S NOT THE END!
WHEN CLARA SAW THAT THE TRAVELERS HAD GONE, SHE WAS HEART-BROKEN. THE DAY BEFORE HER WEDDING, SHE LEFT HER CLOTHES ON THE BEACH AND SWAM OUT INTO THE OCEAN.
SHE WAS NEVER SEEN AGAIN.
BOO!
HER GHOST IS SUPPOSED TO WANDER THE WOODS, CRYING AND LOOKING FOR LOST LOVE!
AHHHH!
IT'S A SAD STORY. SHE WAS NEVER FOUND AGAIN, BUT ONE THING IS CERTAIN. THERE'S NO GHOST HERE!

Preview of Chloe #1 "The New Girl." Follow Chloe as she fumbles to find love, popularity, and confidence!

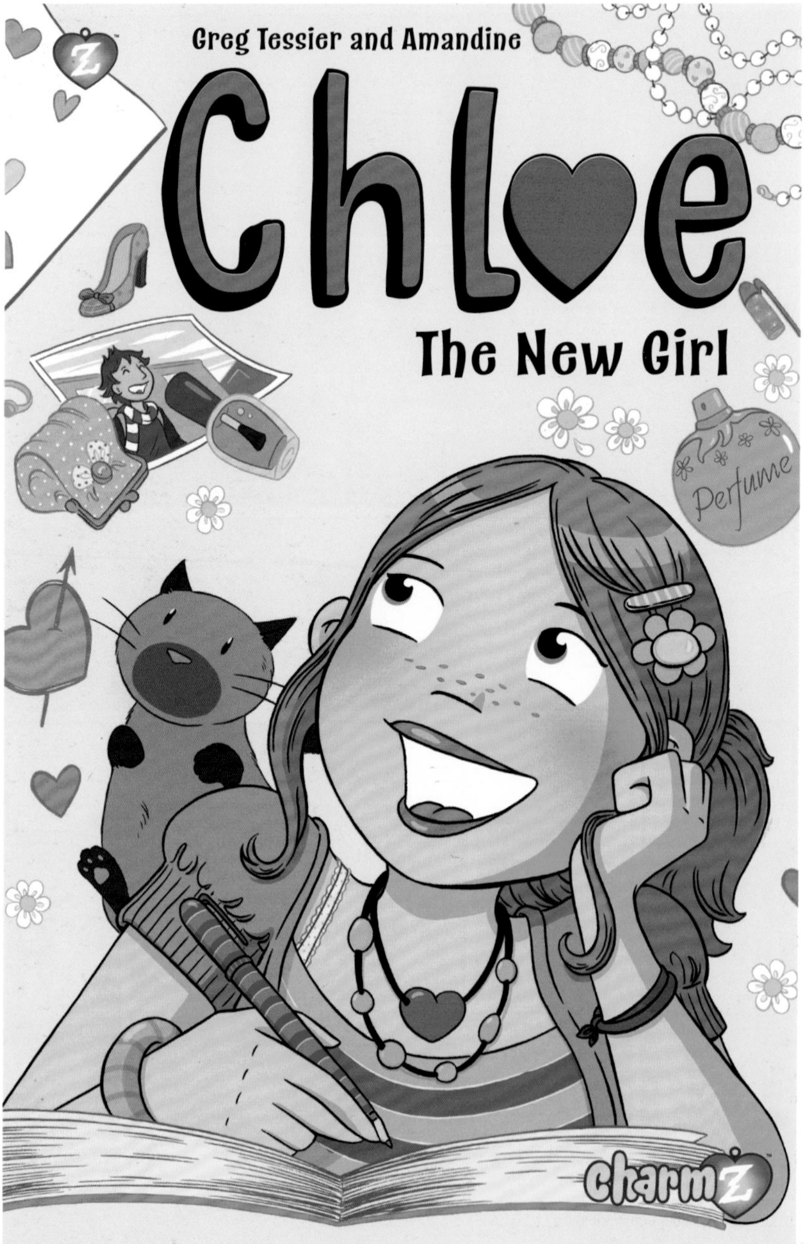

Greg Tessier and Amandine
Chloe
The New Girl
Perfume
charmz

An evening before school starts up, in an ordinary, small town.

IT'S HARD TO BE THE NEW GIRL.

I HOPE I CAN MAKE MYSELF SOME NEW, COOL, FRIENDS. RIGHT, CARTOON?

IT'S TIME TO GO TO BED!

QUIET DOWN, I KNOW WHAT TIME IT IS! DON'T COME IN MY ROOM!

I WILL IF I WANNA!

IF I WANNA!

IF I WANNA!

STOP!!!

CALM DOWN IN HERE! ARTHUR, LEAVE YOUR SISTER CHLOE ALONE. SHE'S GOT ENOUGH STRESS WITHOUT YOU ADDING TO IT!

COME ON OUT AND NO ARGUING!

SWEET DREAMS, LITTLE MISTY!

GOOD-NIGHT, MOM.

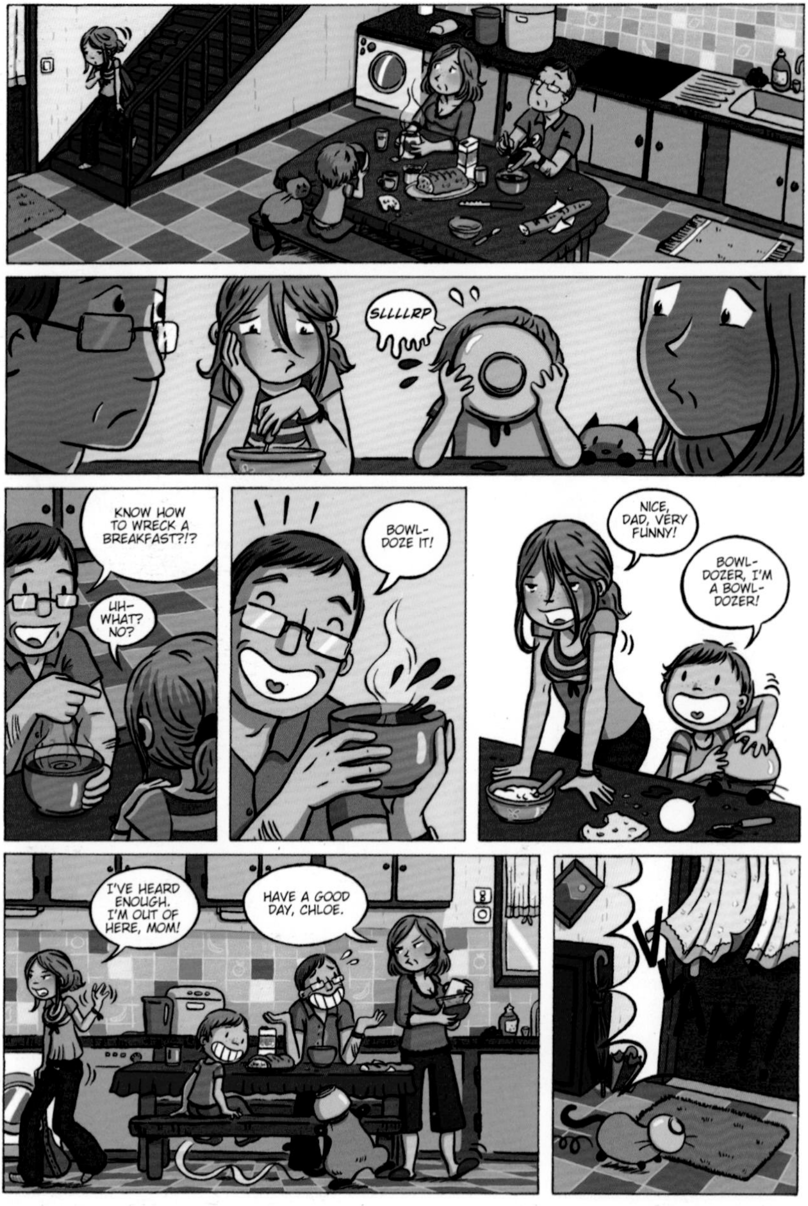
SLLLLRP
KNOW HOW TO WRECK A BREAKFAST?!?
UH-WHAT? NO?
BOWL-DOZE IT!
NICE, DAD, VERY FUNNY!
BOWL-DOZER, I'M A BOWL-DOZER!
I'VE HEARD ENOUGH. I'M OUT OF HERE, MOM!
HAVE A GOOD DAY, CHLOE.

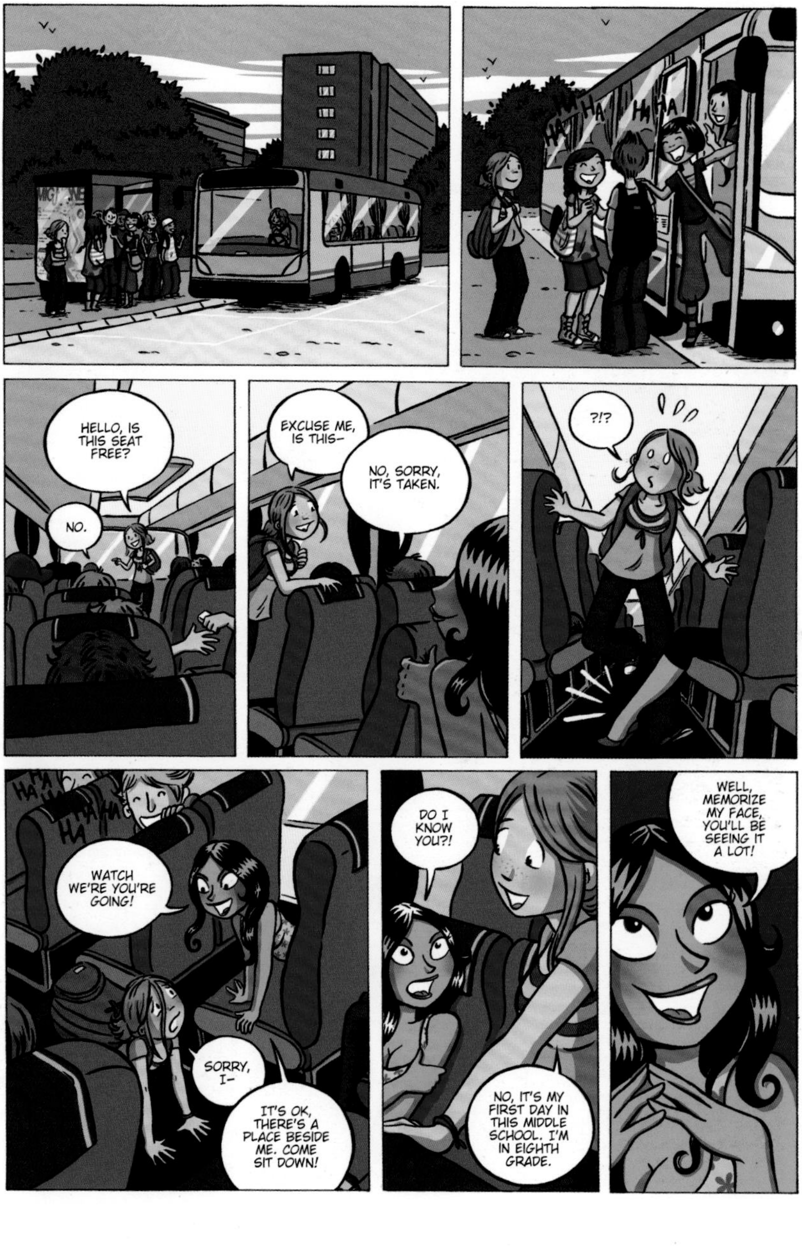
HA HA HA HA
HELLO, IS THIS SEAT FREE?
NO.
EXCUSE ME, IS THIS-
NO, SORRY, IT'S TAKEN.
?!?
HA HA HA HA HA
WATCH WE'RE YOU'RE GOING!
SORRY, I-
IT'S OK, THERE'S A PLACE BESIDE ME. COME SIT DOWN!
DO I KNOW YOU?!
NO, IT'S MY FIRST DAY IN THIS MIDDLE SCHOOL. I'M IN EIGHTH GRADE.
WELL, MEMORIZE MY FACE, YOU'LL BE SEEING IT A LOT!

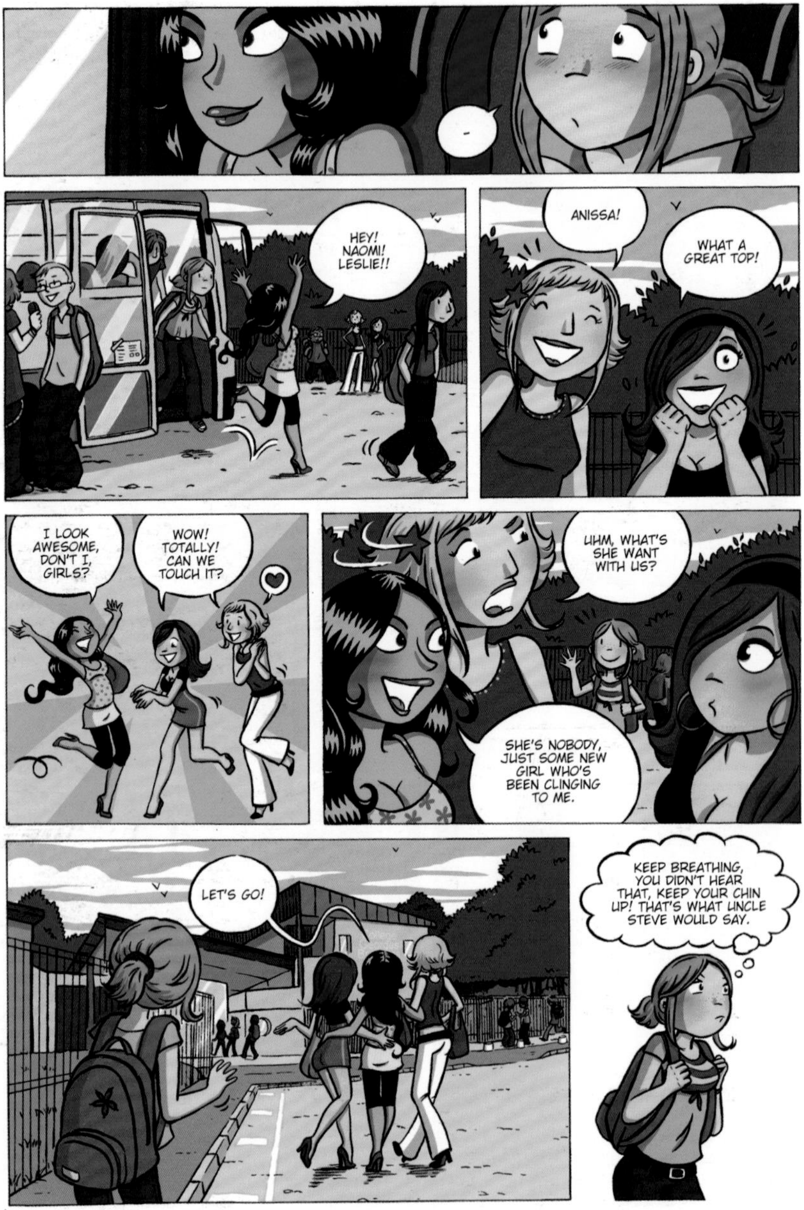
-
HEY! NAOMI! LESLIE!!
ANISSA!
WHAT A GREAT TOP!
I LOOK AWESOME, DON'T I, GIRLS?
WOW! TOTALLY! CAN WE TOUCH IT?
UHM, WHAT'S SHE WANT WITH US?
SHE'S NOBODY, JUST SOME NEW GIRL WHO'S BEEN CLINGING TO ME.
LET'S GO!
KEEP BREATHING, YOU DIDN'T HEAR THAT, KEEP YOUR CHIN UP! THAT'S WHAT UNCLE STEVE WOULD SAY.

Check out more in CHLOE #1 "The New Girl"! Available now!

NANCY DREW GRAPHIC NOVELS AVAILABLE FROM PAPERCUTZ

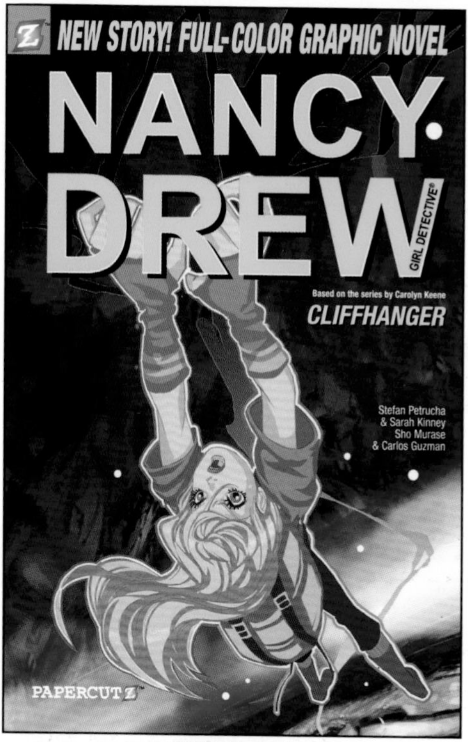
NEW STORY! FULL-COLOR GRAPHIC NOVEL
NANCY DREW
GIRL DETECTIVE
Based on the series by Carolyn Keene
CLIFFHANGER
Stefan Petrucha
& Sarah Kinney
Sho Murase
& Carlos Guzman
PAPERCUTZ

#19 "Cliffhanger"

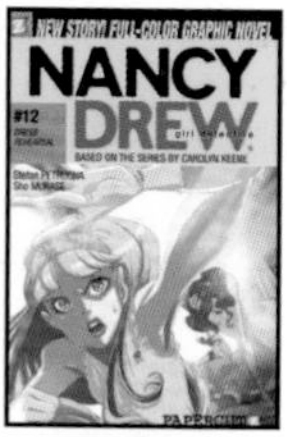
NEW STORY! FULL-COLOR GRAPHIC NOVEL
NANCY DREW
#12
PAPERCUTZ

#12 "Dress Reversal"

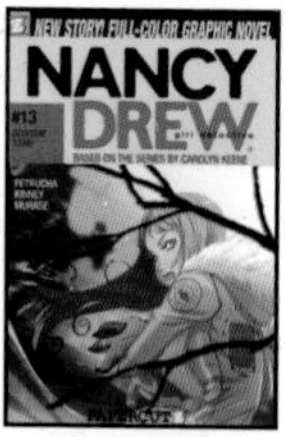
NEW STORY! FULL-COLOR GRAPHIC NOVEL
NANCY DREW
#13

#13 "Doggone Town"

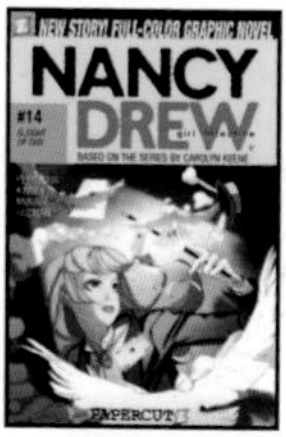
NEW STORY! FULL-COLOR GRAPHIC NOVEL
NANCY DREW
#14
PAPERCUTZ

#14 "Sleight of Dan"

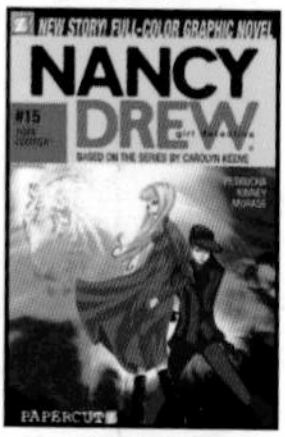
NEW STORY! FULL-COLOR GRAPHIC NOVEL
NANCY DREW
#15
PAPERCUTZ

#15 "Tiger Counter"

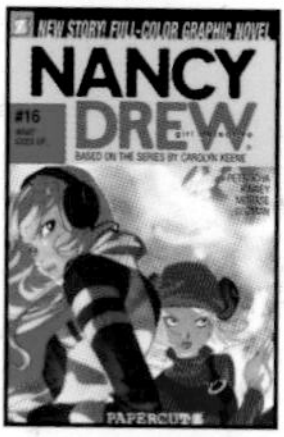
NEW STORY! FULL-COLOR GRAPHIC NOVEL
NANCY DREW
#16
PAPERCUTZ

#16 "What Goes Up..."

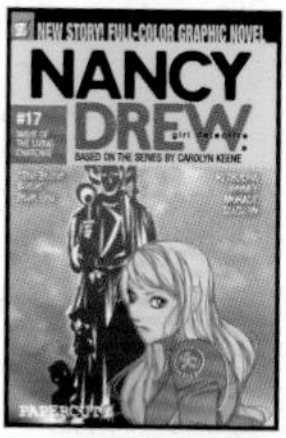
NEW STORY! FULL-COLOR GRAPHIC NOVEL
NANCY DREW
#17

#17 "Night of the Living Chatchke"

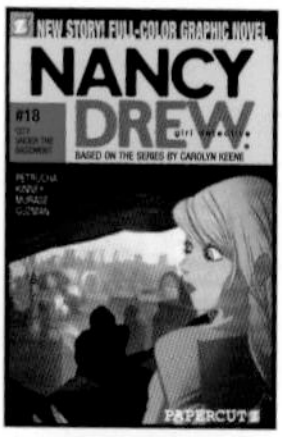
NEW STORY! FULL-COLOR GRAPHIC NOVEL
NANCY DREW
#18
PAPERCUTZ

#18 "City Under the Basement"

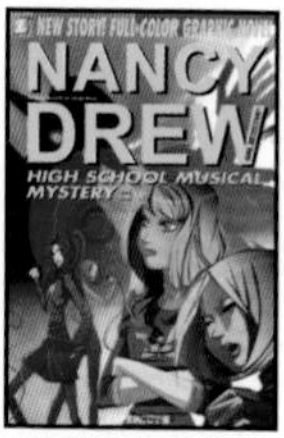
NEW STORY! FULL-COLOR GRAPHIC NOVEL
NANCY DREW
HIGH SCHOOL MUSICAL MYSTERY

#20 "High School Musical Mystery" 1

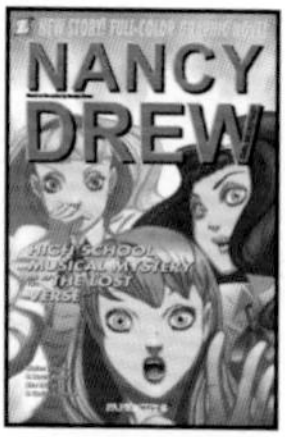
NEW STORY! FULL-COLOR GRAPHIC NOVEL
NANCY DREW

#21 "High School Musical Mystery" 2

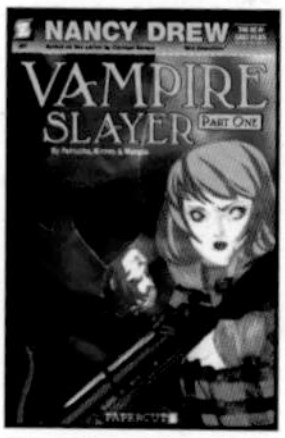
NANCY DREW
VAMPIRE SLAYER
PART ONE
PAPERCUTZ

The New Case Files #1 "Vampire Slayer" Part 1

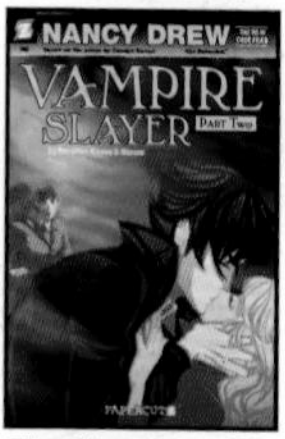
NANCY DREW
VAMPIRE SLAYER
PART TWO
PAPERCUTZ

The New Case Files #2 "Vampire Slayer" Part 2

NANCY DREW graphic novels are available at booksellers everywhere.

NANCY DREW AND THE CLUE CREW graphic novels are $7.99 each in paperback, and $11.99 in hardcover, except #1, which is $6.99 in paperback, $10.99 in hardcover. NANCY DREW GIRL DETECTIVE graphic novels are $7.95 each in paperback and $12.95 each in hardcover. except #20 and 21, $8.99PB/$13.99HC. NANCY DREW THE NEW CASE FILES are $6.99PB/$10.99HC. You may also order online at papercutz.com. Or call 1-800-886-1223, Monday through Friday, 9 – 5 EST. MC, Visa, and AmEx accepted. To order by mail, please add $4.00 for postage and handling for first book ordered, $1.00 for each additional book and make check payable to NBM Publishing. Send to: Papercutz, 160 Broadway, Suite 700, East Wing, New York, NY 10038.

NANCY DREW GIRL DETECTIVE graphic novels are also available digitally wherever e-books are sold.

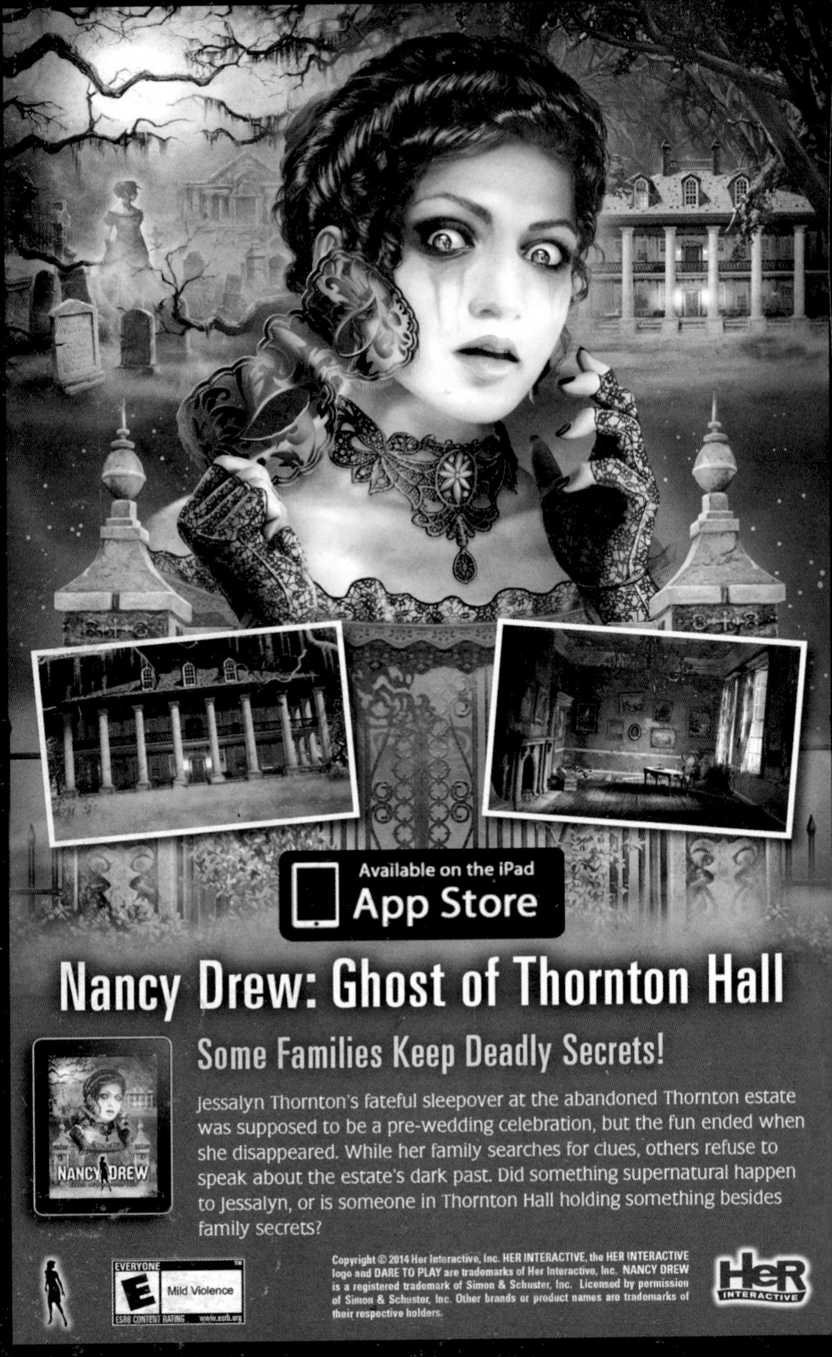
Available on the iPad
App Store
Nancy Drew: Ghost of Thornton Hall
Some Families Keep Deadly Secrets!
NANCY DREW
Jessalyn Thornton's fateful sleepover at the abandoned Thornton estate was supposed to be a pre-wedding celebration, but the fun ended when she disappeared. While her family searches for clues, others refuse to speak about the estate's dark past. Did something supernatural happen to Jessalyn, or is someone in Thornton Hall holding something besides family secrets?
EVERYONE
E
Mild Violence
ESRB CONTENT RATING www.esrb.org
Copyright © 2014 Her Interactive, Inc. HER INTERACTIVE, the HER INTERACTIVE logo and DARE TO PLAY are trademarks of Her Interactive, Inc. NANCY DREW is a registered trademark of Simon & Schuster, Inc. Licensed by permission of Simon & Schuster, Inc. Other brands or product names are trademarks of their respective holders.
HeR
INTERACTIVE